Martin Kettemann

11/5

novum ⬛ pro

www.novum-publishing.co.uk

© 2018 novum publishing

ISBN 978-3-99064-200-9
Editing: Allyson Filippi
Cover photos:
Juri Samsonov | Dreamstime.com,
Martin Kettemann
Cover design, layout & typesetting:
novum publishing

www.novum-publishing.co.uk

Sunday Morning

July 27, 2014

"I am sorry; we had a nice evening. But it makes no sense that we see each other again."

"Why?"

I am sitting in front of the computer at my parents' house. I see the cloudy sky through the window, and it is humid. I have a can of green jasmine tea on the computer table and, I rub over my unshaven face. I didn't expect to get a response from this woman I met the other night. So, I have been almost a bit surprised that she writes, "I am sorry ..." It is just normal and what I learned over the last years. If I am investing a lot of time in writing emails and messages on dating sites I could meet here and there a woman for something to drink, maybe even for a whole afternoon or evening. But it seldom happens that a woman contacts me again or even wants see me again. It's about the same if I would apply for a new job. The talks are nice, but because of so many applicants, they can chose you only if you are absolutely perfect for this job. At least companies are decent enough to write after it that they are not interested in you. But these women on the dating sites are just jumping to their next dates. Though I don't mind, it is always frustrating.

I sip on my cup of tea, sign out and login to Facebook. Ah, there is a message from Ana! She asks how I am doing and writes that a trip to Hong Kong at the end of September wouldn't be too bad. The rain season would be hopefully over, and she wouldn't be too busy at that time.

I don't know why, but for me it is always easier to get in connection with people who are living far away. It is kind of strange. More than once, I had the luck to meet people on pen pal sites, became friends with them and after some time, I met them where they live. And all these contacts were women. Of course, it was almost never about getting into a relationship with them, but they were interested in me. This is different to all the ladies around here. My most far away connections were to Americans. It was probably because of my passion for travelling there. I didn't have any similar good experiences in other countries. But Ana is from the other side of the world. She is a Filipina who is working and living in the former colony of the UK. Hong Kong always interested me, and I wanted go there already three years ago. This was also the only trip I cancelled in my life. Shortly before my planned departure date in March 2011 happened the nuclear accident in Fukushima. The news was terrible in those days and the media excluded nothing. But there was also another reason that made it easier for me to cancel that trip. To the same time when the nuclear disaster started in Japan, I met a girl online who later became my first girlfriend. I'm sure that this would never have happened if I would had been in Hong Kong. Only because she had the same time off as me and I cancelled my trip, she could have visited me for a whole week from Munich. Without this time range, it would not have ended as it did, an eight month, long-distance relationship. Maybe it would have been better never to start this relationship, but I didn't know. Veronika wasn't that kind of girl who I would fall in love easily with after an afternoon together. It was the intensive exchange by phone calls, emails and messages for about two weeks before she came here and I saw her for the first time. She opened up her heart to me, and she didn't hide her sad and dark past. But it was more, I was about to have my first chance in 37 years to get a girlfriend. On that Friday at the end of March 2011 as she came here, I thought in the first hours that this couldn't go into anything. But her sureness about me and the big desire on each side made it happen that we ended up in a relationship.

I'm still staring at the message from Ana. It could be really cool to make my long-distance trip to Hong Kong this fall, I think. There is still something in me that doesn't want to push the idea away of flying to America once again. But I don't know where to go there. I can't visit someone of my old friends there, and there isn't any new pal at a new place I could visit. Time is also running away because my vacation time is planned from the last days of September. About Hong Kong, I am very excited, but what I know is that it would be hard to find an affordable place to stay. I know that Ana wouldn't be able to help me much with this. As she said, she lives in a flat of a big apartment building with the family for whom she is working. Thousands of Filipinas and girls from other poor Asian countries are working in Hong Kong for Chinese families. They clean their rooms, cook for them, watch the children or care for their pets. She told me that many of her friends are treated badly, but she is doing well and this Chinese couple doesn't have any small kids. There is just a cat she has to look for. The only thing I find odd is that the room of the cat is bigger than hers.

I know if I want go there, I have to check hotels and flights soon.

Saturday Afternoon

August 16, 2014

"Hi Ana! I have booked the flights! ☺"

"Wonderful, Thomas! When you will be here?"

"I will leave Germany on September 29 and will be in Hong Kong one day later. I still need an accommodation there. Do you know any inexpensive places to stay?"

"Mmmh … there is one on Chatham Road, but you have to look on their internet site. How long do you plan to stay here?"

"My flight is going back on October 11. I want check the Airbnb site. I'm sure that these private places are cheaper."

"You will have enough time here to see a lot. As you know, I usually only have off on Sundays, but if you would find a place to stay close to my neighborhood, we can meet in the evenings and on October 2 and 3 I have off because of Chinese holidays here. I don't know anything about Airbnb, but you are the traveller. ☺"

"Well, I have booked twice with Airbnb. My first time was in Boston two years ago. The hosts, three Korean girls, were nice, but the place was small and kind of dirty. I had good experiences in Ireland this June. At least the first place in Dublin was wonderful. A teacher, from Canada, was the host, and she cared a lot about me."

"She cared about you?"

"Yes. She took me from the airport, gave me advice about what to do in Dublin, dropped me off one day in the city and even baked a cake on my birthday there. ☺ But it was not only this, I had also some nice conversations with her about spirituality. Since her husband died, she into Buddhism and meditation.

She recommended that I go to a meditation group in Dublin one evening there."

"I wish you could stay at my place. Do you know what you want see here?"

"I still haven't any plans. Of course, I would like to go up to the Peak, go in the center of Kowloon, try some typical Chinese food, maybe go on a hike on one of those green islands there … and maybe go to a fortune teller. ☺"

"You can do all this and much more because you have a lot of time. I will ask my female boss for a place we can go to eat and where they have menus in English. There are a lot of fortune tellers are Hong Kong, but I have to look where the good ones are. Have you ever been to a fortune teller before?"

"No. I'm just curious, and I read in my travel book that it is very popular to go to one in Hong Kong. And you know I'm always curious."

"It's late here; I have to go to bed."

"Ok, have a good night and you will hear from me when I find a place to stay. Have a good night Ana!"

"Thank you, have a good afternoon Thomas. See U!"

I often spend too much time in front of the computer. I am already in the middle of the afternoon now. But on this afternoon, I make something that makes sense. It was about my Hong Kong trip. Instantly, I go on different hotel searching sites. But even hotels on big roads or in bad locations are hard to get under 100 euros per night. Also, the hotels on Chatham Road are on this price level. I noticed this before that Hong Kong is even more expensive than New York City where I was a couple of years ago. I login to Airbnb, and I saw quickly that it gives places to stay where it is cheaper. I find out that the difficulty will be to find a room with good ratings, and it should also be close to Ana's place in Tsim Sha Tsui. At the main site, I see a lovely place on Lamma Island. Why not book in two places? First Tsim Sha Tsui and then Lamma? I am getting excited about this idea. Usually, I need a lot of time and ask other people what they think, but on this afternoon I'm fast and book seven nights in the city center and four nights on Lamma Island! I am just not sure if this place in the center is close enough to Ana. The rating seems to be very good, and the price is about 36 euros. On Lamma Island, I get it for 25 euros.

I know that Ana is sleeping there now, but I write the news in a message on Facebook.

I check my emails. There is the flight info, the Airbnb confirmations and two other emails. One is from Susan. She is one of my American friends. She belongs to those sort of pals that I met in the past. To be exact, I met her in Missouri 11 months ago. I booked that trip last minute too. I was writing with her for just about two months. The email contact to her was very different than all the other pals before. With most, it was like an email friendship. But with her, I was fast in a kind of pre-relationship. It was new and exciting, but also a bit strange because this happened just through emails. She was nice and friendly, and we shared emotional things. Also about things you usually talk about with people you know only in person. Weird that she sounded in many ways very dissimilar to me. She lives separated from her husband, has a daughter, smokes, is a night person and is addicted to getting new tattoos. I don't know, but maybe this different life made me fascinated with her. The big disappointment came as I arrived there. Already after the first hour there, she told me at a dinner that she would feel suddenly so empty. I told myself before this trip that I don't have to expect anything. But after such an intensive email conversation, anything in me hoped for more. Fortunately, I was only in Missouri for five days, and ten days in Las Vegas were following. After a few weeks at home again, I comprehended that it made no sense, and we switched quickly to a friendship level. I am still in contact and sending her emails, postcards from trips and sometimes packages on birthdays and Christmas for her and her daughter. Now we are on the same level as I am with my other US friends. But with her, I am almost daily in conversation. With some old friends, there isn't that intensive connection anymore.

The other email is from Elisabeth, a brand new pen pal from North Carolina. Because of my Hong Kong plans, my many other pen pals and also because it is frustrating sometimes to invest so much time in making friends or whatever through in the internet, I'm not too excited about a new pal. But it is already her sixth email in just a week. I have a quick feeling to see who is friendly, who is interested in me and also what kind of contact can lead into anything or not. It is too early to say anything about Elisabeth, or Elisa as she likes to be called. But single, no kids and open to talk about different subjects makes her curious to me. Further, she writes that she would be a highly sensitive person too. It is nice that there is no need to explain that a highly sensitive person doesn't mean to be sensitive in a general way, that highly sensitive means to have a wider perspective as others and that the stimulation from the environment can be overwhelming. She doesn't have my green tea passion, but she is interested in the teas I drink and much more.

I write both women back and decide then for a small tour with my bicycle out to the fields. I need some movement and fresh air after this whole afternoon inside.

5 Days Later

Ana indicates in her messages that the place I booked in Kowloon wouldn't be so great. Not because of the location, but because it would be a bit away from where she lives and she would have to find out how to get there by bus. I notice that it is not easy to reach from the airport or to get to the subway to get around in the city, or MTR as is it called in Hong Kong. Damn! Why didn't I research enough before I made the booking. I check my bookings on Airbnb again and see that the cancel fee isn't too high if I don't wait too long with it. But before I do this, I had to find a better place. There were several accommodations in busy Tsim Sha Tsui. They were all good to reach by MTR. I look again for the ratings, and they were not as good as the place I booked. Plus, they were more expensive. I selected the best and sent the address in a message to Ana.

Besides these Hong Kong plans, it is an usual work evening. A groundhog evening and also the whole day was a groundhog day. I often felt like the main role in this popular movie from the '80s. I couldn't get out of the things in my life. There are always these worries and problems from my parents, especially from my mom. She has one health issue after another, and she always makes the close people around her responsible for anything in her life. The people who care the most about her, but mainly my dad. I am wondering about his strength. He works so much, has endless patience with his wife and cares intensively about her and his family. But these worries have left their mark on him. He had more serious health issues in the last years than my mom, from cancer to heart problems recently. The only thing that makes him happy is to see his grandchildren, my brother's kids, and going on trips. Also, this becomes more difficult with my mom, but as soon they were away they were both enjoying it. My relationship with my parents is good and strong, but not always healthy. I probably would need more distance, as a highly sensitive person, I was too concerned about anything with them.

And there is my job. I am at same company since I left school many years ago. There were good and bad phases, it depends on what I'm doing and especially who I am working with. It is not what I dreamed to do as a kid. But these last five years until summer 2014, I had a kind of comfortable workplace. I did well with my coworkers in something like an internal call center. I'm absolutely not a phone talker, but I always like to be in contact with other people and help them. But three weeks ago, I got told that starting in September I would have to work in the investment group of the department. I was not happy about this news, but it is something I can't do anything about. I just hope for the best and know that I will make my job as good as possible. I don't love my job, but I appreciate it. I get my money every month for not doing anything too hard, and the big benefit is my many vacation days every year. These vacation days are needed for my trips. My only passion I have, except for the green tea. In the last years, I mostly travelled alone. I found out that it was more uncomplicated as any arrangement with my friend Michael. When we were younger, he only needed me on trips to do things that he wanted, and it always seemed that he never heard the word 'compromise' in his life. He has stolen my only passion during some trips, and I showed myself and others in the past 10 years that I am doing pretty good alone.

Also a part of my groundhog life is writing with these many women in the internet over the years. I almost could call it a hobby. Or maybe addiction fits even better. It is sometimes frustrating and boring, but also hopeful and exciting at the same time. Though I am spending too much time in front of computers, it is often also my only hope to change anything and meet new people.

In these days, I wouldn't need to chat on my typical internet sites because my Hong Kong trip is coming soon, and Elisa started to keep me busy with her writing. Her emails got longer and more intensive in the last days. It is nice, but I don't want overvalue it yet. People who are writing so much need attention, and they are sensitive. About this I am sure. As soon somebody is interested in me in this way, hope starts in me if I want it or not. But I know that the contact with Elisa is too new to say anything. She didn't travel much in her life. As a young adult, she travelled once with her school class to Germany. This was her only official pleasure trip abroad, and she didn't travel much in the United States either. Overall, almost any trip to another place had been to do with a movement to another place to live. She lived once in England and once in Ecuador. She indicated that it had to do with a guy, and it didn't go well. Elisa wrote that she couldn't imagine travelling like I was doing. She would be afraid, and as a highly sensitive person, she wouldn't be able to deal with the crowds at some places. With this, she is referring to my Hong Kong plans. I know that this is untypical for a highly sensitive person, but I have this sensation-seeker gene in me. I need distraction from my groundhog days at home. When I am on my trips far away from home, in another country and culture, I feel excitement and often more happiness than at home. I need these "sensations" to break out at least a couple of times every year. Also when I don't know from what I have to escape.

Sunday Morning

August 24, 2014

It is unusually cold for the season. Last night, I was out with my brother Mark and his wife at the wine festival in the village called Erlenbach. Most of the year, this place is a dead village. A bunch of people you see are just in the Besen there. Besen are traditional locations where you get local Swabian food and drinks. But most guests drink wine there because the owners are farmers and offer their own alcoholic grape juices. The other highlight is this wine festival where the mass of people come from everywhere. After a walk through the festival and having something to eat, we had to leave the village early again because heavy rain started. To be honest, I was not sad about it. Because I don't drink wine and alcohol at all, it was just boring for me to stand there for hours and watch others get stupid and drunk.

Now I am sitting at the computer at my parents' house with a cup of jasmine tea. My parents left in the early morning for their summer trip to Austria. I could be also at home in my condo, but it is just comfortable for me here. I had breakfast with them, and the internet connection here is much faster than my wireless stick at home. I switch on my favourite radio station that I listen to when I am here. They are playing a song I like, and I have never heard before. I'm going on the internet site from this station, and there they have the playlist. It's "Prayer in C" by Robin Schulz. I'm sure that Susan would like this song too. She is into this electronic kind of music. Last year, we made some music CDs and sent them to each other. It's something I generally like to do with friends who are living far away. But I didn't exchange with others as many CDs as I did with Susan. I check the song on YouTube, and instantly, I see that they made the video in Berlin. I recognize some of the streets. It is just five months ago, as I was there the last time on a trip. I'm writing an email to Susan and put in this link from YouTube. Short before I am finished, they play "Hey Brother" from Avicii on the radio. Also a favourite song from her, but this one she put on a CD for me.

There is also another new email from Elisa. She really seems to like to write me. I had these times with intensive email exchanges at the beginning, not with many, but with some other friends before too. She puts a smile on my face, and it feels good that somebody is interested in me and my life. This is something that never happen when I date a person in real life. There is maybe a superficial scan on me, but seldom more. She asks about my Hong Kong plans, about work and what I will be doing this weekend. Though I am not the most active person in the world, I'm getting the impression that a lot is going on here in comparison to her life in North Carolina. She wrote me before that she would live alone with two cats in a big house and that she doesn't have much contact to her family. I still don't know why, but I also don't want to squeeze her like a lemon. There were also some health issues she told me about. She would get rosacea on her face when she wouldn't be careful about what she eats, and she would have the Myofascial pain syndrome. I haven't heard about this before, but she explained to me that it would be similar to Fibromyalgia. Just that it would be not all over the body, instead there are some sensitive points in the muscles that cause pain. I don't know if this makes it any better than Fibromyalgia. She would treat it with magnesium and with healthy nutrition. I notice that she knows a lot about healthy and good food. This is interesting for me; I also was caring about what I was eating sometimes. She seems to have a huge knowledge about vitamins, proteins and what our bodies need.

As I reply to her, I ask for her address. I got the idea to make a little package for her. Usually I am not so fast with this. But she seems to be a really nice person, and I am preparing a package for another friend anyway. This friend also lives in North

Carolina, and I have known her about for three months. This is the normal time range when I start to exchange packages. But with Elisa, it is going pretty fast. Because I feel good in the emails with her, but maybe because it is always the same procedure with new friends that I want send her something. I know how to make a connection stronger, and something personal in the mailbox box makes everyone's day nicer.

Yesterday Ana was letting me know that the location of the Airnb place in Tsim Sha Tsui would be very good. She was even enthusiastic as I said that I want go there instead of the other place. Of course I understand that Cameron Road is much closer to her street. I cancelled the other place, and I got the confirmation for the new place yesterday. I only lost about 30 euros, and I am thinking that it is better to be closer to Ana. I don't know how much time I would spend with her or if I would get along with her. But, she is the trigger for my trip there, and it would be a shame if I would be too far away from her. I have everything planned for the trip now. From looking how to get to the city from the airport, buying some small gifts for Ana, packing and so on I have still time until the last days before the journey. I also have a travel book, a travel magazine about Hong Kong and a novel for this trip. When I was younger, I just had travel books with me. But being alone on a trip often means being lonely on evenings, and it is good have something to read. I even found something that fits great to Hong Kong: "The World of Suzie Wong" from Richard Mason. A story that takes place in Hong Kong.

Saturday

I start the day with meditation. But I don't know if could call what I am doing meditation. I have my doubts if I have ever been in a real meditative condition. It is always hard to keep my mind quiet and to concentrate only on the natural breath. But I believe in meditation, and when it doesn't work as it should, I think it is at least good to do in the times where I try to mediate other activities, like being on the computer or so. How well it works is also depending on what I did before or what else was on my mind. Morning times are generally harder for me because I am a morning person, and I always feel a lot of energy in the first part of the day. Tiredness in the early evening times sometimes helps, and I can try my meditation practice longer. On this morning, it is not easy because I feel some arising excitement in me. The Hong Kong trip is just about three weeks away and Elisa wants to call me today.

I make a Pai Mu Tan white tea for myself. White teas should be healthier than green tea. But these health aspects were never the main reasons for me to drink these teas. I don't like coffee, and I need another caffeine kick. Over the years, I'm loving the taste of this stuff, and I always like to try new types.

I'm excited as I see the email from Elisa. She writes about what a wonderful guy I would be and mentions the songs on the CD I sent her in the package. I put my all-time –favourites for her on it, sent some German gummy bears and a couple of postcards. In the days before, she revealed a bit more about her family issues. Her dad died some years ago from an illness, but she indicated that he wasn't the best person on earth. But mostly, she was the one who cared about him in the days before he died. She mentioned her brother also. He has some drug problems, but he is still the only one who she has contact with in her family. Elisa seemed to suffer the hardest with the fact that there was no contact with her mother anymore. She lost the connection to her when she came back from Ecuador. I now know why she was in Ecuador for several months. It was because of a man from there. She gave up everything for him in the States and tried to get settled down there. But obviously, it didn't work out for them. This man was even violent to her. She came back with nothing and didn't get the support from her mom that she needed. I don't know why her mom treated her like this. She also wrote something about physical, mental and sexual abuse. This shocks me. Not only because I feel bad for her and that I hate people who doing such things, but also because it reminds me on Veronika. Sexual abuse from her dad, getting pregnant from him, losing the baby, escaping from home, borderline syndrome and almost no contact to her family was determining her past too. I know that such terrible things happen more often than people think, but it is weird that my new friend Elisa maybe has a similar past.

I push the thoughts away. As she wrote in the last days that she would like have a phone call with me, I hesitated a bit because it's something I don't care much about. I am also anxious that I could express myself wrong. I am much better with writing, and it is also because of the language difference. But for her, it looks important to talk with me, so I agreed. I said to myself, there is nothing I have to lose. My main goal is the trip to Hong Kong now. Also, in the German language, I don't like phone calls. For me, the best invention is to text with cell phones, or yes, of course, writing emails. So I am nervous on this Saturday. She confirmed with me my suggested time. Eleven a.m. in North Carolina and 5 p.m. in Baden-Württemberg. In our last emails, we also exchanged pictures. We have seen one another before on this pen pal site where we met originally, but the visual impression gets better if you exchange more photos. The recent pictures she sent have also been more private. She wrote that she made them only for me. Elisa had long, dark brown, almost black, hair and bright-blue eyes. In these pictures, she put a red lipstick on her lips. It looks like she has soft and pale skin. Silver earrings were dangling on her ears. In two pictures, the upper buttons on her shirt were open, and it looked almost a bit erotic. She was looking beautiful, and I noticed that she was that kind of girl I felt attracted to. But I don't want to allow myself to feel more. I still don't know her very well.

As the time comes closer, my pulse gets higher. I am telling myself that there is no reason to be nervous; I have nothing to lose in any way. But I always feel this tension, even when an old friend from here is calling me. And this is Elisa from the U.S.! A woman who is interested in me and who looks attractive. There are just a couple of minutes left until five. My hands are getting sweaty; I wonder if she would call me right on time or bit later. From many people, I'm used to them calling later or when they come. I'm usually the one who waits for everyone.

4:58, 4:59, 5:00 … The phone is ringing.

"Elisa … ah Elisabeth?!"

"Yes, here is Elisa, or Elisabeth … however you like to call me. Hi, Thomas! How are you doing?"

"I'm doing good. Nice to hear you. How are you?"

"I am doing great. I love how you pronounce my name. I don't like how the people here around say my name. Therefore, I prefer to be called Elisa. But out of your mouth with your accent, it sounds nice."

"I like your voice and understand you well."

"Thank you! But my voice isn't special. Some years ago, I liked to sing. But I became worse."

"I'm sure you have still a good voice to sing. You mentioned in one of your emails that you sang to the songs on my CD?"

There was some laughs. "Yes, I tried it at least. But the German songs aren't that easy for me since I don't know your language. But thank you for your nice words, Thomas. If you want, I can sing a song in the next days and send it you by email."

"Yes, do this Elisa." I smiled.

"I want to send you a CD with my favourite hits. But it will still need some time. I'm busy at work actually."

"This is no problem. Just make it when you can. Did you eat something for breakfast?"

"Not too much. I was playing with Lucy and Carla, you know, my cats. I was feeding the outdoor kitties, three to four are showing up on my porch every day. Then I made some green juice with my extractor and had toast."

The phone call took about one and a half hours. I surprised myself with the time range. It was not boring, but Elisa spoke more than me. Sometimes very fast, but as long as I can understand the content overall in English then it is okay for me. I'm relieved that the call went well, and I am happy that I made it. She also said that she would like to call me another time before I leave for Asia.

One Day Later

I'm used to being very well prepared for a trip, especially when it is an individual and self-organized trip. It was my third trip to Asia. I have been to Dubai and Thailand before. I don't count Turkey. Geographically, the most part of the country belongs to Asia. But it's not really far away from Germany by plane, and I did, as millions of Germans, a package holiday to the Turkish Rivera many years ago. I am excited about Hong Kong, but the conversations with Elisa keep me away from having full attention. At least once per day we are exchanging emails and, on some days, even more. This was an excerpt of her email today:

> I mentioned on the phone that for the past three or more years, I've been a bit of a hermit, really. I have not been open to the idea of meeting a new person. And I was still pretty much in that mindset when I suddenly got the notion to get on the pen pal site. There was no thought behind that for me, really, and I didn't question why I was doing it. It was just something that suddenly seemed like a good idea. Maybe there is some divine inspiration there. So what I'm trying to say, here, is that your correspondence has really been a gift to me, and you really have my attention!
> Like I said in on the phone, I like you, Thomas. I really like you, and I think about you a lot. And I don't know how all this has happened, but I won't question it. I just will continue to enjoy getting to know you. I hope you feel the same!

Also, just to say, I know you told me that you had only the one relationship that didn't work out, and I know I told you that I've had some bad experiences in my past, including in my last relationship. But what's good is that none of that has any bearing on us or what we want to do. It doesn't for me, at least, because when I hear from you, and now talking with you, I am just thinking about you and us and the time we will maybe spend together one day. The road ahead may be unknown, but I feel a very positive energy about it.

So you are definitely not like other guys I've known, and I hope you understand I mean this as a great compliment … completely! And I guess maybe most of my life I have felt different, or got treated as being different, for sure. But in talking to you, I feel like maybe there is nothing so wrong with how I am. So thanks, again, for being nice and welcoming with me. It's pretty awesome …

I feel good about what Elisa is sharing with me and how she talks with me. What she was telling me about her life in the last weeks is nothing unusual. But there are some things that she is just indicating. I am the person who always opens up pretty fast when I notice that I can trust someone. But not so typical for me is the kind of sureness about myself. I know that women need time to be sure about a man. And most I met were never sure about me, they were never completely honest with me; they never wanted let the things flow. Except for Veronika. She has been fast also … to know how to feel about me. And now Elisabeth, though she doesn't know me in person yet. I know that this can be something different. As long as you see somebody as a friend, emailing is a great way to get connected with someone new, someone you never would have met in real life. But just as soon, there are hopes and expectations in a connection, and it can lead into disappointments. I had these experiences with some women from dating sites around here and also with Susan from Missouri. It is hard to believe in anything if you never had positive experiences. I also lost self-confidence over the years about if there is still somebody out there who could fit to me. I thought hundreds of times, What's the matter? What is so bad about me that I don't deserve a chance? Family, friends and workmates often told me what a good guy I would be. So, where is the point? Maybe because I am too nice, maybe I don't have enough hair on my head or maybe because of my handicap I have since my birth. It's almost unrecognizable, and it also doesn't matter. I can lead a normal life without limitations. There is just a little limp while I am walking. There is nothing to talk about. But if a 'perfect' woman meet me, it can be a reason to lose interest in me. Of course, a woman never said this to me. But, I had one to three very good connections with a lot of hopes many years ago, where there wasn't any clear reason because they were letting me down.

About two months ago, I talked about this with my best friend Christine. She is the person with whom I can talk about anything that has to do with relationships, feelings and more. I always listen to what she has to tell from her life, and she is doing the same for me. We understand each other very well, though she is more the extrovert kind of person and her life has been quite different. At a younger age, it was never difficult for her to find guys. But she met the wrong guys and jumped from one relationship to another. We always talked about our uneven experiences. Finally, she found a guy who she married, and one year ago, she became a mom for a second time. From her second child, I am the godfather. Our talks continued; I just got the impression recently that she just tells me what I like to hear. I don't know, maybe she really has the same opinion. But it doesn't help me much. The good thing is that I could still trust her, and she doesn't start to fight against what I am saying like my parents are often doing. Anyway, two months ago I asked Christine, do you think that my handicap could be a problem for women I am dating? She said that for her it would never be a reason to not fall in love with a handicapped person. But she also said that it could be a problem for some women. It was probably honest what she told me. But it makes no difference for me to know this because I can't change anything.

And now I see these very courageous words from Elisa. "I like you, Thomas. I really like you, and I think about you a lot." She writes these words so sure after this short time that we have known each other.

Sunday afternoon

September 14, 2014

I am sitting at home in front of my laptop with a half can of cold sencha tea by my side. I already drank a lot of green jasmine tea at my parents' house in the morning and after breakfast. But I need more green tea today. I was out last night with my friend Michael at the wine festival called Weindorf in Heilbronn. It's the nicest festival in the city every year and probably the only time where you even see tourists there. Like in Erlenbach too, people like to drink wine, mingle and eat local snacks. I didn't want to stay late, but I also didn't want to leave before Michael's train came. Every year at the Weindorf, he took the train so that he could drink. When I go to bed late, I have a short night. I never can sleep long, and I'm definitely a morning person. I made the sencha as I came home from my parents' house in the late morning, but I had no more time to drink one or two mugs. I usually don't have green tea in the afternoons, but if I have it in front of me then it is hard to resist.

I am still very surprised about what happened in this past week. It started as I mentioned, in an email to Elisa that if I would have known her a couple of months before, I eventually would had booked a flight to the States and we could meet this fall. What I indicated was a mix between what I really did in the past with other mates and with the curiosity about how Elisa will react. I know that many women are careful and guarded if a guy is writing something like that after such a short time. Her reply was positive, and she wrote something back that I didn't expect. Elisabeth said that she would rather come to Germany and visit me. She would like to do this as soon as possible, but because of my big upcoming trip to Hong Kong, she could not do it before the first quarter of the next year. I answered that I would have still some vacation days left after my Asia trip so that she could still come this year. I said this more in a funny way because I was not used to a woman who didn't know me in person would visiting me from America. I have always been the one who visited people I didn't know before! And when I got invited there from someone, there was much more time between the first email and a visit. If the time range was shorter, the girls only met me, but did not invite me to their homes.

But Elisa was very serious about my suggestion and said that she would have to check when she can get off at work. She made two options: either at the end of November for nine days or even longer over Christmas into the New Year. I was special surprised about this second time range. Does she really want travel to a place where she has never been before? And spend the holidays with a guy she never met before? I was always adventurous in meeting new people. But the thought of spending the traditional holidays with somebody I didn't know was even too much for me. I know that it would also become difficult to explain it to my parents. Further, I don't know if I will get off between the holidays at my workplace, and I didn't want to ask. In another response, she understood that it would be better to come at the end of November. Everything went fast then. I asked at my workplace, got the yes for the off time and one day later Elisa sent me the booking confirmation about her flights from Raleigh to Atlanta to Stuttgart. Wow, it is amazing! This even breaks my records for how fast I booked a flight to somebody "unknown." I start to wonder about who this woman is. The price for the ticket is also expensive. I gave her the option to fly to Frankfurt if she gets a better offer there. I was sure that the tickets to Frankfurt were cheaper, but she took the destination airport that is for me better and easier to reach. Of course, on November 27 it could also have some snow. So Stuttgart is definitely the better option for me. This flight data has a double meaning for her. Elisa's father died on that day a few years ago, and it is Thanksgiving in the USA. I am both excited and nervous. Maybe also a bit anxious. Further, I am feeling a bit overwhelmed. There is this big Hong Kong trip coming soon, and now I start with plans about my next off time, just five to six weeks after when I will be back home again. I get some wet hands and wondered if I can push away my "Elisa subject" in Asia. I know if I want to have great time there, I should start to exchange more information with Ana, read travel books and search in the internet.

Saturday afternoon

September 20, 2014

It is sunny and windy as I arrive at Christine's condo in the town called Öhringen. I always liked to meet Christine. But today is one of these duty events. It was the birthday of her son, to who I am the godfather. It is not that I wouldn't like to see her boys, but I never feel too comfortable around a bunch of people. Especially around some I know, but not too well. Christine behaves a bit different to me when there are other people. Sure, she has to talk with her other relatives, friends and guests too. But in comparison to me, she can enjoy it and have a lot of fun with more people at the same time. If I have no one by my side who talks with me, I often felt lost in groups. Though it is nice to watch the children and have some good food on this afternoon, I am missing the conversations that I have at other times with Christine and feeling kind of lonely there. I am playing a bit with little Joe, but even this isn't easy because he is the birthday kid and everybody wants to spend time with him. I have the feeling that I do not belong to this party. This impression of myself isn't new for me. It happens from time to time at different locations, and for me, it is just a sign that I can't participate anywhere when there are more than three people in a room. Fortunately, Christine knew me very well already and is noticing how I am kind of suffering. She announces to the room that she needs to make a stroll with Joe so that he falls asleep. She looks in my direction, "Thomas do you to want give me some company?" This is my rescue on that afternoon! As soon as we are outside in the fresh air and Joe is getting tired, I feel much better. I tell her, full of excitement, about my Hong Kong trip, meeting Ana there, but also about Elisa and that she booked flights to visit me. I see it in her smile and in her eyes that she is the person who is really happy for me. Talking with her makes me aware of myself and that I have some exciting things ahead of me. As other people do, Christine admires me because of my trips and how I always make it to meet people internationally. This part of me doesn't fit in the impression that relatives, friends and coworkers have about me. I think some couldn't even believe it. This is the most exciting part of me, and I need my trips as I need the air to breath. Getting friends from other countries was a combination between making my travels more authentic and specific, but also maybe filling the lack of the contacts I would need where I live at home.

Christine is telling me about her "normal craziness" as she calls it. She mainly means her life as a mother of two little kids. It is always something she wanted to be, a wife and a mom. Her husband is working hard, and the older brother of Joe keeps her especially busy with his hyperactive behavior. Her mother-in-law worries her too since she always wants. Her own mother died 6 years ago, and the connection to her father and brother wasn't that great.

As I am leaving the party two hours later, she and the others are wishing me the best for my trip.

Sunday afternoon

September 28, 2014

It is beautiful outside. Warm, but not hot. This is the best weather that could be at the end of September in Southern Germany. Some leaves were turned a bit into yellow already, but it is still more the summer color green that I see. It would be an ideal day to spend the time on a walk, on the bicycle or in a café or beer garden. Yesterday I was sitting with Michael in a café in the pedestrian precinct in Heilbronn. But on this Sunday afternoon, I don't have any time for those kind of things. It is the day before my flight to Hong Kong. My baggage is packed, and I just can't forget my bath bag with the shaver, toothpaste, shower gel and the other small things in the morning. And there is my old alarm clock. I have this little colorful thing with the world time set since Christmas 1988. It went with me to almost every trip in my adult life. I rarely needed it on my trips and or at home. I have something like an alarm clock inside me that wakes me up before this colorful thing starts ringing. But it is for safety. In the last days, I also bought some small gifts for Ana: a book about Germany, a cream and a perfume, a towel, a little bag and gummy bears. I often had chats with her about food and cooking on Facebook. But of course I can't take any fresh food on this trip. Even the German chocolate that she would like to try is not possible to get in this season. In Hong Kong it is still too warm. I chatted with Ana in the morning last time. She wished me safe flights and that she should hear something from me when I am there. It sounds like she is an easy-going person. She also never says more than necessary in a moment. Weeks ago, she already mentioned that she could not take me from the airport because she would have to work. I am not sure how I can get in touch with her when I am there. Our conversation was mainly over Facebook. Writing emails isn't her thing. I have her cell phone number, but I am sure that calls, and probably even texts, would be expensive there. Ana also didn't mention much about the student demonstrations there. I didn't have much time to watch the news recently. My parents are a bit worried, Michael talked about it and Elisabeth is concerned. My emails to her got shorter because of my busy schedule in the last few days, but it is still an intense connection with her. She writes a lot, and I am wondering how much she cares about me. I never thought that somebody can do this better than my mom. But she is, the American lady who I still don't know in person. On one side, she keeps me distracted from more excited thoughts on my trip, but on the other side it feels very good. As usual, I am thrilled and nervous about the trip. I'm used to travelling alone, but it is always something new to fly in a direction I have never been before. Also a bit excited, but not nervous anymore, when I am on the phone with Elisa. She found a way to get connections with her cell phone to mine via Skype. I don't understand how much she pays for it, but it would be much less and she could talk without limitation to me, she mentioned.

Right now I am reading a second time her email she sent an hour ago.

Hi my Dearest Thomas!

You are just so sweet! I look forward to talking with you today ☺ Yes, I hope you will not worry one bit over me during your Hong Kong trip. I want you to know that in our communications and in our connection there is something unique that I haven't experienced before. Of course there are times I get home so late from work, and I rush in trying to get the cats fed and stuff done so I can sit down and read an email from you. And I'm always so happy about it! But there is a sense in me, for the first time, of this comfort and ease with you. And so sometimes before I check my email I will make dinner, or like this morning, get up, feed the cats, put in some laundry and make breakfast. I feel the connection, and thus, I feel assured. I know you are there, and so I can go on with the normal life things and still know we're there for each other. What this says to me is that our connection is quite special. I don't feel any anxiety if you haven't written because I trust you. I know I will hear from you. And as you know, you'll probably get a bunch of emails from me in that time! I do think of you all the time, and there is this certainty I feel with you. So I will be drawing upon that sense, when you are in Hong Kong, and sending all my best thoughts to you, as well! ☺

I appreciate you telling me your feelings on why you want to be cautious, Thomas. I understand the need to protect your heart. And please don't feel the need to downplay any of the pain you went through by comparing it to what I may have experienced. It's not ridiculous! Emotional pain is the deepest kind of pain, and having a broken heart, it's the most terrible thing to go through. I know there is nothing I could say to take away all your fears. But what I can say is that I don't feel just friendship for you, it is definitely more. And there is no reason for me that it should change when we meet.

I will admit that back in 2012, I was going through a period of loneliness. I came upon this idea online for making a 'dream board' or a "vision board." I guess it comes from the 'Law of Attraction' which I sort of think may be onto something but is an idea that has become far too commercialized. But at it's heart, it say that the energy you are in is what you attract to yourself. So I was somewhat afraid that I would be attracting more negative things for myself if I didn't clean up the loneliness and also fear and mistrust I had around relationships. To note, this needing to clean up those feelings is one reason I decided I didn't want a relationship at all … because I needed time to fix in me what led me to those past relationships. At any rate, I found this site where you could make a dream board. Mine was about a relationship with the one I call "My Love." So I took pictures of couples walking hand in hand, together in the mountains, lying in green grass, smiling, holding each other looking off into a sunset. I put some quotes in it, and I wrote a list of attributes down the side of the dream board … all the things I know that I will have with the person I am to be with. In the center of the list was "Divine Connection." There were other things like: Respect, Honesty, Interest, Caring, Joy, Empathy, Happiness, Passion, Adventure, Sharing, Understanding … And at the top of the dream board was the phrase "The Right Place at the Right Time."

Well, maybe 3 months ago, I was cleaning out my computer files and stumbled across this dream board. Though it's all true, I was feeling at the time that I would not again have a relationship in this lifetime. I had sort of settled on that fact. Because I know I won't again be with someone who doesn't possess the attributes I think are so fundamental. For me, this is like a spiritual thing. I will never be in the situations I once was. I am worthy of more. And I'd resigned myself that in this lifetime, unless I would meet and recognize that person, then I want to spend my days as a single person. And I was okay with that. So I found my dream board, and I decided I didn't need it anymore, and I deleted it. It's gone. The site I created it on isn't working and the profile I'd made there no longer has the file on it. I can't recover it from my computer. So why am I telling you this? I think, when I made up my mind that it will be a true connection with someone or nothing at all, and I let go of longing for something I didn't have, that's when I fully cleaned up what was haunting me about past troubled experiences with men. Maybe that's why I could hear a soft, still voice say, "Get a Penpal." This is not said to put pressure on you that you need to be anything for me. I just recognize that I've met a wonderful human being in you. It's a familiar feeling with you, which makes no sense, since I've never had this feeling before ☺ So I know that your past is full of hurts and rejections, and mine is too. But for me, there is a feeling that I wouldn't have suddenly and unexpectedly met a person like you, when I wasn't looking for anyone, and then experience this deep connection with you, all for nothing. The Universe is saying clearly to me, "Pay Attention." I'm very aware of how I've been in the past, when I'm seeing an illusion and just wanting it to be real, so that I won't be lonely. And this is definitely NOT that kind of situation. As I said, I've let go of those patterns, because above all, I respect myself and want to be true to myself. So you know how I am feeling, Thomas. But all that we need to do is just continue on with this journey together, enjoying all our great conversations, reveling in how we seem to speak and think so alike, finding interest in each others' experiences and ideas, and for once just relishing the moment of feeling a heart-connection between two good people, without all the fear that comes from those who were not right for us and who made us question our own worth. And as for your heart, your feelings, I do understand, believe me I do, and I want to protect that heart too. I accept you for who you are, and I feel you have felt the same way towards me. That's just what I want to say, and I am sorry, in advance, if I say too much. But it's just where I'm at ☺

And yes, Thomas, I would have no secrets from you about my past, though I won't dwell in those things. As you know, the hardest thing I've been dealing with is the loss of family. That is one I still need time with and to work on more because the heart is very much not mended yet in that realm. But the other past relationships, there has been time and perspective now, and I don't feel much about those things anymore.

You are wonderful and special, most truly! I'm so glad that I'm coming to Germany … in only two months now! It's just awesome!

Sweet hugs … talk to you on 11/5! ☺

Elisa

Again, I am surprised about this American woman. Her words are feeling very good inside me. I'm open, she probably noticed this and is open to me as well. But it is her sureness that makes me a bit anxious. Anxious for myself, but also for her.

It is shortly before 5 p.m. and I am waiting for Elisa's call in my living room. Exactly at five, my phone is ringing.

"Hi Elisa!"

"Hi Thomas! How are you doing?"

"I'm doing fine. My baggage is packed. I just need a shower after our call and will go to my parents' house for dinner."

"I will miss you, Thomas. Even though you are at home far away from here. But when you are on a trip then it's something different, and I definitely will miss your emails!"

"I will miss your emails too. If I can, I will write you. But I don't know when, I don't know where I will have internet access, and further, I am busy on trips."

"I know this Thomas. I want you to enjoy your trip and have a lot of fun. Just when you can, it would be nice to hear from you. I have some worries about you because of the demonstrations there. I have seen some pictures in internet. Please, promise me, stay away from that."

"Yes, sure. I don't want to get in any danger. How are you doing there, Elisa?"

"I'm doing good. As I said in my last email, I'm doing my usual chores. But you are on my mind, Thomas. It's so nice to read your emails; I think of you very often."

"I think of you also. Normally in times before such a big trip, there only the trip is in my head. But you find a way in my thoughts all day."

"This is so sweet of you, Thomas."

The phone call goes almost two hours. We give each other compliments, and it is almost like what I would say to a girlfriend here before leaving for the next ten days. The connection with Elisabeth after a such a short time is so incredibly deep. I am wondering if she will go to the back of my mind in Hong Kong.

The Hong Kong Trip

Monday early morning

September 29, 2014

After a quick breakfast at my parents' house, we are going to my dad's car. I have, from my hometown, a good train connection to the airports to Stuttgart and even to Frankfurt. But before a big trip, it is always nice if somebody takes me to the airport with my baggage. My smaller red suitcase with the rolls is easy to handle, but I enjoy the comfort of a car ride. Though on a Monday morning, you never know about the traffic on the roads.

Many years ago, my dad took me to the airport once as I had booked a trip to the Dominican Republic. He got almost a heart attack as we ended up in a traffic jam, and I almost missed the flight. Because of a car accident on the Autobahn, nothing went on anymore. Just then, I got an idea in this moment to drive over a forbidden field from the A 81, and with luck I got that flight in the last minutes.

Through this experience, we all learned it's better to leave too early than too late. Also, my mom is in the car now. They want take their off day to spend some time in the Stuttgart area after taking me to the airport. Shortly after the interchange in Weinsberg, we are hearing in the traffic news, 12 kilometers of traffic jam in our direction. My dad wants to stay on the Autobahn, my mom and I want to leave it and take the small roads. Sometimes the traffic news is wrong or it isn't as bad as they talk about it. But you never know, and I am afraid to be stuck in a jam as years ago. Dad takes what we said, but it is then very slow beside of the Autobahn too. We were hitting every traffic light, and it took an eternity. But because we left so early, I am right on time at the airport. It is my first time that I am standing at a British Airways check-in desk. I have never used them before. But they were the cheapest and it is from the flight time still possible to make it for me.Though, it is almost double the time as a nonstop flight from Germany. But the price for the nonstop ticket would be double. So I have chosen a connection that is going first in the wrong direction, to the Northwest instead of the Southeast. The check in goes fast, and I say goodbye to my parents. The security controls for this flight don't take too long, and it is not to compare with a flight to the U.S. I'm at the gate and still have almost two hours left. I start to eat a pretzel and look a bit in my Hong Kong magazine. I bought it three and a half years ago when I wanted go the first time to Hong Kong. Actually, I always want to have the newest information about a place I go. But I had no time to read much before this trip. Besides this magazine, I also have an older travel book and "The World Of Suzie Wong" with me. I enjoy sitting at an airport and watching all the people. There are still not many passengers at this gate. I think that mostly business travellers will take this morning flight to London. Suddenly, I feel the vibration of my cell phone in the pocket of my pants. I thought, hopefully not my parents to tell me that I have forgot something. No … it is Elisa!

"Hi Elisa?!"

"Good Morning Thomas! I just wanted check if everything is going well."

"Yes, everything is good. I am sitting at the gate right now. But, wow, it must be in the middle of the night there?!"

"It's 2:30 a.m. here. I want make sure that you are doing good and let you know that I think of you."

"This is very nice of you. But you must be tired and have to go to work in the morning there again."

"Don't worry about this. Our connection became so important for me, and I just care about you."

"I don't think anybody did this before. Except for my parents. Thank you! You are so sweet."

"Thanks. You are sweet, too, and I will miss you. I have seen on the internet about the demonstrations in Hong Kong again.

Please be careful, Thomas, and if it is not possible to get by bus to your hotel or whatever it is, then take a taxi.

"Yes, I will be careful, Elisa. It's nice of you that that you think so much of me. But you don't have to worry, ok?"

"Yes, but send me a text or a message when you are safe there. And if you need any kind of help, you know I am here for you."

"Thank you, Elisabeth! But go to bed again, you will need your sleep."

"Yes, I will do." I heard her smile.

I smiled too. "Thank you for your concern and try to catch some sleep."

"I will try. Have good flights, Thomas. Bye"

"Bye, Elisa."

"Bye."

Still an hour later, I am surprised about her call. She really cares about me. She stood up in the night there and just wanted make sure that everything is going well with me! It makes me feel very good, that a woman misses me. Even when it is a bit strange to be missed from somebody I have never met in person.

In the meantime, there are some people at the gate. It is shortly before the boarding, but it doesn't look like the plane will get full.

Right in time, the plane is taking off, and I have booked my seat on the window. It was funny to fly to London when I wanted to get to Hong Kong.

But it was just a 50 minute flight, and we land with rain at Heathrow. More, my issue was how to spend around seven hours in one terminal? The last days at home, I checked on the internet if it would be possible to get to the city and back during my layover. But other travellers on a chat board didn't recommend this. All the procedures to get out of the airport, to the city and back would take too long. I didn't want risk anything, so I decided to stay at Terminal 5. It is indeed a large terminal. I am wondering about all the money exchange points. Who is seriously interested in getting British pounds in an international transfer terminal? Quickly, I noticed why. All the price tags in the shops were in pounds. Typical England! I don't want to buy anything, but of course I want to sit down and eat something. I am strolling in both directions, but there is just a fine restaurant, a fish & chips place and a kind of burger restaurant. So many shops and almost no restaurants! I am going to the burger place, which looks quite busy. But the waitress is friendly, and I get my burger with some salad and fries. Fortunately, I can pay with my credit card and don't need any British money. I also give the young girl a tip. I don't know if this is usual here or not. Maybe not, because she makes a surprised expression and she start to talk with me.

"I am Maria. Where are you travelling?"

"I'm Thomas. I will fly to Hong Kong."

"Oh Hong Kong, I have never been so far way. I come from Portugal originally. From here to Lisbon is the only flight I sometimes take. Where are you from? And are you going to Hong Kong for business?"

"From Germany. No, I'm on vacation. So for pleasure."

"Ah … holiday?" She says with a big smile. "I have to work again. Have a good flight!"

It is easy to see that she was Portuguese. Black hair, big brown eyes and pale skin.

I am leaving the restaurant and login at a Wi-Fi spot with my cell phone. But the connection isn't good. The signal comes and goes. With some effort, I can send my dad and Elisa short emails. She writes back and wishes me a good flight again. I am in London, one time zone closer to her. She is on the way to work now. I want sign in to Facebook to send Ana a message, but it doesn't work. The connection gives me too much trouble. I am at the gate for my Hong Kong flight. I am almost on my feet a whole day, but the long flight was still coming. It's an exhausted and excited feeing at the same time. I see the big plane outside. I don't know much about airplanes, but I think that this must be the biggest Airbus, the A380 with the two decks. The gate is crowded and many special Chinese people are already standing in the line for boarding. Some are wearing face masks. Is this typical in Hong Kong? I think. It still takes some time, but they are using two or three gate entrances, and because of the two decks, the boarding goes faster than I expect. Again, I get my reserved seat by the window on the upper deck. There was enough space with a little board between the seat and the window. On my left is an older Chinese man with a moustache. My excitement is growing. Sitting in this airplane and flying to a place where I have never been before makes me nervous and excited all in one. I think, Hong Kong, I am coming! This city had to wait three and a half years for me! I am checking the entertainment display in front of me. As always, I'm not interested in movies or games. I want to check what kind of music albums they have. And there is a lot. I start to put the songs on a playlist to listen to later. There was something from Lady Gaga, R.E.M., U2, Pink, Fleetwood Mac and also Simon & Garfunkel. Simon & Garfunkel reminds me of Ana. They are one of her favourite bands, and she said in her chats that she likes to sing their songs. More in a funny way, I said already four years ago when I met her on internet that she has to sing for me when I am there one day. I am smiling when I think on this. She always answered that I have to sing with her, and I replied that the streets of Hong Kong will be empty when people would hear me singing.

The plane is leaving the gate now. About ten minutes later, we are going up, but it is slow how the big plane rises up in the sky. It is interesting to see the River Thames out of the window and then the estuary in the North Sea. It gets dark quickly. After an orange juice, chicken with rice, a salad, a little chocolate cake and black tea, I am feeling as comfortable as I could be on an airplane seat. I start to read in "The World of Suzie Wong," but after half an hour I am too tried to read more. I'm not sure if I can sleep, but I want to try to relax with my created playlist. In the map of the display, I see that we are over the Baltic Sea and in direction to Russia. I am closing my eyes, and I'm dosing with the music through the headphones. I listen to Simon & Garfunkel sing "The Sound of Silence …"

In restless dreams I walked alone
Narrow streets of cobblestone
'Neath the halo of a streetlamp
I turned my collar to the cold and damp
When my eyes were stabbed by

The flash of a neon light
That split the night
And touched the sound of silence

And in the naked light I saw
Ten thousand people, maybe more
People talking without speaking
People hearing without listening
People writing songs that voices never share
And no one dared
Disturb the sound of silence …

Tuesday

September 30, 2014

A child is crying a few rows behind me. As I look on the display in front of me, I see there that we are already somewhere over Southern China. I can't remember if I have slept much, but it seems that I had my eyes closed for some hours. I missed the whole flight time over Russia. The stewardesses start with serving the breakfast. My music gets boring, and I read in the book again. I find it amazing how some old books are still popular today. This one was published in 1957. I am sure that Hong Kong changed in these many years, but a novel always gives a specific feeling about a place.

There are just 30 minutes until the landing time. I get more nervous and hope that everything will go well after my arrival. Between the clouds, I see water, but also some green islands. This could already be a part of Hong Kong! A few minutes later, there is nothing to see anymore. Then I am hearing and feeling the noises that indicate that we are landing. But there isn't much to see out of the window; it is like a yellow fog. After ten more minutes, we are reaching the airport building. The sight to the outside still isn't very good. I am wondering if it is really fog, smog or both? Finally I can leave the plane, and I am following the signs. The controls are pretty fast, and I get a stamp in my passport. As normal, it takes some time at the baggage claim. Once again, I'm feeling the vibration of my cell phone in my pocket. Elisa!

"Hello!"

"Hi, Thomas! Here is Elisa! How are you doing?"

"Hey, Elisa! Thanks, I am doing good. I'm standing at the baggage claim right now."

"I have seen on the flight tracker that your plane landed as planned. Do you know how you will get to the city there?"

"If I find the right bus stop, I will take the bus as Ana and the host of this place in Tsim Sha Tsui recommended to me. It must be in the night there in North Carolina?"

"Yes it is. But I wanted give you a call when you landed there."

In this moment, I see my red suitcase coming. Other people are watching me while I am talking on the phone.

"This is nice of you. But right now my baggage is coming … Wait a moment …"

I pick it up. With all these people around me, the suitcase and Elisa on the phone, I am feeling a bit overwhelmed.

"Here I am again. I picked it up. It's very loud here, and I have still a pressure in my ears from the landing."

"I don't want to hold you any longer on the phone. Be safe and send me a text or an email when you can, Thomas."

"Yes, I will do. But as said before, don't wait for it. I don't know if I will always have the chance and time for it."

"Sure, I understand. I let you go now. I will think of you."

"Thank you. Think of you too. Bye."

"Bye."

I enjoyed her call in Stuttgart at the airport, but for this one, the timing wasn't the best. I don't like when I stand in a bunch of people and somebody calls me. I don't feel well when coworkers listen to my phone calls or my parents either. But it is amazing how much this woman cared about me.

I am looking for a bank now. I want to follow the advice in my travel book. I need some Hong Kong dollars, but I don't want exchange too much at the airport because the rates in the city should be better. A few people went to ATMs, but I am searching for somewhere I can exchange my cash. After walking around in the arrival hall, I'm exchanging 50 euros. This should be enough for the moment. Then I am following the public transportation signs. As I am going out of the building, I'm running like I am against a wall. The air is hot, very thick and humid. I see the bus stops, but I am noticing that I want buy the Octopus Card. There is a little kiosk, but the man behind it makes it clear that I can only get this card at the train station in the airport. I am walking back, and until I am outside at the bus stop again, I am sweating a lot. As my printout shows, I have to take bus A21 to Kowloon.

After a short waiting time, a bus with this number appears. Not many people are going on the bus, and only Chinese or other Asians take it. It is a double decker, but I prefer to stay on the ground floor and sit on a seat where I see a big screen that is showing the following bus stops. Because the bus is almost empty, I have my red suitcase beside me and not on a baggage shelf. I am feeling a bit relieved; the first task was made – sitting on the right bus. But one of the more difficult things will come when I have to leave the bus. The host wrote in a message that I should get off the bus at Chatham Road near the Park Hotel. But I don't know the name of the bus stop and knew from other trips that it is never easy the first time in a big city. The screen that I am staring at shows Chinese letters, but also every 10 seconds, it shows the names in English. The bus drove over a big bridge. I assume that it is the bridge to the mainland part of Hong Kong since I know that the airport is at an artificial island and belongs to Lantau. The view out of the bus is still misty, but it is better as we near the arrival. I see green and thickly wooded hills, but also the first big apartment buildings close to the road. When I am somewhere for the first time, I always try to find out which other place a city or country reminds me of. These big tasteless blocks looks a bit like the former Czech Republic; they look socialistic. The obviously bad air reminds me of this too. But all the green and tropic climate doesn't fit to that. I am feeling excited to be somewhere new that I have never been before.

After sometime on a big highway, I see water on the left. It is very busy, many ships and boats, and in the back is a part of an island. The buildings become bigger and everything gets narrower. This is probably already Kowloon. But suddenly, the big screen is black! I get nervous, how will I know where I have to get off the bus? From what I know, it will still take some time, and Chatham Road must be in the other direction. This big road where we are driving now was probably Nathan Road. Before us, the street is blocked and the bus turns to the right. Maybe because of the demonstrations? After some more minutes, I ask another passenger where I have to get off the bus. But he says I should ask the bus driver. I do it as he stops again. I don't understand this Chinese-English or maybe he also doesn't understand me? If I understand him correctly, then I should get off at the next stop. I do it, and I am standing with beads of sweats beside a big road.

I am taking my map and the direction paper out of my backpack. I think that this road must be Chatham Road, and in front I see the Park Hotel. I can't be wrong. Just after a few steps, I see the street sign, Cameron Road. I made it! At least almost, I still have to find the place. They call themselves a hostel orwhat not fit to the Airbnb thing. Usually Airbnb people are private. Cameron Road is a busy one-way street with three lanes, many stores, neon signs and lot of people. It looks definitely Chinese and not too international. I am walking on this crowded street, and after some meters, I see on the opposite left side the hostel sign. It isn't easy to get over this road with my suitcase. On the other side, I go in a small dusty corridor and to an elevator there. A Chinese woman smiles on me as I am arriving at the sixth floor. She wants to have my passport and the booking confirmation. After she made a copy of my passport, she says that I would have go to another place on the right side of this road. I would be booked there. I am a bit surprised because it is exactly the house number that was written at the Airbnb site. After some time, I am on this busy road again. I walk a few meters, but I don't see the sign she talked about. There are hundreds of neon signs on this road. I ask somebody at a money exchange place, but I just hear a "No." Then I see the sign. The entrance is on the left of this exchange place. Maybe the lady doesn't understand me? Again, it is a small corridor with an elevator. This time I am leaving it at the fifth floor. Now I am right. After I'm paying a caution for the room key, the Chinese man says that he will show me the room. It is on the secondfloor of the building. I am not shocked because I heard that everything in Hong Kong would be small. The room was just a little bigger than the bed. On the left side of the bed is absolutely no space and on the right side is no more space than the size of my small suitcase. Near the door is a board on the wall to put on some small things, a water cooker and a flat-screen TV. That is it, but fortunately the room has daylight and a large window above the bed. At the window there was a a cheap air conditioner. The air in this little room was very hot and muggy. I think, Welcome to Hong Kong! But even better is the shared bathroom. There is a single sink and the toilet and shower is in one. I am not demanding, but this could get something dirty and ugly if more people are using this bathroom. The good thing on this place is that I have a free internet connection. I sit down on the bed and check Facebook. There is a welcome message from Ana. She asks if would still meet her on that day. It is in late afternoon, and I am excited and overwhelmed, but not tired. So, why not? She wrote that she would come on my road at 7 p.m., and we can meet in front of a drugstore. I am not sure about this drugstore, but she said it wouldn't be far away from my place, and I would see it. I send an email to my dad at home that I arrived safely and also send another one to Elisa. I'm happy that this place has at least a free WLAN spot. I am thinking that with this, I have a connection to Ana over Facebook and also to my parents and Elisa.

Now it is time for a shower. Nobody used the bathroom, so I jumped in fast, and it looked clean so far. This shower/toilet isn't really a good thing. I think that it would be bad enough to have something like that in your own room, but to share such a shower/toilet thing with strange people is awful. I clean the wet toilet cover. Back in my room, I am sweating even more than before. I put some deodorant under my armpits. I see that it is already 6:40 p.m. I am getting excited to meet Ana. I put on a fine shirt and long jeans. I know that the jeans are too warm, but I don't know how people walk around here at evening times, and I also want to give Ana good first impression. I take all the things I brought for her from Germany in a plastic bag and put on my baseball cap. Years ago, I only wore these caps when it was very sunny. Then I wore it when it rained and now I am wearing them often, to hide my bald spots on my head. It is shortly before 7 p.m.; I am never late when I meet somebody. I go down and cross the road. There is the drugstore in front of me. And this must be Ana! She is already there. She looked in the window, but from the pictures she sent me, that must be her. Slim and tall for an Asian woman, long black hair, a black dress with red flowers on it. I slowly got closer. She turned around.

"Ana?"

"Yes … Thomas?"

"Yes, I am. Hi!" I tried to hug her. But it maybe looks odd. I am not used to hugging somebody.

"Hello. Welcome to Tsim Sha Tsui! Are you tired? Are you hungry?"

"I am not too tired, also not too hungry. But I didn't have anything for hours. So I think that I could eat something. Nice to meet you!"

Her first very serious face is changing into a big smile.

"Nice to meet you too!"

I am smiling back.

"There is restaurant right here at the corner. They have an English menu, and it's popular with tourists. Do you want go there?"

"Yeah, why not?" I reply.

We are walking just a few steps, and we are already at the restaurant. It is close to the bus stop where I arrived in the afternoon. The place is very busy. Ana walks in, and I follow her. Everything is modern and clean; it looks a bit like a fast food place. A waiter came and gave us the menus.

"I have already eaten. As usual, I cooked for my boss and his wife and ate with them."

The menu was more like a photo book, and it helped me to choose what I want.

"Ana, could you recommend anything?"

"I was not here before. But do you like chicken or fish? They also have duck. You can also get a combination with two types of meat."

"Good. I think I take this roasted chicken and roasted duck."

Everything is going fast at this place. Ana is lifting her finger like a school kid and points at the chicken/duck picture in the menu. The waiter says, "For two?"and shows two fingers. Ana says no and shows one finger.

After the waiter left, I asked her if we would order anything to drink. She says that we would not have to order anything extra and tea would always be served.

"I have something for you from Germany, Ana." I gave her the plastic bag. She looked a bit embarrassed.

"Thank you! Are Chinese restaurants similar in Germany?"

"Maybe a bit different. I am curious about the food."

Just a few seconds later, we have a tea can and cups in front of us, and I get my chicken/duck plate. After a short time, Ana asks me, "And is it like in Germany?"

"Yes, I'm surprised that it is not really different. I just have to be careful with the little bones in the meat. In Chinese restaurants in Germany, the meat is mostly boneless. I don't say anything, but I think that it tastes alot like flavor enhancers and glutamate. I say, "This salad with the oyster sauce is different and interesting. In Germany, you have oyster sauce already in the meal, and when I cook Chinese by myself, I also put the sauce in the meat and vegetable while cooking."

"Yes, to take lettuce leaves and put some oyster sauce on it is typical here at some places as a side dish. Do you like the tea?"

"Yes, it's not bad. But it isn't green tea. I think it's oolong tea."

"I don't know. People call it Chinese tea here. But you are the tea expert."

"I doubt if I am an expert, but yes, I already drank a lot of different teas." I laughed.

After I paid, we went outside into the hot and thick air again. Ana wants show me some things. We are crossing Chatham Road over an upper pedestrian bridge, and between some malls, we reach a big fountain. From there, we are walking to the promenade of Tsim Sha Tsui.

"Wow, all these skyscrapers on the other side!"

"Yes, this is Hong Kong Island. And here on the promenade, I am here almost every evening after work."

I remembered that she mentioned in our Facebook chats that she went out for a walk on the water. I am looking astonished over the water to the other side. There are hundreds of skyscrapers all around and very close to each other, hundreds of ships and boats in the water. The view isn't clear, and I wondered if it is still so extremely humid near the water. There is no wind that could make it a little cooler. Ana is sweating, and I notice that this girl didn't look bad from the side.

"Thomas, are you tired or do want walk along the promenade?"

"I'm overexcited and couldn't sleep. So let us walk on."

"Here in this part it's quiet. But as we get closer, we will come to the South point and it will get busier."

We don't talk much in the next minutes. But it is a special feeling and atmosphere to walk with Ana along this promenade. It was now about 30 hours ago since I am not in a bed. But for that I am still feeling good. We don't go too far and are walking over the Salisbury Road to 1881 Heritage. We are going up to a little tower, and I am fascinated about the scene. I enjoy being in another world, far away from home.

Ana says it would be time to go back again. Her boss and his wife would be worried if she would stay away longer than usual. She takes me back to the corner of Chatham Road/Cameron Road. She smiles and points to the neon sign of my hostel. "Can you find the rest of the way?"

"Yes, thank you for taking me here. And thank you for the evening."

"It was nice to meet you. Just send me a message on Facebook when you are awake in the morning. You know I have the next two days off because of the Chinese holidays. I can show you around."

"This would be great! Have a good night!"

"Have a good night too and get some rest. Until tomorrow. Bye!"

And fast, she is gone in the crowd of the people.

My room is hot and humid. I forgot to switch on the air conditioning before I left. I login to the internet with my cell phone and write Ana a thank-you message. It is funny to send her a message, as many times before, after she went back from her night stroll. The distinction was just that I went with her on that night stroll, and I wasn't six hours apart from her!

Elisa has emailed me too. She is 12 hours away now! It is amazing how much this woman cares about me. She is wondering what I am doing and is using a more private notations. She writes things like "My dearest Thomas, mention a couple of times how much she would miss me, and ends the email with 'Big Hugs.'" I like it and write in the same way back. I am glad that I could write her via email from here after such an impressive day. Also, I get a short email from my dad.

The air conditioning is very loud, and anyway, I don't like to sleep with the cold air. I generally don't like air conditioning, but I noticing at this place that it is at least necessary before I go to bed. At the bathroom, I see that in the meantime several guests probably used the toilet and shower. As expected, it looks ugly.

As I lay down, I notice how loud it is from the outside. The cars are driving, the people talking and many other noises. My thoughts and feeling are running in my head like in a fast carousel. It takes a long time until I fall into sleep.

Wednesday

October 1, 2014

It is still very early in the morning. It is hot, and all the night it was loud from the street. I turn around; I am still dozing, but I can't fall in a deep sleep again. The air is standing in the room. I am thinking that the bathroom probably still looks dirty, but I need another shower.

There is no space in this little room for the wet towel and my used clothes. I hang the things behind the door. I notice that I have nothing to eat for breakfast. Fortunately, I exchanged some euros into dollars last night. As I get down to the street, I see that it is quite empty now. This seems to be the quietest time of the day in this area. Just one small supermarket has opened. I'm buying some green tea bags, water, a fruit juice and two apples. This isn't really something for a breakfast. But on the work days at home, I am also used to not eating much. When I am at work, I always drink a can of green tea and have an apple, an orange or any other fruit. As I come back in the room, it is cool; this time I switched on the air conditioning before I left. I make some green tea, eat the apples and go online. Again, a nice email from Elisa, and Ana is online.

"Good Morning! When do you want to meet?"

"Good Morning, Ana!" I'm already up for some time. We can meet as soon as you are ready."

"Didn't sleep you well?"

"No, it was too loud from the street."

"I'm sorry! I thought this could happen. Maybe you should buy earplugs."

"I usually don't like such stuff. But yes, I think it's necessary at this place."

"I can be at the fountain at nine. Can you find it again?"

"You mean this big fountain where we were first at last night?"

"Yes, it's not far away from Cameron Road. You should find it. ☺"

"I hope so. ☺"

"Okay then, until nine."

"See you!"

I am not sure if I can find the fountain easily again. Therefore, I want leave my room now, short before 8:30 p.m. It is still very humid outside. Usually I'm good with my orientation sense, but the many people on the streets and the fact that I just followed Ana last night makes me confused. Sure, I know that first I would have to go to Chatham Road again, and then it must be behind a big mall. I'm sweating again and trying to find my way through the crowds.

Only ten minutes later, I'm reaching the fountain, and it is easier to find than I thought. As I sit close to the water and try to figure out where Ana would come from, I notice again that my orientation isn't the best in this city. I have a good view into two main directions, behind me is the fountain and the square. I'm turning around a few times and watching people. I don't see many Westerners. My impression is that most are Chinese. Ana said last night that she would see the differences between mainland Chinese people and Hong Kong Chinese. It would be easy to see by what they wear sometimes, but always how they behave. Though Ana couldn't speak Chinese, she said that she would hear the distinction between Cantonese and Mandarin. I wondered if these two families beside the fountain where mainland Chinese. It is 9 p.m., but I still don't see Ana. After ten more minutes, I get nervous. When I met anybody at home in Germany, I started to doubt if the time and place was right. But this was also typical for me that I wait. I wait for other people mostly. It is 9:20 p.m. as Ana suddenly is standing in front of me with a yellow summer dress and colorful points on it, a big white bag over her right shoulder and a shy smile. I smile back.

"Hi Ana!"

"Hi Thomas! I am sorry that I'm late. Are you interested to see some temples today?"

"Oh, yes I would like to see it."

"What did have for breakfast?"

"Not too much. Two apples and some green tea."

"I see, the green tea drinker. But you must be hungry. Do you want to try something typical here? Do you see that stand over there? Let's go."

Ana doesn't wait for an answer. I just follow her over the pedestrian zone to the next street. We are at the stand, and I have no clue what food I am seeing. They have big soup pots, then there are little balls swimming in a very greasy sauce, and they have pastries behind glass. But it seems to be popular because people are waiting in a queue. I don't know what to take. Ana talks for me and points to something white. It looks like steamed yeast dumplings at home in Germany. They are packing it in a bag, and I pay. I don't understand what I have to pay, I just give a note and get some small change back.

"These are lotus rolls. I hope you like it, Thomas."

At a bench, we sit down. The rolls are still warm, the dough is soft in the middle and is sweet, obviously lotus paste. It tastes different than anything I've had before.

"It's good. It's not as sweet as I thought, and I know from pastries I've eaten before in other countries."

"Fine. When you are finished, we are going to the MTR station."

I am following her again. Since I arrived here yesterday afternoon, I didn't look into any map. It is easy for me, but it doesn't help my orientation. Especially in the big MTR stations, I don't know where I am walking. My eyes are only focused on Ana. We are changing twice the MTR lines and get outside at a station called Diamond Hill. After some steps, we are reaching the entrance of a garden. It is the Chin Lin Nunnery. It is a beautiful garden with a little waterfall, a waterwheel, bonsai trees and a big temple. The temple and the nunnery buildings are made in dark woods with red columns. It is a Buddhist temple, Japanese style, and it looks very natural. Ana asks after every corner if I would like to have another picture of myself. I say that I am not photogenic, but she disagrees and takes a lot of me. She also enjoys when I take photographs of her. Though there are big apartment buildings around the garden, it is a relaxed oasis. We are far away from the city centers, but even around here Hong Kong is busier than many other places in the world.

As we get to the exit, Ana says that the Wong Tai Sin Temple would also be close and that we could walk there. But she is also now a bit confused about the directions, and we have to ask two passengers. As we are arrive, there hundreds of people streamed in this Taoism temple. Ana explains that it would be one of the most popular temples for mainland Chinese, and because it is a holiday, they are coming with buses. It is very hot in the sun; everything is colorful and soppy; I'm smelling the scent of incense sticks everywhere; Chinese music is playing from boxes, and there is almost no chance to take a picture without having a bunch of people in it. But, I enjoy it. It is how I imagined a Chinese temple.

"Are you hungry?" Ana asked me.

"Yes, a bit."

"Over there is a mall. I'm sure that we will find something … Ah, Thomas, do you see? Here are lot of fortune tellers. Do you want go?" She smiles, and I don't know if she means it serious or if it is just a joke.

"No, not now. I am not even a full day in Hong Kong. I am sure I will have another chance in the next days. Let's go to the mall!" I smile back.

The mall is the contrast to the Chinese temple. The mall could be anywhere in the world, with the same stores and fast food places. We decide on a Japanese fast food restaurant. They have green tea and food; it is nothing I'm used to having. I ate a bowl with tuna, spawn and rice. Ana pays for the lunch. I don't want it, but I appreciate it. She probably has less money than me, but I still would get my possibilities to invite her too.

Our next destination is the Ten Thousands Buddha Monastery. For this place, I was already excited to go some time ago as I read about it at home in my travel book. Fast, I understand that there are many more Buddha statues than 10,000. We are both sweating incredibly as we are climbing up the many stairs to the hill. At the top, I am wet like after a shower. But the way up was worth it, and there is a great overlook. Hong Kong looks different in this corner than I have seen before, a lot of green hills and mountains around. I ask some girls if they would take a picture of Ana and me. Ana felt a bit embarrassed, but for me it is just nice to have the first picture of me and my Asian friend. I'm asking her about the nationalities of these girls here. She says they would be Malaysian and would have a big advantage because they can speak Cantonese. Filipinas like her would always need an employer whose family knows English.

From there, we are walking to the Hong Kong Heritage Museum, which is very close to the monastery. I'm tired, and with museums, I am like a kid. I like to touch things, or it must be exciting anyhow. Maybe it is also the jetlag and the heat, but I notice that Ana wants to sit down too. Outside again, I am buying drinks for us. I want to try such a flower – chrysanthemums drink that everybody is walking around with it. The first taste is interesting, but it is mostly just sugar, and I don't want know what all artificial is in it.

We are strolling along the river like many other people too. My impression there is different than the city center of Kowloon. It feels even more Chinese. I also don't see any Western tourists. On the way, near the river, older people are dancing to traditional Chinese music. It is interesting to watch them, and it is so different than anything else I have seen before. We are taking a break at another bench, and though we are having no profound talks, it is nice, easy-going and always funny with Ana. For both of us, English isn't the native language, and though we have different accents and a different vocabulary, we mostly understand each other very well.

We are riding back to Tsim Sha Tsui and looking for a Chinese soup kitchen Ana's lady boss recommended to her. The location looks pretty simple, but very original Chinese, so original that the owners don't have an English menu. Ana has a paper with

Chinese characters on it so that we can order something. But I see it also works to point with the finger on some pictures with the dishes. The soups are coming fast. Except for some chicken, I have mostly vegetables in my soup. In Ana's bowl, there is more meat and also fish balls.

"Thomas, you want make your soup hotter? You can take this one." It looks like the red spice sauce you find in every Chinese restaurant in Germany that I always take. I don't hesitate, but I notice immediately that it is much hotter as the one I was used to.

I croaked, "It's hot!"

Ana laughs, "You have to be careful … Do you want to try pig ears and tongues?"

I tried it with my chopstick. It isn't easy to use chopsticks for things in a soup. Ana laughs again.

"I can eat it, but will not be my most favourite food." I'm saying with a skeptical view.

"It's also not my favourite food. But I'm used to people utilizing anything of an animal. It's the same in the Philippines."

I am thinking about how it is nice that I do well with Ana. It could also be different. But already after this first day, we are used to each other. In comparison to other pen pals, I don't have the longest conversations over the internet with her.

"Do you know where we have to go to get to the hostel from here?"she says outside on the street again.

I know that it can't be far away, but I'm still very confused about the streets here. With the many neon signs, every street looks special at night like the other.

"Not really," I grinned sheepishly.

"Go on and try to find it."

I feel a bit uncertain, but I almost find it. I am on the right street, and as I look to Ana and want to say that I don't know, she points to the other side of the street.

For the intensive and long day together, the goodbye is very short. She disappears in the crowds of Cameron Road. I notice that I forgot to buy earplugs, but maybe I would sleep better now after this interesting but exhausting day. I'm going online with my cell phone and replying to another email from Elisa. It is an excited, but also a strange feeling to be on a trip far away, having fun with a new friend, a new girl, and at the same time, another woman cares about me and gets more intimate in every mail.

Then I wait until Ana is online at Facebook.

"Thank you for the wonderful day, Ana."

"Did you like it?"

"Yes, it was very impressive. It's nice that I have such a good guide!"

"Thank you. ☺ But I haven't been at some places for years, and as you have seen, I had to ask for the directions once."

"But you have been good. You also wore a nice dress today. ☺"

"☺ Ah … Thank you for you gifts. I just found the time to unwrap it. I like the Germany book."

"Would you like to come one day to Germany?"

"Yes, I would like it. But I don't know if I can ever make it."

"Why? You would have a host there."

"But the flight is expensive, and with my nationality, I can't travel everywhere."

While the small talk with Ana is going on, I am writing my dad a short email.

Thursday

October 2, 2014 – Hong Kong Island

Again I woke up very early in the morning. It was hot and loud again in the night, and I was regretting that I didn't buy earplugs. I am checking my emails, and there was another one from Elisabeth.

Hi my dear Thomas ☺

I am sorry to hear it is so loud there! I am a very light sleeper when it comes to noise, so I understand. I know that is a tough situation, with the time change and no decent sleep. I pray that last night was better for you! You need your rest!

I'm glad you got to visit the temple, today, and that you can easily stay away from the places where the protests are going on. I hope that things will not get any more dramatic while you are there … I want you safe!

I wish I could be there too, and that I had more than nine full days when I get there to Germany. I know it won't be enough, but it will be everything we can make it be, I know!

I found several pictures of Heilbronn. I know they will look different in winter, but I imagine us walking through those places together, and it makes me happy. I want to know all about you Thomas. I want to be close with you too, and I am open to what will happen between us. I want you to feel good with me, and I want to take care of you too. You are very special to me, and even at this distance, I feel so good with you! I think

often to the time ahead, when we first meet in person, when
we first embrace. We have all these moments to discover one
another, and I get butterflies when I think about it. But I am
so looking forward to our time together!
Please have a wonderful day today. I hope you get to visit more
places you want to see and have fun! I miss you so much!!!

Hugs and sweet kisses to you Thomas!

Elisa

P.S. Just keeping it real. I have felt this way for some time
and decided I want you to know I feel I am your girl! ☺ And
dreams are good … we can make dreams happen, you know! ☺

Oh, yes, it feels like she would be my girl. And it feels almost like I am cheating on her in Hong Kong. I have no clue how this could happen. I made Elisabeth simple compliments like I made to many other girls in emails too. It is not that I lied, but she replies to every nice word with something nicer. It flatters me, it gives me hopes, it turns me on, it makes me happy, and she is so serious. But she doesn't know me yet! There has never been anybody in my life who said to me the same in emails as in real life before. And what happens if I don't find the connection with her? It is much too early for thinking about this. Many things can still happen until the end of November. Now I'm still in Hong Kong, and I want enjoy my time here. Elisa knows about Ana, but she never asked much about her or any other friends or people in my life. Ana just knows that I have friends everywhere. But there isn't a reason for me to tell her specifically about Elisa.

With Ana, I am fixing for our meeting point, 9:30 a.m. at the fountain. I'm still a bit uncertain, but I find the fountain fast this time. She is late again and comes with another nice colorful summer dress. The plan on this day is going over to Hong

Kong Island and there mainly to Stanley. Ana searched for destinations on her off days that would be more difficult for me to do alone. Not getting over to Hong Kong Island, but to Stanley. We are walking to the promenade and along to the ferries. It is the first time that I see the amazing skyline by daylight. Taking the ferry to the other side seems to be pretty easy. We just press our Octopus card at a point like in a MTR station and go in. Every five minutes, the rides are running. I enjoy the ride and take several pictures to the Hong Kong Island side, but also in direction to Kowloon. It is like being between two huge cities, and I'm feeling, Wow! again. Skyscrapers are at the one side, but also on the other side. From the ferry terminals, we are walking to Connaught Road. Hong Kong looks very international here in the Central District. The big bank buildings remind me of downtowns in America. Just the Chinese letters on some signs and the Peak, if I get a view between the buildings, is letting me know where I am. It is also the first time that I see a part of the protests. There is nobody protesting on this morning, but the big Connaught Road is blocked. Some people and Ana and I are walking in the middle of this big city highway. The banks and some luxurious stores are closed. It is an unreal atmosphere to be in the center of Hong Kong, and it is strangely empty. It is so empty, as no other place I have seen since I'm here. The protesting students are still in their tents at another square nearby. Only some are controlling the checkpoints at a few corners. Like other tourists, I take some pictures of the scene.

We are walking in the direction of Sheung Wan and get on a bus to Stanley. The bus seats are comfortable and the air conditioning is working. The ride along the coast takes almost an hour, but it is very interesting for me. As we are arriving there, we first walk along a nice path near the water to a little temple called Pak Tai. It is on a ledge with a beautiful look to the sea and the bay of Stanley. I am thinking that if there wouldn't be this high humidity, it would be almost Mediterranean. Just a bit away from the Central District, still on the same island, and it looks so different again. I'm feeling very good with Ana on my side. At the temple, we take a lot pictures again. On this day, she has a camera with her. Back at the Murray House, I am amazed with the Bavarian restaurant. Ana is wondering if food would be in Germany like that. I say that you can get this kind of food, especially in Bavaria, but it doesn't really fit to Hong Kong. We are on the Black Pier, walking further along the Stanley promenade and going up to the Shui Sin Temple, another typical, small Taoist temple. The first time on this day, I feel a little breeze. Ana is joking around that I should be a photo model and take out her camera. I'm laughing and say that I would be far away from her model appearance. We are walking through the Stanley market, and I buy some nice postcards. For a late lunch, we get a sushi box at a supermarket. We share it and a bottle of cold green tea on a bench at the mall square and watch the people.

It is the first time realizing where I am. On the other side of the world, at a beautiful place and with Ana whom I met on a pen pal site many years ago. The last two days have been so busy that I didn't have the time for that. What Ana was thinking about me? It seems that she likes me as a friend, but is there anything more? An old friend in Chicago that I visited in 2006, who could be my mother from the age, told me once that a woman I would meet would always consider me as an eventual partner, even if the circumstances wouldn't be ideal. I was never sure about this statement. Because I often had female friends in the past, my friend Christine was also a good example of it. But a single Filipina girl who probably never spent so much time with a guy from the West?! I don't know. I am surprised how good I can talk with her on the same level. Though she didn't have the best education in her life, she is intelligent and smart. In comparison to women in Germany, she is less complicated, not so serious, but funnier. But she is definitely not cheap. Women from the Philippines sometimes have this reputation.

Back in Sheung Wan, we are going to the Western Market. The buildings are nice, but for someone from Central Europe, the shops there aren't too special for me. Ana wants to show me a

German bakery. For some products, they have given them German names. But I don't feel like I do in a bakery at home.

"Is it like in Germany, Thomas?"

I whispered, "Not really. Maybe overall European. The bread looks French, and the pastries English or even American. Would you like to have something from here?"

"Yes, let take us get two pieces."

We take a chocolate muffin and something like a tea cake.

Then we are walking up the hill and sweating a lot. This is again a part of Hong Kong Island that is not to compare to Western metropolis. Also, not every other big city is flat, but these small, steep roads seems to be typical for Hong Kong. We are reaching Hollywood Road and the Man Mo Temple. Even in my travel book, this place was full of people. Ana says that maybe because of the protests the tourists would stay away from Hong Kong Island. Just over the street under some trees are benches. I'm getting out our stuff from the bakery. I'm wondering if the chocolate in the muffin is melted. The cake is dry and hard to swallow. Fortunately, we still have some tea and water with us. We both don't care that it is warm.

Two hours later, we are in busy Tsim Sha Tsui again. We walk a different way than before, but we are in the mass of people. I'm thinking, Welcome home!

"What do you want to have for dinner?"

"Maybe a typical soup kitchen would nice again, Ana?"

"Yes, I know one place close to here. Come on."

It looks similar to the other one the night before. I had a soup with fish balls, shrimp and mushrooms. I'm getting better with using the chopsticks.

After dinner Ana shows me the hostel, and I wonder how close we are. A short goodbye and she was gone in the crowds again. On that evening, I don't forget the earplugs and buy them in a pharmacy. Besides this, I need some drinks. I take some water and cold green tea bottles to my room.

I haven't seen anybody in the hostel since I arrived here, but in the bathroom, it is visible that others are using it too. After a short shower, I'm devoting my night to routines. I go online, sign in on Facebook and look in my mailbox. I am already nervous and excited about another new email from Elisabeth, and here it is:

Oh Thomas ... reading your email, again, and I miss you so much!

I feel so good with you! I understand what you are saying to me, completely, and I feel the same way. It is not weird at all! I think we are kindred spirits, and somehow we found each other. That's how I have felt for some time. The quality of person you are is amazing, and I think the world of you in so many ways!

I really have never met any man of your caliber, who also understands me and is just a kind and good person. We share so many interests, thoughts, and ideas too, which is incredible! You have so many qualities that are attractive to me, and I think you're just a beautiful person! I feel so blessed and thankful to have met you!

So, yes, I would be more than honored to be your girl and have you as my guy ☺ And I hope we will be as close as possible in the nine days we have to begin our time together in person. I have such feelings in my heart, and I want to express them with you! You are a very dear person, and I want to be tender with you, and hold you and kiss you, and follow what feels right for us, when we are together. And I am open to whatever that will be for us. I trust you, I feel safe with you, and I know that would never change. I want to make you happy, Thomas, because you make me happy! And you can always say to me what you want to say. I want you to feel free with me. My heart is very much open to you ☺

It makes me feel very special, all the things you tell me! I know your sincerity, and it touches me. Also, how you thought of me in your travels through the city. oh, I wish I could be by your side right now, Thomas. But one day I think we will travel together to places like that. You are on my mind so much, and when I can't be in my thoughts all the time, I carry the feeling of you with me ☺ I want to know your experiences and the places you've seen and how you feel about things. I want to know what makes you feel good, what things you enjoy, and learn new things from you too. I want to support you in the things we go through in this life and the things you care about. I wish I could be there for you in more ways now, but just know I hold you very close to my heart and want all good things for you!

I won't keep you on this email, but just want to say that I believe there is a place and time for us, and this is only the beginning! Stay safe, my dear Thomas. Take care and enjoy this exotic land you are in. I'm with you in mind and heart and spirit. I will probably write again before I go to bed, but just wanted to respond to your wonderful message, once more!

All my heart,

Elisa ☺

Wow, this is like a love letter! What I am doing with this girl? I am friendly as always; I make compliments, and yes I am writing nice things to her too. But in every email, she is overdoing it. It is exciting, and it is as if she would give me another new positive kick with every new email. It feels very good, she seems like she is understanding me. But are these only hopes and fantasies or could this lead into anything real? I am used to being in contact with Americans, but I know that there is a culture, language and special a geographical barrier. Even if everything would work well in these nine days at the end of November, what happens then?

I try to push these thoughts away, and it is easy. I am recognizing that I'm in another hot night in the middle of Kowloon, and there is a new message from Ana on Facebook.

"Hi Thomas, is everything okay there on Cameron Road?"

"Yes, Ana ☺! Just the mess in the bathroom here."

"It would be better if you would be in a hotel."

"Sure, it would be more comfortable, but also more expensive."

"I'm sorry that I can't provide you a room."

"That's okay. I know that you have no space and that you can't do it. Do your boss and your lady boss know that I am here?"

"No. They think I am meeting a female friend when I am out with you."

"Ok … I have some earplugs for tonight now."

"I hope that you can sleep better … What do want do tomorrow? You know I have to work. We can only meet in the evening."

"I don't have any special plans. But I want walk around here in Tsim Sha Tsui and maybe in other parts of Kowloon."

"If you want send me a message on FB, you can go in a McDonald's. They have free access for about 30 minutes or so if you have any questions."

"Ok … You wore another wonderful dress today."

"Thanks! ☺"

Ana is never complicated, but kind of shy like a young girl. She is some years younger than me, but she doesn't have this pride and arrogance some German women have in her age.

By the speed of her answers, I notice if she is only chatting with me or also with some relatives and friends in the Philippines. Since I am here, she was mostly very fast with writing back again.

I'm tired and try to sleep at about 11:30 p.m. with the earplugs this time. I wonder how good they block the noise. But it hurt in my ears a bit, and I don't find the best sleep again.

Friday

October 3, 2014

I wake up early, totally sweaty, and go to the toilet/shower before other guests would use it. Probably because I get always so early up, I don't see any other guests.

After reading another email from Elisa and one my dad, I am leaving the hostel. Here, it is a normal day again, while at home in Germany there is the national holiday. But I wonder if it makes any difference here if it is a holiday or not. I buy two apples and sit down at the big fountain. The first day I would spend without Ana until the evening. I'm walking to the promenade, and I enjoy once again the great view to Hong Kong Island. I found my way here, but I would need my maps for other discoveries. I stroll to the ferry terminals, and then I decide to go over a food bridge to the city again. I reach a blocked street where students have piled up a bunch of trash bags. Many are sitting on the streets with umbrellas and posters, mostly with Chinese characters on them, but one reads: "Democracy Now." I don't know for sure what is going on with these protests. But it is obvious that they are demonstrating against the influence from Beijing. I am also curious about how free Hong Kong is? But at least some people still dare to say what they think. Already twice I have seen that some activists from Falun Gong were quietly protesting with posters at a bus station on my way to the big fountain in the last days. Ana told me that at this bus station tourists are arriving from China every day. So people in Hong Kong are maybe still free, but I doubt that somebody who is spreading open opinions against the Chinese regime would have fun on a trip to the mainland.

I look on my map because I want go to the Kowloon Park now. I'm sure that it isn't far away, but these streets here are a little labyrinth for foreigners. Then I see the tower of the mosque, and I know that I'm right. Kowloon Park is an oasis from the busy city life. People are practicing Qigong and Tai Chi, tourists and mothers with their kids are walking around. I sit down on a bench with a table and start to write my postcards. This is my routine that I do on almost every trip. My family and friends like to receive my mail. I try to send them as soon as possible so that they are at the receiver's address before I come back home from my trip. But it doesn't always work. Elisa is new in my address list, but Susan still gets cards from my trips. I also don't mind if I get postcards from other people or not. I just do it because I liked to share my experiences. Shortly after I'm finished with the last one, it starts to rain. It takes just a minute for the light summer rain to change into a heavy tropical shower. Like others, I run to the next kiosk to get some shelter and stand there for almost an hour. As the sun comes out again, I take my postcards to the post office I saw on my map and go into Chungking Mansions at Nathan Road. It is lunchtime and I want get some food. Something Indian would give some variety to the past days, I think. There were a lot of Indian food places, but they aren't really busy. I decide on one place finally, and an Indian guy sat me down in the back on a very simple plastic chair. Close to me are three Indian women in traditional clothes and typical jewelry. After I order Chicken Vindaloo, I am wondering why the guy is calling somebody on the phone. I don't understand, just that he says, "Chicken Vindaloo." Then he makes a second call and a boy is bringing a plastic bag. He serves me the food out of this bag on a Styrofoam plate. I wondered where the food came from? The taste isn't bad, but not great either. The Indian women are giggling behind me and are talking fast in a strange language. I'm thinking first that they maybe are family members of the guy, but they talk to him in English. The youngest woman was nice and smiles to me sometimes. I order a coke because the food is spicy. After the women are gone and I'm finished, I am paying. Wow, 110 dollars for this cheap food?! This was more than 10 Euro! I saw that the guy had calculated the rice and the naan bread extra. For a lunch in Hong Kong was this expensive. Even in Germany, it would be too expensive for such a meal. He probably knows that I won't come a second time anyway. As I get outside again, it is the first time cool since I am here. But the rain is light, and I walk North on Nathan Road. I first thought that I should take MTR, but I always enjoy walking until my feet are hurting. As I see a McDonald's, I think of Ana and go in. It is difficult to find a chair to sit down. Ana isn't online, but I leave her message. I write where I am and ask for tonight. I go outside again and walk across to the street and over to the Tin Hau Temple. It is a bigger one. After I visit it, I sit outside at the little square on a bench. The sun was shining again. My travel book and the map show that I'm close to Temple Street and the Night Markets. I don't know when they will open, but I want look there since I am so nearby. On the way, fortune tellers are preparing their stands for the nighttime, and around the corner is Temple Street. Most stands are already open and the owners want people to buy clothes, toys, souvenirs, jewelry and other things. After strolling down between the stands, I turn around, and this time I walk behind the stands on the right side close to the building's front.

"Hi. Do you want have a massage?" I turn to the left and see a woman with a lot of makeup leaning on a house wall.

"No," I reply a bit irritated. After some meters, another woman stands with a short skirt on the wall and also asks if I would like a massage. I don't know, but they look like prostitutes, though they aren't pretty. I want get off of this street and walk down Nathan Road again.

It is already late as I arrive in my quarter in Tsim Sha Tsui. I want eat something before I met Ana. I'm sure that she will eat at home with her bosses. Then I see the soup kitchen where I was with her before, and I decide to go in. Every table is full. I feel a bit embarrassed because I don't know if it's better to go again, wait or ask if I can share a table with others. Some of the guests

are noticing my unsureness. A young Chinese guy makes a movement with his arm and says in English that I should sit down anywhere. At one table, there are just two girls. I ask guarded and
politely, and one replies friendly that I can sit with them.

"Are you from here?"

"No, we are from Singapore. Where are you coming from?"

"Germany."

I have a nice talk with the girls. I order through pointing at
a picture of a bowl of soup. The Chinese guy who talked to me
before claps on my shoulder as he leaves and says, "Take it easy"
and smiles. I was unsecure as I came in, but did I make such an
impression? The girls are laughing. I talk with them about the
places I have been since I am here and what I want do eventually in the next days. It seems that they are mainly in Hong Kong
for shopping. We are staying for the same time. The old waitress
makes a sign with her hand and indicates the question if I want
to pay for the whole table. The girls are giggling.

"When we meet again, I will invite you," I say to them, but
I doubt that this will happen in this busy city.

We said goodbye, and I walk fast to my hostel. Fortunately, I
find it easily this time. On Facebook, I read that Ana is ready to
meet me again. I have no time to take a shower. I just use some
deodorant and go to the fountain. This time, I'm even a few
minutes later than the time we said, but she isn't still there. It is
cooler this evening, and I am watching the people around me.
Maybe ten minutes later, Ana appears. It is the first time that she
comes without a dress. She wears short, dark pants and a simple white shirt. But I notice that everything looks good on this
woman. From the distance she makes a very serious impression;
as she comes close, she smiles.

"Hi, Thomas! How are you?"

"I am doing good. I am just a bit tired from walking around
the whole day. How are you?"

"I'm doing good too. Maybe we can sit down on a bench on
this pedestrian bridge, which goes to promenade … there where
the kiosk is. Do you still know it from the first evening?"

"No. Sorry. But let's go there."

She smiles and it seems to always be fun for her that I don't know where the things are in this city.

It isn't more than a five minute walk to that place. Ana wants to know what I did the whole day and is surprised that I did everything by foot. It is dark, and we just have some light from a lamp next to us. She likes when I give her compliments. But she never gives any compliments back. I am noticing that she always tries to change the subject. The only subject we are talking about on this evening is about my experiences alone during the day. But it is never boring with Ana.

"Can I touch the hair on your arm? I have never seen so much hair on a body before." She is grinning.

"I know I have more hair on my body than as on my head."

Ana laughs out loud.

Softly, she strokes my arm and is touching, very cautiously, some hair on my left knee like she would touch a very thin glass. I think that she maybe was never so close to a white person from the West before and is noticing the physical differences to Asians. Without asking, I am touching her elbow with my fingers.

"From where do you have these scars?"

It looks like she didn't expect that I would touch her too.

"Ah … these are from my childhood. You see I have more on my left foot … these ones are also very old. Your hair is special."

"I really wish I would have more on my head." I smile. "If you want, you can have some from my arm."

Ana laughs. "Yes, maybe on your last day here."

"I know I asked you this before in our FB chats. But why does somebody like you not have a boyfriend?"

She is getting obviously embarrassed. A thought comes up in my mind, that with white skin, she would probably be blushing. But I see that she is sweating a bit more.

"I don't know. But do you think it is not normal that I haven't one?"

"Ahm … I just think that an attractive girl like you would have a boyfriend in Germany or would even be married in your age."

"In the Philippines, many women in my age are married too. Even in a much younger age. But maybe because I am away from home I don't have many friends here."

"You mentioned a guy once."

"Yes. There was one from a befriended family of my parents at home. But I wasn't interested in him and was enjoying life here. I just miss my family sometimes."

Ana indicates that she has to go back again. We are walking to the fountain together, and there she disappears in the crowds of Tsim Sha Tsui again.

As I walk back to Cameron Road, I'm feeling a bit familiar with the place for the first time.

It is a normal evening in my room with chatting some time with Ana and sending Elisa a new email. Also the night is as the nights before. I can't sleep very well.

Saturday

October 4, 2014 – Hong Kong Island

I'm feeling a breeze on the ferry boat to Hong Kong Island. It is another day that I start without Ana. I already knew before I came here that Saturdays are her busiest days. She always has to make fresh Chinese dumplings for her bosses and eventually guests. Because of this work, she would be able to meet me later in the evening, as she said last night. I want to discover more of Hong Island and go up on the Peak today.

As the ferry arrives, I am walking to Connaught Road first where I have been with Ana before. The road is still blocked from the students. In my travel book, I read about traditional food stores and markets in the area around Des Voeux. I'm also searching for a bakery because I'm hungry. I step in the next one and don't really know what I buy. I have two rolls, but the surprising thing here is always the filling. I put them and a soy bean drink in my backpack. I want to eat it later at a nice place where I can sit down.

Now I come to the quarter with the stores I read about. Once again, I get the impression that Hong Kong Island isn't as busy as Kowloon on the other side. People are walking around, but there are not too many. The stores look interesting to me. They have a big selection of dried food, but I don't know what it is. It looks like dried herbals, fish and meat, but most is indefinable for me. On the outside are hanging sausages, and behind windows are greasy chickens and ducks. I walk back a bit again and then go up in the direction to the mountainside. I am starting to sweat again. On my left, I see the entrance of market hall. I always like to see markets with fresh food in any country. This hall is on different floors, and on the signs, it is easy to see what to get on each floor. Vegetables, meat, fish ... I first go through the vegetable floor. Some things I know from Asian supermarkets in Germany, but there are also a lot I don't know what is it. I am walking to the fish and seafood department. I heard before that Chinese like to have animals alive as long as possible, but I have never seen it until this moment. In small boxes, there are crabs and fish. Some still very lively, but some are hurt. I am not an animal protector or even an activist, but it is hard to see them suffer. I decide that I don't want to see anymore of the fresh meat department, and I am going outside again. It was a long walk until I walked over Hollywood Road, saw the Man Mo Temple a second time, crossed the Escalator, walked through upper Central and reached the Hong Kong Park, finally. I sit down on a bench in this beautiful green oasis between the skyscrapers and take out my bags from the bakery. The rolls were filled with something very sweet; I don't even know what it is after eating it. I'm still hungry, and I know that I would need something again later. From a little lake or big pond in the park, I'm shooting some wonderful pictures. The contrast between the green plants and the skyscrapers in the back is amazing.

"Do want to have a picture?" A Chinese-looking man asks me.

"Yes, why not!"

He takes a few pictures of me. While in European countries, you to have ask politely, Asians seem to notice if somebody might want to have a picture.

A rain shower comes down again, but it is a very short one. I'm not sure if I want to go up to the Peak. It is already early afternoon, and the weather isn't the best. I see clouds on the mountains all the time. But I still want to check where the Peak tram station is. As I arrive at the station, there are many people standing in long queues. Employees are coordinating how the people have to stand in the lines.

"How long does it takes get up there?" I ask one of these employees.

"About one and a half hours. It's the weekend."

"I see. Thank you. I better come another time. I still have a whole week in Hong Kong."

It is an easy decision for me. I never like to stand in queues, and hopefully I will find another day to go up there. I'm looking at my map and think that I could go to Wan Chai. In my travel book, I read that it would not be as international as Central and Admiralty on Hong Kong Island. It is also the part of the island where the story in the book "The World of Suzie Wong" happens. It reminds me that I still haven't read much in this book, just these 30 pages or so on my flight to Hong Kong. But I didn't find anymore time.

Hennessy Road was blocked from the protestors in the direction to Admiralty. I am not sure where the center of Wan Chai is. I'm just following the stream where the most people are going. And, yes, then I see busy side roads with market stands. I immersed in the crowds, different smells from every side, and it feels good to be a part of all this. I am thinking about what I could eat. I'm always interested in trying anything new, but I also want to know what I eat. This is the difficult part because it seems that the people here would not speak much English. At a little restaurant, I look at the pictures of the food on a menu on a wall. The waiter or owner sees me.

"One person?"

"Yes." I sit down on a table outside, and I order a soup with chicken. At home, I am not much of a soup eater. But here, it seems to be popular, and it is also more than a soup in Germany. Here, it is a main dish. It is interesting to watch the people and the busy street market from this place. About 40 minutes later, I am leaving and strolling for some time through Wan Chai. My feet are starting to hurt, and since it is already early evening, I decide to go back to Tsim Sha Tsui.

Though I met Ana on that day first at 8 p.m., I have to hurry at the hostel to be right on time at the fountain. As I get there, I'm sweating again, but Ana isn't there as usual. As she finally comes, she smiles from the distance as she sees me this time.

"Hello, Thomas. How are you? How was your day?"

"Hi, Ana! My day was good. I'm just a bit tired from walking around. How are you?"

"Have you been up on the Peak?"

"No. The queue was too long, and the weather was also not too great up there, I think. I hope that I can make it another day."

"I am a bit tired too. My bosses had unexpected guests, and I had to make a lot of dumplings. Are you hungry? I have some dumplings for you in a box."

I smile. "Oh yes, I would like to try your dumplings!"

She opens her bag, and then a little box, and gives me a plastic fork.

"Mmmh ... they are yummy!"

"You like it Thomas?"

"Yes, really ... they are bit spicy ... but you know I like spicy food. You are a good cook, Ana."

"Thank you. But I have been making them for a very long time."

After I'm finished with Ana's delicious dumplings, she takes me to a place with soft drinks and desserts in the center of Tsim Sha Tsui. I order a coconut-lemon drink. In every drink, are like little silicone balls in different colors. The drink is a bit strange for me, but at least it is very refreshing. Ana has a red fruit drink, but also with these balls in it. Together we share a piece of Durian cake. Ana always talked about this fruit in our chats before, but she is disappointed that in this season she can't give me any fresh fruit to try. At least we have a Durian cake now. I like it, but it is also not a cake I would die for.

After a short, but nice, evening, we said goodbye and Ana was gone in in the stream of people at Cameron Road again.

Up in my room, I'm starting with my evening routine. Elisa has sent another email. She wrote about the situation at her workplace and that another company would take them over. Many would lose their jobs, but the chances that she and her co-workers could work for the new company would be good. She mentioned that it would be hard for her on some days to do the household chores. She has bad muscle pains. Further, she talked about her brother Sam; he is a good guy despite his drug problems. He is the only family she has. After writing her back, I go to Facebook and have my evening chat with Ana.

Sunday

October 5, 2014 – Lantau

I have set my alarm because Ana told me the night before that we should leave at 8:30 a.m. at the latest from the fountain. She has the whole day Sunday for me, and we wanted to go Lantau Island. But it was unnecessary to the set the alarm. I was already up in the early morning hours.

Ana is reaches the fountain only five minutes later than me. We take the train to Tung Chung. From there, we use a bus. Instead of the bus, there would also be the option to take a cable car up to the Big Buddha. But I think the bus is cheaper because Ana has chosen it. The landscape is getting nicer with every kilometer. As we get off the bus up in mountains in Ngong Ping, the air is a bit fresher and clearer. The big Tian Tan Buddha was already visable from the distance. At the ticket office, we pay for a ticket, including a vegetarian meal in the monastery. We are not the only tourists as we are climbing up the stairs to the Buddha. As Ana tells me, they are mainly mainland Chinese people. The view up to the Buddha, but also down to the mountains around the cable cars and the monastery, is wonderful. Also, Ana is beautiful in another nice summer dress. She is crazy about taking pictures of me with her camera. But I don't miss any moment to ask others to take pictures of us together. As we are going down again, we make a short visit at the temple of the monastery and walk to the restaurant. It looks like a mass canteen, and in Germany I would go quickly away from such a place. But, we have already paid for it, and it is interesting to watch all these people. The food is very insipid. It is just cooked or damped simple vegetable with rice. Ana stands up and takes some spices from behind a desk. With this, it is possible to eat, but it isn't great food. After this, we are walking to the Wisdom Path. I knew these wood boards with Chinese signs from my travel book. But, it is a very nice place, and I enjoy being here with Ana. Old Chinese people are walking around with little radios.

"This is typical here, Thomas. Old Chinese like to listens opera music if they are on a hike." She grins to me.

"Do you also like this music?" I ask jokingly.

"Yes, sometimes … la-la-la … la-la-laaa." She tries to imitate an opera singer. I get a bit embarrassed as the old Chinese folks are looking at us.

We take another trail and, except for the mosquitos around us, I enjoy the afternoon a lot. We are talking about the nature, about her life in the Philippines, about food as always, about music, and she mentions that it has been a long time since she has been here. Back at Ngong Ping, we are walking through the village. But it reminds me more of an entrance area of an amusement park. Ana asks if I want to buy any souvenirs. But I am never interested in such standard souvenirs. They are dust collectors at home, nothing more. As we are standing at the bus stop, Ana says that she forgot that a nice fisherman village would be close to here, but it would be too late for it now. Just after she speaks these words, a bus with the letters Tai o arrives.

"This is the bus! We can still go there if you want!"

"Ok, if we are not too late, we can do it."

At about 5:30, we reach Tai o. It is a lovely place. We are walking through the main alley, and the locals are selling fresh cooked food and handmade things. The path was turning smaller, and over a bridge, we are strolling into a quieter part of the village. I take some pictures of the waterways and the small houses on stilts. It is beautiful, but we both agreed that we wouldn't like to live here. It is very simple, probably cold in winter and night times and too warm in summer. We are walking until the end of the village, and I see a little temple on the other side of the water. In this moment, the atmosphere feels very special. The sun is already low, and it is a nice light. There is also not much noise. We are walking slowly, and we are stopping after every couple of seconds at the railing. The mountains are in front of me on the right and water on the left, behind me the village and Ana by my side. I am aware that without her I wouldn't be here at this beautiful place. We are talking a lot about love and relationships this time. I tell her about my only relationship with Susan and how hard it seems to be to find a girlfriend. Ana explains what would be important to her in a relationship, but she is doing it only because I ask. She always makes a relaxed impression and doesn't seem worried to not have a boyfriend. She is incredibly uncomplicated and easy going. With the time, I get a bit nervous that we could miss the bus back again. But Ana is relaxed. Slowly, we are walking back and get to the bus right on time. It was definitely worth coming here, and it's now more than two hours after we arrived in this village.

It is already very late as we arrive in Tsim Sha Tsui. For dinner, we are going to a Malaysian restaurant. I never had Malaysian food before. I am ordering a curry called mixed plate. In comparison to an Indian curry, it is mild and I doubt if I have chosen the right food. The meat tastes strange, and I don't want to know what I am eating.

As we are leaving the restaurant, Ana is walking with me still a bit in the direction of my hostel and is then going home. I know that I will not see her tomorrow. My plan for tomorrow is to do a day trip to Macau. It's the only day where I can do it.

I see that there is a long email from Elisa again as I am back at the hostel. I notice how important I became for her, just through emails. I don't know how it will be when she visits me, but I'm feeling like I'm almost in a relationship with her, at least when I'm writing her.

Hey my sweetest girl!

I enjoyed every word of your long email. I know you understand that I can't write in the same way back now. But I wished and would love to send you the same "novel" because I feel so good about anything you write.

Bur today I was on a whole day trip on Lantau Island, and tomorrow I have plans for the only time to leave Hong Kong for a boat trip to Macau.

First, thanks for sharing your dreams and wishes. You know I have the same, and I am sure that we will go straight into all the things you mentioned. I am so excited for our time. I never get from anyone so much love already before and also not when I have been with someone in person.

Elisa, I want to also say that you are in safe hands with me. I want to really care about you. I'm looking forward to it and not only say nice words in emails. I want to be the one with who you can share everything and take care of you. I hope that 2014 will bring something very life changing for you. And not only because of me, I want that you get confident by yourself. That you see in my and your eyes how wonderful you are.

It's not bad that you have a lack of intimacy experience. I also don't have much experience with it. But I am sure that I can lead us. As long I feel a reflection in you, and we are on the same page it will happens with anything. Elisa, I think it could happen already in the first 24-48 hours that we feel like a couple. But if either of us would need more time, there would also be nothing to worry.

Before I end this email again, I want tell you some other thoughts. It feels already that you are my "girlfriend"☺ and it seems that we are going straight in this direction. But I think and hope that you understand that I want to wait with this until we meet. It's something we have to do in person. You know, I want to have a real and not a virtual girlfriend. ☺

But I know with the things we are sharing that it feels this way already. And maybe even more.

There are even things in my mind I never thought that I will ever consider. ☺
Some things I thought that they would never happen with me.
Anyway, I want to be close to you my girl.

Thinking of you

Many hugs and kisses,

Thomas

I am very tired and don't think too much about what I am writing. But I'm surprised by myself with what I am sharing with this woman in America. During the day, I enjoyed time so much with Ana here, and at night time, I am like in another world with Elisa. Ana is more real, I know her in person, but with Elisa I have a strong connection. I had good connections with girls through emails and chats before. But these hopes never went true in the past.

With these thoughts, I am falling into sleep.

Monday

October 6, 2014 – Macau

It is something after 8 a.m. as I'm standing in the Macau Ferry Terminal at Central. I heard something about the ferries also running from Tsim Sha Tsui to the former Portuguese colony. But I didn't find enough info about it and know that the ferry traffic is more frequent from here.

On the ticket office is a sign TRIP TO MACAO ONLY WITH PASSPORT. I'm so glad that I have my passport with me. Ana couldn't say if I would need it, and in my travel book there is nothing written about it. Overall, there is not much info about Macao in this book. I'm also not sure if I have to exchange money in Macau or not.

The procedure to buy a ticket, the passport controls and the wait take some time until I'm sitting on the big boat. During the one hour trip, I'm eating a roll from a bakery, drinking some water and watching out of the window. The closer we come to Macau, the browner the sea gets. I wonder if it would be generally dirty or muddy from the Zuhjinang River which flows in the sea here?

Some big buildings are hard to see, and the boat docks on at the ferry terminal in Macau. The terminal is very busy, and the first thing I do is search for an exchange kiosk. I am the only customer, and I have my doubts if I would really need to exchange some money. But I do it and go out and search for a bus to the center. I'm not sure until I ask somebody. On the bus, I walked in and "Almeida Ribeiro"is written. I have no clue if this is right, but the lady I asked pointed to this bus. Also, most people went into the same. On a paper sign, I see "2.00 Patacas." I put the money in a box. I observe that some people paid in Hong Kong dollars and some paid nothing. It is a bit confusing. The bus drives on, and a board is showing every bus stop, but only in the Chinese characters and in the Portuguese language. I'm getting nervous because I even don't know where I want go exactly. I am looking out of the windows to recognize what could be the center. I try also to orientate with other tourists in the bus. When the most jumped off, I'm following them. I get upset with myself that I didn't inform myself more about Macau before. But just after a few steps on the sidewalk, I see a big square, an old building that is obviously the post office and something that looks like a city hall. I am thinking, that it must be the center! Crowds are walking around in the hot, but not so humid, air as in Hong Kong. I am first going into the building that I thought could be the city hall. Then I walk over the street to the square and follow the crowds in the pedestrian zone. The buildings around are nice. They look old and Southern European style. Just the bright colors of some façade and something in the middle of the square I couldn't identify, looks Chinese. These corny things don't fit to this old town center. Around the corner are some candy stores. They seem to be very popular. Now I see signs. The big square is Senado Square and in the direction where I am walking are the Ruins of São Paulo. I know from my travel book that this must be one of the most favourite sightseeing spots here. I take out my camera, and after the next corner, I am standing in front of the ruins. It isn't easy to take pictures without having someone's head or hand in the shot. Then I walk up to the Fortaleza do Monte, the big fortress on the hill. It was a great overlook. I see the whole city, the big casinos, the Macau Tower, the sea and in the back is probably the Chinese mainland.

I am going down to the old center again and searching for something to eat. I think that it would be interesting to eat something Portuguese, but I don't find anything and end up in a Chinese place. I order some damped dumplings. The food is good, but it isn't much, and I am leaving the restaurant hungry again. I'm walking now in the other direction and going into the big Wynn casino. I am not into gambling, and my Las Vegas trip was only two years ago. After walking around in the full casino, I leave and find a bench to sit down and drink some water. I am thinking that it would be nice if Ana would be by my side now, but at the same time I'm thinking about Elisa. It would be nice to relax, but when I am somewhere I have never been before I am always impatient and want to explore as much as I can. I see a lighthouse and something like a church on another hill and decide that I want to walk up there. But I went in the wrong direction and need an hour or more until I am up there. I'm sweating out of all my pores, but it is worth. The view is wonderful, and it is so quiet up here like no other place in the city. Tired, I walk down on the other side from the hill and notice that a cable railway goes up to the hill. It is already in the evening, and I am thinking about getting to the ferry terminal again or having dinner before. As I read, the boats are running all the time and I wouldn't have to worry to get back again. It is better to have dinner because I am hungry for the most part of the day. I'm searching in the same corner as lunch time for a place, but go into another simple Chinese restaurant. I am having fried noodles with chicken and ordered the obligated tea as in Hong Kong too.

It is already dark as I'm arriving at the ferry terminal. I find out that I have to exchange my Macau patacas back again. It should not be possible over in Hong Kong. I also know now that I could have paid with the dollars in Macau too. But I'm also paying a fee for the exchange, and now I still have some small money left I couldn't give back. I buy something to drink and a chocolate bar before I go on the boat. Everything goes well, but it is already after 10 p.m. as I arrive at my hostel in Tsim Sha Tsui finally again.

In my mailbox is another new email from Elisa that she wrote the night before.

Dearest Thomas,

I hope your trip to Macau will be wonderful! I thank you so much for writing me, I know it is late at night for you.

I'm just doing laundry and trying to clean the house today, and wishing I could also spend this day with you ... although where you are, not doing laundry here hahaha. But I know our time is shortly approaching. I'm going over to my friend Martha's place tonight to spend some time with her, which is good. We were going to go out, but it was a bit overwhelming for her, and I suggested to just bring some food and we can watch a movie.

Everything you are saying is very good to hear, Thomas, and I trust you. I have worked pretty hard over the years to try and improve my life and feel better about it. Maybe that is why the timing is right for us. I know I have more to learn and improve, but for once I also am looking forward to what is next. That has a lot to do with meeting you and learning to follow my instinct, get that ticket and come see you ☺ And I'm also really excited to see where you live and experience what it is like there. One of my biggest interests is in other languages, cultures, customs, and meeting people from other places. Because I am a shy person, I've not been one to travel alone. It's really amazing that you can show me many things, and that together we can travel a bit too. I know in the nine day, we may not be able to travel far, and even if we couldn't travel, I know it would be wonderful. But my spirit for adventure also loves the change to see any of your hometown and experience it with you! I know you've already changed my future in this year, Thomas. You gave me the chance, even just when you first met me in friendship. And now unexpectedly, you've touched my heart too. I can't imagine what the months ahead might bring us!

I understand what you mean about not wanting me as a 'virtual' girlfriend, Thomas. But, still, if anyone were to ask me, I'd tell them I'm with you. And I'm here for you when you *need me. Maybe we won't be sharing all those things a couple would share, until we meet and are both ready. But to me, I am loyal to you, and I feel I'm yours. So whatever it is labeled, for me, meeting you will solidify it, but meeting you won't be starting at the beginning. We've gotten our beginning in a virtual world, as two very real people lol … but because of it, I've got this plane ticket and we'll see each other soon now! So I'm pretty darn thankful for the internet! But for anything official, for telling others, for being absolutely 100% sure yourself, I understand you want to meet and then decide if we are a couple. It's okay, and I have faith that all will work out the way it should, between us ☺*

You have a GREAT time tomorrow … take care of yourself, my sweet!

Hugs and Kisses!!!

Elisa ☺

I send a short reply to her and go on Facebook. There is already a message from Ana.

"Thomas, let me know when you are back safe again, ok?"

"Hi, Ana! I'm back again. I had a great time in Macau, everything went well … I just missed you. ☺"

It took only three minutes until I got a response.

"I am glad that you are safe in Tsim Sha Tsui again and that you had a great time. Thank you for missing me. ☺"

"I have also a little souvenir for you from Macau. But maybe you still know I will go to Lamma Island tomorrow."

"I know. When do you want go there?"

"Well, the host there isn't at home. She wrote me before I left Germany that she would put the key in her mailbox because she would have to work and come home late … So it doesn't matter when I go there."

"I can get off some time in the early afternoon. If you want, we can meet."

"This would be nice. I'm sure that it will be more difficult in the next days."

"How is it with 1:30 p.m. tomorrow?"

"This is fine. I think I have to leave the hostel at 11 in the morning. Maybe I can leave my suitcase at the reception desk. This would be easier, and I wouldn't have to walk around with it.

"Good. You can tell me more tomorrow about Macau. I think you are tired now."

"Yes I am. Looking forward to meeting you tomorrow again. Have a good night!"

"You too. Sleep well, Thomas!"

Tuesday

October 7, 2014 – Lamma

It is about 10:45 a.m. as I am checking out at the hostel. It isn't a problem to leave my suitcase for another couple of hours there. I was already in the city in the morning, bought apples and cookies at a supermarket and took some last postcards to the post office. I checked and sent emails to Elisa and my parents because I wasn't sure if can go online on the island easily. Further, I checked the Airbnb site if there was any last info from Julia, the host on Lamma Island. After these busy last days, I am relaxed for the first time on this sunny morning in Tsim Sha Tsui. I am looking forward to meeting Ana again, and I'm excited about the island. I'm used to my forehead being wet again after I am leaving the hostel and turning into Chatham Road. I want to stroll around still a bit before I get some lunch. I am aware that it is not my last day in Tsim Sha Tsui. At least I would have enough time on Saturday before I fly back Germany. But I want be clear where the tea shops are so I would not have to search for them on my last day. I wanted buy something for myself, but also for my dad and my brother's family at home. I see two shops not far away from the fountain.

An hour is quickly over, and after some thinking I chose a restaurant in the basement of a big mall, close to the square with the fountain. It seems to be a modern restaurant, but with typical Chinese food. I order a chicken dish with vegetables and rice. Tea and a broth are included before. For my taste, it could be just a bit spicier. I am missing the red chili sauce from Chinese restaurants in Germany on the tables. It went pretty fast in there, and already at 1 p.m. I am sitting outside at the fountain. I don't want to walk around again because I know that I will still walk a lot today. I am just sitting, watching the people around me and waiting for Ana.

She comes with her obligated delay, and this time with short pants and a pink T-shirt. In her right hand, she is carrying a big plastic bag.

"Hi, Ana!"

"Hello, Thomas! How are you?"

"Good, and you?"

"I'm good too. Did you have something for lunch?"

"Yes, I have been down at the restaurant over there." I pointed with my finger.

"I have never been there. How was the food?"

"I liked it. The lunch dishes were cheap including a soup and the typical tea."

"This is nice ... the bag is for you. I hope you like it." She smiles.

"You don't have to give me anything, Ana. But thank you!" I grin back and go on. "I also have something for you in my backpack. But it's only something small from Macau."

"This is nice of you. But let us find a bench under trees behind the malls."

We walk over there and sit down in the shadow. Except for us, nobody else is sitting in this corner. This is a nice thing in Hong Kong. You could be in the busiest roads and squares, and behind the next block, you can sit in the greens and enjoy the silence. In the bag from Ana are different candies, a lotus cake and three sorts of green tea.

"Wow, Ana ... just before we met I thought of buying green tea! You know what I like." I smile to her.

"Yes, sure. I don't know if the quality of this tea is good. I got this one tea from a friend. This is Genmaicha tea, the other a Sencha and the third I don't know. But we can go tea shopping in the next days if you still have time."

"I probably don't need so much more anymore. But yes, maybe some good jasmine tea would be great." I get in my backpack and give her the little bag from Macau. "This is for you, Ana. But just something small. A postcard and coconut candies."

"Thank you, Thomas. I didn't have them before … and you even wrote on the postcard?!"

"Yes. As I maybe told you once before, I write always cards from my trips. But it made no sense to send you a card from Macau." I laugh.

"How was it in Macau?"

I tell her about my experiences there and that I walked too much. I am noticing that Ana is used to hanging around with me after these past days. I think that it would be nice to have her at least as my guest in Germany.

"Would you like to visit me one day in Germany, Ana?"

"Yes sure, but as I said before it's not easy for me to travel there."

"What you would need is the money for the flight tickets. But anything else in Germany I would like to take care of. If necessary, I would also vouch for you."

"I am sure that this would be necessary. People from the Philippines can't travel to a Western country without connections or that someone vouch for them. But first, I would need the money for the flight."

I hesitate to go on with this subject. I'm sure that I could have a good time with her in Germany too. But what would happen if we would fall in love with each other? I doubt if this would make any sense to get too connected with a Filipina girl. And there was Elisa. Though I don't know her in person, it feels like as she would be my Elisa and I would be her Thomas. We go on with more funny and simple subjects again.

At 3 p.m., we decide that it is better that I start with my trip to Lamma Island. As usual, she is saying short goodbye and is gone in the stream of people. I'm going, for the last time, back to the hostel and take my red suitcase. I walk with it all along the promenade until the ferry terminal in Tsim Sha Tsui. I am sweating. On the boat, I am getting excited and a bit nervous about the new place. I hope that everything goes well. It isn't difficult to find the Lamma Terminal No. 4 on Hong Kong Island. The pier number is on my printout that Julia sent me after I booked at her place. I just have to be cautious to take the right side of the pier to be in the right boat. I see on the time schedule that they run fewer ferries between Kowloon and Hong Island. But I don't have to wait too long. The boat gets full with school kids and a lot of Westerners. But they are not looking like tourists. I read before that Lamma would be popular for Europeans and American expats to live in Hong Kong. The ride takes more than 50 minutes, and the sun is already very low as the boat drives in the little harbor of Yung Shue Wan. The view this evening is beautiful. The setting sun colored the village in a yellow light. The landscape of the island and the harbor village reminds from the distance of Italy, but not of Hong Kong. Just two big chimneys in the back are bothering the view a bit. The boat docks, but nobody is hustling to the pier. Everybody seems to be relaxed.

As I am leaving the boat, I get on the side and take my descriptions to Julia's place out of my backpack. I'm walking along the post office and two fish restaurants. Right behind there must be public toilets and stairs going up, I thought. Yeah! There were the toilets and the stairs. If I found the hostel in busy Tsim Sha Tsui, this place should be easy to find. Now comes the heavy part: going up these stairs with my suitcase. As I am reaching a small way, beads of sweat are running over my face. I look on my papers again. Don't go up the first stairs, take the second, was written there. But instead I see three options. Stairs, after a few meters on a small flat path stairs too and after a few steps on this small path a third time stairs. I'm a bit confused. I think about taking the second stairs, but an older Chinese man in a garden above the way is shaking his head. He speaks something in Chinse, but of course I don't understand him. In the moment, a little schoolgirl comes behind me. She says to me that the man says that I can't go up there. Another teenage schoolgirl who looks European stops and says that the man wants to make it clear that these stairs would lead into nowhere. I try to explain that on my paper is written that I have to go there. The older girl is polite, but suggests that I should take the first stairs. Okay, I think, lets try this way. I go up until I end in a court of three houses. My T-shirt is sticking on me. This can't be the right way! I am walking all the way down again. I am at the same place as before. The old man isn't there anymore. I go up the stairs into the "nowhere." Fast, I notice that they were right. I'm standing in front of a house door; this is maybe the property of the Chinese man. Again, I go down. I am starting the get desperate. If I have the totally wrong directions, only the third way can be the right way now, I'm thinking. I'm climbing up these stairs. The way up there is even longer. This time, I'm ending in woods. I walk the way back down to a little crossing from two other small ways. Where I am here? I have no clue where I was standing. In this moment came a text from Julia.

"Hi, Thomas! Did everything work well? Are you in my house? Julia."

I'm feeling embarrassing and frustrated and write "Hi, Julia. No, I don't find your place. I don't know which stairs I have to take."

Just after a few seconds, a text came again. "Do you want me to call you?"

I reply, "Yes, please!"

My phone was vibrating "Hi, Thomas! Where are you?"

"I don't know exactly! I am at a small crossing, on the right is a big wall."

I'm very confused, nervous and have problems understanding Julia's English on the phone.

"You passed the public toilets, went up the stairs …"

In this moment the older school girl came again. She is wearing other clothes and has a small dog on a leash with her. She smiles and probably noticed that I am desperate.

"Oh … you are still searching?"

"Yes … I have my host on the phone … Could you talk with her? This is maybe easier …"

To Julia on the phone I said, "Julia, there is someone who maybe knows the way better …"

Without waiting for Julia's answer or listening to what the girl is saying, I just give her my phone.

The two talked with each other, and the girl seems to know the neighborhood very well. She says to me that we can find the way. We are going together on the stairs again; I am following her and the little dog on a small overgrown path and wondering if we are a right. After three more minutes on the right a woman on the top of a house is waving at us and shouting that we would just have to go around the next corner and then we would be there. As we are arriving at the house, the woman introduced herself as the neighbor above Julia. She has Julia on the phone and hangs up as we are standing in front of her. She says that for the official way I should walk to the right at the crossing and take other stairs which would lead right to the house. I say thank you to the girl, and the neighbor gives me the key from the mailbox. I'm feeling very embarrassed, but happy at the same time that I am where I want to be now.

The house has two floors, in the first floor is Julia's apartment and above the one from this neighbor lady. It is a nice apartment and the size of it reminds me of my condo at home. Everything is clean and so quiet in comparison to the hostel in Tsim Sha Tsui! Lamma Island has no streets and no cars, except for some small power cars from the police, hospital and other providing companies. The house is almost in the woods and from one window was a great view down to the village and the sea in the back. The guest room where I would sleep the next four nights was also much bigger than the one in the hostel. This really looks like a Airbnb place. I also notice that I could login with my cell phone to the internet too. I take a shower, change my clothes, send Ana a message on Facebook and actually don't want go out again, but I need something for dinner. It is dark as I am leaving the house. As I am walking down in the outside stairwell of the house, toads or frogs are croaking. The lady above told me that I never should turn on the light there because of the animals. Julia had written already in her description that I should never open a window or door at the night time. This place is so different than Cameron Road; it is just two ferries away! Cautious, I am walking in the direction of the village. There are less lights, and I try to remember so that I can find the way back again. The center of Yung Shue Wan is busy. People are coming with another boat and streaming in and through the little village. The few shops are still open. I notice that I have seen nowhere else in Hong Kong so many Westerner faces before. The people probably come home from working in Hong Kong Island. I'm searching for a restaurant. There are some fish restaurants, but all with lively fishes in tanks in front of the restaurants. Since I have seen these fishes at the market hall the other day, I am not keen to go to such a place. After walking in every direction in Yung Shue Wan, I decide to go to a Thai restaurant. Guests are leaving when I am sitting down and others just take their meal for at home. I'm the only guest then. My Thai curry with chicken and vegetables is going pretty fast. I'm sure that it is not fresh cooked. But the taste is not bad. Outside again, I'm buying drinks, apples and oranges for the next day. It is a wonderful full moon over the small harbor. Though I enjoy the evening atmosphere, I'm too tired to walk around longer. I'm a bit nervous as I walk up the stairs again, but I find the house from the right side now. Julia is still not at home. As a little gift, I put two bags of German gummy bears on the table in her living room.

I go online with my cell phone and read the email from Elisa she sent the night before.

Hi my dearest, sweetest Thomas!

Thanks you for the emails you've been sending me … it means so much to me, I can't even begin to tell you. You don't have to feel bad at all about not being able to respond fully now. What you say is so nice to hear, and I'm sure we'll talk more when you are back, and fill in the gaps! ☺ *Again, being able to hear from you has been such a gift, as I didn't think we'd be able to communicate much at all, while you were there.*
I'm very happy your trip to Macau was good, but I understand how tiring it must have been. I also read it is the most densely populated area in the world (or one of them), and so some of that must have been draining, along with the boat trip to and from there. I'm glad you get to see another island, and I hope

the place is nice for you, maybe quieter, too! If I don't hear from you, I will try to text you. My texts will be very small, as they take so long, and I only have 130 characters per text on this phone. But if by tomorrow night I see you cannot email me, I will send a text. Please don't worry to reply. I'm not even sure if I will receive your texts back. You can try, but if you don't hear back or my next text does not say "I got your text" then it will mean it did not go through. But I will continue to text you each day, even if that is the case ☺ At some point, maybe before your flight home, I will try to call you, when I think you might be at the airport. If I can't get through, that is okay, but I will try, Thomas. You have no worries for me if we cannot communicate back and forth during the next few days, though. I know you will email me when you are home and let me know, too, when I may call you. I want you to have no worries at all. I'm here thinking of you, always!

If feel the same, Thomas. The things that go on in your day, the things you see and experience, they matter to me too. I'm interested in hearing of those things as much as any conversation about meditation or green tea or travel or things like that. It's anything you want to share with me that I will be glad to hear about too! And I'm glad if my things don't sound silly to mention ☺ Yeah, my brother has friends around the globe; I think he met through IMDB (internet movie database) boards, who he sends and receives movies to and from. I think one person is in Pakistan and another in Norway? Or some other places. My brother goes to the University libraries here and finds rare and esoteric films and researches them. He has hobbies like that. So hopefully he will find me some interesting films ☺ And yes, he's my only family now, so I hope you can meet him one day. I have told him about you, obviously, since he's going to look after my cats when I see you ☺

Oh I am very glad to hear you say that, Thomas, that I am your one too. And I will follow your lead when it comes to making it formally known or official, when I am with you. I am sure how I feel too, but I know it is very important to have that known between us when I am there. 51 days, and I am on a plane to see you. It's not long now, my dear!

Yes, I am thankful for the internet, but I agree. If I could be there now, I would. I want that time with you in person to be now ☺ I know patience is a virtue, of course … but I tell you one thing, I am so grateful I got the plane ticket this year! Oh Thomas, I want to be that person by your side, and I want your dreams to be reborn! You're doing the same for me. You can't imagine! God, tonight driving home, so many emotions just welled up and poured out of me. A conversation at lunch today brought back something very dire and tragic from my childhood, and I dampened it down, even forgot about it for a while. I got into the car to drive the long drive home. I was singing songs, and the one I'd sent to you on the email eventually played. It was "Bird of Sorrow". Such a powerful song! I was singing it, and I was thinking of us finding each other. I was singing it to us. And this experience from so many years ago, and all the tragedy and suffering around it, it just came rising up through me, and I'm crying out the words of the song and just wanting to give it all over to the Heavens, cause there is just no space for it anymore. I don't want to continue the good fight I've been in all these years, trying to protect that little girl in me. I just never, ever thought I'd be understood or held dear to someone's heart, someone who sees me and thinks well of me, thinks I'm something special. I never thought I'd belong to anyone like that. You just never know the power you may have in someone's life to give them hope, even by just smiling on them and being yourself. You are a beautiful soul, Thomas, and I don't just want to have you to make things better for me, I never would take from you. I know I have to make it right for myself. But being close to you in this connection, that recognition, that being near someone so lovely, that sharing and understanding between us, it's such a balm to my heart. It gives me such hope that the long fight can soon be over, and I can lay that part of myself to rest, at last. At some point, I can explain what I mean by all this. It sounds so dramatic. But honestly, it is. It's pretty profound to know that you are not alone, when that's all you've ever known. And I just really want to give you the best I have to offer. I want to give you a reason to smile every-day. I am so grateful for you. I look at your pictures, and I bring in the feeling of your energy and all the words you've written, which also have energy, all the things we've shared, your voice on the phone, and all the hopes and dreams arising in you and me, and I close my eyes and bathe in the feelings. I don't know if you know what I mean, but being away from you, I just go to that space sometimes, and there I feel this knowing, and I feel this comfort, and it is a very warm, calm place for me. It's not like anything I've felt before. It feels safe and good and loving. I feel a belonging with you, and I want to stay with you there. It's really wonderful, Thomas. You are the one person I can feel this with, and maybe that's why you're the only person I can say this to, even if it sounds strange. Needless to say, I want to give you so much happiness. You deserve it, Thomas. We deserve it! You're still mysterious with the 'crazy' thing you speak of. But whatever is in store, whatever that means, if it is something you may want, if it would be meaningful for you, then what-ever you want or need, I'm in … I honestly have no idea what you are talking about, this time … lol … But you don't have to explain it or say it unless it feels right for you ☺

Yes, if I could hold you and kiss you, now, that would mean the world to me! I am also so tired, so I must go to bed. I hope that you will have internet access on Lamma Island. If not, I will miss you all the more, but again, I'll be texting you, in that case. A warm embrace and soft, passionate kisses for my man!

Yours truly,

Elisa

Her email gives me a warm feeling around my heart. I never en-joyed reading someone's emails so much. But that her brother Sam being her only family worries me and reminds me of my ex-girlfriend Veronika. Her only family has been her grandparents. I write Elisa a short, but also nice email back. I am sure that she loves to hear from me and that I have internet access on Lamma. Then I go in a short chat with Ana. She likes to hear from me and asks when we would see each other again. I'm sure that I would miss her on the next day, but I want stay on the island. I think about taking a hike. If I'm here on this island, I also want take the possibility to discover Lamma and not go to Hong Kong Island or Kowloon again, at least not tomorrow.

I feel tired, and it is already after 10 p.m. Julia isn't at home yet. I go to the bathroom and get ready for the night. It is about 15 minutes later, and as I am getting ready for bed, I hear the door. I think, is it better to go to bed or say hello even when it's odd to meet a woman in her own house in my sleeping clothes for the first time?

I go out in the living room and a tall, blonde good-looking woman turned around.

"Hi, Julia! I am Thomas."

I'm a bit embarrassed and think maybe it's better to not shake her hand. I am not at home in Germany, and in my clothes I appear goofy in the night.

"Hi, Thomas. Nice to meet you. I'm sorry that you had problems finding the house."

"With help from the school girl and your neighbor, I made it." I grin abashed.

"I thought my description was good enough. Maybe I have to work on it again."

"Have you been at work for so long?"

"I was long at work, but after it I was still at the swimming club. Do you need anything?"

"No thank you, I am fine. I am just tired. I have for you here some gummy bears from Germany." I pointed to the table.

"Thank you! Have a good night … Also in the next days, I will be out long. Just so that you know it."

I see that she is tired too.

"Good night!"

Wednesday

October 8, 2014 – Lamma

It was a good night and so quiet at this place! But I'm up early. I make some green tea in Julia's kitchen, and after it I am leaving. It is just about 8:15 a.m. I didn't see Julia, and the door to her bedroom has been closed. I suppose that she is still sleeping. It is a beautiful morning. I see the view to the village and the water below. I am walking down the stairs. I want to hike over the island on this day. But I don't have a map and already last night I wondered where the trail starts from this village. I go up between small houses on the other side of Yung Shue Wan. But the way ends sudden. At least I can take some pictures of the scenery from this side. I walk down again and ask myself once, what happens with my good direction in Hong Kong? Everybody can ask me everywhere, and I know always the way, but I here get lost in this village! Down on the main village way, I go in the only direction I didn't walk before. It is the way where I just went until the Thai restaurant the last night. The way winds up the hill now. On the side are little shops and the village looks quieter and different than down in the center. I am already sweating again. In my backpack, I have water, some green tea soda, apples and the oranges I bought the night before. Finally, I see the sign LAMMA FAMILY ISLAND WALK, and it seems that I'm right. I am crossing a bigger way, what looks like an old road and then meanders the way into greens. I'm feeling good, and I start to get excited about my hiking day. Some joggers come towards the way. It doesn't take long until I reach a little beach. Something like a beach bar is still closed, but two people are already swimming. I sit down on a stone table that is a bit above the sandy beach and take out my oranges and water. I see the chimneys very close now. I saw them the first time at my arrival with the boat yesterday. The chimneys belong to a power station and blight the view in this direction.

After my break, I go on hiking. The path is beautiful and looks exactly like the pictures I saw in my Hong Kong magazine. On the right is the water and everywhere are green bushes. After some time, I come to a sitting area overdrawn with a typical Chinese roof. It is again a great view. At the opposite side, I see Hong Kong Island and on the right in the little bay this must be Sok Kwu Wan, the other village on the island. I'm passing a little temple and arrive around noon to the village. I'm hungry and end up in a restaurant with a terrace over the water. The place was nice to sit, but the menu wasn't a hit. The food is a westernized and international. I take a Japanese soup that is okay. Before I go on my hike, I buy new water bottles and another cold green tea soda. On the footpath, I have a travel group with older Chinese guys in front of me. They walk very slowly. I don't want be impolite, so it takes some time until I can pass them all. The path goes up and then down again. Some little gardens came, simple houses, and it looks very tropical. There are some palm trees and reed. Then I reach a little crossing with the sign "Ling Kok Shan." I don't know if I should go, but I continue to follow the bigger path. The landscape is changing almost at every next corner. Again I see a bunch of simple houses, an older woman is greeting. And then around the next curve, I see a wonderful beach. The hills and mountains on the right look barren and much different than before. The closer I get to beach, the clearer I see that the sand is full of trash. I haven't seen so many plastic bags and scrap in all of Hong Kong as here. It could be the nicest place without these things. In the middle of the way along the beach is a tent, but I don't see anybody. After the next corner, the way goes into the inland of the island again. I am totally wet from sweating. The path went straight and steep up the mountain now. At the horizon on the left, I see a look-out with the typical Chinese shadow roof. As I reach it, exhausted, another man was up there. Except for him, nobody else was there to see. After a break and drinking something, I walk on and see at a the crossing another sign with the name LING KOK SHAN. It dawns on me that I would be on the other side of this mountain now. The path goes straight up. Though I am feeling tired, I want to go up this exciting looking path. I meet two older Chinese couples on the way. Up on the mountain is something like a transmission mast. The path is changing into stairs, and I'm making some beautiful pictures in the direction of Hong Kong Island. I think that I would probably come to the crossing again where I have been one and a half hours before when I go went in this direction. So, I turn around and walk back to where I came from. From there, I walk on the path and come down to the temple close to Sok Kwu Wan again. On my way back, I'm doing a detour to Lo So Shing Beach. Some people are there, but not too many. I notice pretty fast that this the most beautiful beach on the island! No power station in the back and also no trash. I stay some time before I hike back to my village. As I am arriving there, it is already dark. I'm exhausted and tired. I also need a shower, but I don't want to go up to Julia's place, the way down and up again. I go in a little Japanese restaurant for dinner. I am ordering a set meal: a soup, a seaweed salad and fried seafood. With it, I get served a fresh sencha tea. The place get crowded, and I am enjoying the atmosphere in this family restaurant. After it, I go up straight up to Julia's. She isn't at home. I take a shower and go online. There is another email from Elisa; she writes the night before.

Awww, you're so sweet, Thomas!

I'm so, so happy to hear from you! I'm really happy you made it there okay. That would have been so troubling to get lost, but I'm grateful the schoolgirl was nice and could help you! I'm doing okay today, my sweetheart. The project boss guy came over and basically told us he would NOT lose us three employees, and if he had to buy out our contracts so that he could hire us on directly, he would. I felt really honored to hear that he thinks so highly of our team, and of course I feel relief that he won't let us lose our jobs. So I know there is a place for me, and I can get the retention bonus, which is great. I want to pay off all my bills by the end of the year, and now I can. Of course, I'll feel completely comfortable once I know the extension of the contract is official. But all this was very good news! Other than that, I just went for a walk today with a friend who now works there. We go on Mondays and Tuesdays for 30 minute walks. But a while after, my neck started to have spasms and so it's been pretty intense and I'm going to have to just lie down flat, soon, to relieve some of the pain. I try to do things to get stronger and fitter, but my body doesn't always go along with the plan. But I'm sure it will be better tomorrow! I'm going to order some of these supplements for muscle cramping (with magnesium and such). I also have a kind of stressful job, so I need to learn to relax, despite the hectic stuff going on ☺ I promise to myself to just keep trying at it. Eventually this condition will improve. And I think when we are together, all the good feelings with you will definitely help ☺

Despite the pain today, I feel really good inside. I feel so very happy about us!

Oh sure, Thomas, I can wait to call you until your text arrives. That makes total sense! If you get a chance, would you mind sending me a text as a test, to see if I get it? I can email you or text back that I received it. The phone company had said I would receive the one text you sent (when I added money to my phone), since it had been made within 72 hours of me adding money, but I never got it. So I want to ensure it works ☺ If it doesn't work, then I can just hold off and not call you, or call at a perdetermined time, but if you can't answer, just have your phone off or something. I don't want it to be any trouble for you, my dear!!!

Oh Thomas, everything you are saying is so true for me too. I want the things you want, and I want to be with you and share our lives with each other. I know that the time together will show this clearly. And of course I'll be ready to talk about any plans for us, after we have the time to be together, like you say. I want to be in your arms. I'm not going to want to leave them! And when the time is right, you just let me know, and we can talk about any of our dreams, wishes, and plans. I know things are unfolding in a very wonderful way with us. I'm so excited to take this step forward, into your arms, into your life in person. It is really a blessing. I can't see how it could have happened that two people like us randomly meet in this great world and have this incredible connection. Life is precious. You are precious! Yes, I've told pretty much all the people I have in my life about you, Thomas! I don't have that many people, but the people I do have in my life, they know about you ☺ Though there is no one I could really explain the level of our connection to, I know it will become clear to them, soon enough ☺ I will tell my friend Cony and Sam you said hello … you are so sweet!!! I feel in my heart we will only be closer and closer, Thomas. I dream about being in your arms. It will make so many things right with the world, when I can be with you that way, just holding each other so dearly! I go to bed at night with your arms around me, in my mind, and when I wake up, you're still with me. It is unbelievable that this is going to be a reality, to be right there in front of you in a short time. I really cannot wait! Macau sounds like a fascinating place. I am so happy for you to be there, where you wanted to go, and seeing all those things. It sounds really wonderful. I know the day likely exhausted you, but I hope today will be wonderful for you!

Oh my sweet, wonderful Thomas, to think you are so far in distance from me yet so close in my mind and heart! You are amazing, and I am dreaming of all we will share when we are so close. I feel a great passion for my man, and I want to take care of him! Take care, today, and know I'm dreaming of you, my dearest Thomas!!!

Hugs and beautiful kisses …

Always yours,

Elisabeth

I'm feeling so touched from this woman, but at the same time I am wondering how a woman can write something like that when she doesn't really know me.

I'm reporting to my parents in an email about my wonderful day on Lamma and write Elisa back.

I sign in at Facebook and there was Ana.

"Hello, Thomas! How was your day?"

I'm telling her about my hike, and she asks if I would like to come to Tsi Sha Tsui tomorrow.

I am tired, and at around 10 p.m. I'm sleeping already.

Thursday

October 9, 2014 – Kowloon

I'm in the same restaurant in Tsim Sha Tsui near the fountain where I was before when I waited for Ana. I am searching in the menu for something spicier this time. As a friendly waitress comes, I order chicken Schezwan style. It seems that most are business people on this early afternoon here. It doesn't take too long again until I get my meal. Oh wow, you can see chili and black pepper on the dish. It looks incredible spicy. I'm loving spicy food, but after some bites, I notice that this is impossible to eat. Not only the chili and the peppers, but the sauce and everything is just spicy. Though I try, I can't finish the meal.

The next 30 minutes I spend by the fountain once again. People are running around this place as usual and as usual Ana is a bit too late without any excuse. But it feels good to see her again. She enjoys my company obviously too. I need still some tea for at home, and we decide to go to a tea shop. I buy three little bags of loose jasmine tea, one for my dad, one for Mark and one for myself. I'm surprised how expensive it is. At my tea shop at home, I don't pay more for a good quality Chinese jasmine tea. Ana tells me that the price would be normal here.

We go back to the fountain and sit together on one of the benches there. As typical, we haven't any deep conversations, but I like this relaxed kind of communication with her. After some time, she says that she should have to go again. I indicate to her that I want walk up on Nathan Road again and eventually look for any further gifts. Ana told me that if I would need any help I could go to a McDonald's and write her on Facebook. It would be nice if she could hear about me from time to time.

As always, she turns around and is gone in the crowds.

I am walking through the busy part of Tsim Sha Tsui, and I see my hostel on Cameron Road. It feels like it is long ago since I have been there. Also on Nathan Road, I am walking the same way as before. At a traditional Chinese shop, I buy two little cans of Tiger Balm. I use it at home sometimes, but I know from another trip to Thailand some years ago that it is cheaper in Asia. It is already very late in the afternoon as I go in a full McDonalds to check Facebook. There is a message from Ana.

"Hi Thomas! I don't know when you want go back to Lamma, but if you are still here until the evening we could have dinner together. What do you think?"

I didn't have plans for this, but I know that I won't see her anymore, except for my last day in Hong Kong before I go to the airport. So I am thinking, yes and why not. I write her back, but I don't get any reply. I write a second message and write if 7 p.m. would be ok, then she should text me. I don't want to stay at this McDonald's forever. As the week before, I visit the Tin Hau Temple, and around the corner I go to the Night Market again. It is about to the same time as the week before. I want to find a souvenir for Elisa, but also a goodbye gift for Ana. I'm fascinated with the Chinese calligraphy cards at different stands and wonder if they have the names of my two girls. I find Ana's name, but not Elisa's. The Chinese seller comes and says that she can paint a card with any name I want. She asks how many cards I would need. Three cards would be cheaper. I am thinking, and I decide to buy an Ana, an Elisa and a Thomas card. I have to pay immediately, and I should come back in 20 minutes. I get the cards with Ana and Thomas and hope that I get the Elisa card later. I am strolling through the market and see some nice bracelets. I smile to myself and think that it would be odd to buy gifts for two girls to the same time. But I convince myself that the things are for different reasons. I just should not give the wrong card to the wrong girl. I buy two bracelets each with black stones. One bracelet just has bigger stones and the other one looks maybe a bit more elegant. I know already because of the weight I will send Elisa the one with the smaller stones from Germany. I walk back to the calligraphy stand.

"Hello Sir … ah … you want to have the card?"

"Yes."

"I have it right here. I have a present for you, three of these key chargers. I see in your eyes … you are a very nice man."

I get a bit embarrassed. But I probably paid more than usual for this, and therefore I get these chargers.

I say thank you and leave.

Ana sends me a text and confirms 7 p.m. Because it is already late, I take the MTR this time to get back to Tsim Sha Tsui. Though I am right on time at the fountain, I wait again. I have beads of sweat on my forehead and face. At home I would feel bad to appear sweat to a date with a woman. But here, it was normal or at least I have no chance to change how it is. Ana doesn't wear her short pants from the afternoon anymore; she has another nice summer dress.

"You look beautiful, Ana!"

She smiles shyly.

"Thank you! You mentioned sometime before that you have never been to a Dim Sum place. Do you want go there?"

"Oh yes, this would be nice!"

We rarely walk side by side. Sometimes it is not possible because of the people. But also when there are less people, Ana walks a bit in front of me. We are immersing again in the busy part of Tsim Sha Tsui. I think that I couldn't find the place by myself. Ana walks straight into a modern looking restaurant, and I am following her. A waiter points to a table, and instantly we get the obligatory Chinese olong tea and a can with cold water. I look in the menu, but I don't know what to order. Ana recommends some Dim Sums, and she then tells the waiter what he should bring. I don't know what to expect, but I trust Ana and I like general surprises. She doesn't order anything for herself. She says that she had eaten at home. On the first little plate are dumplings filled with prawns, and then I get some rolls that look a bit like Mexican enchiladas. They are filled with meat. The third one is mixed vegetable. I am offering some to Ana so that she can also try if she wants. It is a taste experience for me, and I have a good time with her. For dessert, I get a soy pudding that I always wanted to try. With this, I am not hungry anymore. We are going outside and walking to the benches on the footbridge in the direction of the promenade where we have been before.

Ana is in a good mood, and I think again that I don't know any other woman at home in Germany who is so easy going and also easy to entertain.

She is always playing with her cell phone, and when she arrives for a date with me, she has headphones.

"What do you listen Ana?"

"You know what I like. 70's, 80's and a bit of 90's. I don't like too much of the new music … Ah, Thomas you promised me once that you would sing with me?" She says this mischievously and smiles.

"I didn't know that I had promised you that I would sing. I told you once before that the streets of Hong Kong would get empty when I start to sing!"

We both laughed.

"But it would be nice if you would sing for me." I smile at her.

"Ok, what do want to hear? The last song on my phone was 'Go Your Own Way' from Fleetwood Mac."

"Yeah, this would be fine!"

She smiles and starts to sing:

"Loving you
Isn't the right thing to do
How can I ever change things that I feel
If I could
Baby, I'd give you my world
How can I …"

She laughs and stops. "I'm not good right now, and I think it's better not go on with this song."

"It was good, Ana! But sing something from Simon and Garfunkel. Your favourite band."

"Sound Of Silence? But you have to sing with me! I want hear your voice."

"But I can't. It's so terrible."

"I want hear you! I will start and you follow me. Okay?"

Without waiting for an answer, she started to sing.

"Hello darkness, my old friend,
I've come to talk with you again
Because a vision softly creeping."
I imitated to sing and tried it a bit.
"Left its seeds while I was sleeping
And the vision that was planted …"

Ana burst out laughing. I am laughing too.

"I warned you before!"

She just laughs for the next five minutes.

I was glad when we changed the subject again. We talk still about many random things. I'm sure that I will miss her when I am in Germany again. But there is Elisa who will visit me in November, and though Ana is a nice and beautiful girl, I know that it would lead into nothing with her. The culture, the distance and overall the circumstances would be too complicated.

She looks again on my arm hair.

"You want some?" I grin.

"Yes."

"Then take some."

She smiles. "I don't want to hurt you."

"I think you can do it better than me."

Very cautiously, she put her thumb and forefinger on my right knee and pulled out two or three hairs with her nails.

"Can I also have one or two of your hairs as a souvenir?" I smile.

"Ok. But you don't pull them out." She grabs on her head and gives me two of her long black hairs. It was obviously more painful than on my leg.

We both are laughing.

"It's 9:15 p.m. Maybe I should go home soon. When are boats departing to Lamma Island?"

"Oh, I didn't recognize that is already so late! I don't know the schedule exactly … But they should run until midnight … but from here it is a long way to the Lamma ferry on Hong Kong Island. I should leave."

"I'm sure that you are not too late, but yes you should go too."

The goodbye is this time a bit different. There is almost nobody around. I don't know if it was a reflex, but I am holding her hand for some time. She gets a bit embarrassed, and as I let her go from my grip, she smiles and turns around.

"Have a safe trip to Lamma!

"I will try. Bye."

"Bye-Bye."

Never before have I walked so fast this way. At the promenade, I am almost running. Why didn't I look at the time schedule of the ferries before? But I didn't expect to stay in Kowloon so long on this day. As usual, the ride to Hong Kong Island is pretty fast. I go to Pier No. 4. I notice that it is very quiet and fewer people hang around. But I am breathing deeply as I see on the board that the next boat leaves at 10:15 p.m. It is late, but no problem to get over to Lamma. The pier is filling with people again, and until the boat arrives, it is once again almost full. I am enjoying the special atmosphere here. I am sitting on the outer deck; some people are drinking soft drinks, some beer. It looks like some are going home late from work, but some have probably just been out. The breeze is blowing through the deck, and sometime after 11 p.m. I get off in Yung Shue Wan. The restaurants are already closed, and I go straight up to Julia's house.

Friday

October 10, 2014 – Hong Kong Island

It is my last full day in Hong Kong. My flight is going on the other day before midnight. But it will be the last day that will end in a bed here in Southwest Asia.

After my green tea and another apple, Julia appears. It is the second and probably the last time I meet her. I tell her about my hike and the things I did in the last days, and she talks about how busy she would be in her job and how in the swimming club there would currently be a lot of events. She would not come home on Friday night, but I could stay as long as I want on Saturday because no new guest would be arriving. I say thank you, but I mention that I probably would not leave so late because I want to meet my friend for the last time.

On this Friday, I want to try my second attempt at going up on the Peak. I don't plan to see Ana. I wish she could spend the day with me on Hong Island. But it is a normal work day for her.

At 9 a.m., I'm sitting on the boat again. As I arrive at Pier No. 4 on Hong Kong Island, I walk straight to the Peak Tram station at Garden Road. The queue at the tram station is very short this time. Twenty minutes later, I catch a good seat in the front part of the tram. It is interesting to watch how fast this old cable car is climbing up the mountain. The ride takes less than five minutes. On different escalators, I go up in the Peak Tower to what looks more like a shopping center. The weather is nice and sunny as I am walking out on the big terrace. The view is amazing! The skyscrapers of Hong Kong Island are directly below, Kowloon behind, the New Territories on the horizon and on the left Lamma Island with the power station in the back. I have the best weather that I could imagine. The many tourists are just a bit irritating. I see two or three other hills around which look even higher from where I am standing. I go down the tower and walk outside. On the other side of the street are a bunch of people, and they are cheering to others in pink T-shirts. Later I see that it is a run against breast cancer. I am walking the same street where the runners go, and then I'm following a small path. I don't know if I am right. I'm just searching for a way which goes up. After some stairs in the woods, I am reaching something like a platform. It looks like helipad. But the view from here is great too. I see the Peak Tower below me, and behind it is the panorama of the rest of Hong Kong. It is quiet, and no other tourists are in sight. I take the chance, sit down in the grass and meditate a bit. It is a wonderful feeling to be so high and enjoy the silence above this huge city. I walk down on the side, come to a road and reach another path to the Victoria Peak Garden. There it is also quiet, but I am not the only one. Some people are strolling around and an obviously just married couple let take photographs. After spending some time in this lovely park and taking some other great pictures from Victoria Peak, I walk back to the Peak Tower. I go further on a road and catch some good views a last time before I ride on the tram again. At the next bakery, I buy some rolls and a drink. I am hungry from the morning, and it is already early afternoon again. After taking my late lunch, I walk the next two hours through the streets of Admiralty and Wan Chai. It is already like the first part of my farewell tour in Hong Kong. I know that I would still have more than 24 hours here, but I am aware that every place I see now will be the last time, at least on this trip. I think about having dinner on Hong Kong Island. But it is still too early for me, and I am too tired to walk around more. So I go to the Central Ferry Pier again.

As typical I go up to the outer deck on the boat. I am enjoying this special atmosphere here. There are almost no tourists, mostly just people who are getting home to Lamma and enjoying themselves. There aren't many conversations as I notice before. People are looking around in and outside the boat. I take my camera, and I can take a beautiful picture of Hong Kong Island by sunset. The view is very clear to Hong Kong in this moment. I am thinking that this could be a picture for my walls at home. Already for years, I make enlargements from the best pictures on my trips and hang them on the walls in my condo. It looks already like a gallery, but I always find a white spot to put on another one. As I arrive in Yung Shue Wan, I decide to go to a restaurant immediately. I don't want to go up to Julia's house and back again. I chose the same Japanese restaurant as before. This time it is hard to get a table. The place is crowded, and there is just a very small one left between two other tables. I order almost the same as the last time, a big soup and fried seafood. Just instead of the seaweed salad, I get a couple of sushi. Tired, as almost every night in Hong Kong, I am walking up the stairs to Julia's place, and as always, my evening program follows. It is important for me to talk with Ana about my last day here. Of course to know when I can see her, but also I want ask her if she can take my red suitcase. I am still here a whole day and with my suitcase it would get exhausting.

I sign in on Facebook.

"Hi, Ana. How are you doing?"

It just takes about five minutes and she is online too.

"Hi, Thomas. I am doing good. How was your day?"

"My day was great! I went up to the Peak. There were no long queues at the tram station this time, and the view from above was beautiful."

"Yes, the weather was nice today. I have been once to the Peak many years ago as I moved to Hong Kong. I'm glad that you had a good day. What are your plans for tomorrow?"

"You know my flight is first in the night. So I still have a full day here. But I don't want to walk around with my suitcase all the day. Is it possible that I can give you my suitcase and I get it back later?"

"When do want give me the suitcase? Tomorrow is Dumpling Saturday; this means that I have a lot of kitchen work."

"Somewhere during the late morning would be good. You know it will take some time from Lamma to Tsim Sha Tsui."

"I have to ask my boss, but it will be no problem. Could you be at the apartment building at 11 a.m.?"

"Yes, this is possible. Thank you! Where exactly should I be? I hope that I can find the building. You showed it to me once from the distance."

"There is a playground near the building; you will see it. To find the building, you just have to walk from the bench on the footbridge where we have been before to the right and go in this direction for 10 minutes, an escalator brings you down and around the corner is the playground."

"Ok, thanks, I will find it."

While I was chatting with Ana, I also checked my emails, and of course there is one from Elisa.

Hi my darling Thomas!

How was your day today, my sweet? I hope you have had a wonderful vacation in Hong Kong! I know this is the last full day for you, and you'll be traveling back tomorrow. I will call you at 10:15a.m./10:15p.m. tomorrow, or when you text me to. I look so forward to hearing your voice! Although I wish somehow you didn't have to endure all the flights!

I'm just getting online for work now, but I wanted to wish you good night and tell you that I hope you have good, restful sleep and sweet dreams tonight. I know you have a long couple of days ahead!

In 48 days, I'll be boarding a plane too, and it won't be long now until we can finally see each other and be together. I can't seem to think of much anything else but our future time together, Thomas! You said it to me, and I'll say it to you now, you've really changed my world. I never could have imagined meeting a man like you and feeling the way I do with you! You say I've got you flying high, but I'm right up there with you, honey!

Oh, I wish I could impart what I'm feeling here and all the reasons why, but I know you know what I mean! I'm looking forward to everything! ☺

Must go get on my work laptop and start the day … but I'm thinking of you!

Many hugs and sweet kisses!

All my heart,

Elisa ☺

P.S. I can't wait to hear about your vacation in Hong Kong!!! ☺

"Are you still there, Thomas?"

"Yes, I just was checking my emails."

"You have really seen a lot in Hong Kong!"

"Yes, I have. Everything that I wanted to see, and I couldn't be more active in this time as you have been."

"Send me a text when you are at my building tomorrow. I will be busy, but we can meet then at 4 p.m. I will bring your suitcase to the fountain, and maybe we will have another hour."

"I'm looking forward to meeting you again, and it's nice that you can take my suitcase."

"You are welcome, Thomas. ☺ I have to go to bed now."

"Okay, have a good night and some sweet dreams."

"You too … until tomorrow."

With a good feeling, I prepare for bed and fall fast into sleep.

Saturday

October 11, 2014

It is about 9:15 a.m. as I am on the ferry to Hong Kong Island. I didn't see Julia again. I put the key on the table in the living room and wrote on a paper, Thank you for everything. I had a good time there, and in comparison to the place in Tsim Sha Tsui, it is a paradise. But all together I didn't see or speak more than five minutes with her.

I'm enjoying the atmosphere on the boat for the last time. People to this time are probably going to work or shopping. I know from Ana that for many people in Hong Kong the work week goes from Monday to Saturday. I sit outside as usual and catch a last glimpse back to Lamma. As I take the other ferry to Kowloon I notice that I'm not too early. Along the promenade on Tsim Sha Tsui will take some time, and I have to find the apartment building where Ana is living and the playground. But it works well, and I am happy as I find at 10:45 a.m. the place. Children are running around, mothers were sitting on benches and I am looking maybe a bit odd with my red suitcase as I sit down on a bench. I am sweating and write on my cell phone a text to Ana. The answer I got immediately, "I come down!"

I see already when she appears that she is in rush.

"Hi, Thomas. I am busy in the kitchen. I have to go up again."

"No problem. Here is the suitcase. I hope it's ok for your bosses."

"Yes, I told them that it is from a friend who is leaving today."

"When will we meet later?"

"I will bring the suitcase at 3 pm to the fountain. I think I have maybe an hour of time."

"Ok. Thank you!"

"I have to go. Until later!"

"Until later, Ana!"

I look after her as she disappears with my suitcase. I know what I want to do now. Since my first whole day here at the Wong Tai Sin temple, I haven't seen any other places with fortune tellers, except at the Temple Street where they prepared their stands. But it is clear that it is the wrong time to go there now. I also have no notion about the prices, but the Wong Tai Sin temple seems to be my last chance in Hong Kong.

I am walking a last time through the busy Cameron Road to take a look at the hostel and go down into the Tsim Sha Tsui MTR station. I take the line to Kowloon Tong and change there into the other. Lok Fu and the other was already the Wong Tin Sai station. I am walking fast through the temple terrain, and I remember that the fortune tellers must be at the exit. I see them and become nervous as I turn into the way with the fortune tellers. Many people at home would probably laugh at me now. I look for the signs where it is written, English. The people seem to be not interested as I am passing their stands. Almost at the end of the way, an older Chinese lady is standing outside. She smiles at me.

"Hello Mister ... Are you interested? Come in!" It is maybe one of my fastest decisions. I don't even ask for the price and sit down on a chair before a table. The lady is behind it and makes a friendly impression. In the back is a bookshelf and some long flags with a lot of Chinese symbols on them.

"Show me you palms, please." I do it. She asks for my date of birth and writes fast some numbers and Chinese characters on a paper.

"You have to take care of your health. Especially with your digestion. You already had some problems with it in the past?"

Is it question or a statement? I am thinking. But she is right; I had problems with my bowls in the past.

"Be careful with your health, but also with your finances. Don't easily spend money on new things!"

I never had problems with money. She goes on and repeats again the health and the financial subject. With the health, she is about right but not with the finance. Then she explains that it would better for me to move away from the place I would be born. I should move to Hong Kong or the USA. It is probably easy to see that I am a traveler, and yes I love traveling. But I never considered moving to another country far away from Germany. Now she changes into the relationship theme.

"There will come a girl in your life soon … At the end of November."

A cold shiver runs down my back. At the end of November is Elisa's visit! I am thinking.

"But this is not good for you. Be careful. Sometime next year … maybe in summer will come the love of your life." She smiles. I smiles nervously back.

She comes then fast to the conclusion of the talk, and she wants 250 Hong Kong dollars. Though I have nothing to compare, I think that it is expensive for Hong Kong. We say good bye. I walk away and am astonished that the girl who would come into my life fit exactly to Elisa's arrival. With some things, she was maybe a bit right, with some wrong, but this is a hit! At least it is from the date.

I'm excited about the talk with the fortune teller. I'm already sweating again, and I walk back to the MTR station. There isn't too much time left anymore to have a snack and go back to Tsim Sha Tsui again. As I go out at the subway station, I am buying a lotus roll at a little bakery and eat it while I am walking to the fountain. As normal, I am there a few minutes earlier. I notice that in last 10 days I got familiar with this place, the fountain and the busy square around. It is the place where I met Ana. I'm also a bit nervous to meet her for the last time. She definitely made my Hong Kong visit pleasant, and I am sure that without her I wouldn't have seen so much. But beside this, she is a nice and beautiful woman. I often feel melancholic when I have to leave a place and head back home again. I'm the opposite like others are. People are getting homesick. I heard some are getting this feeling even shortly after they left home. With me, it is never like that. I have these feelings when I am leaving a place far away from home. I'm still in Hong Kong a few hours, but I feel that the time of farewell is starting.

Ah, Ana is coming in a green summer dress with my red suitcase.

"Thank you for taking the suitcase. I hope it was not too heavy for you", I shout over to her.

"No, fortunately it has rolls." She laughs and sits down with me. "Are you hungry?"

"I have eaten a lotus roll. I want to eat something before I go to the airport."

"With your suitcase, we won't be able to walk around much, and I don't have too much time since it's Dumpling Saturday."

"I know, maybe let's just walk a bit and sit down somewhere again."

"Yes, let us go to the bench on the footbridge."

We are walking to the place where we have been twice before. It doesn't feel like this is the last time I would see Ana. The conversation is funny and easy going like the whole time. At the bench, we are listening to some of her favourite songs on her phone again. But I make it clear that I won't sing anymore.

"Do you know where I have been before, Ana?" I ask her cheeky.

She smiles, "Where?"

"I visited a fortune teller at the Wong Tin Sai Temple!"

"Oh, fortune teller! Cool! What did the fortune teller tell you? How much did you pay?"

Though Ana says that she also would have no notion about the prices, she indicates that it was expensive. I tell her everything about my experience, except for the girl and relationship part.

Ana checks her watch, and I notice that we might not have much time anymore. She asks me things like when I would like to leave for the airport, where and when I would like to have my dinner.

I think then it would be right the time to give her my gifts I bought the days before. The same gifts I have for Elisa. As I grab in my backpack, I make sure that I have the right paper bag with the bracelet and the card with Ana's name in my hand.

"This is for you!"

"Oh, Thomas you gave me so much already. Thank you!" She says this with her shy smile.

"You are welcome, Ana."

"A bracelet with stones … nice! And the Chinese calligraphy card! Thank you."

"I hope you like it."

"Yes, I like it. But it would not have been necessary."

"I know. But I have to say thank you to you. For all the time you spent with me. For all the things and places you showed me. You have been a fantastic travel guide!"

"Thanks. You are a nice visitor and a good person. I feel sorry that you couldn't stay at my place … I have to tell you something …"

"What?" I asked curiously.

"Before we met on your first evening here, I was very nervous. I doubted if you would even come and we would meet. You know you planned once before to travel to Hong Kong."

"I understand. Usually, I am always doing what I am saying and people can trust me. Why I didn't come three and a half years ago was under other circumstances."

"I also never met a man from so far away before and didn't know how you would be."

"Then I am glad that I didn't disappoint you. I told you before that I already have some experiences with meeting people far away at another place. I had luck, and I always made good experiences. But until you meet somebody, you never know how they are in person. You can email a lot, you can chat on Facebook and you can even have phone calls with someone, but spending time in person is always different. But you are a very nice and beautiful woman."

She smiles, and I notice that she is starting to sweat more. She reminds me of a shy little girl, and it is still similar as when I met her on the first evening. But this time, she looks at me with her big eyes. She is really beautiful, I think.

We are going down with the escalator to Chatham Road. She takes me to the bus stop where the airport busses leaves, and I figure out which place I will go for dinner on the opposite side of the road. I notice that Ana has to go back home. We say goodbye, and she doesn't refuse a big hug this time. Even our cheeks are touching each other. She gives me a last smile and disappears in the crowds of Tsim Sha Tsui.

As the traffic light switches to green, I go into a modern style restaurant. The furnishing looks almost like a fast food restaurant, but it isn't. There are mostly small tables, and at some there are single people also with travel baggage. So it is the right place for now, I am thinking. The menu is typical Hong Kong cuisine, and I am ordering a soup bowl with different vegetables and chicken. Ten minutes later, I have the hot bowl in front of me. It was spicy, but on a level that I like it.

There is still some time until my flight. But I figure out that it doesn't make much sense to hang out longer around here. I know that the bus ride will take some time, and I want be earlier rather than late at the airport. I get a bit nervous then because it takes more time for the right bus to come than I thought. I get a seat on the left window side. The bus is cruising through busy Kowloon. My melancholic feeling comes back. It is already dark outside, and as the bus drives on the big bridge up North, I have a last gaze over the water in direction to Lantau and see many boats in the water.

The bus arrives at the airport, and the first thing I am doing is bringing back my Octopus card. I calculated well; except for the refund fee, there isn't much money left. Then I change the Hong Kong dollars back into the euro currency. The check-in goes fast, and I get my boarding cards for seats at the windows once again. I could login at the free airport spot and send Ana a message on Facebook that I arrived on the airport. Then I send Elisa a short email that I checked in and that she can call me now if she wants. It doesn't take five minutes, and my phone is vibrating.

"Hey, Elisa!"

"Hey, Thomas! How are you doing?

"I am doing good, thanks … everything worked well on my last day here in Hong Kong, and now I am already checked in at the airport. How are you?"

"I'm fine. It's so nice to talk with you!" I hear her smiling through the phone.

"It's nice to talk with you too!"

"I missed you. I know we have been in contact every day by email, and it was wonderful that you have been able to send me all these emails from there. I didn't expect them before. But it's great having you on the phone again. It makes me happy that you seem to be doing good, and you are back on the way home to Germany again. Also because I know that time will be running now, and it doesn't take long until I will enter an airplane and fly to you! To you, you sweet man!"

The call takes about an hour until I say that I should go to the gate. Once again comes this feeling up in me that I feel amazing and comfortable with Elisa, but I am wondering again how a woman who has never met me can bring up so much trust, sureness and positive energy to me.

It is boarding time. Again I have my seat on the second floor of the big A380. As soon the multimedia computer in front of me is working, I start with putting my playlist together. I look shortly at my book "The World Of Suzie Wong," but I am sure that I probably will not read much on this flight back. I remember that I bought a book for another trip before and read almost nothing. But I had definitely no time in Hong Kong, and I had many other things on my mind. The plane is ready for the take off. The heavy ship went up to the sky. After dinner, I am closing my eyes, starting to doze and hear in my headset …

And in the naked light I saw
Ten thousand people, maybe more
People talking without speaking
People hearing without listening
People writing songs that voices never share
And no one dared
Disturb the sound of silence …

Sunday

October 12, 2014

It is the same as on my flight to Hong Kong. Also now on the flight back to London, I obviously missed the part over Russia. I can still remember to see some Chinese cities in the screen in front of me, but now the line from the airplane is already over the Baltic Sea. Breakfast is being served, and it isn't long anymore until the landing in Heathrow.

As the plane touches the ground, there are blurred raindrops on the window. It always has a special feeling to arrive in the early morning at an airport. But this big airport is already very busy. Soon, I am at my Terminal 5 again. This time my layover is not as long as on the flight to Hong Kong, but there are almost five hours to spend here again. I promised my dad to send a text when I will be in London. I take the next free seat in a full waiting corner and switch on my phone. After the phone shows the right time, I write my text. But I can't send it! Why? I try it a second and a third time. Then I get a text that I don't have enough money on my pre-paid account anymore. How could this happen? Before this trip, I had almost 40 euro on this card, and because I could use the internet with the phone, I sent less texts all the time! But could it be that I got charged for Elisa's two calls? I don't know, but I have to try to get access to the internet again. After some attempts, this works and I send dad a short email. But I know that he might not check his emails. For this case, I send also Mark an email. Further, I sent a short one to Elisa. The thing with the cell phone sucks. Elisa always calls via Skype. And I know that I didn't pay anything at home in Germany. Maybe it is a difference where I am?

The plane to Stuttgart is right on time, and it looks like the flight isn't booked out. On this short flight, they just serve a drink and a chocolate cookie. The sun is shining as I am arriving on this Sunday at noon in Southwestern Germany again. My parents are waiting as I come out with my suitcase. My dad tells me that he got a call from my brother, and he informed him about my email. As always, I am excited to tell them about my trip. But I want also hear how my parents are doing and how the things have been here. It is always good to hear when everything was ok, no new illnesses or other problems. My dad is more patient, but mom is that kind of person who also likes to speak out as fast as possible about what happened, especially including complaining about any new worries about dad or about herself. This time she is telling about problems with her eyes. And as usual, she didn't visit a doctor. I assume that she probably talked about it all the time to my dad while I have been to Hong Kong.

Shortly after entering on the Autobahn the county of Heilbronn, we are stopping for lunch at a Besen. I am not too hungry, but it is good to come as soon as possible in the German rhythm again, also with the meal times. I think, what for a difference after 10 days of Asian food to now get something solid Swabian! Often I eat a Besen fried sausage with sauerkraut and bread. I don't like the other typical Besen food too much. Things like the popular slaughter plate with blood sausages or liver sausages and mostly a greasy piece of cooked bacon. But now even, I don't want any sausage. I order a schnitzel with potato salad and bread. It's something you get everywhere here, and it's not even something Swabian; it's an all over German and Austrian dish. But I think that this would be a good start to get used the food here again. During the lunch, I finally can talk a bit about my trip. My parents are mainly happy that I am safe and healthy and back again.

We drive to my parents' house. My mom is offering to wash the clothes from my trip, and I need to check my cell phone account in the internet. I don't trust my eyes after I log in. I'm about 100 euro in debt! How could this happen? I have just a pre-paid card and no contract with them! But on the connection list, I see that they made me pay for Elisa's calls. I am wondering, because even if they are right that I have to pay it, how was it possible that I went with this simple pre-paid card in this much debt? But I also recognize when it is very annoying, and I don't like it, but I have no other chance to put the money on the card again if I want keep my number. I do it and immediately send a complaint email to the provider. Further, I send a message to Ana and an email to Elisa. I write to both that I am safe at home again. Elisa seems to sit in front of her laptop there too. I get a response instantly from her. She writes that she feels very bad about my costs and says that we could speak on the phone about it later. In my email back, I suggest at 11/5 and she agrees enthusiastically.

I walked with my backpack home. I am breathing in deep the fresh and clear, but still warm, air in fall. I smell the scent of the colorful, wet leaves in the bushes and the greens beside the street. I notice also how clean and tidy the gardens, houses and entrances are. These are the things that foreigners often speak about Germany, but Germans doesn't notice as long there were not on a trip far away. Though I can imagine in my fantasies to travel the whole year, a trip only for 10 days helps already to see things at home with different eyes, also to appreciate the seasons, I am thinking.

The same impression about a clean and neat environment I also have as I step into my condo. My white stone floor, the white walls, the accurate pictures on the walls and not much is standing around in the entrance area and corridor of my condo. But I also know that I have been special with this. My place doesn't look much different to the time when I moved in here many years ago. People who haven't visited me in years would probably get something like a déjà vu. I often say to myself that I am leading an alibi household. I sleep here, use the bathroom and the toilet and spend my time in my book and computer room. I'm only really living here when I get guests. Anyway, this neat and maybe even sterile looking place is my home.

I open my backpack, sort my documents from the trip and put out all the things and gifts from Hong Kong. As always, I want that my condo looks like before I arrived again as soon as possible.

I open a package from Elisa that I obviously got while I was on my trip. She sent me a cats' card with some nice words and a music CD with her favourite hits for me. I am listening to the music from her instantly. The most songs I don't know, but the one from Coldplay called "A Sky Full of Stars" I have heard before.

But it is already close to five again! I get a bit nervous and exactly at five o'clock my phone is vibrating.

"Hello?!"

"Hi, Thomas. Here is Elisabeth, how are you doing?"

"Hey, Elisa! I am doing good. I think I am bit jetlagged, but expect for this I am fine. How are you?"

"I'm doing good as well. I feel so sorry because of the issue with your cell phone. I should not have called you."

"It's not your fault. I forgot that this could happen. But I still don't understand how this can happen with a pre-paid card. I sent an email to the provider."

"Okay, good. But I can give you the money or at least the half of it."

"No, Elisa! Thanks for your concern, but it's not your fault."

"Then I invite you for dinner when I am there with you, my dear Thomas."

"You don't have to. But if you want you can, my dear Elisabeth." I smile and she smiles too at the other end of the line.

"I like how you pronounce my name with your German accent … It feels so good to talk with you."

"I also enjoy talking with you. You know that I am usually not a phone talker."

"I know! And I appreciate this a lot. You are so wonderful to me, Thomas."

"You are also very nice to me. Though I already met many people through the internet, I never had an experience like this with you before."

"I think as I told you, before we were starting to write each other, I was done with everyone. Not even in my dreams I did expect to meet someone like you. You are amazing!"

"Thank you. But you still don't know me in person."

"Yes. I will give you and me all the time we need. But I have this feeling in me that I never had before that we are meant for each other."

"Yeah, we will need the time in person. I am sure that we will know more about us after these nine days at the end of November."

"They will become our nine days! I can't wait to meet you, fly there and be with you all the days and nights."

"I'm looking forward to it so much! I came right back from a fantastic trip and another wonderful event is ahead!"

Elisa is giggling on the phone.

"Ah … and I almost forgot to say thank you, Elisa."

"Thank you for what?"

"For your package with the nice card and the CD!"

"I hope you like the songs. Did you listen to it already? I hope you like at least my most favourite song. When I hear that song, I always think of you … 'A Sky Full of Stars.'"

"This is funny. Because it's the only song I know." I am laughing, "But I like it!"

"Good. Tell me more about how your flights have been, Thomas."

The call takes about one and a half hours. I'm tired after it, but I'm feeling good after the welcome call from Elisa, my Elisa.

After a dinner at my parents' house, I'm going to bed early.

Sunday

October 19, 2014

It is a rainy afternoon and the perfect day for what I am doing. I'm preparing a package for Elisa. I put in some German candies, the bracelet and the calligraphy card from Hong Kong in it. I didn't mention that I would send something to her. I always like to make surprises. I want to bring the package to the post office on the next day, my first work day again.

The past week went fast. Yesterday, I met my friend Michael and told him about my trip. On Tuesday, I was with my parents in Heidelberg. One of my most favourite places here in the state. Except for these activities, I spent a lot of time in front of the computer. I wrote with Susan, Ana and gave many of my other pen pals a Hong Kong report. But the most time, I have been busy with reading emails from Elisa, writing her back and sending pictures from my trip. She wrote in the nicest words about me. Usually I didn't like to share too many pictures of me. But she wanted them and always gave me the sweetest compliments. She also sent me pictures about herself. She looked cute and had a big neckline and her red lips; they had some erotic touch.

I heard more about her physical issues and her past. Her rosacea, the Myofascial Pain Syndrome and how she tries to treat it by nutrition. She writes also about the bad health system in the US and that though she would have a good income, she couldn't afford to pay for physical therapy. I told her how ridiculous it would be and that in Germany every legally standard health insurance pays such a therapy for a lifetime if necessary. I told her how good my physical therapist would be, and Elisa said that she would like to go there with me one day.

I knew already that some not so nice things happened in her past. But I just heard that she has no connection with her mother and something didn't work out with a violent boyfriend in Ecuador. Now she mentioned that she has been married once before. I asked her what went wrong and in email and she wrote back:

Oh, as for the marriage. I was 19 when I got married. Well we had a plan to marry here in America before my 20th birthday, but we did paperwork wrong, and so he came here and was turned around and had to fly home. So the immigration people felt sorry for us and suggested I go to England and marry and then we'd still be able to make the church date. But we didn't make that date. So I married in a civil ceremony in England in October over a holiday weekend, while I was in college, at age 19. Then I came back to America by myself, and it took nine more months for him to get here. But we were together maybe another year, and then got separated. Not meant to be! So technically we were married three years, but two years we were apart (Three months when I came back to America the first time and then nine months after I got married to him in England). My grandmother actually came to me when we were separating and told me she wanted me to try to get the marriage annulled. She thought he was gay, and apparently so did my parents! I guess I was very naive to it all. But I didn't want to hurt him to get an annulment over that topic, so we got a divorce instead. This is all pretty embarrassing in some sense to look back upon. But I was very young and naive, yeah, so I have to kind of laugh about it and forgive myself too. Still I don't know everything of her past, but I have the feeling that there was still more. I push the thoughts away and tell myself that however it goes on I have to wait until she would be here at the end of November.

With every day the conversation between her and me gets more romantic. We are calling each other darling, honey, my guy, my girl and more.

She always shows an interest in learning German and using short phrases in emails. She wrote in another message at the middle of the week:

Hi my darling Thomas ☺

I hope you are winding down for bed or already asleep ☺ *I know that you've not had enough time to recover from the time changes after your holiday yet, especially with all you are doing every day.*
It's good of you to be there for others, but soon I want to be there for you and help in any way I can too.
I just want to make you feel nice!
I'm still at work and have something to finish, so I'm keeping this short.
Take care tomorrow, my sweetheart. We'll talk again, soon, I'm sure.
Du bist mein Schatz ☺

Your girl, with love …

Elisa

Saturday morning,

October 25, 2014

My first work week has been over again. It was busy, but even busier was the email exchange with Elisa. On some days she wrote several times and mostly long letters. I like it and tried to respond in the same way. But I am starting to feel overwhelmed. I'm also wondering about where this will be going, if we already have this strong connection to each other now. Fears come up in me. I am thinking that at one side I can end as a "victim" again like it was with Susan before, or as the "culprit" to the same time and I would hurt her. I get doubts if this girl is really the one I could be with together. We write already about an eventual move for her to Germany. She is emphasizing that nothing would hold her back in the US. In her last emails, she talks a lot about her cats. It would be hard to leave her outdoor cats, and if she moves to Germany, she can do this only with her two indoor cats. I do have nothing against animals, but I am not used to them and can't imagine having two cats in my condo. Another subject has been that she seems not to be interested in having children. Of course it is something that is early to go into, but I'm not sure why she doesn't consider this. Bad experiences in her past? Her health issues? Being too old? Or maybe she just doesn't like kids at all?

Another question that makes me nervous is how I could get used her. Nine days are maybe enough to know who the other person is, but not enough to find out if she would be a good match for life. As far I know, Americans can be in Germany only for three months with a tourist visa, but not longer. This reminds me again of her past. She seems to be a person who makes quick decisions. Twice she moved or even changed her life totally because of a guy. This makes me very nervous, but on the other side, it give me hope that she is serious with me and her words are maybe not only empty promises.

Today another call is planned. But I want to read all her emails from the week once again and want to write her clearly what I think. At least as clear as I was capable for. I'm feeling a pressure in me. The people around me know that she is coming, but nothing more. I indicate something to Christine in my texts and Stefanie, my sister-in-law. Stefanie is always supposing that something could go on just when I mention a new woman. But of course I talk nothing to Michael or to my parents. They would think that I am complete crazy.

It took some time until I was finished with my email:

Good morning my darling Elisa! ☺

Wow … I really wonder sometimes from where you can take this energy to write me all these emails? ☺ *You know I love to write you too, and you set many energies free in me.* ☺ *I could write you also endless. But I always need a kind of day plan so that I get not overwhelmed.*

Okay, now I want go straight to our subjects. I'm very aware that we are right now where we are because of our feelings for each other, my honey. This is amazing, this is wonderful and much more. Your feelings brought me through my Hong Kong trip, through the last couple of weeks and make me think about things I never thought before.

But as we mentioned before, we have also a rational and a logical side in us. By all these wonderful feelings, I can't ignore this other side completely. I think it's important too. But to this I come a bit later in this email. I want to talk first about the fears, which came up in the last days. You know as a HSP you see it every day a little different, so I can't write you exactly what I felt in the last two days.

One thing that I want say you before I go on in this email is that you have promised me that you ask me before you get worried. I know myself very good that our mood can go down fast if we don't like to hear anything or if we interpret something different. You know you can talk about anything with me and you can trust me completely.

Ok, talking about my fears. One fear is probably related to my last and only relationship in my life until now.

The most people I met new in the last years I always met over the internet. So also that one, my only ex-girlfriend. There is nothing to compare with you, but the way that it started was similar. Because she lives in Germany, it went faster. But though, it was a long distance relationship. We emailed or talked on the phone almost every day. But it was not something I wanted; I felt even stressed with the time. It was like she is living her life there and I life my life here. I never thought this before, but it was relief for me as we broke the relationship.

You know now a little bit more why it's hard to deal with a long distance relationship for me. I know it will be different with us because if we want it, we both will try everything so that it works.

I'm a very matured man, and I know what I want. But my experiences with relationships are on a level of a 20-year-old person. Maybe even less.

Maybe you can understand this all makes me disappointed over the years. No woman gave me so much as you give me already now, Elisa. You probably noticed already that this is also a vulnerability of me. I know that you are different, and I'm sure about you as far as I can be sure right now. But though, I think there is a rest risk when we meet. And I don't want to push this away. We are doing well, and I think there is a big chance for much more, my darling. But we shouldn't see this as 100% for sure. I hope you understand this. I have no doubts in you, my girl. Everything that I say and what I feel for you is very, very honest. But we have to meet in person. We have to know each other in person. When you are here, I think we are going fast on that level where we are now. But we should be in a flow. If the flow is faster or slower, it doesn't matter. But I don't want that we think that we have to do this and that and that we think it must be that way. Nothing must be in any way. I just want that you are happy and that we have a wonderful time.

Through our emails in the last two weeks, we got expectations. Very positive expectations. Because we are on the same wavelength, I don't think we have to worry about it. But though, we should be aware that these unconscious expectations are very high. We are talking about things I never thought that I would talk with someone before we have ever met. We are with many things in our mind already behind these nine days. Elisa, again ... this is wonderful! But we need these nine days and especially in the first couple of days we have to be relaxed. We have to know us in person.

One thing that makes you a bit confused in my emails is maybe that I can't wait until you have moved here and to the same time I am guardedly, aren't I? Because you are sensitive too, I think you can understand it. That I am thinking like you how you can get here and how we can make it, is my feeling side. With this, we are already much in our future. But the careful side has to do with my past, but also because I think we shouldn't over jump these significant nine days.

My darling, we can go on with talking about our plans and our thoughts. There is nothing to worry about it, as long we don't forget that with the decisions we have to wait until these nine days. It's a little hard for myself. But I don't want to hurt you. I want to protect us both. I don't want that we find us in December in a situation where we are totally overwhelmed and we can't go back anymore.

The situation is wonderful in which we are now. I just want protect this "little plant."

As for your many thoughts about your move here ... I appreciate this so much on you, my honey!

Getting a visa and finding a job here is maybe something we have to see as one thing. But if it's necessary, we have to see it also different. Anyway there are two options in my mind.

1. *You can work online from here in your old job. This would be of course the easiest way. You would be here officially as a "tourist." You can stay with your passport here for three months, and I think it will be no problem to expand it for further three months. So we would have again at least a half year. In this time you could improve your German skills, you would get used to everything around here and we would see how you can find a job here. What is possible, what we have to do next ...*

2. *You are getting a working visa for Germany. This is the safest way. If you would have this permission, you would be official here as a resident. We wouldn't be in any hurry. Such a working visa would be valid at least between 6-12 months. The problem will be to get such a visa. Either you would get it because you work for an American or German company here or get just the visa (but this is probably hard to get).*

Okay, then there is the language subject. I know you already know a lot. It's so nice that you start already to learn a bit online! And yes, you can always ask me if you have any questions. I'm sure that you will able to learn German. You will notice every week that you spend here that your German is more improving than learning it in the US. You have here much more opportunities. Beside for me and that I like to teach you, everything is German here. The media, people around me, if we go shopping, you could attend here a German class, we could go to a German language group and more. Just for example, I'm sure you learn here in a month much more than when you learn for three months from there.
You mentioned your cats. I know that I probably love your cats, honey. As I said to you, though I don't have any expe-

riences, I like animals. I'm open if we have cats or any other pets. But I didn't expect that you want bring your cats over here. I know this is logistically not easy. Further, I still don't know if we can have cats here in my condo. It's my own condo, so I think it should be anyhow possible, but I still don't know. I live on the second floor, and I have only a balcony. My apartment isn't too ideal for cats; it would be better if I would live on the ground floor. I don't want push this subject away, but it's something we should talk about another time again. Latest when you are here, then you see the circumstances here.

Another subject you talked about is your health, your doctor appointment and family planning. The most important thing for me is that it is going up with your health, my darling. I hope that you can get more active. I will support you with everything I can. Health is the most important thing for you and also for us. I mentioned before that it would top everything if we could still have a child. It's something that has been always in my dreams. But I want to say now that your health is more important for me. If we are meant for each other and decide to spend life together and the baby subject would be the only thing that not works, you don't have to worry about it. I will get through it.

I know you are already making many thoughts about how you will do it with your house and generally the financial aspect is also in your mind. The idea with giving the house to your brother is good.

My honey, you know I am with you and I can't wait to have you here.

I don't think we have any reason to get nervous. Everything is fine. But on our level and the speed of our connection, it's maybe good to talk also a bit about worries. And though you want the best for me and I want the best for you, it's important that we can also talk about our fears. And maybe it's just because nobody else means it so serious and honest with me before as you my love. ☺

You know I want be here for you with everything. For your
visit that is ahead, for your moving plans, for your past, for
everything positive, but also negative. I think if we can share
good and bad things we both are just great. ☺
Is it okay for you if you call me today a bit later? Instead of
11/5, at 12/6? I forgot the time while writing this email and
should do some cleanings.

Until later.

Your Thomas

I'm feeling a bit relieved to write everything down that has been
on my mind. I knew that it was too early to speak about most of
these subjects. But there is such an incredible speed in the connection with Elisa and I didn't feel well in the last couple of days.

For lunch, I went to my parents' and maybe two hours later I am back at home. I am cleaning in my bathroom as I am
hearing the vibration of my cell phone on the little metal trol-
ley in my corridor. Who is this now? Christine, my brother or
have I forgotten something at my parents' house? I am rushing
to the cell phone and Elisa is showing on the display! It was
just 2:54 p.m.!

"Hi, Elisa!"

"I have to call you now! I am very irritated about your email!"
Her voice sounded different than normal.

"Wh …?" I hear her crying on the other end of the line.

"How can you write something like that!? I will never leave
my cats alone!" she says harshly and whiny at the same time and
goes on, "This my commitment! I have almost no friends, almost no contact to all my family and you indicate that I should
move there without Lucy and Carla?! It will be already hard for
me to leave the outdoor kitties!"

She cries again.

"I am sorry, Elisa!"

"You made a list that I have to do! I don't like this. I am the one who would leave everything behind me. The only thing that I have in my life are my cats ... and you are just afraid about the white walls in your condo!"

"I am so sorry!"

"Why did you say this to me?"

I got very nervous.

"I just want write down what is in my mind. I felt a bit over-whelmed in the last days. But I am sorry, I didn't want hurt you. Sorry for being so insensitive."

This was probably not the correct explanation, but I don't know what to say. I notice that I'm missing the English vocabu-lary to express myself correct and her crying, groaning and fast talking doesn't make it easier for me.

"I can't handle such emails from you!"

"I understand what the cats means for you. I didn't want to hurt you, Elisa."

I try to justify myself and notice what I did with my email. I also get aware of how vulnerable she seems to be.

The call goes on in the same way for the next 20 minutes. The only thing that I could say and what I repeat again and again is that I am feeling so sorry. Then her mood changes.

"Thomas, I feel bad that I upset you. I even didn't ask if the call time was ok. But as I woke up I read your email once, twice, and more times. I need to talk when I don't feel well."

"It's okay, Elisa. It isn't nice what I wrote."

"You still don't know everything from my past. But I have a special connection to cats, and it's my commitment to care about them."

"You know you can talk about anything with me. Also about your past."

"I know, honey. You are such a nice man. But I don't want do this now or in emails. I hope that I can do it when I will be there with you next month."

"You don't have to. But if we trust each other and share everything I want to be here for you about not so nice things."

"Sure I trust you. You know I never before felt such a connection to someone as to you, my darling. The reason why I didn't tell too much about my past is because I have handled it for myself. I could fall in a depressive mood. But I am sure the moment will come when I'm able to tell you more."

"Take your time, my Elisabeth."

"Oh, you are so nice and good to me, my sweetheart!"

She starts suddenly to giggle. "You know I like how you pronounce Elisabeth."

"Yes, though I am just saying your name as I think." I am smiling, relieved.

After two hours, the line breaks up. We notice during other calls before that after two hours we have to wait a minute and Elisa has to call me again.

About a minute later, my phone is vibrating again and this time it is just a nice and even romantic talk time. After we hang up, it is 6:50 p.m. Wow, I can't imagine that we talked the whole Saturday afternoon! Fortunately, the day ends happy with Elisa. But I am exhausted and we don't figure out the issues. But I am feeling very bad about myself. Maybe the cat subject and other subjects are issues, but how could I write about something like that with someone I still didn't know in person? Further, I think that I am always the nicest man to women. But I hurt her. I hurt somebody who likes me and even loves me. Somebody who considered to move from America here. She never asked before if she can take her cats here. For anyone else this sounds maybe odd to move with cats to another country. But as she told me, the cats would be everything that she has. I don't want to think again about her past.

One hour l later, I am checking my emails a last time today, and there is another new email from her. She is apologizing for her mood on the phone and writes how happy she would be to know me and that she can travel to me soon. She says thank you for my package that arrived there and that she forgot to mention it on the phone. She likes the calligraphy card, the candies and the nice bracelet she would wear on her arm since she opened the package.

I am looking to the right, to my bookshelf and see my Chinese calligraphy card there. I smile and think that Elisa, me, but also Ana in Hong Kong have such a card. I wonder how she is doing there. Because of the intensive contact with Elisa, I reduced the writing with Ana, Susan and the other pen pals and friends.

I go out on the road; I need a walk and some fresh air.

Saturday

November 1, 2014 – All Saints

The holiday is falling this time on a Saturday. For somebody like me who works only from Monday to Friday, the holiday isn't then too special. But at least better than on a Sunday. But I like it when all the shops are closed and it is quiet outside.

For lunch, I had invited my friend Michael and his girlfriend Joan. Or I better have to say, his ex-girlfriend. I don't know if they are still together. Joan is originally from the Philippines but lives already many years in Germany. Michael didn't end his relationship with her. He has the ability not to talk about it and reduces the connection very slowly. It was first hard for Joan, but she seems to get used to it in the meantime. The "process" started already two years ago and is still going on.

Anyway, because Joan asked also about my pictures from Hong Kong, I invited them together for lunch and viewing my pictures. When I get guests, I cook something Asian for them in my wok. I love to eat Asian, but I also like to cook it. I made fried chicken in oyster and soy sauce with soybean seedlings, bamboo shoots, belly peppers, leek and carrots. As for the starter, we had some spring rolls and for dessert, ice cream with lychees. They enjoyed my food a lot. I made it maybe a bit too spicy, but Joan loves spicy food.

As we are watching the Hong Kong pictures, she has of course questions about Ana. Where she would come from exactly, if she would be nice and she says that Ana looks beautiful in the pictures.

Sure she is beautiful … but there is another woman in my life now, I am thinking.

After some cookies and coffee, tea for me, they are leaving at about 4:15 p.m. I don't want to throw them out, but it is perfect for my weekly call with Elisa. I wrote her before that I would not be sure if she can call me at 11/5 and that I will send her a text when my guests left. It was okay for her, and though we mostly have our fixed call time, it is never a problem for her to change it eventually. I think also that I never meet anybody before with who I can rely so much. She is never late with her calls and is very flexible to my time schedule. As she tells me that I was the highlight of her weekends, and it seems that I was often the only reason to look forward to the next one. She says that she cleans in her house, cares about her cats and sometimes she meets her friend Cony for a dinner. I don't have the busiest life, but in comparison to her my weekends are sometimes packed. But I know this isn't just a difference between Elisa and me, this is also a difference between Germans and Americans. I know from other friends there that many Americans have often busy work schedules; they are tired on the weekends and care about their houses. Many Germans love to go out on every off day, meeting friends, family and doing a lot of outdoor activities.

Now it is 5 p.m. and exactly to the second, my phone is vibrating.

This time, we have a very nice call again. We give each other compliments, and she tells me how much she is looking forward the end of the month. Yes, the end of the month, I can't believe that there are just a few weeks left! I talk about my holiday, Michael and Joan. She says that she has a cold and had some muscle cramps in the night. But it sounds like she has been up for a long time. I notice in the last weeks that with this she has been generally different to me. While I was always tired at night times and have go to bed relatively early, she can be a night owl. When she is obsessed with something like learning German, it sounds that she is sitting the whole night at her laptop. She mentions also about a therapy she attended it the past called Human Design. Elisa says that she writes about it in an email to me, but because it was already 11/5 she didn't send it, but would do it later.

Just 15 minutes after our call, a long email arrives:

Honey, you are the best! Thanks so much for the time you shared with me today. I hope you have a wonderful dinner! I'm going to go grocery shopping. It says we may have freezing weather with ice between now and Monday, so I need to go buy a few things. I hope the power stays on!
I think you are a wonderful man, and I can't wait to have you in my arms! Thanks for everything you are and everything you do, Thomas … you are so lovely!
Sending you many hugs and kisses, always!

Your girl,

Elisa ☺

P.S. Below is the email I finished before our call, but didn't send.

Guten Tag mein süßer, süßer Thomas!

I just want to say that your emails and all you say is really so wonderful for me. You really lift me up, Thomas, and you make me feel so good! You support me in a way I've never experienced, and I want to do the same for you, my love!
I appreciate all you say about listening to my silly work situations. In America, we're supposed to be social at work, and so I think there can be more situations where people are thoughtless. Although I don't think it would be easy, on the other side, to have everything be just business, if people were harsh all the time too. I just wish we had a more polite society, and that people would take responsibility for what they do, but also give a little more trust, as well. But that's a utopia I'm speaking about … not going to happen. But yes, I have been in trouble with authority figures in jobs that did not treat me well. I have left several jobs

in my career because I won't deal with abuse or control that is far beyond what is reasonable. I've also pissed off some managers because I will be very forthright about what I think is wrong with a situation, and not everyone likes honesty, apparently. I don't think our personality types find an easy time in the normal politics of work life. But we have to adapt. It seems you found a way, honey, and I'd love to know more. Like you, I'm starting to see that my job is just a job. I won't put on a job that it has to fulfill my life because there is more in my life that matters, especially now. I want to do a good job, but I can't take it too seriously. And also, I've never had a job that fit me. That I may have to leave for another lifetime! But you know, maybe one day you and I can have one of those travel blogs or cooking blogs and write a few e-books or whatever. Some people make very successful livings doing that and enjoying it. I don't know if I really am a 'blogger' type of person, and I don't really like social media. But maybe there would be some freedom in it. I think about trying it, sometimes, but I just don't know exactly what to write about ☺ The outdoor cat Jonny with the infected ear is doing well, thanks. I really hope my treatment helps him! Lucy is dealing with having her inside for a few days ☺

Thanks so much for supporting me about my issues, Thomas. I've gotten pretty far with getting over much of the abuse itself. But it's the family dynamic, with my mom and stepdad and my mom's parents, that has been the most painful and traumatic for me. When I came back from Ecuador, things fell apart, and I started to feel suicidal. I decided I must get help. I wanted to find a therapist who worked with Energy Psychology and trauma (my previous experience with the Psychology community was very negative, so it took a lot of research for me to find someone I could trust). I had to literally beg my mother for 80 dollars, since I hadn't gotten my first paycheck, yet, to get an appointment scheduled as soon as possible. It was ridiculous to have to guilt my mother into helping me when I was in a crisis … and I did pay her back. But I went to this therapist, a LCSW, Stella Meyer, almost weekly from early 2011 to 2014, up until a few months before we met. I finally decided, in 2013, that I didn't need to go as much, so I went every other week or less this year, until I was like, I know I'm ready to continue the healing on my own. The support I got from her was very helpful, but it is expensive to get therapy, and I had begun to feel I'd reached a level where I'd gotten the most benefit from it I could. I've processed a heck of a lot of stuff in the last four years. I've move out a lot of trauma energy from my system. I'm proud of the work we did together. She was a really good fit for me because she treated me as capable person, who could learn to trust my own process of healing. She uses energy medicine techniques and also neurofeedback in her practice, both of which have shown great promise at treating trauma and PTSD. This was the lady I wanted my mom to see with me, but my mom didn't want to go with me or talk about anything, and instead chose not to see or contact me. Yet my mom feels sad, according to my brother, that she may never see me again. It's ridiculous. When stuff goes wrong and wrecks your life, you have to deal with it. You have to have some courage to make things better. But my mom and I are different, and I have to feel sorry for her for giving me up, rather than facing it, because in the end I can't imagine that would make her happy. But maybe she is happier without me. I'm just at a point I cannot continue to let this situation have a hold on me. I deserve to have a happy life, even without my mom or family in it. And I really believe, me getting through these things and all the work I've done is part of what has opened up my life. Maybe in some way I had to prepare to be ready for you, Thomas. I had to clear out a lot of negative ideas and thoughts about myself, and start loving myself, before I could be open to have true love in my life. I know I still have a ways to go, but in these past few months of knowing you, of getting close to you, I can feel myself stepping through a door, and on the other side I'm no longer carrying this stuff … I'm stepping through and I feel really good and much stronger than I've ever felt before. I feel more resilient, and I'm not getting caught in past thoughts as much or getting as upset by them. I also have to tell you something interesting that I came up with at the beginning of this year. It's a healing technique I suddenly woke up and had in my head. It somehow relates to Germany, actually, so I want to tell you about it. The more I think about it, the more amazing it seems. It will make better sense when I tell you! ☺

I have some grey in my hair too, Thomas ☺ But like most women, I can 'correct' that lol … but yeah, I feel as you do that I want you to just feel good with wearing what you like and being comfortable with yourself. But I would go shopping or shop for you, of course, if you like. I'm not a girl who finds material things that important, but it is nice to enjoy what you wear and feel it looks good on you. But I'm not this girl who has to do my hair up and have perfect makeup and jewelry and fancy clothes all the time. I would say I'm not that vain. Of course there are things I want to improve about myself, and if I had the money I might have nicer clothes too. But I'm pretty easy to please and don't require a lot of things to make me happy. I do like the idea of having a home that feels really warm and inviting to come home to. But I wouldn't care if I got stuff second-hand if I liked it. In fact, I'd rather do without someone I really like than spend a ton of money on it. And it's more important to do things you like than have nice things, I think ☺

I hope it goes okay when you visit your grandmother. You are so dear for doing that, and I know it's not easy for you to have to see her that way. But I believe it makes a difference, to the spirit at least, to have that support. You are such a good person, Thomas. I want to be there for you through all this too. Oh honey, I can't wait to hear your voice. Mine might sound a bit different, with this cold … but still, it will be great to talk with you!

I'm going to go get some things done. I send you all my love, and I will speak to you soon, honey!

Sweet kisses,

Your Elisa ☺

Thursday

November 27, 2014

It is eight in the morning, and I am still in my bed. I think that it would be better to get up as soon as possible because there are a lot of things to do on this off day, on this last day before Elisa's arrival! But the memories of the last weeks are running through my head. There were again ups and downs with her. She has been twice confused and emotional on the phone again. She said once that I would pull her close and would push her away again. I know what she meant. But it has been because I was at one hand very serious about the connection with her, but on the other hand I was afraid that she wouldn't love me or that I couldn't love her for some reasons when she would be here. Obviously, this made her unsecure, and she wanted to demonstrate in her emails and calls that she is very sure about me and told me about her plan to learn German there at a school and how she could immigrate to Germany. She even mentioned once that she would like to marry me soon if necessary to move here. Things like that scared me still, and I felt a lot of pressure. The one night, I had even sleeping problems because of her. I met Christine once and talked about everything. I know that she is the only one with who I could talk very open about it. As usual in the last months, she agreed with me, probably mainly to reassure me. I told Christine that I just wanted focus on the nine days. I even repeat this again and again to Elisa in the last 10 days. Two weeks ago, she cried on the phone and asked in her desperation if she should cancel the flights. Of course I didn't want this. If she would do this everything would had been in vain, and I am not that type of person who cancel trips or even would unload guests. I have a strong conviction when I start something then I have to finish it. And there is no reason the end this wonderful connection.After her emotional moments, she always apologized for it again and felt very sorry.

But now it is time to get up. The sun is shining, and it is looking like a perfect day in late fall. I start with cleaning the bathroom. I am going on with the floors and the kitchen. As typical, it needs more time than I thought before, and when I look on my kitchen clock, I notice that it is already after 12. I am driving to my parents' house for lunch. As I am entering the door and walk in, I instantly feel that the mood of my mom isn't good.

"Why are you so late, Thomas?"

"I cleaned a lot, but I also didn't think that lunch would be ready."

"I am not even ready. There was a lot of work in the morning, and I have the feeling that everything gets too much for me." I notice on her desperate and frustrated tone that there is more, and I even had a notion before she is saying it.

"I have such a bad headache, and I don't think there is anything with my eyes because I am seeing so blurred sometimes … I hope that there is nothing in my head."

"There will be nothing in your head. But it's good that you have the appointment in the hospital next week."

"But I still have to wait for it a few days!" She almost cries.

I got louder. "You waited so long with getting an appointment, you will be able to wait until next week!"

In the meantime, my dad came and I notice on his view that he seems to be angry too. I think, it's no wonder, my mom probably bothered him the whole morning with this subject. I don't have the nerves since there is still so much I have to do on this day. Anyway, my mother manages that we get something to eat. After lunch, I am cleaning the dishes with her, and I am able to reassure her a bit. Sometimes it works, sometimes not. I have the ability to understand almost anybody, even my mother. But maybe we are on the same wavelength when we are into any bad things.

I am checking my emails upstairs. There is another email from Elisa; she wrote before she went to bed last night. She was still out with her friend Cony for dinner and wrote that everything would be packed and prepared now for the trip.

I write a short email that I am looking forward to meeting her tomorrow morning and that I am very excited. It just took 15 minutes until I get a reply from her. She is also very excited and a kind of nervous. I write back that I will be right on time at the airport, but if for any reason I wouldn't be there, she just has to wait. I also mention that she shouldn't forget her passport and that I have to go now. Have a good flight, honey!

I drive to a place to clean my car, and then I drive to Kaufland (a big grocery store). As I am driving home, it is already dark again and I notice how much time I spent with cleaning the car and shopping. The car wasn't too important, but the shopping was. I need a variety of food at home, at least for the next days. For tomorrow night, I have planned to cook something Asian. It will be Elisa's first day here, after a long flight. She will be jetlagged and we won't go anywhere. I remember that my mom wanted to help me with the last cleanings, and I have to pick her from my parents' shop.

As I arrive there, she is in a better mood than at lunch time.

It is 8 p.m. as she left my condo. But I need still one hour more until I am finished.

I am now definitely prepared for Elisa's arrival. I know her flight schedule, so I know where she is now. Elisa must have arrived from Raleigh in Atlanta and should be already on the gate for the flight to Stuttgart. I feel the excitement for the next days, but I am also nervous. But on this busy day today, I could push away my worries. I know also that it is Thanksgiving in the U.S. today, and it has something sad for Elisa. Her dad died on Thanksgiving, and for many years ago she never had family around her on this holiday. But therefore there are also hopes in her because she flies exactly on this day to Germany and meets somebody she dreamed about in the last months: me.

Friday

November 28, 2014

I wake up because my phone is ringing. I look on my alarm clock, and it is still about one hour earlier than I wanted to get up. I kept on my cell phone over the night, just in case if there would be anything with Elisa. I jump out of my bed and see on the display of the phone that it is my dad.

"Thomas, we saw at the videotext on TV that the plane will arrive one hour before!"

"Oh really?!"

"Yes, as you wanted, mom checked it on the screen."

"This is unusual that a plane comes so soon before the planned time, but I see I have to rush … Thank you!"

"But be careful on your drive!"

I didn't expect something like that. I put on my clothes, brush my teeth, clean the washbasin accurately and check the videotext page of the airport on my TV once again.

"Wow, the plane arrives now at 7 a.m. instead of 8:25 a.m.!" I say aloud to myself. It is already six, and even if the traffic would be good, I won't be before 7 at the airport, I am thinking."

I'm looking around fast if everything is neat and tidy in my condo and almost run down to my car in the garage.

Fortunately, the streets are very clear and without much traffic. I am driving faster than usual. The last thing that I want is to be late.

As it is 6:40 a.m. and I am close to the airport, I know that I will make it.

It's good that the Stuttgart airport isn't that big, and I know exactly where I have to park to be close to the arrival area. I walk in and feel my heart beating. Now I am here, near the exit and the big glass front where I can look inside and see the baggage claim. Above the screen and it shows now, Atlanta 7:30. Okay, I still have 40 minutes to wait, I am thinking. But it is better than if I would be too late.

People nearby are opening a big banner with "Welcome home – Wilkommen zu Hause!" It looks as if they are waiting for their kids. In the pocket, I have folded a paper where I printed out last night, "Welcome Elisa" with a little red heart below.

The time passes very slowly ... now still 10 minutes.

I get more nervous, my palms a bit wet and I am observing the other people around me.

Now, I see the first passengers through the glass. It is some distance to them, and I am not sure if I will recognize Elisa from here. I unfold my paper and hold it in front of me. I look to the baggage claim and think about whom could be Elisa. There is one woman on the other side of the claim. I don't see her face, but from the hair and especially because of a blue scarf, this could be Elisa. She mentioned a blue scarf before. Again, it feels like an eternity. I have this woman in focus, but I'm also making a look in direction to the exit. Now the woman with the blue scarf is moving to the exit; I am walking there too ... but where is she? I know that there are also restrooms still inside and the custom checks.

The woman with the blue scarf is standing in front of me. She is smiling; it's Elisa! I smile back.

"Oh, how nice Thomas ... Thank you for the welcome paper!"

"Hi, Elisa!" Shortly after speaking it, she hugs me tightly.

"How was your flight? Are you tried, hungry, thirsty?"

She just smiles. "The flight was faster as you see. I am not hungry and thirsty, and I am wondering that I'm also not tired."

"Let's go to my car. It's not far to walk."

I take one of her big bags, and we both are smiling. I pay for my park ticket and offer Elisa something to drink from my trunk.

"This so nice of you! But I would prefer water instead of the soda."

We sit in the car and are driving on the Autobahn. Elisa slowly touches my right thigh with her left hand.

"If you get distracted, you have to say."

"No, I don't think so." I smile a bit nervous back.

It gets brighter outside, but it's foggy.

"It's going to be a foggy day. Yesterday it was still so beautiful."

"This doesn't matter to me much, Thomas. I am so happy that I am here with you!"

I smile and touch her hand that is still on my thigh. Elisa makes a happy impression, and she tells me a lot about the flight, with who she was talking and also that her brother took her to the airport in Raleigh yesterday.

"I am sorry that I am talking so much."

"That's fine, Elisa … It doesn't take long to my house anymore. I will stop first at a bakery and buy something there for a late breakfast."

"This sounds good!"

It is probably her first time at a German bakery, and Elisa doesn't know what she wants after I asked her. I take pretzels, rolls and some sweet pastries.

I don't drive in the garage and park outside, because my plan is that we will leave later again. As I know from my trips, it's important to stay awake after an arrival from the U.S. here to get as fast as possible in the German time rhythm.

"Oh, your condo looks so bright with all these pictures on the walls and everything is so tidy and clean!"

"Thank you!"

"Give me your bags; I put them right to the bed in the bedroom."

Elisabeth walks around astounded. My condo isn't that special, but I know different to many other people's condos, also here in Germany.

I start with preparing the breakfast, and I am telling her she should just relax. But she doesn't, she is with me in the kitchen and walks around me. She continues talking a lot, this time about my condo. She lightly touches me at my back and my shoulders.

I make coffee and green tea, eggs and take the things from the bakery but also marmalade, a chocolate cream, honey and peanut butter to the dining table where I put plates, cups and some nice napkins before.

We start to eat and Elisa is curious about the German bakery things, but also about the chocolate cream and the peanut butter.

"Actually I shouldn't eat too much from these things, you know my rosacea ... but I love to try it ... I wonder also if this peanut butter tastes as the ones in the States."

"Try it."

"Mmhhh ... it's good, but different than the peanut butter at home ... I like also your green jasmine tea, Thomas ... but I think I need a cup of coffee also." Elisa is laughing.

"Sure, I will bring you some from the kitchen, it should be ready."

As I am on the way, she also stands up behind me and says, "I can do it also by myself!"

I grab the glass can of coffee and turn around. Now Elisa is standing in front of me with a tender smile, red cheeks and some small silver earrings are dangling between her dark long hair from her ears. She touches my left body side. I look at her and put my left hand on her right side. She pulls me close and we hug and hold each other very close.

"Do you feel good, Thomas ... is everything okay?"

"Yes I am doing good. I'm glad to have you here! How are you?"

"I am feeling wonderful!"

She is pressing her head against my chest. Then she releases me and turns around. She walks a few steps away from me, I look at her and grab her left hand to pull her close. She kisses me on my mouth carefully. I reply to it, press her stronger to my body and stroke her on her back. She presses me against the kitchen counter behind me. While we are kissing, it's suddenly more intensive and I am touching her thighs.

We are stopping. "I see you feel great too, my dear Thomas!"

"Yes I do, honey." We smile at each other and sit down at the table again. I didn't expect that it would go so fast with Elisa.

While I am cleaning the dishes, Elisa unpacks her things and takes a shower.

Two hours later, we are ready to drive into the center of Heilbronn. I park the car at the parking area at my workplace. Without any hesitation, Elisa takes my hand. I am feeling a bit embarassed because I am not used it, but also because we could meet somebody who knows me.

"Would you like go to the Christmas Market, Elisa? They opened it first yesterday."

"Yes … but I would also need something to eat. I know we had breakfast, and you want cook for me tonight, but I still haven't too many calories today." I am wondering a bit because never before had a woman told me that her 'level of calories' would be too low. But I say, "Sure, we can go over there in a Turkish kebab shop."

"Oh yes, I want try this!"

I order a usual Turkish kebab, and Elisa wants to try a falafel sandwich. She likes it, and we try from each other.

Then we are going outside. Elisa is packed like an Eskimo. She is wearing a wool hat she got before from me, her scarf, her winter coat and thick gloves. It is a bit chilly, but still not really cold. We are walking through the crowds in the pedestrian zone and getting closer the Christmas Market.

"I am not used to having these temperatures at home, and it's not good for my condition."

"We don't have to walk around long. I just want you to see the Christmas market. It's also good if you sleep better tonight, and it gives us a little program before we are at home again. It's still too early to cook dinner."

We are walking a bit around the Christmas Market, but I notice that Elisa wants to go back. I am hoping that it will be a bit more possible with her in the next days. I know that she struggles with her condition and people in the U.S. often are driving everywhere, but if you want to make some experiences and want to see things in Germany, you have to walk a bit.

At home, we are getting close to each other again. It feels good, and it's been long ago that I have been touched from a woman before. Elisa seems to be in her element and very happy. I still don't see any clue of tiredness in her eyes.

I start to prepare my Chinese food for dinner. She is helping me to cut the vegetables small. I soak the turkey meat in soy sauce and add some fresh garlic and cashew nuts. This kind of Chinese dish I have made already for many guests in the past. But the situation that someone helps me with the preparing reminds me of my ex-girlfriend Susan. I even feel a small déjà vu. Elisa opens a board and sees the many candy and chocolate I have there.

"May I try something from this white milk chocolate?"

"Sure … but you know we will have dinner soon." I am a bit surprised about it because before in our phone calls and in our many emails, she often told me that she has to be careful with her rash, but also with her condition what she is eating, special sugar and bread, would be a big issue. Of course I like when she wants eat. I even had worries that it could get difficult to have the right food at home for her. But now it seems to be no problem at all.

"Oh, this chocolate is so yummy!"

"You like it, Elisa?"

"Yes! The quality is much better than the stuff we have in America. It's so creamy!"

"And this chocolate isn't even something expensive. I know you would pay a lot for this at home. Here you get even for a very low price a high standard of quality with almost any food."

"Sometimes it really sucks to live in the States. It's not only about chocolate and food, though you know healthy food is an important subject for me. But it's also because of many other things too. Like the politics, that nobody cares really about the environment, the conservative views of so many people and so on."

"Yeah I know. A party like the Republicans there, would be called Nazis here! And they are one of your two big main parties."

In the meantime, the white chocolate bar is gone.

"I can't hold myself back if I start to eat something good like this."

I smile. "It's often the same with me too … but I can't do it before I am having dinner. I hope you are still hungry."

I start with cooking. I put some sesame oil in my big and heavy wok, add chili and some other spices. When it's hot, I throw the soaked turkey in it and stir around.

"This my Thanksgiving dinner for you, different as the traditional American dinner, but it's turkey." I grin.

"You are so sweet, and you can't imagine how much I enjoy this moment with you, and I am looking forward to my first Thanksgiving dinner for ages!"

I put the meat with sauce and the nuts in a bowl and put it in the oven. I clean the wok and heat it again. Now I throw all the hard vegetable like carrots, belly peppers and bamboo sprouts in the wok first. At the same time, I switch on the rice cooker. The basmati rice I had put in before.

"It's smells already so good, honey!"

"I hope you will like it."

Now I am adding the softer vegetables like mushrooms, the bean sprouts and leek. I pour some fish sauce and oyster sauce in it, stir around and let it cook for some minutes. The rice seems to be done, and I heat up the meat in the oven once again.

"I probably made too much, as usual."

"It's not bad if we have some leftovers."

I put the vegetables on an extra plate, and we take everything to the dinning table.

"Do you want eat with chopsticks, Elisa?"

"Yes, sure … You are so prepared with everything. The napkins, the Asian bowls, chopsticks and this Chinese music fits perfect!"

"It's actually Tai Chi music … but yes, it fits and it's very relaxing music."

While talking, I lit up the candles on my candle holder.

"Oh, honey you are so wonderful! I never had such an experience before!" She is stroking my hand, and I am feeling very good.

It takes almost one hour until we are finished. I couldn't eat as much as usual. Though I am feeling good, I am kind of nervous.

"Of course I cooked too much, and we could fill everybody in the whole street."

"But we can also eat it still tomorrow, darling."

I remember that it is more common in the U.S. to have left-overs. Here people either eat it or throw it away. To offer a guest two days the same is almost a no go.

"You want to have a dessert, dearest Elisabeth?"

"I like so much how you pronounce my name … thank you, but I think I am full."

"I can do the dishes, and you can go to bed if you want. I guess, you are very tired."

"Yes, I am. But I would lie down with you, honey."

"You know I prepared the sleeping room only for you to-night. I want that you get a good rest on your first night here. I can sleep on the coach in my computer/book room. The size is the same as the bed."

"But it would be nice to be close to you. Don't you want be close to your girl, Thomas? I waited so long for this first night."

I don't want anything too fast, and it went already so fast since she arrived here in the morning. But I also don't want to disap-point her. It's something like a flow we are into and maybe it would be stupid to say to such a nice woman, no.

"Ok. I will get to you in the bed. But go ahead, I do the dish-es and I come later."

"Nice. I am looking forward to have you by my side."

It takes something more than an hour until I am finished with the cleaning and using the bathroom.

I walk into my dark bedroom and go around the bed to the left side. Elisa is lying on the right side as she said that she would do before. It's the same side where Susan was lying more than three years ago. I slip under my bed cover and softly touch Elisa's arm on her right side. I notice that she is still awake. She is turn-ing around, embracing me, pressing me against her body; I am wrapping my feet around hers and we starting to kiss each oth-er. First softly, but then stronger.

For the sleep, it isn't a good night, for both of us I think. I am too nervous, excited and aroused to sleep. Elisa falls into sleep in the meantime. Sure she must be very tired because of the jetlag but also spending the last night in the plane. Sometime in the middle of the night, I touch her again softly. Though she slept before, she awakes fast again. We are getting close to each other, this time much more passionately. I can't resist that she touches me everywhere. I didn't want this before, but it is like an automatic flow which goes out of control. She knows how to make me feel good.

Saturday

November 29, 2014

It something around 7:30 a.m. I am wake again, or still wake. I really didn't sleep much. I am feeling a kind of emptiness in me. It's like if I would have done something wrong the past night. Things went much too fast!

Elisa wakes up too.

"Good morning, my darling." She is whispering with a smile.

"Good morning, honey." I respond.

"Did you enjoy what happen between us?"

"Yes, sure it was wonderful what you did with me."

"Great! You are my man, Thomas!"

"It was really nice, but I don't know if it was too fast."

"I know it was fast. But there is nothing to worry. I knew before that we are made for each other and I am so sure about you. Aren't you?"

"Well, I just need probably a bit more time."

"About what are you talking? For what do you need more time? We got intimate and now you have doubts?"

I feel that she suddenly is annoyed. Yes, I should know before I get intimate with her, if I am sure.

"I am sorry. It was really wonderful. But right now, I'm feeling a bit empty."

I notice that was also the wrong expression.

"Are you kidding me? You feel empty? Did I make anything bad?"

"No, you didn't! As I said, it was wonderful."

"I am sorry that I am a bit upset right now. But you are confusing me."

Anyhow, the mood gets better 30 minutes later as we get up. I am preparing the table for the breakfast, making some toast, coffee, tea and boiling the water for the eggs.

"Honey, I will walk down to the bakery ... I will be back soon!"

"Okay, until soon, my darling!"

It's a short walk to the bakery down the street. The sky is grey like the day before, and I am thinking this is typical November weather in Germany. At the bakery, I take some other rolls and pastries than the day before.

As I come back, Elisa is still in the bathroom. I am finishing the breakfast table.

"Breakfast is ready!" I call in direction of the bathroom.

"I am coming!"

Elisa's hair was still wet. Her skin was a bit pink, her eyes bright and she was smiling. She comes close to the chair I'm sitting, put her hands on my shoulder and kisses me softly on my forehead. I stand up and embrace her.

"It feels so good to be here with you, Thomas! I liked as we have been in your kitchen last night and then the wonderful dinner, now being together at the breakfast table again. I have missed something like that probably my entire life. You are so nice to me. You are so thoughtful with everything. Again you have nice napkins on the table and all these yummy things from the bakery. Oh, and you lighted up the candles again. You are so sweet, my guy!"

"I also like that you are here, honey. It's good that you are feeling comfortable. I enjoy being around with you too. Sit down ... you want coffee?"

"Yes, please. I know your green tea would be healthier for me. But I needed at least one or two cups of coffee. You see on my skin that all the sugar yesterday wasn't too good for me. I should be more careful. But it's hard here."

We have an extended breakfast. Elisa is telling me that she doesn't have these routines with the meals at home.

We decide to go to the Christmas Market in Bad Wimpfen. I told her in my emails before that this historic old town is a must-see place. It's the only old town which is still intact in the county here, and they have one of the nicest Christmas Markets.

As we sit in the car, I am asking her questions, "Would you mind if we make a quick stop at my parents' house? It's on the way."

"Oh, I am not prepared for this. Why didn't say this before?"

"It just came right now in my mind, and I am not talking about a visit, just to say a short 'hello.'"

"I am bit nervous, but okay … what do I have to say in German again? 'Guten Tag, ich bin die Elisabeth'?"

I smiled. "Yes, but you don't have to do it."

I go out of the car and am getting nervous too.

"You know, it's better to not hold hands now. I don't want to confront my parents with this situation now."

She releases my hand and smiles. "It's hard for me to not touch you, but I understand."

I didn't announce us at my parents' house before, but they are smiling too as they open up the door and ask us to enter.

My dad and my mom saying almost to the same time, "Hallo!"

Elisa doesn't hestiate, "Guten Tag, ich bin die Elisabeth!" She turns to me, "Is this right, Thomas?"

I grin, "Yes, perfect!"

We talk about her arrival yesterday, that we want go to Bad Wimpfen, my mom mention the worries about her MRI appointment next week and Elisa is making a very open, friendly and extroverted impression. Almost the opposite of I mostly behave when I meet somebody new. My parents invite us also to go with them to a Besen tomorrow for lunch. The Swabian style of a local restaurant.

In the car again, Elisa makes a relieved impression. "How was it going? What do you think?"

"It's was going good, honey. Especially my mom seems to like you."

"I think also that it went good. Your parents are friendly."

"You have been friendly too."

The Christmas Market is still not so crowd as I have expected it, but I am sure that it will change later. We are walking hand in hand through the streets with the cobblestones and everything is as festive as usual to this season here. In the windows of the old half-timbered houses are candle arches and other Christmas and Advent decorations. The stands on the markets are decorated beautiful with many green brushwood. It smells like cotton candy, sugared almonds, roasted chestnuts, but also like grilled sausages and Glühwein.

"Would you like a Glühwein and maybe a sausage, Elisa?"

"Yes, I would like to try it, I never had it before!"

"It gives a different kind of Glühwein here. Maybe you try the regular one first. Hot red wine with Christmas spices."

While Elisa has the Glühwein and a red sausage, I had a non-alcoholic punch and a white sausage Thuringian style. But we are trying from each other. After an outlook over the Neckar Valley, we are going back to the center of the market and Eliza wants to try the fire tongs punch. I am warning her that it has a lot of alcohol.

I am feeling very good with Elisa on my side. I always like showing people around and going to a Christmas market. But with a girlfriend, it's something different than with family or other friends.

"Oh yes, this Glühwein is too strong! I can't drink it anymore. I know you paid it, but is it okay that I throw it away?"

"Sure, before you feel bad, throw it away!" We put our Christmas cups in our coat pockets. On the Christmas Market here, no return is possible. People have to bring their own cups or have to buy it. But especially for someone like Elisa, it's a nice souvenir.

"Thomas I have to tell you something ..." She turns around to me, grabs my left and right hand, getting close and looks in my eyes. "I love you. You are the best thing that could happen to me"

"I love you too, my Elisabeth."

She is laughing like the happiest girl on earth.

"There is a nice, popular old café down the street here. They are famous for their cakes. You want go there?"

"Yes, it would be nice to go somewhere inside. I am freezing."

The café is very full, but on the big round table two people are getting up.

"I know this place is very different than restaurants and cafes in the U.S. We have to sit with other people on this table. Is this okay?"

"Yes. It looks very cozy here, and wow, the old walls are with paintings and it smells very good like coffee. Let us sit down."

I don't know if it is the alcohol, but Elisa was talkative to the strange people at the table. They know some English, and some words I have to translate. Is she really highly sensitive? I am thinking. But we having a good time and Elisa is taking the bill for the Black Forest cake, the strawberry-chocolate cake, a coffee and a green tea.

As we are leaving the place, it's getting dark and the crowds are streaming in the old town. We agree that we are going to the car now.

At home, it is still too early to prepare dinner. I am also not sure and a bit embarrassed if I can offer the Chinese leftovers from the night before.

"What do want for dinner?"

"Of course the leftovers from yesterday. It was so good, and it would be bad to throw it away."

"Good, but we can still wait a bit with it."

"Yes, just let us sit down and relax … I want be close to my man."

"Wow, I am noticing that I lost the time feeling … It feels like you would be here already for some days. But I can't imagine that you arrived first yesterday! This is amazing! I am always into time, every hour, sometimes even every minute."

"I think this is a good sign, darling … what I feel is also a kind of strange, but very wonderful! I feel so familiar to your place. I feel so comfortable. It's just as my soul would have waited for this moment now … Please come closer to me …"

She kisses me softly. First on my mouth, then all over my face. I reply with some stronger kisses also on her neck.

"Be slow, Thomas!" she said with a wide smile.

Sometime later, we have dinner and after it we are sitting on my colorful couch and eating gummy bears together.

I am still a bit nervous and as we are going to bed, but I feel more relaxed than the night before.

Sunday

November 30, 2014

I didn't sleep too much again. That my futon bed is so small makes it easy to get physically connected with Elisa, and there isn't much space and time to relax. I am feeling once again so empty and asking myself in my thoughts if it is really good what I am doing with her. But since she arrived, there wasn't any time to think much about anything. I just stayed in the flow what she wanted to do with me. And physically, it always felt very good, especially in the night times. But is it the right thing from the mind and the emotional side? I can't speak out about what I am thinking. Every single doubt and uncertainty will make her upset.

"Good morning, darling ... you are already awake again ... how did you sleep?" she says sleepy in my direction.

"Good morning, honey. The first part was okay after we got close ... but I woke up early in the morning again."

"I am so sorry ... my night was good after we got intimate to each other."

"It's not too bad, I am glad that your night was better."

"What time is it? Should we get up?"

I look over Elisa to my little nightstand on her side where my old fashioned world time alarm clock is standing.

"It's 7:30 ... we have still some time. Because we drive with my parents already something after 11 to the Besen for lunch, we won't need much for breakfast today."

"That's fine. We need our showers, and I have to make myself pretty for you."

"You are already pretty, sweet girl."

"Thanks! But I am not. Do you see my rash?"

"Yes, but though you are beautiful."

"You are so sweet … come here, I want cuddle with you before we get up."

She doesn't notice my doubts this morning.

Sometime after 11, my parents are in the street in front of my house with their car. We got ready right in time. Elisa has her big smile as we are going to sit down in the back of their car. Both women, she and my mom are in their elements and talking a lot. I am the one who is busy with translating. My mom wants to explain everything that we see right and left on our drive while Elisa shows a lot of interest. In the Besen, it goes on this way. It seems that my mom likes her. But I know her, it can be also a bit played. My dad is friendly too, but acts a bit more careful. Instead of the usual tender touches from Elisa, she pokes me many times. My parents recommend to her what she should try, and she is following their advices, a schnitzel with potato salad and fresh farmer bread. I ordered brat sausages with kraut and bread. As the food is there and we eat the first bits, Elisa wants to share her food with me. I recognize on the view of my parents that they are wondering because usually I don't share my food with someone else. But they don't say anything. The time at the Besen is very harmonious. My parents have chosen a very big Besen, and we sit alone at a big table. We are explaining to Elisa that in Besen, people have often sit together because it's full and they don't take reservations.

After lunch, my parents are taking us home again. Elisa and I have planned to go to Heidelberg, one of my most favourite places in Baden-Württemberg. She put on a second pullover, and we are soon ready for the drive. I decide to take the beautiful route through the Neckar Valley. We are passing Bad Wimpfen again, Gundelsheim and coming now in the nice part of the valley.

"Is this a castle up there, Thomas?"

"Yes it is, one of some on this route. But we won't have the time to stop at any. Some are also private and have special opening times. I just wish that the weather would be nicer. Since your first day here, it's grey in grey."

"I don't care about it, honey. I am so happy that I am here with you. That I am seeing things I never have seen before. You know, the only place where I have many years once before is Heidelberg. I wonder if I will recognize anything there."

"Yes, sure. It would be just a bit nicer if the sun would come out a bit. But if you like it already now, then you will love it in another season with better weather." I smile.

"Do you know that for me it is really important to be here with you my man, listening to music on the radio, driving and doing this day trip."

"I'm also happy that you are here, and I am looking forward to Heidelberg, darling."

She is stroking my right thigh, is smiling and yes there is no doubt that she is in love with me.

At the early afternoon, we are arriving in Heidelberg. I'm parking at the same place as always when I am here. I am just hoping that she has enough power to walk because where we are is out of the old town. Elisa looks as if she would step out in the coldest winter with a hat, scarf and gloves. I first don't want to take my gloves, but she resists. We are walking hand in hand in the direction of the pedestrian zone. It's cool, but not winter cold. As typical, there are crowds of people in the main street of Heidelberg. I always like the mix of cultures here, tourists from everywhere, international students who live here and old Heidelbergers with their dialect and accent. Heidelberg has some different small Christmas Markets, and the main and biggest one is at the university square. Elisa has a Glühwein and I have a punch. I walk with her on the main street to the church and the city hall; we see two other Christmas Markets and as the big castle on the hill is appearing to us, I am wondering if Elisa is able to walk up there. But she wants to, and I am positive surprised about it. With a bit exhausted girl, I arrive at the castle. We agreed that we don't want pay the admission and go inside. The best thing here to see is the castle and ruin from the outside, and the most special thing is the outlook to Heidelberg and the Neckar Valley. It's already dark again, and we are enjoy the beautiful view down to Old Heidelberg, seeing all the lights from the streets and Christmas Markets and hearing some laughter and music in the distance. After these more than 100 steps up here, we both feel hot. I see in the light of a street lamp that Elisa has cute red cheeks. We are taking pictures with her and my camera. I ask a Japanese tourist if he can take a photo us. Elisa seems to be proud that she made it up here with her condition, and I am proud of her!

We walk down the steps again, and I say to her that we should not miss going to the Old Bridge. It's also the bridge where Elisa is sure that she has been before with her brother on a school trip. As we get there and we see the Ape of Heidelberg, Elisa recognizes it.

"I have been here before! I have exactly this picture with me and the ape in the back still at home! You have to take photo of me here!"

"Ok, just wait until these tourists gone."

"We can also walk on the bridge and do it then. I never thought that I would come back here once again. And now I am here with you, my dearest man."

"This is nice, my woman."

"You are so sweet, honey." She says with a wide smile.

"Are you knowing the history of this bridge in 1945?"

"No ..."

"On one of the very last days of the War, German soldiers used explosives to render all of Heidelberg's Neckar bridges impassable, including the Old Bridge."

We walk back from the bridge through the big gate, and I take several pictures of Elisa.

It was already 7:30 p.m. as we are on the way to the car. We are think about where and what we can have for dinner. We are deciding for a Thai restaurant on the street where my car is parked. We both are loving Thai food, and I know from my brother that this place should be good.

Already before we are ordering, Elisa makes it clear that she wants to pay it and we have to take what we want after this wonderful day. Indeed it was a wonderful day. We had good time with my parents and this trip to Heidelberg was and is awesome. After ordering soups and the main course, we are holding hands on the table, and I look deeply Elisa's eyes. I'm thinking that this day was also so wonderful because there were no worries or any other problems. And to be active and get around is my element.

It is almost 9 p.m. as we are leaving the restaurant happy. For the home drive, I take the Autobahn. Now we want be at home as fast as possible.

As I am driving on the middle lane of the A6 and after some quiet minutes, Elisa turns to me.

"Thomas … I have a question …"

"Yes, sure, ask." I know this kind of starting a subject already from her phone calls before. Sometimes it is something important she wants tell me. But sometimes it is just something she is curious about. But it always makes me a bit nervous and aware that I have to listen exactly now. And this is probably also her intention with it.

"Would you mind if we start Skype when I am back in States again? It would be nice to see you sometimes if we are far away from each other. I know you still don't have the technical condition for it at home. But you can easily make a contract."

I am starting to swallow a bit hard.

"Mmh … honestly I don't need it. I'm fine with our emails and your calls once a week. I would need a contract and don't want to or have time to spend more time in front of the computer."

"It wouldn't be more time in front of the computer. It would be instead of emailing!" she says suddenly in an angry tone.

She is going on, "What is your problem, Thomas? I don't understand you! I am your woman … and you don't want Skype with me?"

"Yes, you are my woman … but I just don't need it …" I say shy and unsecure.

"I absolutely don't understand you! Why I have to beg for something normal like that?" She sounds aggressive now.

"I … don't know." I see anger in her face.

I continue, "We had such a wonderful day. Why are you talking in this harsh tone to me now? I don't know, I am just not this Skype person. You know I would like to have you here. But I see no need for Skype. I don't want spend more hours in front of a computer. I am sitting the whole day at work on a computer and also at home!"

I notice that I became also loud and couldn't concentrate much on traffic anymore.

"Is it not normal that your girl wants see you?"

"I appreciate this … but why you come up on every second day with another problem? And today it's hard because we had such a great day!"

She starts to cry, then it's silent and we don't exchange many words until we are in my garage at home.

The air is chilly as we walk through the big garage. At the door to the stairwell of the house, Elisa stops, looks to me and starts to cry again.

"I am so sorry, Thomas! I am so vulnerable and emotional sometimes. I didn't want spoil our wonderful day!

"It's okay. I am sorry that I got loud."

"You don't have to apologize."

She touches my right shoulder and then I take her in my arm.

She whispers, "I love you, Thomas. You are everything for me."

"I know, Elisa. And I love you too."

After sitting embraced in front of the TV in the living room and eating some gummy bears, we are deciding to go to bed.

That she freaked-out in the car is still in my mind and I am feeling it in my bones. It always comes so suddenly, I am thinking. She is not wrong when she want Skype with her boyfriend. I also don't know why I have a problem with it. But that she gets from one minute to the other totally upset scares me. I noticed this already on some of our phone calls before. But this seems to not be different in person. I have to be careful, and it is something I don't want to have in the next days again. I want to enjoy these days with her, and hopefully I will get completely sure about my feelings for her. I don't need these ups and downs anymore. Not through her pressure, but also not through my own doubts.

Monday evening

December 1, 2014

At about 10 p.m., we are lying in the bed together. Elisa has her head on my chest, and I am holding her. I feel her warm breath on my neck. I am wondering how she is already so tired again. We did almost nothing the whole day. We got up late, had breakfast, just hung around with each other and late in the afternoon, we went grocery shopping. Elisa said that she would have muscle cramps, and it was too much in Heidelberg for her, so she has to relax one day. For me it is hard to relax a whole day. But it was nice that I could do all the walking with her yesterday, and it was very understandable for me that she needed this staying at home today. We both noticed at the store that we are very familiar with each other, and once again I had the feeling like she had been here already for many days. Elisa also enjoyed preparing and having dinner with me a lot. It is something she doesn't know and gives her a family feeling. We had baked Maultaschen (Swabian pasta bags) with green salad and bread. It was nothing exciting, but a taste of Baden-Württemberg for Elisa and something that is good and simple at once. I also enjoyed the day with her, with my girlfriend. There are really good things between us. If there wouldn't be my doubts. But it was a peaceful day between us. Nothing bad came up. When Elisa is so close to me as now, I get aroused fast. But I want let her sleep, and I feel foolish to have sex with her, but being to the same time not sure about my feelings. Elisa is turning around in the other direction, and I am doing the same in my direction. I hope that I can catch also some sleep tonight.

Tuesday

December 2, 2014

"Good morning, darling … are you already awake again?" She is turning around to me, her eyes still a bit closed, but with a relaxed smile on her face. It is shortly after 7 as I see over Elisa's body on my alarm clock.

"Yes, I am honey." I am smiling back.

With a sleepy voice she is saying, "I don't want that you catch so less sleep every night when I am here! Maybe I am taking your space in your bed."

"No, you aren't. Of course it's just a futon bed and rather for one person. But I generally to tend to be early riser. And to be honest, I am not used to sharing my bed with such a beautiful woman."

A big smile is running over her face and her eyes are from one second to the next wide open.

"Oh, you are so sweet my man! … Please come closer and hold me from my back side. You know I like this a lot."

I slip over to her and carefully put my left hand and arm under her shoulder, with my right hand I'm going over her right side, pressing softly on her tummy and pushing me softly against her back.

"I like this so much, Thomas!"

"It feels good being so close to you, Elisa."

"I feel the same."

I'm touching her upper back with my mouth and start kissing softly on her neck.

"Ah … you are so wonderful."

She is touching my right hand and leads it to her breasts. I am pressing her stronger against my body. Then she suddenly turns around, holding my heads and starts kissing me on my mouth.

She is smiling. "Sorry I have a bad taste in my mouth … I have to go to the bathroom."

Her left hand is going down on my body. She knows exactly how to do it.

"Oh, I see honey … you are ready for more!" There is a glowing in her eyes and with her two big front teeth, she is biting on her lower lip like she would has a mysterious plan in her mind. She is leaving fast the bed, smiling me and saying, "I am right back!"

About one hour later, we are still lying in bed and holding hands.

"I hope you enjoyed it, Thomas."

"Yes, I did. I had never such experiences before, honey."

"I want to make you happy; I want show you that I am your girl."

"I hope I can make you happy too, Elisa."

"It makes me happy, if you can enjoy it. That you feel a pleasure is what I want."

"And what's with your pleasure?"

"This isn't too important. You have to know that women are different with their sexuality. It's mostly not like you see it in the movies. The most pleasure for me is if you are full of joy."

"Ok. Should we get up?"

"You can't relax. But get up, you can use the bathroom first."

"I can go down to the bakery and buying something for breakfast."

"This is nice of you, darling. But do you want that I make some bacon and eggs for you? Since we were shopping yesterday, I should be able to make you a real American breakfast. You also have toast, butter, marmalade and peanut butter. So you don't have go to the bakery today."

"Fine, I would like to have an American breakfast from you today, honey." I smile.

"My mom never taught me how to cook. She only opened cans and showed me how to use the microwave. But I learned from my dad how to make a good breakfast."

"I also have a little surprise for you."

"I am curious … but you know I am not materialistic. I am just so glad to be here with you, that I booked this flight, that you invited me and that I can be here in Germany with my man."

I am laughing and getting up.

Sometime later, we are together in the kitchen.

"Here is my surprise, Elisa!" I give her a chocolate advent calendar.

"Oh, is this such a calendar you told me about before?"

"Yes. It's a German chocolate advent calendar. It has 24 doors. I forgot to give it you yesterday. Every day you can open one door until Christmas Eve. Every day you get a chocolate and you a see a picture behind every door. Every child in Germany has it and many adults too. You can get such a calendar in different sizes with different chocolates and also with other things behind theses doors."

"You are so sweet, darling!"

"Usually I also have one every year. I get one from my brother, and he gets one from me. But we still haven't time see each other. Maybe it works tonight."

"I don't like that I can open this door now, and you don't have a calendar."

"Don't worry."

She grins with her long wet hair like a child under the Christmas tree, holding my hands and starts kissing me.

At the breakfast table, I am thinking that this girl is really beautiful with her blue eyes when they are sparkling, her cute nose, her lips which are strongly red even without a lipstick, her sensitive skin and her dark long her. Elisa isn't slim, but her body is very feminine and everything seems to be in the right place. She is the woman I always dreamed about it. Not only because how she looks, also because I felt more attracted to American girls than to Germans and especially also that she would do anything for me. I don't want think about my doubts.

"Do you like it, Thomas?"

"Yes, it's great honey!"

"It's nice to hear this. It's something I wouldn't do for you every day when we live together, but sometimes."

"I know it's also not the most healthy food, and it's not something I would want every day. But you are great with making breakfast."

"Thank you!" She is smiling and touching my left hand. "I didn't care much about what I ate since I am here. But I can't resist the good food here, and it makes me happy to eat with you, darling … But I should be careful, the rash on my skin doesn't looks good."

"I understand, but it didn't look too bad."

"I want look nice for you, and I know that dairy products, sugar and too much gluten doesn't help."

"I know that you have to be careful, but though you like nice."

She smiles again like a little child. "Come on Thomas, let us go over to the couch."

Without a comment, I sit down in the corner of my colorful couch. Elisa is following me quickly.

"Lean back and relax." I do what she is saying. She is sitting with her knees over my thighs, putting her hair to her left side, bending her face to me and is softly taking my face in her hands. I close my eyes, I feel her warm lips on mine and she starts kissing me slowly. I'm replying, and since she is here I know how she likes it. Not too fast, eagerly and greedy.

Time slips by, and it's already after 12 o'clock until we a finished with cleaning the kitchen, the dishes and Elisa is dressed. I suggest driving to Öhringen in the afternoon. It's not too far way, Elisa will like to the old town and there is eventually the chance to visit my friend Christine there.

"Yes, let us go there, Thomas! This plan sounds good. It would also be nice to meet Christine."

It wasn't too cold for December, but it was still another foggy and very grey day.

While car driving, I say to Elisa, "This sky is so frustrating, I wished you would see also some sun here. The weather forecast doesn't sound better for the next days."

"Thomas, I said to you before that this isn't important for me. What counts is being with you, 24/7. We had such wonderful morning together, and I am so happy to be here with you!"

"Yes, you are right, honey. I just thought that some sun would be nice too."

She is lying her left hand on my thigh, and soon we arrive at the parking area in Öhringen. I am calling Christine on my cell phone and tell here that I'm with Elisa in her town and if we could visit her after a stroll.

"What did she say, Thomas?"

"We can come to their condo. Today in the afternoon her mother-in-law would be there. But she said that this would be good, then she has some time to talk with us and her kids are busy with their grandmother."

"This is nice; I am curious to meet your friend Christine."

"Let's walk to the historic town of Öhringen. It's not too big here, and we can do it by foot."

"If it's not too much, I can do it. The rest yesterday helped to relax my muscles and my hips."

We are walking hand in hand through the city park, or it least what is possible to enter. I am telling Elisa that Öhringen is getting the 2016 garden show, which is every year in another town of Baden-Württemberg and that because of this they are already busy with making new things here.

We are climbing up the stairs to the market square, and I am noticing that it is a bit hard for her. But though, she is smiling. We are passing the square, see the city hall and the church. Elisa is enjoying walking with me around there. We are making a round in the old town and walking back to the car again.

Five minutes later we are at Christine's condo, and I am ringing the door bell.

"Hi, Christine! Here we are! This is Elisa!"

"Hello! Hello, Elisa! Please come in!"

"Hi, Christine! Nice to meet you … you have a nice place here."

Christine is acting a bit more formal than usual, but very friendly as always. We are also saying hello to the kids and her mother-in-law. We are sitting down on the big couch in their living room, and Christine is offering us self-baked Christmas cookies, Elisa coffee and me some tea.

"I have to excuse if you understand me not too good, Elisa. I haven't English since school. But Thomas will help to translate … I think."

"Oh no, your English is great, Christine … I wished I could speak so well in German."

The two women seemed to be doing good with each other, and I knew before that Christine can talk anyway with anybody. Elisa is in a very good mood, her eyes are sparking and she looks in change to me and Christine. She definitely doesn't make any shy impression, enjoying her coffee, the cookies and I don't recognize any indication of a highly-sensitive person. When Christine disappears for a short time kitchen, she is softly stroking my thigh and grinning at me.

"Your Christmas cookies are wonderful, Christine."

"Thank you! I made this year the first time such a wide collection of them, and I am surprised about myself that they are good." Christine smiles.

Mostly Elisa is leading the conversation. She mentions the things that we did in the last days and is talking about the less vacation days in the U.S., the bad health care system there and how much she likes all these things in Germany. Christine is listening, asking sometimes short questions and needing the one or other word from me in English.

After about one and half hours, we are leaving again, and on our way home, we stop at a grocery store to buy some Maultschen and salad. Elisa loved this Swabian food so much on the evening before that she wants to have it again for dinner.

Originally, it was planned that I would go with Elisa to my brother's house and introduce her to his family. But my little nephew Ben was sick, and therefore, my sister-in-law doesn't want to have guests. My brother Mark texted me in afternoon that he would come over with Larry, my four years old nephew, tonight.

We still had some time left, and we are sitting on the couch.

"Thomas, didn't you say that your mom has her appointment at the hospital tomorrow?"

"Yes, it is tomorrow morning. You are right."

"Wouldn't your dad like to go there with her?"

"He can't close their little shop. Someone has to be there."

"Couldn't we do it?"

"Mmh … I don't want that you have to spend your time here with me in their shop."

"I just think that it would be nice if your dad would go with her. I would like to do this with you."

"Really?"

"Yes, your mom probably doesn't feel well, and this is what we can do."

"Okay, this very nice of you, Elisa! I will call them."

My dad likes this suggestion. He didn't want it, like me too, but he said yes.

Sometime later, Mark arrives with Larry, and they are bringing me a nice self-made advent calendar with a picture of Larry and Ben on it. Then I give my advent calendar for Mark, and they also have a little Christmas thing for Elisa.

"Oh, this is so nice of you. Mark, say thank you to your wife also." The conversation is about the same we had with Christine in the afternoon. Mark needs also some translation help from me and Larry is shy.

They are leaving after 40 minutes.

"It was nice to meet your brother and your nephew. It seems that he didn't feel too good in my presence."

"He is shy, but he behaves like this in the first 15 minutes also with me or when other familiar people around him. It has nothing to do with you."

Elisa touches me on my shoulders.

"I love you, Thomas."

"I love you too."

We are kissing each other softly.

After a couple of minutes, we are preparing dinner together. This time we make the Maultaschen not baked with cheese as the day before. Elisa mentions that she can't handle so much cheese because of her skin. So I cut them in small pieces, roast it in a pan with fresh onions, add two eggs to it, and separate I grilled some brat sausages. Elisa makes a mixed salad. She enjoys this situation with me in the kitchen so much. I am enjoying it too. But it reminds me of similar situations with Susan three and a half years ago. Also there was the time in the kitchen, preparing food together and cooking for each other, nice and special with comfortable moments.

"I am finished with the salad. I set the table, darling. What do like to drink?"

"Apfelschorle. You know, some apple juice with sparking water." I am smiling.

"This is so good, that you don't drink too much soda over here."

I lit up the candles; we start eating.

After cleaning the dishes, we sit down at Elisa's favourite place, my couch.

"Thomas, you have to know that I am missing this so much at home. Of course, everything with you. Waking up together in the morning, being around you all the time, spending a nice time with you, going together to bed at night, but especially also this, cooking and having dinner together. I don't even have chairs at home on my dining table. Since I moved in this house, I have been always busy. When I am at home, I just care about my cats and working on the computer upstairs. But I also never have guests. It was not necessary to have chairs. There is also still so much to do at my house, inside and outside."

"I like all these things with you too, my dear Elisabeth." I smile and I know that she likes it when I say her full name. "Sure, I am used to having meals together with my family. But I also seldom cook here at home. Only when I have guests and this happens a few times every year, but not too often. I also don't really live in this place. Sleeping and sometimes spending time in my book and computer room. But because of the internet, I am spending often a lot of time at the computer in my parents' house."

"But it's so nice that you are having family, and they are all very good people … Well, maybe I can tell you a bit more … but I don't want to disturb our wonderful vibration today."

"It's okay, Elisa. You know I want that you share the bad things in your life also. Please be free to talk about it when you want. I am here for you."

"You are so sweet to me. Nobody behaved like this to me before." She pauses a short time and is going on.

"I told you already some of my past. There was no stability in my life. We also moved a lot around when my brother and me were kids. We lived some time in California, and we drove all the way by car. These moves were the only trips we did in our family. My mother cared always more about herself. As we have been back to North Carolina again, Sam and I hang around with our cousin. He was violent and often made stupid games. I think he was also not nice to my brother. But Sam didn't notice or didn't want see what he did with me …"

She pauses again and continues with a shaky voice. "I am sure that he did this with other girls too. My uncle, his son, our cousin, visited us often. We played a kind of hide and seek game. He was following me in my room, he closed the door, as I was sitting on my bed he jumped on me, pressed me down, hit me in my face, he pulled down my pants and raped me."

Elisa has tears in her eyes and starts to cry. I try to comfort her and stroke over her shoulder. But she rejects me, and I feel that she wants to go on.

"This happened more times! You know my brother is younger, but he had to notice it. I couldn't tell anything to my brother. My cousin threatened me to tell it to no one."

"How old were you, Elisa?"

"I can't tell you when it started. But I was then around 13. This was also the age where I became pregnant."

"Pregnant?!"

"Yes, I didn't want to tell it to my mom. I noticed it as my period was gone. First after it was obvious that I was pregnant, she went with me to the doctor. My mom, my dad or the doctor didn't ask what happened. But for my parents, it was clear that it was my guilt. It was already something in the 14th week, so it was officially too late to abort it. But the doctor gave me pills. Nobody talked about it with me."

Elisa cries and needs a break again. I feel very bad for her, but anyhow I am not surprised, maybe because I know about the same stuff from Susan.

"All these things what happened at that time were also the reasons that I didn't want contact with Sam anymore. He must have known what our cousin did with me. But he was only quiet. First two years ago when I came back from Ecuador and my mom broke up with me …" she is sobbing … "he indicated in a talk with me that he got raped from our dad. I am not completely sure about it. But it could be, our father was a bad person too. Before I went to Ecuador, my dad was dying. I have been there in his last hours with him because nobody of our family cared about him. He died painfully of cancer."

She breathes deeply a few times.

"But back to my childhood … My parents ignored everything, my whole personality. Though of my problems in school, I have been very good and got the best marks, but this didn't help me much. I became teased from classmates. I always liked to be at my grandparents' house, but there I wasn't much welcome later anymore. You know as I started the relationship with this guy from England. I also had three suicide attempts in my life … But the hardest is that my mom didn't want any contact with me since I am back from South America. She probably gives me the fault that I moved because of this guy to Ecuador, but for her I am for everything guilty. Stella, you know the therapist, said to me that it would be better not to try to be connected with my mom anymore."

Elisa is crying, and I take her in my arms.

"I feel so sorry …"

"You don't have to feel sorry. It's nice that you are here for me, darling. You are the first person to who I could tell all this."

"I am glad that you did it. I can't help you with it, but it's good that you talked about it."

"I know that you can't help me and that I have to do it by myself. But you give me as nobody else the feeling that I can trust and that I can share anything with you."

"Yes, this is right. You can share anything with me. I am here for you, honey."

It was also kind of confusing for me what I understood. Maybe because I am not used to having such deep conversations in English, but maybe because she didn't tell me everything. I could question, but it is sad enough what she told. I think it's better not to go deeper; we both are feeling uncomfortable. I don't want to ask about her suicide attempts.

Wednesday

December 3, 2014

Right on time, we are at my father's little shop at 8:30. My dad explains to me and Elisa how to use the coffee machine, and my parents left to the hospital. It's not really busy on this Wednesday morning.

"You are thinking probably of your mom, honey?"

"Yes, I do. She is often too deep in her anxiety, mostly the things have been good in the past. But I understand her worries."

"I understand it too. I am the same if I have any pain and don't know where it comes from ... Do you think I can make a coffee?"

"Sure, my dad said that we can use his machine ... Maybe we can also take something from the next bakery ... but I can't leave now."

"I can do it! I am nervous, and I don't know if they understand me. But I can try it." She is smiling.

"Yes, if you don't mind ... I would like to have pretzel."

"Explain to me where the bakery is and what I have to say."

I am laughing a bit. "Ok, you just go out of the front door, cross the street and walk until the traffic light, there you cross the street again and on the left side you will see the little bakery, it's very close ... You have to say, eine Bretzel, bitte!"

"E-i-n-e pretzel bidde? But I am still not sure what I want."

"Yes, eine Bretzel, bitte ... just point what you like to have, and they will understand you ... Do you need money?"

"No, I have still some."

It doesn't take long until she is back again with a paper bag and a wide grin over her face.

"I did it! The lady was very friendly. I told her that I would be from America and pointed to something ... how do you call this?" She opens the paper bag.

"Ah, this we called a Flammendes Herz – Fiery Heart ... as you see on the outside part, the dough is covered with chocolate and inside is marmalade."

Just 30 minutes later, my dad comes again.

"How is mom doing?"

"The MRT went fast, but she has to wait for the results and this takes time. I can't wait so long."

I translated it to Elisa.

"Should we go to hospital, Thomas?"

"You don't mind, Elisa?"

"No, I just think it is better if somebody is there with her."

My dad is also happy that we want go there.

As we are arriving at the hospital, we see my mom coming towards us. My mother is smiling, "Everything is fine; they found nothing. I should let them check my eyes. But I am relived that nothing is in my head."

I was relieved too and told it Elisa.

"What are you doing here?" is my mom asking me.

I am laughing, "Taking you from the hospital. It was Elisa's suggestion."

"I could have walked back. But if you are here ... are you busy or would mind driving me to the grocery store? I would need some things."

We are not in a hurry so we do it, and my mom asks Elisa if she would like to have any chocolate. To my recommendation, she selects a big box of Mon Cherie. My mom invites us also for coming to their house in the evening.

For lunch, I drive with Elisa to a Chinese restaurant in Heilbronn. They have a lunch buffet. I know this place is very good and have been with Michael and other people before.

We are both enjoying our time there a lot.

"What would you like to do in the afternoon today, honey?"

"I just would like to relax with you at home. I am tired and should spare my muscles, Thomas."

"I thought that we could go in the city when we are already here."

"You need always something to do, darling. Can't we just relax?"

"But we didn't do much today and in the last two days."

"Mmmh …"

"Ok, if you don't want to walk, we can drive up this hill over there … You see?"

I pointed out of the window to the Wartberg, and other things around are good to see from this Chinese restaurant on top of the building.

"It's a nice view from the Wartberg, though we have again a grey sky. There is also a good restaurant up there. Of course we are full, but maybe we can drink something there."

"Ok, we can do this. It sounds good."

Thirty minutes later, we are at the top of the Wartberg. Again I regret the bad weather, but though the city of Heilbronn and the area around was good to see from here. We couldn't let it be to order to our drinks, a coffee and a green tea, also two pieces of cakes. Outside, we both are takingpictures of each other. Elisa wants to take a selfie while we are kissing each other. She gets embarrassed as other people walk by.

"They don't care about us, honey!"

"Though I don't like to do intimate things in the public."

"I can ask them to make a picture of us while we are kissing," I am laughing.

"No, no … this is private what we are doing" and her cheeks are getting red.

At home, Elisa is happy about our privacy again and pulls me on the bed.

Until the evening, we are relaxing. Then she gets nervous about the visit at my parents' house.

"Hey, what do you think I should wear tonight, darling?"

"You look good already now."

She is smiling and gives me a kiss.

Twenty minutes later, she comes out of the bathroom in a white summer dress with black balls on it, big silver earrings, a dark red lipstick on her lips and some make up.

"What you think?"

"Mmmh … you look good."

"Honestly? You have to tell me … I want to make a good impression … I don't know what your parents like."

"It's important that you feel good what you are wearing … maybe it's a bit too fine."

"Too fine? This is the best thing I took with me here." She says in a sharp tone.

"It's really nice what you are wearing, honey. It looks good on you. But we are just going over to my parents' house, and it's winter time." I try to sound relaxed.

She gets angry. "I know that it is winter! But it's one of the least new dresses I have!"

I can't suppress that I am getting insecure. "I am sorry …"

"I will change it … but it's already late!"

"We are just going to my parents … it doesn't matter if we are five minutes late."

"It matters to me! It's not nice if we are coming late." She closes the bedroom door behind her.

I don't know, did I say anything wrong again? Or could it be that her behavior is typical woman behavior?

Ten minutes later, she appears in a red sweatshirt in front of me.

"Okay?" She asks rhetorical.

"You look great!"

She takes the bottle of wine and a bag of coffee she bought on Monday while we were shopping. She insists to have some small gifts for my parents.

My mom is ready with cooking the dinner as we arrive. We have chicken schnitzel with baked potato wedges and salad. Elisa is very talkative again and is enjoying the food, and me too.

Later we are going to the living room. My mom already has a lot of Advent and Christmas decorations around in the room. Also the first candle is burning on the Advent wreath. My parents offer us Christmas cookies and Elisa some wine from the region. It seems that she likes the atmosphere with my parents. My mother is curious and asks her some things. I am busy with translating, especially from English to German. My dad smiles, but is mostly quiet. I notice that my mom likes her; my dad is a bit guarded.

Maybe Elisa gets a little drunk because with the time she is touching me a few times and she is almost the only one who is talking, except my translations.

"You look again like Einstein, Thomas." She says with a smile and is adjusting my right eyebrow. She did it and said this already some times in the last days. My mom is reminding me always of my long eyebrow, but of course without touching me or calling me Einstein.

I think that my parents have recognized that there is more between her and me.

It's a weekday evening, and I see it on the tired faces of my parents that they want go to bed, but it's hard to stop Elisa with talking. I am indicating to her that we should go now. After some further 15 minutes, we get up and walk to the car. She is almost glowing with a big smile on her face.

"It was a nice evening. How have I been, darling?"

I smile back. "Yes, it was a nice evening, and I think my parents like you."

"Maybe I talked too much, but I felt good, and I liked the atmosphere there with your parents. They are nice people."

"You touched me a few times; I think they noticed something."

"I had probably a bit too much of this good red wine. I am sorry. I hope you don't mind?"

"No, I don't mind. I think that my parents noticed already something on Sunday as we shared our meals in the Besen. This is very untypical for me."

At home it doesn't take long until we are in the bed and cuddling close together. I am feeling better and more relaxed. There weren't these ups and downs as in the last days.

Thursday

December 4, 2014

"I'm thinking about what we can do today, honey. It's already 12:30, our breakfast took long."

"Oh Thomas, I am just enjoying the time with you and like to hang around. I don't need any big plans."

"Yes, this is nice. But I also want that you see something here. Even if it isn't the best season and the days are very short, and I want show you around at least a bit."

"We have been already to Heidelberg, Heilbronn, Ohr-inken, Baad Wimpfen … do I pronounce it correct? And also here around … what do you thing we could do this afternoon?"

"For a trip to France and Strasbourg, I thought before it's too late, also to Baden-Baden which is near the Black Forest, it's already too late. Maybe Würzburg in Bavaria?"

"What is like there? Is it a lot of walking? You know with my condition I should be careful."

"Well, it's a city, we have to find a parking spot, and yes it will be some walking. You know how it has been in Heidelberg. We can also make in this direction a trip to the River Main, to Wertheim or Miltenberg and driving through the Odenwald … it's another forest, back again."

"This is sounds good!"

"It's of course also not the perfect weather for this, but I won't be able to change the weather, and it won't change in the next days as long you are here."

"Ok, I still need an hour until I am ready to go. Is this good for you, my sweet guy?"

It is 3 p.m. as we are arriving in Wertheim on the River Main. The sky is as usual grey since Elisa landed in here in Germany. But on this Thursday, the fog clouds are very thick, and it looks like it gets darker every minute.

"Uhh … It's cold … but this town over there looks nice!"

"Yes, this town is called Wertheim. We are still in Baden-Württemberg, but on the other river side and around us is Bavaria. But not this typical Bavaria people often think when they hear the name of this state, this region of Bavaria is called Franconia. Let us walk a bit along the river and then we can turn left to the old part of the town."

Elisa looks, in her outfit with a winter hat from me, a scarf, her coat and the gloves, like the temperatures would be much under the freezing point again. But they aren't. Though it isn't pleasant and with this wet air it feels colder than it is. Because she said I wear gloves too.

"There is a ship … where they are going, Thomas?"

"It comes from Würzburg. I don't know where they are going. But in the River Main are still coming the cities Offenbach, Frankfurt and Mainz. In Mainz goes the Main into the Rhine. So theoretically the destination of this ship could be many other cities in Western Germany or even the Netherlands! But it would be also possible to drive up the Rhine to Basel in Switzerland!"

"Wow! It's very quiet here."

"Yes, it's the season, the weather and because it's Thursday. On a nice summer day on weekends, you will find the crowds here … but maybe we will see some more people in the town."

But even in the small streets between the old and historic buildings are just a few shoppers to see. We decide to go to a café. Each of us has a cake, Elisa a coffee and me a cup of green tea.

Until we are back at the car, it's already dark and early evening.

"I wanted to show you much more in this area … but as you see it's already dark again! I am just thinking how we get back. We won't see much in the Odenwald now anymore, but I also don't want to drive exactly the same way back."

"Just do it as you think, darling. What we will have for dinner today?"

"It depends when we are at home. When we cook something, we should stop at a grocery store, but we can go also out for dinner. Let us take the route through the Odenwald. We have more options, maybe we can still stop at a Christmas Market or stop for dinner before we go home."

I don't feel too well on these curvy roads and the temperatures were dropping as higher we get in the Odenwald. I don't want to see any ice on the roads. But Elisa is doing the best to entertain me. She is switching the radio stations and to some songs she is singing. She has really a good voice, though she says that it was much better when she was younger.

"Elisa, we finally made it safe through Odenwald." The town of Mosbach is ahead. Do you want go to the Christmas market there? I think, but I am not complete sure, if they are open on a week day."

"Honestly, I don't want to go out in this cold again. Could we find something for dinner?"

"Yes, we can. Bad Wimpfen is also on our route. They a have a good Thai restaurant there. But I don't know if you want to have Thai food a second time?"

"I loved the Thai in Heidelberg, let us go to the Thai here too! I want to invite you."

"You don't have to do it. But yes, we can go there. They also have a special Thai room, where you sit on the floor."

She is touching my thigh, and we are both smiling.

We are walking hand in hand over the wet cobblestones in Bad Wimpfen. It doesn't rain. The stone are wet from the thick fog. But this town with the half-timbering houses is always nice. Especially for an American, it must feel like in another century, I am thinking.

As we enter the restaurant, we see that the Thai room is already crowded. We just get a small table in the bar room. This doesn't make Elisa hesitate to order the best four course menu for us. We start with a Tom Kha Gai soup. As our large appetizer plate with deep-fried vegetable, prawns and calamari is coming, another bigger table gets free and the waitress conducts us to sit there. I feel better there, and we are no longer the center of attention and have more space. We are almost full as the main dishes with chicken, duck and fish arrives at our place. I like the spicy green curry sauce. For Elisa, it is a bit too hot. But we are both enjoying the great meal a lot and eating is definitely something we both love. Before her visit, I had my doubts if I would find the right food because of her diets she told me about. But she seems to eat almost anything I like too. After the ice cream and fruit salad, we are leaving the restaurant full and happy. Elisa invests every cent from her travel budget on paying for things for me. She is not a lady who is into fashion or wants buy anything expensive for herself.

Friday

December 5, 2014

"Good morning, my Thomas!" Her eyes are still a bit closed, and with a grin she is turning to me and continues, "How are you feeling about me?"

"Good morning, honey … I am feeling good."

"I mean … are you sure about me and our relationship?" She looks in my eyes questioningly.

I remain silent a few seconds. The past night is running through my mind. We have been once again very close and intimate with each other. It felt good for me. But not for the first time, I woke up with a kind of empty feeling inside me. Do I just imagine this empty feeling? Or do I imagine the love for her? What is wrong with me? This woman is giving me so much!

She is interrupting my thoughts, "I am sure about you and me for 120 percent!" It sounds like a request to confirm it. In my life, I always try to be honest and clear about what I think and I feel.

I just bubbling out, "I think am for 80 or 90 percent sure."

"You are not sure about me?"

"Maybe it's 100 percent, but I need time." I am saying, uncertain.

"I am doing everything for you, I'm thinking about moving here, I want to make you happy and you are not sure?!" She is staring at me with big eyes.

I notice that I said something wrong.

"I am sorry, honey."

"Don't say sorry!" Tears are running down her cheeks, "Why are you doing this to me?"

"I just want be honest … and things are taking time with me."

"I can't believe what you are telling me!"

She is jumping out of the bed and then I hear her going to the bathroom.

Why I did say this? Since Sunday night, there were no big problems anymore.

She is the girl who loves me as nobody else before. Having a girlfriend I dreamed my whole life. And now she is here, Elisabeth from America. Beautiful, is ready to do almost anything for me and she attracts two big things for me, girlfriend and USA. But why do I have doubts? Why I am not sure?

Elisa comes in the bedroom again, grabs her blanket, and I hear that she going in the direction of the computer and book room. I wait some seconds, get out of the bed and follow her. She is lying with tears in her eyes on the couch.

"Elisa, I am sorry … come back to the bedroom again."

She doesn't say anything, but gets up and is going with me back again.

"Have you any clue how I am feeling? You are everything for me. I came over here only because of you, and you are not sure after one week?"

"I am sorry, I don't regret anything and all that we did together was great. I enjoyed every moment. Really. But I don't know why I sometimes have these empty feeling after a nice night with you."

"You mean by empty that you are not sure about me?"

"Not sure about my feelings."

We are having breakfast with fresh rolls from the bakery, but the mood is tense. We are just talking about what is necessary.

"Elisa, what do you think about driving to France today?"

"I don't think that I am in the mood for it. And isn't it anyway too late now? How far is it?"

"Well, it depends where we are going. For Strasbourg, it's probably too late. And it would mean some walking there."

"No, this isn't good. I don't like to do anything."

"But today is the last day where we can make a trip. I doubt that we want do it tomorrow on your last day here. We could drive to the German Wine Route in Rhineland-Palatinate. In the South, the road goes to France. Just right after the border is a little nice town."

"If you want do it, Thomas. I am not convinced, but it's your decision."

Two hours later, we are sitting in the car and cross the Autobahn bridge to Rhineland–Palatinate. It's foggy and grey outside, like the mood in the car. Elisa is saying nothing, she just changes the radio station sometimes. On the time, I see that we are already late, and I didn't check any distance before. In my mind, I skip to drive along the Wine Route. We are too late, and with this weather it makes no sense at all. I just hope that we are arriving soon in Wissembourg, the little town in France. But still we are some kilometers away. I don't feel well; Elisa's silence push me down.

"I am sorry, that I am not talkative. But I feel almost depressed. It's not your fault I can't handle this day."

"It's of course my fault, Elisa! I was the one who started to ruin everything today in the morning."

I am already very impatient as we arrive one hour later in France. It is still hard for me to endure the silent and tense mood. Close to the parking area in Wissembourg is a small old house with the sign *Flammkuchen* outside.

"Is the this French pizza you talked about before, Thomas?"

"Yes, it's very popular in the whole region of Alsace here."

"Do think it's a nice place to go?"

"I have never been in there, but it looks nice and cozy. If you want, we can eat something there."

I am not really hungry. It is sometime in the middle in the afternoon, and after sitting two hours in the car, I would prefer to walk around as long it is not completely dark. But my main goal right now is to lift up Elisa's mood.

We are sitting down at an old wooden table, and the place looks really very rustic, friendly and comfortable. But some of the old signs on the walls are in Bavarian and remind me more of cottage in Bavaria than a restaurant in France. The little menu is Alsatian. We are ordering a Flammkuchen together, for Elisa an elderberry juice spritzer, and I take an Orangina soda drink. Elisa is warming up a bit again and is risking a smile.

"I like it here. The walls are interesting with all these signs."

"I like it too. But though Alsatians have such rustic furnishings too, it looks more German or even Bavarian. The waitress speaks also a standard German without any accent."

"What you do think about the other visitors here?" She is whispering.

"Interesting … this one guy seems to be something like a German businessman who has been here before, at the other table they are a mixed culture group. They speak German and Spanish, maybe students. But except for the menu, nothing here is French or let me say Alsatian."

"I studied French, but it was long ago."

"As a German, you don't need French here in Alsace. At least most should understand German. The old ones still speak the old Alsatian German dialect and kids are learning German as their first foreign language in school."

Elisa is holding my hand on the table until our Flammkuchen comes. It tastes good and is aromatic. We order a second one, and we leave the place about one hour later with some better moods.

Outside it's getting dark. We are walking first along the main street where we are looking in windows off different little shops. Later we are crossing the creeks in this pretty town, and she is taking some pictures of the church there. At a bakery, Elisa is fascinated with the different chocolates in the windows. We are going inside and she wants sit down, but the women are saying that they will close soon. Elisa is talking to them about the chocolates and is buying some. Obviously the owner and her daughter or employee are very friendly. While I speak to them in German, Elisa practices her French.

It's already something after six as we reach my car again. On the German side again, we step into a drugstore because Elisa would like to buy chewing gum and some other little stuff.

"Where do you want go for dinner tonight, honey?"

"Mmmh ... you mentioned this Mexican place in Heilbronn before?"

"Oh yes, Enchilada! We need about two hours until we are back again. So it's better to find something near home, and it's maybe also better as to cook today."

At around 8:30 p.m. we are walking in the Enchilada in Heilbronn. Of course it's full on a Friday night, and we don't have a reservation. But a waiter tells us that we have to wait for five or ten minutes and a table would be free.

"In the U.S. is this common and 10 minutes isn't really long."

"I know. Here people are not used to waiting. Either you just walk in and sit down where you want or a place is full and you would need a reservation before."

"I am already curious about the menu, Thomas."

"I'm also curious what you are saying. I know that the food here and at the most Mexican restaurants in Germany isn't authentic."

We didn't get the best place, it's close to the door, but we are sitting comfortably.

"Here is the menu, honey!"

"Let me see ... Taquitos con Pollo, Quesadillas, Enchiladas, Fajitas ... is this all?" She smiles. "And what's this? Burgers, Buffalo Wings, Steaks, Chili con Carne ... this sounds more American than everything else!"

We order two different plates and some nachos before.

"Are you serious Thomas ... we really have to pay extra for these nachos?"

I am laughing. "Yes we have ... I know that in the U.S. such appetizers are for free. Germany is a service desert in comparison to the U.S. The good thing here is that you don't have to tip. Sure, you are giving some tip. But it varies from a couple of cents to the next euro or some more, if you ordered a lot and you are very content. But you don't have to pay the waiter like it is in the U.S."

"Yeah, in my country you pay 20 percent or sometimes more for the service."

The meals arrive; we are hungry and eat fast because we are both tired. We are leaving as soon as we are finished.

As we are walking hand in hand to the car, I turn to her.

"So Elisa, what do you think about this place?"

"The interior is nice, the staff was friendly, the food was good, but it is far away from real Mexican cuisine. It's even not what we call Tex-Mex. I don't know what it is … something American."

"Yes, I thought so before too."

At home I open a bottle of regional white wine as we are sitting on the couch.

"But I don't want to drink more than one glass, Thomas … but it's sweet of you that you want to drink with me."

"You know I usually never drink, but I will make an exception tonight."

The mood is much better again as in the morning, but still not as before.

Saturday

December 6, 2014

"What time is it, darling?"

"As I see over your back, it's something after 8:30."

"What are we doing today?"

"Well, it's your last day here. What do you want to do? Maybe we can go to Heilbronn if you want and you can buy some souvenirs. At night we can go out for dinner … maybe also visit my parents once again."

"This sounds good. I don't think that I haven't much money left to buy anything. But I would like to have something for my brother and my coworkers."

"Don't worry about the money. I can take care of it."

Tears are running over her face. She is touching my arm and hand.

"I am so sorry for yesterday!"

"You don't have to apologize for it. It was my fault."

"No … I have been depressive, and I also had doubts about our relationship and everything. If I feel this way, nothing and nobody can help. Though you treated me nice and drove with me to France. I liked this little town. And you opened a bottle of wine for me at night, and I couldn't enjoy it."

"It's no problem … I am glad that you are feeling better again, aren't you?"

"Yes, I think so. I want to enjoy this last day a lot with you."

We are starting to kiss each other.

"I have to get up and prepare something, honey."

Five minutes later …

"You can stand up, Elisa!"

She is walking out of the bedroom and looking around.

"Do you see anything?"

"What should I see, Thomas?" She smiles.

"Look in the direction of the wardrobe."

"Oh, what's this?"

"Today is December 6. This means Saint Nicholas Day in Germany. Boots got filled over the night."

She bends down to the shoes.

"Oh, a Santa Claus chocolate, some other chocolate and in this bag is tea?"

"Yes, it's my favourite organic jasmine green tea."

"You are so sweet!"

After each of us had a shower, I walked down to the bakery and Elisa made some scrambled eggs and bacon. We are enjoying our full and late breakfast.

In the early afternoon, we are driving to Heilbronn. The city is very crowded, which is typical on these Advent Sundays before Christmas.

"I want to buy you something … what would you like to have?"

"You gave me already so much and you don't have to buy anything, Thomas."

"You spent all your vacation money on our food, and it would be nice if I can give you something. Do you want go in this bookstore?"

First she wants to buy a book for her brother, but then she decides to give him the green tea she got from me and take a Swabian cookbook in the English language.

"I don't think that the recipes are easy to make from this book. Food like Maultaschen is often bought ready-made, even here."

"But I think I can make it, I would try it before, when you are visiting me some time next year."

"This would be nice! But only take it if you like it by yourself."

The book was on sale and very cheap.

"Elisa, do you want to have anything else?"

"You are so sweet, Thomas. You don't have to buy anything more. You know I am not one of these many American materialistic girls."

"I know. But with this cookbook you think mostly about me. I would like that you have something for yourself. Christmas is coming soon, and it makes no sense to pay a lot of shipping costs when I can give it you now."

"Mmmh, maybe a scarf?"

"Yes, why not?! Over there is a department store ... they should have scarves."

In the department store, Elisa doesn't need much time to pick a red scarf. She asks me a couple of times what I think, which one I would like and if it wouldn't be too expensive. The red one is one of the cheaper scarves. I am noticing how modest this girl is.

"Thank you so much, darling!"

I smile "You are welcome, honey."

"When did you reserve the table for dinner tonight?"

"At 6:30 p.m. If you want to take a shower before, we should drive home soon."

Right on time, we arrive at the restaurant in Neckarsulm. As usual, the rustic place is crowed, and I am happy that I reserved a table before. I wanted to take Elisa out on her last evening to a restaurant with Swabian cuisine.

"You have to tell me what I should order, Thomas."

"I think they also have a menu in the English language. But I can translate and we don't need it ... What's about with the Schwabenteller? Pork medallions with Spätzle, Schupfnudeln and Maultaschen."

"I know Späa-tzle and Maul-ldaschen ... I love them, but what is Schuuupf?"

"They are also in your new cookbook," I laugh "Schupfnudeln are thick noodles made with potato dough."

"This sounds good. I will take it! And what do you like?"

"Maybe I will take the pork loin with mushroom sauce and Spätzle."

We are sitting at one of these higher tables close to be bar. A scent of Swabian and Bavarian food is in the air. A waiter is a carrying a big pork knuckle with sauerkraut and dumplings to a table; the place is very loud.

"Never eat this when I am with you!" She says pertly.

"I had this before. It's not something I would like to always have." I grin.

As the friendly waitress brings us our plates, we start to eat, and as typical, we try from each other.

"Do you like it, Elisa?" I ask carefully.

"Oh yes, it's good … what do think?"

"We should have taken something more different. The meat is pretty much the same from our dishes, the sauces are salty, and I am disappointed about the Spätzle."

"Why?"

"I doubt if they are fresh and homemade … they taste and look more like noodles."

"You are the expert … but I think it's not bad."

"Yes, overall it's not bad … but I would have liked something a bit more special on our last evening together."

"Don't remind me that it is our last evening! But Thomas, do you know what? I am so happy that today is our last day, and it was not yesterday … This would have been terrible if I would fly home after such a day and today I enjoyed a lot."

"Yes, you are right, honey. I am also grateful for this."

As the waitress comes again, Elisa wants to order the desserts for us. She is pointing with her finger on the menu and gets a bit nervous.

"Ich möchte ein Apfelstrudel mit Vanille Soße, and …"

The waitress is interrupting her with a big smile. "You can order in English." Elisa sighs and smiles back. "And for my boyfriend this ice cream with the red berry sauce."

"Ok … Where are you from?"

"From North Carolina, USA … Your English is pretty good."

"Thank you!" she is walking away again.

"Darling, you have to tip her for me. She is very nice."

The desserts are good, and we are leaving the restaurant with full stomachs.

At about 8 p.m., we are at my parents' house and sitting on the couch in the living room again. While I am having apple juice with water, Elisa is drinking fresh-made Glühwein. I see again that she feels comfortable and talks a lot. This means for me that I have a lot to translate.

After an hour, we decide to go. I know that she still has to pack her things for her flight home, and I would like to spend some time with her alone.

As we stand up, my mom is coming back from the kitchen.

"Das ist für Dich, Elisabeth."

"Oh ... this is so nice!"

She is taking a big Christmas bag from my mother. In there is coffee and a big chocolate Santa Claus.

She is smiling like a little child. "Today in the morning I found a Santa Claus in my boot and got green tea ... Translate, Thomas ..."

"Thank you ... mmh   Dankeschön!" she says out loud.

My parents are smiling.

"Bitteschön." My mom replies.

At home we are sitting on the coach in my computer room together. Her eyes are sparkling, we are holding hands, and her head is lying against my shoulder.

"How are feeling right now, darling?"

"Good, with you on my side ... but I know that you are leaving tomorrow."

"Yes, but we will see each other as soon as possible again, I think. Between many couples is a distance, and I am sure we can make it too."

I don't say anything, and we are in silence for two or three minutes.

Then we start to kiss each other, and it turns fast into a passionate affection.

Suddenly, Elisa presses her right index finger against my lips.

"Wait, darling ... I will be back immediately again." She is leaving the room fast.

I'm tired, and I think that I am not in the perfect mood for having sex now. I am really wondering about myself again. At least with the erotic part, I never had a problem until she was here. My thoughts are stopping as Elisa is standing in front of me, only clothed with red string underpants and a red bra. She looks beautiful. She is moving closer, opens the buttons of my shirt, pulls the belt out of my jeans, and opens the zipper. I feel a mix between arousal and fatigue. But I hope that she doesn't notice anything on this last evening. Also what I learned in these nine days is that she has the same sensitive antennas about thoughts, face impressions and behaviors of others as me. But I have luck, that she is more centered on herself.

After it I go in the bathroom and get ready for the night. Elisa is still running around and is stuffing her clothes in her travel baggage. I set my old alarm clock for 5:30 a.m. This should be enough for the plane at 10:30 a.m. I think anyway that we are much faster at the airport in Stuttgart on Sunday morning than on a week day.

It takes 30 more minutes until Elisa is in the bed too, and it's already late. She just gives me a short kiss and we are saying good night.

Sunday

December 7, 2014

"Are you already awake again, darling?" She says with a sleepy voice.

I also reply tired "I don't think that I slept too much."

"What do you think, how much time do we have until the clock is ringing?"

"Probably soon ... but let me look over your shoulder."

"You know I don't see anything without my glasses."

"Mmmh ... I thought it would be later, if I read it correct it's something after 4:30."

"Really? I also have the feeling that it would be later already ... I want to check my cell phone ... Do you see my glasses?"

"Yes, they are lying close to the alarm clock."

"My cell phone is showing 6:30 a.m.!"

I jump out of the bed and run to the alarm clock.

"Oh ... you are right, the alarm clock has stopped!"

Elisa is asking very nervous, "Can we still make it to the airport?"

"Let me think ... we are getting up one hour later than planned ... just in case, I always calculate two hours to the airport, but we can be faster and it's Sunday morning! So yes, we can do it!"

Elisa jumps out of the bed too.

I just clean my teeth fast, make coffee for her and also make two sandwiches.

At 7:20, we are leaving the condo.

The Autobahn in the direction to Stuttgart is empty.

"We are fine, honey. If there aren't any accidents, we will reach the airport right in time."

She is relaxing and putting her hand on my thigh.

"I think that I put everything in my baggage, and if not, it's not important."

"Do you have your passport?"

She is smiling, "Yes, I have it. You reminded me already by email of my passport as I left home on Thanksgiving Day."

I am smiling back. "Yes, because it's the most important thing."

Exactly at 8:30, I park my car in front of the airport building.

I know from my past trips to the U.S. where the Delta check-in is.

"It's good that this airport is so small, Thomas."

"Yeah, this is the reason why I also like to fly from here, and it's the nearest airport from my hometown."

I get an uneasy feeling as Elisa is standing in the check-in line. Soon it will be time to say goodbye. I see in her face that she has the same feeling.

After 15 minutes, she is coming over to me again.

"Do you need still anything? There is a little shop over there."

"Maybe some water. But you have to pay for it."

For a couple of minutes, we are sitting on bench and holding hands as usual, then Elisa is saying, "My dear darling, I think it's better if I go in there through the controls now."

"Yes, I know … I will miss you."

"I will miss you too, and I love you, Thomas!"

"I love you, too Elisabeth!"

Her eyes are glassy, and I hold her a last time in my arms. She is turning around, and I am waiting until she is through the controls. Then she is waving at me, and I see that tears are running down her face.

She is gone.

I'm walking back to my car, and it feels strange doing this alone after having her the last days always by my side. I am writing her a text, My dear Elisa! I miss you already. Have a safe flight. Your Thomas."

It's getting bright as I am driving back. But the sky is still grey as the last nine days too. I notice that my thoughts are confusing. Do I really miss her? At one side, yes. But do I miss her as I should miss a girlfriend? I am not sure. The last days have been very intensive. I maybe never had such an intensive connection before. There were some very nice, but also tiring and emotionally desperate moments.

I am back even faster from the airport as the drive was to it.

At home, I am looking around in my condo if there are any clues from my guest left. She forgot a cream and her magnesium jar. But the rest is just trash. As usual when I have guests, I am instantly starting with cleaning and pulling the covers so that everything looks as before.

I'm not in a great mood as I walk for lunch to my parents' house.

My parents ask if I have driven her to airport, if everything worked well and when she will be at home, but there isn't any hint about Elisa and me, no curious question.

Can it be that they didn't recognize anything? Or are they just ignoring it?

But I am not in the mood to tell anything.

After lunch, I don't know what to do, and I am feeling more confused than ever before. I would like to go home and not leave my condo anymore. But I know that it isn't a good idea. I decide to walk out in to the fields; movement is always better I think. It's also what I wanted do with Elisa, walk to the old farm house with the big trees around. But after her hip problems, I was glad that she was able to do what we did. The farmhouse and the vast area around I like to go in summer times when I need some distance from everything. But it is not too cold on this second Advent in December and the ground is dry. A fresh breeze is blowing around my nose. It would be maybe good to talk with Christine now, but she has probably no time with her kids and husband and what do I want to tell her? She will also not be able to tell me if I love Elisa.

I pass the terrain of the old farmhouse and walk up the hill behind it. The wind is blowing a bit stronger here. But I don't feel cold. Probably the strongest wind wouldn't be enough to blow my mess in my head away that it becomes one clear thought. I am talking to myself and to the universe or whatever energies exist out there. Why do I have these doubts about such a wonderful woman? Yes, she seems to be a kind of emotional wreck, and it's no wonder after all that this poor being made through in her life. But she is sure about me, she loves me as nobody else before. She wants to change her life 180 degrees for me. Isn't she the person I dreamed of all my life? A sweet American girl who wants to move here just to be with me!

Tears are running down my cheeks.

I walk back again and take a nap and meditate at home.

As I am up again, it's already early evening. I need to talk to somebody and dial Christine's number. I thought before that she will be busy, and yes, I hear the kids crying on the phone. I don't have the time to talk much and I don't want to moan. While I try to explain my confusion with my feelings, I notice that another call is coming in … it's Elisa! I say a fast goodbye to Christine and pick up the other call.

"Elisa?!"

"Hi, Thomas! I just wanted let you know that I arrived safe in Atlanta, and I am waiting for the other flight to Raleigh. I miss you so much!"

"I miss you too." I say a bit hesitantly.

"Is everything okay with you, darling?"

She notices something in my voice.

"Mmm … yes, I am ok. I just didn't feel too great in the afternoon. But I have been out on the fields for a walk and took a nap, maybe this helped a bit."

"I am sorry. It was hard for me in Stuttgart after we said goodbye. I thought now that it is still not too late in Germany, and I took the chance to call you. It will be late until I will be at home, but I will send you an email … You are every second on my mind, darling."

"You are also always on my mind." That isn't a lie.

"What are you doing tonight?"

"Not much, going to my parents' house for dinner and early to bed."

"Did you talk about us with your parents?"

"Not yet. As I said, I didn't feel well and it wasn't the right moment."

"Just do it when you feel that it would be a good moment ... But you said that your parents had a good impression of me?"

"Yes, I think so. You have been very nice and friendly to them, and I am sure that my critical mom likes you."

I hear some laughs on the phone.

"I think boarding starts soon. Have a good night there, my man. I love you!"

"I love you too. Have a good flight, and I hope that your brother takes you as planned from the airport in Raleigh."

"Thanks. I hope this too. You never know with him. Bye."

"Bye, honey"

"Bye, darling."

I still write an email to Elisa, though I am not sure when she will read it.

Monday early evening

December 8, 2014

My first workday wasn't too long, and it's getting dark as I look out of the window of my computer room and see the next street lamp. The stars begin to sparkle. It's a clear sky after a sunny day. It's kind of ironic; it was the first nice day since November 27, the day before Elisa arrived. In the last nine days, there was not a single cloud gap in the sky. But now it seems all the clouds and fog go away.

But still not in my mind. This workday helped me to get some distraction, but I don't feel that I got a clear mind.

I am checking my emails and find two from Elisa. She wrote still last night from her home:

Hi my darling Thomas!

I'm finally getting a chance to read your letter. I also got the postcard you mailed me before my trip with the duckling ☺ So sweet of you! Thomas, you are so, so wonderful to me, and I love you so very much. I also had a lot of sadness today, leaving you to return to America. As I told you on the phone, the second I rounded the corner after waving goodbye, I immediately started to cry. I tried to have you see the happy side of me when we parted, the part of me that feels so loved by you, the part that loves this wonderful man who I've been so blessed to meet out of the blue. And now you are my boyfriend, and I am your girl-friend! And honey, I feel so good with you. I must be with you again soon. I'm dedicated to you, Thomas, and I love you so!

I thought of you also when I flew over Canada because I imagined you had traveled the same exact route when you came to America ☺ Maybe I was picking up on your wavelength, honey! We did get to Atlanta early, but had a wait before the plane could get to the gate. But I was able to figure out what to do for the next flight (rechecking bags and all). I have many ideas to streamline things for my next visit ☺

I did forget the chocolates, so I was glad you gave me a few this morning! But I got your advent calendar! Also, I know I left a few things, but didn't realize that I left that much. But it's good because they are there for me when I come back. And darling, I want you to know that I want to come back! You are my man, and I need your love and your sweet kisses, and I want to wake up in your arms and go make breakfast with you and enjoy our days and evenings. You are so special, Thomas! I need you! But mostly, my love, I need you to know you've got my love and support here. You've got a woman who wants the best for you. I know it's sad that we will have some months apart, but we've got each other now. It won't be long, I feel, until we are together again, with no more distance! But as you know, I will wait for you, Thomas, because you are worth it to me! You are incredible! So we can encourage each other to take comfort in this love and not let the sadness take root. I don't want to associate my love for you with sadness, but with gladness and anticipation of all the great things that are in store for us! I'm really glad you got some meditation and a walk, my darling. You are taking good care of yourself, and that makes me happy. I am holding you so tenderly in my thoughts. When I'm feeling sad, I see us smiling so brightly at each other. There are so many precious moments in our nine days to remember! And Thomas, thank you so much for being my boyfriend. To me, you are so much more to me than that word can convey. I love you until my heart is must bursting!!!

That is incredible about the alarm clock, honey! I really do think these synchronicities mean something special! It's like the universe is giving us signs ... seriously ... how can you explain that!

I must get ready for bed. I'll tell you more tomorrow when I call you at 6 p.m. your time. Also, no worries about talking to your parents right away. I'm sure when the moment is right, it will come up in conversation. But explaining it all when you are feeling sad, that's hard. I hope, my love, that you are sleeping well as I write this, and that you have a good day. I look forward to talking with you tomorrow night!
I love you!!!

Your girlfriend …

Elisa ☺

And the second one:

Hello Thomas, my sweet darling!

It's our four month anniversar, from the first time you wrote me ☺ But like we've said, it feels like we've known each other for so long now ☺!
I've been up since 4:30 a.m., here, but I got about six hours of sleep, so that is pretty good. I've been unpacking, paying bills, doing some laundry and spending time with the cats.
I wonder how your day is going, honey. I think about your beautiful smile and how happy I feel when I look into your eyes. I miss your sweet kisses, my darling. I miss us cuddling in bed. I miss us making meals and eating together. I'm missing everything about you! But I'm also so happy that you are in my life, that I'm your girl!!!
I want to tell you that I'm certain that if you decide you want me with you in Germany, I will be able to come be with you in 2015. Of course, I will give all the time you need, honey. If you can visit me here, that would be wonderful too! I can also plan to visit again. It's all about whatever works best for us,

honey. I really love you and want to be with you, whenever you want me there! I've done my budget, and I should have almost a year's worth money saved up for expenses even before the end of the year (for the partial house payment, student loans, as well money as for my cats and towards food, etc., for us). That way, if I come to Germany in 2015, I can focus on getting fluent in German and finding a job there, while there is money in the bank to take care of these things. I will still try to find some online work too. My brother Sam also said he and his buddy Jim are interested in the house. I say all this not to pressure you in any way, but to let you know I'm serious, honey. I'm your girl, and that means I need to be with you, there for you, there to wake up with you and take care of you and have fun with you. You've given me so, so much that I never believed was possible to have with someone, and I'm just dedicated to you, Thomas! I can't wait to learn how to cook the foods you like and make a Swabian meal for you! I also want to take walks with you on the farmland, by your house. I want to be there to have tea and a nice meal in the evening. I want you to teach me and show me more about the German culture. I think maybe, eventually, I would even go to a sauna with you … if I get brave enough! Of course, I want to be close to you and make you feel good ☺ That is so wonderful for me! But mostly, I just want to be near this dear, wonderful man of mine. I just want to give you my heart and all of me, Thomas! You are the best!!! Oh, I must get ready to get online for work. I will call you at 12/6 p.m./ ☺

All my heart!

Your Elisa ☺

Wow, these emails are once again overflowing positive! I see there is no space for my doubts. Anyway, it's 5:45 p.m. and she is calling soon.

Monday Evening

December 23, 2014

I am sitting with a can of ginger tea in my computer room and writing Christmas and New Year's greetings to my friends here in Germany, to Ana in Hong Kong, to some other old friends in the U.S. and of course also another email to my girlfriend. To all my mail friends there weren't any conversations for months, but now for Christmas I should do it. There was no time. I was and am so busy with the emails to Elisa. We mentioned that we could fill books with our letters. Since last Wednesday, I have off. I have to take some vacation days. It's only possible to take five days into the next year, but not more.

Emotionally, I didn't feel good in the last weeks. I played like a double game. In my emails, I behaved like she wants and needs it. Be her man. But inside me, I nearly despaired. There was also nobody with who I could talk or with who I dared to talk about it. Christine has not too much time. She always understands me and agrees with what I am saying, but this doesn't help. With my parents, I can't and don't want to talk. One week after Elisa left, I mentioned that I would be together with her. First they didn't take me serious, and then they didn't want to understand me. My mom and I got louder, so I noticed that it isn't good to come with the subject again. They assured me that she would be a nice person, but a relationship would be ridiculous. They are thinking that way because of the distance, but also because of her past. I was disappointed, but I didn't wonder about the re-action. It was the same as when I was together with Veronika. There are just my brother and his wife who have a better understanding for my situation. But I also don't want bother them too much, and at the end I have to know by myself what I want. It's what I wanted to find out in the last weeks. But no walk, meditation, book or prayer took me closer to it. I am aware how precious this connection is I always wanted, but I have to be sure about my feelings.

Today I was in Heidelberg. This wonderful place gave me some distraction. I did some last Christmas shopping, went for lunch at an Asian restaurant, walked up to the Philosophers' Way, was at the Christmas Market and had something to drink at Starbucks. I wrote postcards and a short email to Elisa in there. Yes, I missed her. But was it in a way I should miss a girlfriend? She also loved Heidelberg as I have been there with her. Today there were some memories as I walked around, but not that kind of special and unique memories. She was also not the first person and woman with who I have been there.

I feel sad for her. She will spend Christmas alone. It will not be her first time alone as she said. For me, it's hard to imagine that somebody is alone on Christmas since I am already my whole life together with my parents on the holidays. I also find it pity there is recently such a bad relation to Sam, the only family member she has still a contact. She told me that he came late to the airport as she arrived there from Atlanta, he drove crazy and Elisa assumed that he doped before. They didn't talk for some days, and he wants money again and she gave him some as usual.

In another email from today, she wrote:

Guten Morgen mein Schatz Thomas ☺

Thanks for writing me from Heidelberg and when you got back home, honey! It's really so sweet of you to think of me in your busy day. I'm glad you got to go to Philosopher's Way and see the view, although it was cold. I'd love to go with you someday, when it's nice out too ☺

My day was pretty easy-going at work. Tomorrow may be more rushed, and I also have to go get two fillings done at the dentist. So I'm not too keen on that! ☺

I'm also a bit tired right now. But I hope to study German a bit more tonight. I found a site. I'm trying to learn 1000 words as my first goal. They say if you learn 3000 words, you can basically get around in a language, but 1000 will get you 80 percent. So hopefully this site will help me build my vocabulary and some basic sentence structure. I can then study grammar more in depth with the books. I do admit I'm feeling on one side a bit blue about Christmas this year. I'm not feeling very good with my brother, and it just shows me that I'm one thread away from having no family anymore. In the past four years, I was sometimes invited to go see friends at Christmas. But since I've moved here to Wendell, I'm farthest away from them, and so I don't really see them much anymore. So it will just be a day at home. Martha hasn't been answering my calls, so I think she must be on vacation too. I'm okay to be alone, but I guess it's just feeling like I wish I weren't at this place in my life where I have a reason to be so alone (physically alone) at Christmas. I also am missing you so much, honey. And I'm really grateful you love me and even want us to talk sometime this week. That means so much. But part of me is praying that maybe this is the last Christmas I will spend by myself ☺ I'd like it to be a special day, again, one day. What makes me feel a bit better, actually, is that each morning I wake up, and I go to the Advent calendar you gave me, and I find the day and have a chocolate. It gives me a moment with you, something you gave me, something sweet (both in sentiment and literally), and I get to do it each day until Christmas! Okay, honey … thanks again for all you do. You're such a sweet man! I love you, and I hope your week is going to be very relaxing and nice for you! I look forward to talking with you again soon!

Your girlfriend with love and kisses,

Elisa ☺

Christmas

December 25, 2014

It's late afternoon, and I am sitting on the couch in my parent's living room and watching my nephews under the Christmas tree playing with their new toys. Everything is going on here as normal.

Yesterday my grandmother was here from the nursing home for coffee/tea and cake. After it, we took her back again and we went for the Christmas mass to an old church in the neighbor village. Christmas Eve is the only day in the year where I still go to church. For Christmas Eve dinner, we had fresh brat sausages with potato and corn salad. After it, we shared the gifts as usual. Not usual was that I sent a text at 10 p.m. to the U.S. as I have been home again. Elisa called me instantly. It was a nice call and I figured out that the day wasn't too bad for her. While here Christmas Eve is the most important day, there it is almost a normal weekday. Because she had a dentist appointment, she worked from home.

But now I have worries about her, I suppose that she will spend the day alone with her cats. I am just physically in this room and with my thoughts with her. We fixed for today our usual phone call time once again, 11/5.

Shortly before 5 p.m., I say that I will go upstairs because I am expecting a call from Elisa.

As typical, she is right on time with her call.

"Thomas … Hi, Elisa!"

"Happy Christmas, my dear one!"

"Happy Christmas to you too, honey!"

I feel relieved to hear her on the phone. I am also glad as she tells me that Sam is coming tonight for dinner at her house. I am telling her about my Christmas Eve, about today and the second Christmas holiday tomorrow. Though I know it, it's always hard to understand for me as a German that Christmas holidays in America are actually just one holiday. Christmas Eve is already at least a half holiday, then the firstChristmas holiday today, tomorrow the secondChristmas holiday and the January 6 is another holiday here which belongs still to Christmas.

While I mention things from my family, she speaks about her cats, the dentist appointment and work. We both say a few times how much we miss each other and that it would be nice if she would be here now. It makes me happy when I hear her laugh. I don't want that she feels lonely.

"Did you read my email from today, Thomas?"

"No, just the one you sent me last night after our call ... But I am in front of the computer ... I can check it. Give me a second."

"Yes, it would be nice if you open it now." She says with some expectation in her voice.

I see that in this email are three attachments. Pictures?

"I am right now opening it ... there are three paintings?"

"Yes, open them and read it!"

"Oh, they are very colorful! Did you make it by yourself? The first says: A massage for my man, the second, a dinner and watching a movie at home, and the third has the title 'Trips to Pilot Mountain, Wilmington and to more places' ... Wow, thank you my sweet girl!"

"It's not a surprise because we talked about these things in emails before, but these are the things I want give you or make with you when you are visiting me here. I took a lot of time last night until I found an online program where I could create these paintings."

"They are very nice; you know I love colorful things, honey."

"I first wanted to send you something, but the shipping costs would be double amount the as the item itself. Ah and thank you again for the cute Christmas card you sent me."

"You are welcome. But I am sorry that it is just this card."

"You gave me already so much as I have been there."

I hear a voice from downstairs.

"Elisa, my mom is calling, I think my brother and his family are leaving."

"No problem, darling. I can wait."

"I can take you with my phone down there."

I walk down the stairs and my whole family is gathering at the front door. I say a bit sheepish that Elisa is one the phone.

"Merry Christmas from my parents and my brother's family to you!"

"Oh thank you! Tell them also Merry Christmas from me."

Sunday

December 28, 2014

It's the late morning, and I am sitting with a can of jasmine tea in front of the computer at my parents' house. It was a cold past night, and we got some snow. It's still freezing outside, but the sun is shining. It would be a perfect Sunday near the year's end, if there wouldn't be my mixed feelings about Elisa and her plans. On Friday she sent me a long email about different options how and where she could study German here and generally that it would be the best thing to go to school here. Because of the mortgage on her house, her job and much more, she would not be able to come here for a three month test as I recommend before. Anyway, she wouldn't test anything. She would need still a year or more to save every cent to have no debts there, and she is sure about me, about this big step in her life and our relationship. Her email was overwhelming for me, once again. How can be somebody sure about this, after being for nine days in person together? Maybe it takes one year or even more time until she can come here and then she wants to study at a school here? Elisa soon gets 40 years old! What's with her cats? If it doesn't work with a school, how can she stay here? Have I to marry her in a short time? And the biggest worries are my feelings for her. I know that I love her in some way, but is this enough?

I always try to be honest, with everybody and also with Elisabeth. But also don't want hurt her. She made it through so much and she means it honest with me. So I found myself yesterday again in a balancing act and didn't know how to answer her.

I am reading now another response from her yesterday:

Hi my dear Thomas,

I'm glad you're not driving in the snow, and I hope it clears up before Monday. I'm sure it is pretty, though. I know you will be careful driving too!

Thank you for your apology, Thomas. I've taken the morning to write you back because after reading your first reply, I did feel hurt. I really was hoping for some reassurance from you, not to hear about how you need more time, how overwhelmed and pressured you felt. I am not making demands on you or pressuring you to make decisions. I'm the one who also said we can and need to take the time. I'd only researched that as an option, in case it would work. But it would be too hard on me. That email was just a response to you offering to sponsor me. I wasn't asking you to make any decisions. I was letting you know that my research indicated it would be a difficult route. That's all. We talk all the time of me one day being in Germany, so I didn't think it would be bad to mention what I found out.

I want to build the foundations with you, and that means giving you time to release whatever pressure you're putting yourself under too. I'm not putting demands on you, Thomas. The things you want with me are up to you. I've tried to let you know my feelings for you are true, and you're worth the wait, for me. I also know this is new for you, honey. But in no way was that email or anything I've ever emailed meant to pressure you. What does pressure me, however, is hearing replies that indicate you are unsure about me. It just hurts my heart. I don't expect you to be 100 percent sure about me, us, our future, right now. Yes, we need time. And love is in some sense a gamble, for any human who ever fell in love! But if you keep holding up a sign that you're overwhelmed, feeling pressure, and need time, especially when I'm not pressuring you or demanding any answers, it will chip away at the foundations we are trying to build. I don't need to see that sign waived at me every time you feel a little pressure inside. I'm doing the best

I can, and I love you. All I hope is to have your support and
that you will want to see me again. I want to enjoy our time!
I want to grow this foundation of love and the care between us.
I hope you want this too.
I hope we can still talk on Sunday.

Your girl,

Elisa

By her writing style, I notice that she isn't in the best mood. Neither am I. I have a bad night behind me, and I was more in my thoughts than in my sleep. I would like to talk to someone about it. But with who? It doesn't make much sense with Christine. She would not give real advice. I wrote recently to Susan about my problems. She is straighter, but wouldn't tell me what I have to do or not.

I sign in to Facebook and there is message from Ana. But she isn't online anymore. She wrote me just something from her daily life in Hong Kong. I am missing the funny and easygoing time there with her. There were no pressure and nothing to decide, except for my daily program.

Ah, I see that Erika is online. It's an older woman in my mother's age that I never met. She is into spiritual and alternative things; I know her by email already some years and always to Christmas and sometimes to our birthdays we send something small to each other, also on these holidays. I had some good conversations with her in the past, but she belongs to that kind of people for who everything is always good and if not you don't see it.

First I don't want to chat about my issue with her, and then I can't hold myself back anymore. I am surprised about her response. If I wouldn't feel good with Elisa, I should let her go. I know that I don't have to do what Erika is telling me. But if I want to or not, I feel some relief around my heart to read her words. She is also saying that I would have to be very honest, even if I hurt her. Otherwise, I would hurt myself.

I am very sad, but something in me knows that I have to be very honest about my feelings to her. I have to say very clear that I am not sure about them. It's almost breaking my heart when I think on this because I don't want hurt her. But I have to tell her this, still today!

I'm not hungry at the lunch with my parents. After cleaning the dishes with them, I decide to walk to the park. Maybe this sunny and nice winter weather helps me to get some energy and be self-confident. Through the walk, I want to give myself a last chance to think how honest I will be with her.

The cold air stings my face, but it's good to feel it. I am getting sure that I will write very clear in an email about my unsureness. I don't want break off with Elisa, but I am aware that it can happen. This nice weather doesn't fit to do something like this. But I can't wait for worse weather. I have to do it.

As I come home, I turn on my laptop and check my emails a last time. There isn't anything new from Elisa, though it's the time she usually writes on weekends. I start to formulate my very sad email for her. Is it too hard? I need about 30 minutes for these words. It's 3 p.m. I check my emails a last time and there is a new one from Elisa! A very long one again. She wrote something about apologizing for her pressure on me. Should I really send my prepared one? Maybe I should delete one or two sentences.

After five minutes, I send her this email:

Dearest Elisa,

Thank you for your long email. I have seen your email as I wanted send you another email I prepared offline. A very sad email. But your email is giving me some hope that we can stay in connection. I could delete this prepared email, but I think it's good to be open and honest … especially at this moment now and today.
So that's it:

Since I sent you my email this morning and read your and my old emails again, I struggled a lot with myself. Not the first time, but in the last two days it was very heavy.

I have tears in my eyes; I feel bad and very sad.

But I think I have to write you this now. I don't want hurt you anymore. I can't hurt you anymore. I know if we are going on as we did, it will happen again and again that I hurt you. This is the last thing I want. I can't let you suffer (and myself). You are such a great person.

I love you in a complete way. I'm sure about this. You are so wonderful in many ways. I like your interests, I like how you are you, I find you attractive and there is a lot of sexual attraction. But I have some doubts if I am (still) in love with you. I know I break with this not only your heart. But I can't risk that we both find us some day later in a much bigger "hole" as it is already now.

There is nothing wrong with you. You are so wonderful. You are the best woman I ever met. But I don't want to hurt you deeply …

That was it … it costs me a lot courage to send you this. But it's like how I'm feeling actually.

If we are going on now on this level where we are now, I think there is still a chance. I don't have doubts about a connection with you. With chance, I mean a chance for more.

I felt also depressed sometimes in the last days. It's good that Martha called you. Don't let yourself down, Elisa. You are a great person. I want support you with your health issues and much more.

I still believe that it is positive that we met.

And yes, I still would like to visit you there next year. You know I work the next two days again, and I will figure out if I can get off at the end of March.

Maybe you need to think after this email again about anything. What I understand. But I think what I can promise you, it doesn't goes any deeper and our ups and downs are

over now. You started it with your recent email already. I ap-
preciate this a lot. Though I feel still sad. But it just can go
up from today again.
I want to have you on the phone again, but I think it's better
to cancel it for today.
I'm sorry that you felt bad yesterday and for this hard email …

But hopefully always,

Thomas

It doesn't take three minutes and my cell phone is ringing. I am even afraid to take the phone; I'm getting wet hands.

With a broken voice I am saying, "Elisa?"

"Hi, Thomas! I read your email and I have to call you. Thank you for your honesty. I understand you. Do you want break off with me? Is there still a chance? I knew before that you don't feel the same and I know since I visited you, that you are not sure about your feelings."

There was no wailing in her voice and she sounds self-assured. I am astonished and need some seconds to find words again.

"You knew it? I didn't want to hurt you."

"Yes, I know that there is not the same love from your side, and I know that you always care about me and you don't want hurt me. Thomas, do you want break up?

"No. I think our connection is very precious. But for me is important that you know that I am unsure about my feelings for you. I had to write you this. If it's ok for you that I am not on the same level with my feelings as you with yours, then we can go on."

I feel relieved, and I heard also a relief in her voice.

"Yes, let's go on. I am aware about our special connection, and I need you as my boyfriend, Thomas."

"I am glad that we met, and I have never been in my life so close to my dreams. I feel sad about my feelings, but I know what for a wonderful woman you are."

"You are wonderful, Thomas!"

Thursday

January 1, New Year's Day 2015

It's the early afternoon and I am sitting with a can of chamomile tea at my laptop. Already for the third time, I have been with Michael at the same club in Heilbronn on New Year's Eve. I think we are much too old for the party people location. But it's hard to find any compromises with him and since it's not far away and I see that it's no fun to sit together with him alone at home in this night, I let myself be convinced again to go to this club. But this New Year's Eve was different. Even before this evening, I didn't feel too well in my stomach, but I couldn't let him go alone there. We had as always the "big ticket." This means it it included a dinner buffet. Just shortly after we sat down, a female colleague of mine appears with a girlfriend and they asked if they can sit next to us. They were some nice company, but my stomach rumbled and my thoughts were in North Carolina. I knew that this holiday Elisa spends alone. It doesn't make happy to know to have a girlfriend there who has just has one person in her life: me.

At midnight, I got a text from her and wrote her back. I have been with Michael outside on the street and watching the fireworks. He lighted his own firecrackers. But it was a big effort for me to enjoy this moment. As soon he was finished, I said to him that I have to go home and can't go back to the club with him anymore. He understood it and wished that I am doing better soon.

And I am doing better today again. After the breakfast at my parents' house, I checked different booking machines for flights to the U.S. Elisa confirmed with me already on Tuesday that I can come for a visit at the end of March. I think I never booked such expensive flights to the U.S. before; I will pay around 850 euros. And this is outside of any pricy summer or vacation season. I didn't find a nonstop flight, not even from Frankfurt. So I decided on a flight from Stuttgart to Atlanta and from there to Raleigh. My trip back will go over Atlanta to Frankfurt. This was the cheapest option I found. I don't have the patient to wait for some more days or weeks to get something cheaper. I am happy, and I can't wait to tell Elisa on the phone about my bookings.

Exactly at 5 p.m. my phone is ringing.

"Hi, honey!"

"Hey, darling! Happy New Year to you!"

"Thank you! Happy New Year to you too!" In the last weeks, I learned to know on her first tone and words in what mood she is in. I am noticing that she seems to be ok now. Not a very excited Elisabeth, but also not bad.

"How has your New Year's Eve been?"

"It wasn't too good for me. I had problems with my stomach."

"Oh, I'm so sorry! When did you guys leave?"

"I don't know how long Michael stayed, but I left shortly after midnight. I just waited until he was done with his firework. But he understood it. The food there was good, but I couldn't enjoy it really."

"How are you doing now?"

"Thanks, much better! My thoughts have been with you the whole night. How was your New Year's Eve?"

"This is so sweet of you, that you thought of me! You know, my dear Thomas, I think also always of you." Her voice gets softer and there is some smile to hear. "But I didn't do anything as you know. For many years, this night isn't anything special for me. I just spent the time with my cats and went not too late to bed. I think it was something before 11 p.m. But as always, I felt a strong connection with you and wished you would be here or I were with you there."

"I have some news!" I say with a smile.

"Oh, what kind of news, darling?"

"I booked the flights for my trip to you!"

"Wow! Really?"

"Yes! I will arrive there in Raleigh on March 26 in the evening. It's the Thursday we talked before about."

"Oh, I am surprised! I didn't think that you would book it. I hear in her voice that she didn't expect what I said.

"I didn't want to wait longer. Eventually the price would come a bit down again, but it could go also in the other direction. So I will pay 850 euro."

"I am sorry that it is so expensive, but I will care about you and everything else when you are here! I will work on this Thursday, but I can drive straight from the company to the airport … It feels great that you are coming! I just was not sure if you would do it so fast after our issues in the last time."

I'm surprised about myself. But I know also that from time to time I am faster with trip bookings as with anything else in my life. Maybe I want show Elisa that I mean it serious and however the things are going on with her, it's just a trip. One of these many trips I made before, and I love traveling to the States. With these thoughts, I am convincing myself that it is the right thing what I did.

Elisa gets more relaxed and nicer with every word, though I feel that she is holding herself a bit back in comparison to former talks.

Wednesday

January 7, 2015

I'm almost at home with my car, the sun is going down, I feel a bit melancholic when I watch outside of the windows. The traffic flows, so I think I will be right on time at home.

It's 4:45 p.m. as I open the door to my condo. It's still enough time to change my clothes before Elisa calls me at 11/5. The time is as usual, but not the day. It's her birthday. She is working from home, therefore she can do it.

4:59, 5:00, 5:01 … the phone rings.

"Hi my dear Elisa, Happy Birthday To You!" I say loud with a big smile.

"Thank you, darling!"

"How are you doing?"

"Well, honestly as every day. And it doesn't matter that I turn 40. I will go out with Martha tonight for dinner to the Mexican place down the road here. Maybe my brother is calling me, but maybe he forgets it. But the nicest gift was your package!"

"You got it today?"

"No, yesterday … but perfect in time. I like the card, all the chocolate and you made another great music CD for me, darling. I listened to the songs already the whole morning. Thank you so much!"

"You are welcome. I am sad that I can't be there with you today."

"Yes, but it's like it is and you will come soon. It's normal that couples are sometimes away from each other."

The conversations go on that level, and we talk about 20 minutes about daily and irrelevant things. Then I notice more and more some tension in her voice.

"Elisa, is everything ok with you?" There is some hesitating on the other end.

"Mmh … not really. I feel lonely, and I have a boyfriend to who I can't express my feelings. Since we had this talk at the end of December, I holding my feelings back!"

She starts to cry. Now I am surprised. I thought everything would be clear.

I stumble on the phone. "I am sorry."

She gets louder.

"I love you so much and I am so glad that I found you, but I can't tell you this! I don't want to put pressure on you." I hear her sobbing.

"I'm so sorry. I wasn't aware about this."

"It's so difficult to handle for me. I am sorry that I am crying on my birthday; it should be different."

I feel very bad.

"I don't want that you hold your feelings back and that you can't express what you want. Please be yourself and so much open as you like, my girl."

"Really? Are okay with this?"

"Yes, I am. It's stupid if you can't tell your boyfriend all the nice things you want to share."

"I love you so much, Thomas! I want be with you! I can't wait until you are here."

"I am also looking so much forward to be there with you."

"I can't wait to have you here in my house, that we take an evening stroll here in Wendell, to cook with you dinner and much more."

"I am already very excited about this. I want go to all these places you mentioned, but I want to mainly spend time with you, honey."

"You are so sweet, Thomas! Sorry again that I cried. There are many things I want do before you come. There is a lot to do in my greens, but also in the house. I need chairs for the dining room and eventually a railing for my stairs. They are dangerous. Did I tell you that I fell down once? It was fortunately just from the third step. But this scared me. Maybe I also need new windows. I live very close to the main road and I don't want it to be too loud for you, honey."

"It's nice that you want fix so many things before I come, but please do only the things you can do physically and also the things you need. You know I come only for a visit. Maybe I can mow the lawn when I am there, honey."

"This is very nice of you! But you will be on vacation. By the way, my house isn't very hospitable until now. As my brother came for dinner on Christmas, we ate in the living room on the floor because there are no chairs! And as I said, for safety the railing is also a good investment. There are some things not good in this old house. I don't trust the pipes. Somebody has to check them and the AC system isn't working correctly as well. This all costs me a lot of money, but I have to do it."

"I understand, but be careful with your physical condition, Elisa."

"Yes … in the last days it was a bit better with the muscle spasms. But I should maybe go a last time to this Chinese practitioner I told you about before. I want to be in a good condition when you come. I am also very attentive with my nutrition. This means no bread, no cheese, less meat and at least every second or third day one to two glasses of juice made with my juicer."

"I am not the most practical man as you know, but I think there are really things I can do for you when I am there. Maybe I can also cook something. At least in the first days when you have to work from home."

"I like this idea with cooking … and I also want go grocery shopping with you, my darling!"

We are more than two hours on the phone. I feel good that I could turn her mood and that she makes a happy impression again- I am a person who needs harmony, and I don't like when she is suffering, especially also not on her birthday.

Friday

Hello dearest Thomas ☺

Honey, I read your email when I was still at work but didn't get a chance to respond.

I just have to start with a point that has stayed in my mind, since I read it. It's about what you wrote, here:

It's sweet of you that you talked with your friend Leni so positive about me. ☺ *But don't make me an angel, because I'm not. Thomas, this isn't the first time you've tried to push back a compliment I've given you by telling me you're no angel. First of all, I'll set the record straight. I know you are human, I know you have flaws like everyone does. Maybe even there is something in your past that might make you feel badly about yourself? I don't know. I sure have things that when I reflect on, I feel pretty badly about, decisions and reactions that I regret. But what I have to say is this. I truly believe that you are a good man. I know and believe that you would never intentionally hurt me. I don't believe you'd ever hit me, or cheat on me, or belittle me in public, or mock my emotions, or do degrading and harmful things to me to please yourself. I don't believe you'd ever lie to me or try to manipulate my emotions to get things from me or have a laugh at me. I don't believe you'd ever put me in a dangerous situation to see how'd I'd react or use what you know of my history against me. I don't believe you'd use me for money. I don't believe you'd tell your friends horrible things about me or ask them to do mean things*

*to me. I don't believe you'd abandon me in my time of need. I
don't believe you'd criticize my imperfections, try to isolate me
from friends, or try to control me. I simply know you are not a
man like that. A man like that is what I'd say is "no angel."
I've had all of the above and more experiences with men, so I
know what I'm speaking about.*

*What I do believe and know to be true about you is that you
genuinely care about my feelings, that you listen to me in a
way I've never experienced by anyone … you actually care
what I'm speaking about. I know that you are honest. You
were honest with me even when you were afraid it might end
our connection because you wanted to have integrity with what
you say and do with me. You've stuck by me, too, when I've
had challenging moments. You've communicated with me to
work through emotions, something a majority of humans have
no idea how to do! I know you to be a very sweet and tender
man. You write me letters, postcards, daily emails without me
ever even asking for those things. Out of the kindness of your
own heart, you've made CDs and sent me candies and cards,
and the lovely scarf. And you took care of me, fed me, drove
me everywhere, sheltered me, and took me out again and again
for those nine days. You scheduled your vacation with me, and
now again, you have bought a plane ticket for 18 days with
me in March/April – even when I had to work some of those
days. You want to take care of me in ways I have never imagined anyone wanting to care for me! I am so adamant about
this, honey. You are a good man. Let me tell my girlfriends
this! They are happy for me. Both of them have also experienced very bad, bad men in their lives. They understand what
a good one looks like! They understand the kinds of qualities
you have are not easy to find in someone! And trust me, they
also understand that relationships are sometimes hard, that men
and women speak different languages sometimes, that no man
or woman in this world is perfect.*

*So Thomas, I hope you will just accept how I feel about you
and know I'm not holding you to some level of perfection that*

is unattainable or unsustainable. I wouldn't change my opinion of you if there were days you were in a bad mood or not communicating or not doing something for me, trust me! We all have the good side and the shadow side of ourselves. We all have good and also troubled feelings and actions and reactions sometimes. If you were a 'perfect' man, an 'angel,' what credit would it be to you for being nice and kind and caring and communicative? All that would be easy, if you were an angel. The credit to your character is that despite being human, you still have all these wonderful ways of being, because you are a quality person who is good at heart and always willing to learn and grow. I find that very admirable! So why not accept that I love you and I know you are a wonderful person, without trying to prove me wrong!

Sorry to get on my soapbox about this, Thomas, but you need to know that I don't take lightly if I hear you basically putting yourself down in this way. I'm not infatuated with you and just seeing what I want to see in you, with rose-colored glasses. I see who you are, and I love and accept all sides of you. You know I'm a flawed woman, and yet you still care for me. I think you can understand why I write all this. It's just as you would and have done for me, if I kept rejecting the idea that I'm the wonderful person you seem to see in me. There is a need to reach out and say, honey, you are beautiful just the way you are! And Thomas, you are so beautiful!

So now, my dearest, since I've spend all my time letting you know that you can't convince me you're not great ☺, I'm actually going to go have something to drink and maybe lie down early tonight. I will respond more to your wonderful email tomorrow ☺ I appreciate you taking all the time to write this long letter, when I know you have had some really long days.

Darling, if I could crawl into your bed tonight, and press my warm body tightly against yours, and melt into your arms, I would. I wish so much to be close to you. You mean so much to me. I need your sweet touch once again. I send you all my *warmest thoughts and feelings, honey. I'm counting down the days until you are here!*

I hope your Friday is a good one. Take care, my sweet, and I will be writing you and also talking with you soon!

Your girlfriend kissing you with soft lips ☺

Elisa

Wednesday

February 11, 2015

Thomas, to be honest, I'm not really sure why you feel empty and ashamed after being sexual with me, even on that recent phone call. I don't know what to say. I'm sorry, but I just don't understand, and this feels awful to know. I've been trying to respond for an hour, but I feel so depressed, I can't figure out why you don't want me. I don't understand why you want to be open, but when I'm open, you feel so terrible. What's going on? Why is what I have to offer you so unimportant to you, and why does it actually make you feel badly? I don't understand! What have I done wrong?

My dearest Elisa!

I don't know if I really express myself always so wrong that we come again and again to this point that you are feeling upset and depressed. I was in very good moods as I wrote you the email last night!
Again honey, you did nothing wrong! And I don't feel empty. I felt a bit empty after some of the mornings when you were here. But with my email yesterday, I wanted say that I am doing very good actually. I wanted say you that everything is going very good right now with my feelings. Probably much better than before. Honestly it makes me sad that you feel depressed again.
You are wonderful! But you cannot feel depressed if I express myself wrong. As I said first last week, again I am not perfect. You have also to respect and accept how I am.

238

Again I don't feel badly. In the last weeks, I felt so good with you as never before!
I am very sorry if I have confused you again.

Have a good day! Your boyfriend,

Thomas

My love Thomas,

Please know I'm in love with you and I'm sorry if my fear of having done something wrong or maybe losing you came up like this. I'm really so thankful for you explaining everything to me. I guess I have tried to piece together what the sequence of events has been and what the changes have been, but I never understood completely. But this helps me to know.
There are many things I could explain as to why my mind went to the place of being afraid. Like I told you, my past has really more personified the terms 'empty' and 'ashamed' about the topic of sex. It's a horrible thing to feel those feelings, so when I saw you say you felt them after being with me, it brought up a lot of fear. I would never in a million years want you to feel this way, Thomas. I just interpreted why you felt those things as they were feelings I gave you by doing something bad in our sexual intimacy. I thought maybe you were saying we must take it slowly because you are afraid you will feel those things if you have sexual intimacy with me again. I just didn't understand that your feelings came from the long distance aspect and not being in 'love' with me. I just had tried to comfort you before to let you know that you don't have to all-at-once be in 'love' to still want to be with someone and grow the feelings you have for them. So when I thought we both agreed that we wanted the relationship that I could have some pleasurable moments with you, even at a distance. So when we had that phone call and I found out you just shut down, it really worried me. I

didn't know if you found me disgusting or as if I were a slutty
girl or if it wasn't arousing and you were bored or if something
was physically wrong or what had happened. I was afraid to
ask you. I just felt like there was something wrong with me. I
thought that I just have to never bring up sexual feelings again.
I felt like I'd done something wrong to you. And I didn't understand why you wouldn't want to feel pleasure with me, if
I'm your girlfriend. You reminded me you wanted to take it
slowly, in emails. But then the most recent one was then saying you wanted to be open, so I got scared that I might try
to be open again and then get rejected and lose you. It's just
been a snowball effect because I didn't understand what was
going on. I was afraid to ask because I thought it would pressure you. I'm just very inexperienced at knowing what to do
with this vulnerable subject, if things have been going wrong.
I think that most of my life, it seemed no one loved me, loved
who I am, but if I were with someone, they only cared about
me as an object. And the only one who never wanted sex with
me was my ex-husband because of his own struggles with his
identity, I think. So this has all been confusing. Also, when
I tried to talk plainly in the past about feeling upset by the
push/pull, you wrote me that break up email. So I've been
worried that if I tried to bring up my worries about sex, that
you might just let me go. That's probably an internal fear of
mine in life. Even my family, my own mom, let me go rather than talk to me about a problem. So I sometimes feel like it
would be very easy for you to do this too.
So these were the things that instantly went to my mind last
night, and then other stuff got triggered about my family, and
then this horrible, horrible image I saw on YouTube. Actually,
I realize now that I saw this horrific image the night before, because the first night I wrote you asking the question was when I
later looked up some stuff about families of sexual abuse victims
abandoning their children, because some stuff with my mom
was coming up inside me. And then I tried to find a meditation online for healing sexual abuse, and I'll just tell you, this

image on a video came up in the search that was so absolutely horrific. It was of a woman, completely naked, who was hog tied with a pole through the length of her body and cooking over a fire, and the title of the video was 'Woman who was raped is cooked alive by Russians,' or something like that. And it was 100 percent real. It could not have been fake, Thomas, and it completely devastated me to see it in that one instance. I'm sorry to tell you, but now I realize I saw this not last night after I wrote you, but the night before, after I first wrote you questioning about your email on being open with me. I saw that image when I was trying to look for help on the abuse issues and things that were coming up for me. And the second I saw it, I started to shake inside so much. I still can't wipe the image out of my mind. That this happened to some poor woman! That there are people who would do this to another human being! And the horrid video had over four million views. I clicked away almost as soon as I saw it, but it so, so upset me. I went to work yesterday, and even driving home that night, I kept seeing this image, and I was just crying and yelling at God for allowing such a thing to ever happen to a human being! So yes, now I remember I came home and read your email reply, and I saw the 'empty' and 'ashamed' words, and I think I just went straight into fear. I feel like while writing you this email now; I just have sort of pieced together a puzzle, Thomas. Because I was already pretty triggered by that vile image and bad feelings when I read your email. I'm so sorry that I didn't recognize why I might be seeing things from such a fearful perspective when I read your email last night. I just know that I had a really horrible reaction that I couldn't seem to contain. I went into depression really fast, and had to make myself go to sleep to stop crying all night. It was probably my brain was completely overloaded. I'm really sorry I couldn't somehow ride it out and reply that I just wasn't feeling well and needed to sleep. But I know I can't change it. I just am so very thankful that you called me this morning and made all these efforts to contact me. I was feeling really lost when I woke up this morning.

Anyway, it's very important that you know I want to go the 'long haul' meaning go the 'distance' with you to see things through. I don't expect us to marry in March, Thomas. I don't even expect us to get engaged, yet, honey. If we ever got engaged, it wouldn't mean I could leave in a day. For us, I just want that we move forward, naturally, over time. I obviously want to be there with you now, and if I just had an apartment and could easily got to school at Heilbronn University, honey I would be making plans now. That scenario would be awesome for us! But they don't have a program I can go into (because I don't speak German), and I have things to do before I could sell my house, and more time I want with you before I'd make that decision, of course. So, I'm doing the fixes on my house, and I'm learning German and saving up money. If it can't happen this year that I get there, then I imagine if you and I are going strong into next year, I will be setting wheels in motion somehow, someway to be close to you, because I have a feeling we will both want this. But if it takes longer, it takes longer. It doesn't mean that I would give up, just because it might take some time. I'm your girlfriend; I'm committed to you, Thomas. I'm not worried that we have to figure it all out now. It seems like we're getting our 'sea legs' building a foundation together. We've come from different backgrounds, but we have things to learn and share with each other, and I can see that it is very healing. Maybe I will find myself a much stronger, happier woman with each day. I know I want to be my best for you and for myself!

I feel like I'm babbling in this email, and I hope I'm not saying things funny or weird. I love you so much, and that's the thing I want you to know! I even came home and got your AMAZING package today! Honey, I didn't wait to open it, and I don't want you to wait to open my letter, unless you really, really want to. I needed to open it like I need to be in your warm arms hugging you right now. It has really touched my heart so much, what you gave me, what you made for me! Never in my life, honestly ever ever ever, has anyone made something like this for me! I'm so honored, honey. It's so sweet and beautiful, and you are so, so sweet and beautiful! I can't believe you took the time to paint me that heart. And I love you for being a person who would do that. I'd never laugh at that. I find it so very precious. And I LOVE the picture of you, my man, with the painting you made for me. You're so sweet and dear and wonderful!

When I wanted to send you something, I realized I'd waited too long to send you more than a card, and expect that it would get to you in time for Valentine's Day. I wanted to send more, honey. But there will be things, when you are here, that I hope will be wonderful for you. I'm just really glad that it arrived in time. And feel free to open it when you want, but even now, if you like. I will be looking at all you sent me over and over again, today, Valentine's Day, and forever!!!

Honey, I must try to get a bite before I go to bed tonight. I admit, I've been enjoying the chocolate you sent. Wow, you are so wonderful! I have never gotten a Valentine's present from a boy ☺ You are my boyfriend, my man, and I thank you so very much for taking such good care of me!

I love you, Thomas! I hope you are sleeping well, as I write this. I send you all my warmest thoughts and would hold you through the night, if I could. Thank you for everything!!!

With all my heart,

Your girlfriend,

Elisa ☺

Saturday

Valentine's Day, February 14, 2015

I am walking from my parents' house home. It's a cold and clear night; there are a lot of stars to see in the sky. I should freeze, but I don't. My thoughts are driving me crazy once again. I sent Elisa a nice package, from her got very nice and lovely letter. But our emails were confusing in the last days as well as the phone talk today at five. She was crying again. Her emotional break-downs are scaring me every time more. Her behavior is chang-ing sometimes from one to the other minute. I understand how she is feeling, but I doubt if I can give her what she needs. I look nervous up to the sky and am formulating a message, a request or a prayer to the universe, to angels, god or whatever can be up there. I need to know what I have to do and need a lot of energy.

Sunday evening

March 1, 2015

It's something after 8 p.m. I came home from Heilbronn about two hours ago. I met my friend Michael, but we didn't have our typical coffee/green tea – beer/apple juice with water drinking appointment. We also went this time to the movie theater. It's long ago that I could convinced him to see a movie what I liked to watch, and he enjoyed it finally too. I read the book "Wild" before two years ago or so, and it impressed me. As usual, the movie doesn't go as deep as the story in the book, but it is very well made. Stories like this always open up my fantasies and dreams. Dreams of traveling far away, of adventures, of America, of freedom and of finding myself. The beautiful pictures of the mountains and the music of "El Condor Pasa" made the rest for me. But in my mind was also always Elisa. I miss her. At the same time, I have worries that I can't reply what she needs and wants. Only 26 days until I will see her! On the phone yesterday, she has been once again emotionally weak and told me that I would reject her in her plans for our future. I started an email where I wanted to explain again how I feel. I am telling myself that I have to be honest with her and myself. But the day, the movie and my fatigue tonight made me soft and I come to the conclusion that I can never reach anything good if I might hurt someone. Someone who loves me, as nobody else before. While I am almost finished with a small email, my phone is ringing.

"Elisa?!"

"Hi, Thomas! Are you okay? I just think of you."

"Yes, I am okay, thank you! I am just very tired. But I think also of you."

"I am sorry for my behavior on the phone yesterday. I just need you so much!"

I feel a relief as I hear her voice, and I'm happy that I didn't write the email I wanted to send before.

"I miss you, Elisa."

"Oh, I miss you too, honey. Is really everything ok?"

I am smiling and feel like some little stones are falling from my heart after this tension over the weekend.

"Yes, everything is fine. It's nice that you call me."

"I didn't plan to call you. But I had such a feeling."

"You know what?"

"What?"

"In 26 days I will be there!"

"Wrong … in exactly 25 days … you can't count today anymore! I can't wait!"

"I am looking also so much forward to it!"

We both just laugh.

"My Thomas, have a good night and have some sweet dreams."

"And you a good afternoon, my girl! Bye."

"Bye. I love you."

I sent the email:

Hey my dearest darling Elisabeth,

I'm sorry that you don't get a longer email tonight. I came home from HN something after 6 p.m. I read your email a couple of times and started then with a response. I wrote about that I understand you, but I also wanted to explain how I feel and think. When I was ready with it shortly before 8 p.m., I read it a couple of times. I came to the point that I didn't tell you anything new, that we both know us very good and it makes no sense to send you that email. I got tired of what I wrote.

In my mind it came up how precious life is and how precious our connection is. Also the movie today in the afternoon reminded me of this.

What I can tell you is that the second chapter of your email made me feel very good. All the things you wrote are true. I maybe miss the feeling of being in love with you, but what I do for you is love. You have to know that I care a lot about you, my sweet girl. I'm a very aware about our wonderful connection! Your nice call right now fit very well to what I feel, and it showed me again how we care about each other. ☺

You are very special for me!

Thank you for being there for me.

Your boyfriend,

Thomas

Saturday Morning

March 7, 2015

After some meditation, I am sitting at my laptop and have a can of jasmine tea. The meditation helped at least put my worries away for about 40 minutes, but now they are back again. I still suffer from the incident with Elisa on Thursday night. She called me without notice while I was watching TV with my parents in their living room. Immediately, I heard on her voice that something is wrong. I went up to the computer room. She asked me if she should register for a specific German lesson and how much she would love me. I just hesitated a second, and she was shouting and crying. I experienced some downs with her, but this one was dramatic. I wouldn't love her because nobody could love her, nobody did and will ever love her. I wouldn't understand her because nobody would understand her, she would make everything wrong and it would be maybe a big fault when I travel there. I tried to talk good with her and convince her that she is a nice and a lovable woman. But she couldn't or didn't want hear this. This dramatic call took about an hour, and I didn't feel that she was doing much better as we ended the call. I had a sleepless night, have been very tired on Friday at work and found a long sorry email as I came home yesterday night. Elisa asked me for forgiveness and tried to explain her "PTSD meltdown" as she calls it. She has been in a spiral down. I would not have been the cause for her problem and would be never responsible for what is going on in her. She apologized for hurting, emphasized a few times how important I would be for her and that she made some appointments at her old therapist Stella. I know that Elisa is a good and nice person; I know also that I became the most important person in her life and her email now makes a decent impression again. But this incident on Thursday night was shocking for me and I am feeling it still in my bones. I never experienced her this way before. All other issues weren't nice, but they got solved in a phone call or in an email. I always believed in the good after it again. But this evening had damaged also something in my psyche. But anyway, she is doing better again, there is no way that I cancel this trip – I can't do this! – and I still have to hope that someone above there is meaning it good with us.

Our weekend call will be today at 11/5 again.

North
Carolina

Thursday

March 26, 2015

My door bell is ringing. As I watch out of the window, I see my dad's car. I open the door and he helps me to carry my baggage to the car. He is wondering about my heavy suitcase. But I have some gifts for Elisa in there and also a lot of different clothes. She said to me in the last days that it was warm, but it depends on what kind of trips we will doing, it could be that I need some warm clothes. As always when my dad is bringing me to the airport, he has been at the bakery before and had some fresh pretzels in the car and tea in a can. Five minutes before 6 a.m. we are on the Autobahn, and it seems to not be too much traffic. It's already getting light, and this is the sign that spring is here. On the upcoming weekend, we will set the clocks also to the summer time here. The U.S. changed the clocks already on March 8. That means in the last weeks our calls turned into a 12/5 call. I start to eat my pretzel and drink some tea. My dad and I are quiet, just here and there he is saying something casual and I give a short answer. There were some concerns about his health still in the last days. He had a doctor's appointment, and they found that two of his heart veins don't look good. As I told Elisa about it, she was more worried than me and suggested even that I can cancel the trip or she would come over here. My mom was worried too, but as usual my dad put the emotions down. There is nothing to worry about, he said. He would get in two weeks eventually another stent, but I can go on my trip. What I have in common with my parents is that for both of us our vacations are very important. Nobody would tell the other side to cancel a trip as long it isn't absolute necessary. Maybe it would had been for another reason better to stay here? But I always do what I have planned. Also Christine, the only person who knows almost everything about my doubts, my worries and about my current status with Elisa, said that I should see my 12th trip to the States like any other trip as I did before. And if things would go wrong, I did my best. Sure, I did my best. I wanted to have a girlfriend, and I believed that there is a reason because I met Elisa. Susan, my Missouri friend, recommend always stay honest and she wished me also the best for this trip.

We are arriving at the airport in Stuttgart. We park the car almost at the same spot as I have been here in December when I took Elisa to her flight. Like I waited for Elisa, my dad waits for me until I have checked in. We say goodbye and he wishes me a good flight and a nice vacation. I go into the security controls. I don't know what he is thinking about me and Elisa. My parents are ignoring my connection with her as they ignored my relationship with Veronika. But maybe it's the best, they would call me crazy if would have told them what I went through in the last weeks and months emotionally with her. The controls are going fast, and the gates are empty at this time. It's nothing new for me. The flight number DL117 to Atlanta is one of the less long distance flights from this airport. As I promised, I send Elisa a text that everything went well and I am sitting at the gate. Though it's the middle of the night on the East coast, I got a fast reply from her. She is nice and thinking of me, always. I am starting to wonder once again about my feelings. It feels different than when I sat last September at this airport on my trip over London to Hong Kong. I have been surprised and very happy about Elisa's call. But how do I feel now?

The gate is filling with people. The grey sky outside reminds me that it was grey on Elisa's arrival here in December, on the day when she left and the whole nine days of her visit.

Right on time, they are starting with the boarding process. It looks like the people came out of the nowhere and now the crowds are gathering in front of the desk and entrance. Ten minutes later, I'm at my seat 37A by the window. It seems that I had luck that I got a window seat because the plane is full. On 37B next to me is sitting a little older lady and I wonder if she is German or American, I tend to think German. The take off is exactly at 9:45 a.m. as planned. I checked the maps in the screen in front of me, and as always, I made a playlist for the flight. Some Pink, Lady Antebellum, Bruce Springsteen and Train.

For lunch, I chose the chicken Thai curry dish. We left Ireland in the air and the plane is now in direction to the North Atlantic.

I feel almost numb. I never before felt so strange on a vacation flight to the U.S. There isn't any happiness in me. I feel depressed. The many ups and downs with her are pressing me down. I should be the happiest person in the world. Flying to my beloved country and the first time in my life my girlfriend is waiting there for me. Maybe is something wrong with me? In this moment, I am not scared anymore as in the weeks before, but I am far away from being happy. I am numb.

After a slight nap, I hear my neighbor chatting with the flight attendant. She speaks English very well, I am thinking. As I open my eyes, I see that she gets another cup of red wine. She looks at me and asks in German where I am going. After a small talk, I know that she is a German who is married in Florida and visiting her mother in Baden-Württemberg every year once or twice. She is funny, maybe because of the wine, but maybe it's also how she is.

I start to read in the two books I have with me. In Eckart Tolle's "Practicing The Power Of Now" and in a book of Bronnie Ware with the title "Leben Ohne Reue." I don't know if I really understand the books of Tolle. But there is something in me that feels that he is right. I read this practice book and the original version already a couple of times. I notice that I forgot the sense of it once again. I just read some single parts on some pages. I am going to the other book. This seems to be more of a "feel comfortable" book. It's a collection of short stories. But maybe it's what I need right now. Through my earphones I am listening to "Angel in Blue Jeans."

And there you are
Like a highway headed my way
Life is but a dream
I was shot down by your love
My angel in blue jeans.

Is Elisa my angel?

In the plane, the lights are going on after they kept the room dark for some time. I see on the map screen that we are passing from Canada to the U.S. A little bit of excitement is growing in me the first time on this day.

The flight attendants are serving a lunch snack. Something like a pizza, crackers, cheese, ice cream and as always drinks. I see that we are now over North Carolina, my heart is beating a bit faster. It's over the Blue Ridge Mountains and the Asheville area. It's another corner to where Elisa is living. But maybe she will go with me here to this area? I have been once to the Biltmore Estate seven years ago. My friend Sandy invited me to visit her and her family as they lived at that time in South Carolina. I knew them from Germany. Her husband is working for the U.S. army, and they have been stationed for three years in Wiesbaden. She once made that trip with me to the Biltmore. I remember that it was a nice and warm day late in October. We enjoyed the beautiful view to the mountains and the foliage of the trees around. I was a bit sad that I couldn't see more of the area there. Sandy did her best for my vacation time, but her kids where still little.

The plane is going down, and sometime later we are at the gate at the Hartsfield-Jackson Airport. We arrived 40 minutes earlier and that gives me some relief. If we would have arrived as planned, my time to the next plane would had been two hours and 20 minutes. My experiences in the past showed that you need at least two hours to be on the safe side because of the controls. But now it should work.

I am saying good bye to the German-American lady as we are leaving the plane and I walk with my backpack through the long passageway with the old carpets. I know already here very good.

"Wilkommen! Waren Sie schon mal in den USA?"

I am surprised as a security woman in front of me talks to me in German. On my 11 trips before, this never happened.

"Ja."

"Dann gehen Sie bitte hier nach rechts zu den Automaten!" She is saying polite and friendly in a good German.

Wow, it seems that there are machines for a self-registration! No lines and it looks like it goes fast.

I take the next machine. I have to answer some questions, take a picture of myself, scan my fingerprints, an officer is giving me some advice, then I go to a desk and another person is checking my passport.

"Have a nice day!"

Done! I'm very surprised about the fast procedure. In the past, it took about an hour or more just to stand in these lines over there and be asked silly, personal and not appropriate questions. I know that there still coming other security controls where I have to take off my shoes, belt and my sweater. But this former unpleasant part is done.

After another 40 minutes, I am already on the way to my flight DL 743 in terminal S. I now have a lot of time to send a text to Elisa, to my dad and Susan. To her, I always sent texts when I am on a trip and especially to the U.S. I'm noticing that I can login for free to the internet with my cellphone. Elisa I sent both, a text and a short email, my dad texted me and Susan sent an email.

Elisa's response:

Hey my darling!!!

I've texted you back, but here too, just in case. I miss you, but we've only a few hours now!!!
Welcome to the USA. my honey! I am tracking your flights ☺
Kisses and Hugs

Your girl!!!

Elisa ☺

And the one from Susan:

Hi!

I know you won't be responding again, but in case you see this,
I hope your trip is great!
I will be thinking of you, and also miss our emails until you
get back ☺
Again, have a great time!

Your friend,

S

After some reading in the Bronnie Ware book, I can board. The
plane seems to be also full.

About 20 minutes later, I am up in the sky again and flying
at least the first part in the direction where I came from before.
My mood is much better than before, and I am getting excited to see Elisa again. I push my fears away and want to concentrate on what I read in my two books. Try to be in the moment,
enjoy everything positive and don't think about anything that
might happen or not. Nobody knows what tomorrow will be.
I start to observe the people around me. It's something I usually like to do. Yes, I am in America! The passengers are different
than on the flight from Stuttgart to Atlanta. On this flight there
were still many Germans, some Americans and other nationalities. People are wearing T-shirts and shorts and ordering soft
drinks with a lot of ice, though the man next to me is coughing.
Typical American. I always wear a sweater on plane trips. The
time is going fast, and the plane goes down for the landing. I
have a clear sight to the ground. When I arrive somewhere, I'm
always asking myself, if this place looks different than where I
came from. I see many trees, lakes, maybe it looks greener than

at home, but not too different. My heart is beating stronger and I'm getting a bit wet hands.

Right at 6:57 p.m., the plane is docking at the gate on terminal 2 at the RDU airport.

Elisa said that she would wait at baggage claim. This is the ridiculous thing in the States. While the check in process is so strict with the baggage, the claims are in an area where everybody else could grab the belongings too.

I am walking away from the gate, and I am following the claim/exit signs. I am going up on an escalator, and I am sure that above must be the area. I am nervous.

I see the claims and am wondering where the one from this flight is.

"Hello, Thomas! I am here!" There are really not many people, but I didn't notice that Elisa was standing there and waving at me.

"Ah, hi, Elisa! I didn't see you!"

We are getting closer to each other. She is smiling, wearing a white summer dress with yellow and black symbols on it, her lips are red, she has some make up on her face and silver earrings are dangling on her ears.

We are hugging, and she is giving me a kiss.

"How was your flight?"

"Long, but good. Nice to see you." I say with a smile.

"Nice to see you too!"

"Where is my baggage claim?"

"It's over there!"

"I see my big suitcase is coming!"

"Oh, it's really big. Do need some help?"

"No, I can take it."

After taking my suitcase, she is grabbing my right hand and we are walking outside the building.

"Wow, this is warm here! It feels like summer."

"Yes, it was already in the past days this way here. Did you hear that the crash of the Germanwings flight was suicide of the pilot?"

"No. Of course I heard of the crash in the French mountains, the medias were full of it at home. But it was still not clear why it happened as my dad drove me this morning to the airport in Stuttgart."

"Yes, this is crazy, how can someone make something crazy like this?"

"I don't know … it's terrible and sad."

"Here, over there is my car. I cleaned it yesterday. I cleaned the car for the first time since I own it."

After we put my things in the car and she offered me a bottle of water, she starts to drive.

"Are you hungry, darling?"

"Not really until now. Especially on the long flight, I had a lot to eat, but I feel still a pressure in my ears."

"I know this too after flights. As we wrote before, we will eat at my house tonight. Is this okay for you?"

"Yes, this is fine. Probably don't need anything too big tonight."

"You are maybe tired now?"

"Not really, maybe it comes later. How has your day been?"

"It was usual at work, but I left a bit earlier and everybody knows of course that I am driving to the airport because my boyfriend from Germany is arriving." She smiles and I smile back.

I am touching her right thigh as she did when she was visiting me. She is grinning and strokes my hand.

"We will need about one hour to Wendell. I hope that there isn't much traffic … what do you think about how it is looking here?"

"Well, from the landscape it's not too different than areas in Germany. I just think that you are with the season one month or even more ahead here. It's greener and all these blue bushes here are already blooming!"

"The most parts of North Carolina look the same, the landscape is boring and not as hilly as at your place. But if we do a trip to the mountains, you will see something different."

It is still a bit light as we arrive at the entrance of Wendell.

"I just need something from this shop near the gas station here and then we are soon at my place. Do you want come in with me? Do you need anything?

"Yes, I will come with you. But I don't think that I need anything."

"I also should have everything at home for the next days. I just need some water and toilet paper.

Ten minutes later, we are arriving at the house. It's on the big main road, some greens are in front of it and it looks a bit like a witch house. Narrow from the front side, white wood and a long red sandstone chimney. Elisa is stopping in front of a wooden gate, which is a part of an old fence. She opens it and jumps in the car again.

"Ah, here is Sally and Randy ... do you see them?" She is pointing to two cats on her porch.

"Oh yes."

"These are two of my five outdoor kitties ... Hello, Sally! You want come over here?"

She is speaking with a Mickey Mouse voice and cranks her window down.

We drive slowly around her house and there seems to be the door.

"I always use this door and never the front door. This is my yard on the left is. There would be so many things to do. But you know with my physical condition it's sometimes not so easy ... Come, we take your baggage and go in the house!"

As typical in the U.S. and known from other trips before, there are two doors.

"Here in front of us it goes down in the basement and this is my kitchen!"

We are walking through a long kitchen strip, I see her juicer on the right, the oven and on the left is the microwave, the sink and a kind of grill.

"And this my dining room! Can you imagine that some weeks ago there were no chairs in there?"

"It looks nice! The big table and the windows around on two sides."

"And here is the living room. I almost never spend time in here. On the right, this is a book room, it could also be used as a guest room, but I never need it since I am here. The other door is a little bathroom. Let's go upstairs! But let me help you with the baggage. You know it can be dangerous."

She takes my backpack while I am lifting up my suitcase. The floor is cracking. I am sweating a bit as I am arriving at the last step.

"Are you okay, honey?"

"Yes, I am."

"On the left, this is my computer and working room. It's the room where I spend the most time and it's also the cats' room. Where are you sweeties?"

She is changing in her Mickey Mouse voice again.

One cat is jumping up to a board and another one is looking behind from an old little brown sofa.

"Don't be shy my girls … this is Thomas!"

The smaller one on the board is growling at me.

"Don't be mean to my boyfriend, Lucy!" She turns to me and goes on. "She needs a bit of time I think, but both Carla and Lucy are nice. "Yes you are?" She talk with her funny voice to the cats again.

Carla is now jumping on the table and sniffs around the two laptops which are standing there.

"Here if you go to the left it's the bathroom, there is a closet. Ahead is the bedroom. I walk in, it's really big. On the right I see the bed, beautifully coated, three windows, one on the right near the bed and two ahead. On the left I see a big mirror and a closet.

Elisa is turning to me, putting her hands on my hips and giving me a kiss. I am holding her.

"I hope you feel comfortable here. I hope that the road is not bothering you. But it's much better since I have the new windows."

"I don't hear much from the outside. It's not too much different than at my place."

"You can take a shower now, if you want. And I am preparing something for dinner. You can come down when you are finished."

"Thank you, my Elisa."

She smiles and leaves the bedroom.

After the shower, I open my suitcase and sort my gifts for her. I take out a bag from my mother with a bag of coffee, a chocolate Easter bunny and some other sweet things. Further a towel, a shower gel, two other creams and a whole shoebox of gummy bears, different chocolates and Kinder eggs. I know that she wanted these eggs for her coworkers, and I thought some things are maybe for her brother or her friend. But it's up to her what she wants to have for whom. I let some small gifts back in my suitcase that I can give to her another time on this vacation.

Two hours later we are lying entwined in the bed.

I am happy about this day. My flight went well, and I am now enjoying the time with my girlfriend. Maybe it can be a great vacation; I am thinking while Elisa is snuggling with her head on my chest and I am holding her tight. In my mind, I say thank you to the universe that this day ended so good.

Friday afternoon

March 27, 2015

Elisa is smiling to me. The cats are running around. We are sitting in her working/cats room. She is typing something concentrated on her work laptop while I am on her private laptop and surfing in YouTube from video to video. I would rather go out in her yard, but it's raining already the whole day. But well, for a first day somewhere new and after a long flight day yesterday, this isn't too bad. Elisa isn't as busy as I thought before when she works from at home. She made me a good breakfast in the morning. Though I wanted to make something for lunch, she cooked a yummy vegetarian dish. We had vegetable oriental style with naan bread and hummus. She cares a lot about me. Five minutes ago, she was sitting on my lap, we were holding and kissing each other. It seems that it was unnecessary that I have been scared for this trip in the last days. She said that she probably can log out from her work at 4:30 p.m. today, and we can go for dinner to the Mexican restaurant down the street tonight. The place she often wrote about in her emails and where she sometimes meets her friend Martha.

Saturday

March 28, 2015

I don't know what time it is, but it's still dark outside. I woke up already a couple of times. Lucy and Carla are active at night. Lucy suddenly runs around at different times. Carla even jumps on the bed. They are probably used to being close to Elisa at night times and now a stranger is lying in the bed.

With a crumpled voice, "Honey, are you awake? Can't you sleep because of the cats?"

"Maybe the cats woke me up, but maybe it's also the jetlag because it's difficult to find some sleep again."

She is touching with her hand my right side. "I am so sorry!"

"It's ok. Sleep if you can."

Two hours later, we are in the dining room. Elisa made a wonderful American breakfast. Bacon, scrambled eggs, toast with butter and different jams, orange juice, coffee for her and tea for me.

"I have just these tea bags, but we will go shopping later. I found a tea shop on Google in Raleigh. I want go anyway with you to Raleigh today. What you think? Is it good idea?"

"Yes, sure … this is a good idea! You know I like to explore and everything is new here for me." I say with big eyes and a smile. My travel passion comes out.

"I think I show you the area here on this weekend. This means mainly Raleigh, Durham and Chapel Hill. So let's start with Raleigh today. I have a kind of plan in my mind."

"I'm curious, honey."

"I know also that you like surprises. I don't want to talk too much and shut my mouth." She says pertly.

After the feeding and goodbye ceremony for the indoor and out-door cats, we are driving out of her property.

"It's a beautiful day, Elisa! I think I told you before that we have a saying in German – when angels are traveling …"

"Yes, you told me about it. So you think we are angels?" She is laughing. "But I hope you have your jacket in the trunk … It's much cooler as the days before, and it can get cold tonight."

"Yes, I have." I'm touching her thigh.

"I am so happy that you are here, my boyfriend!"

"Me too, my girlfriend."

"I miss you so much in the last time. And as you know, I had just one goal in the last months. You! Only you …"

"I missed you too. It's so difficult that we are living so far away from each other."

"Yes, I know, but there are ways, nothing is impossible."

She is changing the stations on her radio.

"The only station I can listen to sometimes is Public Radio. The have some good reports. But all the other stations here are trash! But if you want I can put CDs in it … wait a second honey … We are now on the 264 … Here it is … do you know it?"

"Oh yes, sure … It's one of the CDs I made for you and sent last year." I am smiling.

From the speakers and out of her mouth I hear:

Wenn man so will
Bist du das Ziel einer langen Reise
Die Perfektion der besten Art und Weise
In stillen Momenten leise
Die Schaumkrone der Woge der Begeisterung
Bergauf, mein Antrieb und Schwung

Ich wollte dir nur mal eben sagen
Dass du das Größte für mich bist
Und sichergehen, ob du denn dasselbe für mich fühlstFür mich fühlst

"Wow, you are good, darling!" I say astonished. "And this music here in North Carolina!" I am laughing. This text fits perfect about what she is probably thinking about me. Is she aware of it?

She is laughing too. "No, I am not really good and some words are hard to pronounce for me, but thanks for your compliment."

"The name of the song is compliment." I laugh. "You have a good voice and you pronounced most great, Elisa."

"What's the name of this band again?"

"Sportfreunde Stiller. It's a kind of strange to hear German music here on a U.S. highway, and my girlfriend is singing the song!"

We both have fun.

While our easy chat is going on, we are arriving at a parking area near Pullen Park. Hand in hand, we walk in the park. It's very sunny, but in the shadows still a bit cold. After the rain yesterday, it's cooler. But it feels more like spring and more natural for me since it was much colder in Germany when I left. I take pictures, Elisa takes picture and gets red in her tender face as I ask someone else to take a picture of us. We are in good moods, and we enjoying our time together. Also her Myofascial Pain Syndrome seems to be ok. She doesn't moan as we walk around the lake and later up to the car again.

We drive to an area where there are different stores and restaurants in a complex.

"I think the tea shop is over there, Thomas. We can park right here."

We get out of the car, and as I see the letters of the shop on the wall, it looks familiar to me. But I don't know why.

As we get in, I notice the big tea boxes and look around.

"What is it, honey?"

"I feel familiar here, and it reminds me of the tea shop where I buy my teas in Heilbronn." As I see the cash register, I stumble. "There is even the name of the shop in Heilbronn?! It's a German tea shop chain!"

Elisa is turning to the man behind the desk. "Hello. My boyfriend is from Germany. He is saying that he knows this all from at home …"

"Hi guys! Yes, I get the equipment of my shop and most of my green teas from Germany, the black teas are from India. Just look around and say if you need any help."

"Thank you. We would like to get some green tea." Elisa is turning to me. "Select any tea you want, Thomas, and also anything else what you want here. We will need a pot and something like a sieve or filter like you have at home. I didn't have loose teas before."

"Thank you. But you don't have to buy it just because of my vacation here!"

"That's fine, honey. I want that you have your green tea here too, and I want also to drink some and use the pot."

About half an hour later, we are leaving with a china teapot, five sorts of green teas, jam and organic gummy bears. I feel almost uncomfortable, she paid nearly 100 dollars! But she insisted to buy these things. I know from my other trips to the States about the big hospitality of many Americans. All my pen pals and friends treated me very nice and well. So I don't wonder too much that Elisa wants to treat me as her boyfriend even more special. Beside that, I am embarrassed I feel also pampered like a child who was shopping with mom.

"Are you hungry, sweetheart?" She is pressing my hand and smiling. "Here is a pasta place and that looks like Japanese noodle bar?"

"The noodle bar looks interesting. But this time it's my turn. I will invite you, honey."

"But you don't have. You are my guest and come all this way to see me."

"But we have just day number two from my two and half weeks here. And I think you have planned still more in the next days." I say with a smile.

"Yes, you are right. Let's go in."

The furnishings are bit a simple, but the location is cool and there is a good smell in there. We are ordering Yakisoba, Spicy Udon and iced tea. Quickly, we have our dishes on our table.

"Oh, it's very good, Elisa!"

"Yes, mine too. And I am surprised and didn't expect something delicious here. Do you want share?"

"Sure, I hope mine isn't too spicy for you."

The rest of the afternoon and evening we are spending in downtown Raleigh. After coffee/tea and fresh made cookies at a café on Wilmington Street, we are walking to the State Capitol, along Salisbury Street, over Hargett Street, to the Moore Park and to Parham and Blake Street. This seems to be the oldest part of Raleigh. Here are some older looking houses and even cobblestone streets. An event seems to be happening tonight around Moore Park.

"Oh, it's so cold!" Elisa shouts out.

"Yes, it is. It was still very nice in the morning and afternoon, but the air is very clear. Didn't they talk something about temperatures under the freezing point tonight?"

"They talked about 30 degrees. Yes, this should be under the freezing point. It was so warm in the last days until your arrival day. And I can't imagine that we had such a cold this season in the last years. What do you think about dinner tonight? I don't want to get home too late. Is there anything around here you are interested in?"

"I don't know. On the other side of this park was something Asian."

"Yeah, I think Laotian. I have been never been there before. But we can check it out."

The place looks good, but there is no chance for table. The waitress tells us on weekends we would have to reserve four weeks ahead. The upcoming Tuesday would be the next day where we could reserve a table. We made it and walk out again.

"Too bad that they are full … mmmh … before I thought that we are going to the Big Easy next week or even the week later. I am not sure if we can catch a table now, but we can go there if you want."

I feel almost frozen as we reaching the Big Easy on Fayetville Street. But we have luck. There are still tables on the second floor available.

"Elisa, you have to recommend something to me. I had never Cajun food before."

"I know and you wanted try it, thus it was one of my Christmas gifts for you going here. I don't know if you like it, but they also have alligator meat. I don't want to have it. But it's up to you. Very famous is the jambalaya. It's spicy, but you will like it."

"I never had alligator meat, but I also don't need it. The jambalaya sounds good. I will take it."

"Fine. I think I will take the shrimp platter. As always, we can of course try from each other."

I am feeling good; I like the location because it's something new for me and not that kind of American restaurant that looks one like the other. The light is dimmed, everything is wooden, I hear laughter and music from the first floor. Elisa has some red eyes. Probably it's from the cold wind outside and maybe she is also a bit exhausted from walking. But she smiles and it seems that we are both feeling well on this cold Saturday evening.

Sunday

March 29, 2015

"Our time together feels in the same way intensive as you have been at my place last year. Though today is just day number three of my full days here, I have the feeling that I would be here already much longer."

"Yes, I know what you mean, honey. I want show you around here this weekend as much as I can. You know, the next two days I have to work again."

"I know, but just two days and you are working from home again. It's nice that you could arrange working from home, three days in a row. Thank you so much for showing me around. How you are feeling physically?"

"I noticed last night that my muscles are tensed. I hope that it works well for me today. I need a hot bath tonight."

"I can give you also massage if you want."

"This is very sweet of you. But I also have to give you massage. You know this is also one of my Christmas gifts. Maybe we see today somewhere massage oils."

"I also have a Japanese mint oil with me. This could be good for your muscles."

"But now we first enjoy our day. Soon we should be at the place I have chosen. It's another surprise. But I have never been before there. I hope you will like it. It's always on the way when I drive to Stella, my therapist. But we will drive a bit further into the country."

It's late Sunday morning. I don't know where she is driving. We were driving on the Interstate 40 to Chapel Hill and now it looks rural. Woods and meadows around, the sun is shining.

"You see these houses ahead? This is Fearrington Village."

Everything seems to be very clean. On the cars and some houses, it's easy to see that richer people are living here.

We walk hand in hand along some houses and enter a park.

"How do you like it here, darling?"

"This park is nice, the landscape around is nice too, everything looks neat and clean. But it looks almost sterile and even if the houses are probably expensive, they are looking like white barracks."

Elisa is laughing. "Yes, you are right. I also don't know if I would like to live here. It's also out in the country and if you are working in Durham or Raleigh it's some drive."

"Do you want go back to the village? There is something like a boutique and a book store."

"Yes, let's go there."

We are leaving the boutique fast. Elisa thinks that it is too pricey. The bookstore is comfortable. She interested about the book from Bronnie Ware. Unfortunately, my book is in the German language. I told her in the last days about some of the stories and said that it is an easy and enjoyable read.

"There are no new insights in this book, nothing but what you know already. But eventually it helps to see the glimpse of joy and happiness in simple things and moments."

Since the original version of this book is in English, I am surprised as the seller is telling Elisa that they don't have this book and that it wouldn't be available to order.

About three hours later, we as sitting in a kind of alternative café in Durham.

"What do think about this place here, Thomas?"

"It's very relaxed and chill. We are almost sitting on the floor on these pads, the music is something like reggae, there is a fragrance of incenses in the air, the cookies are good and this Japanese sencha tea too. Further, my wonderful girlfriend is next to me." I say with a smile.

She is turning around a bit shy and kisses me.

"You are wonderful! I like this chill atmosphere here too. I am glad that you like it and that I can be here with you, honey."

"I am surprised about this good and fresh green tea everywhere."

"I also didn't know this. As you know, I am usually not that tea drinker and I didn't come around here in the last years. I know Durham and Chapel Hill very good, but it's because I studied here and because of my different workplaces. So it's long ago that I walked here around where we have been the last hours. We will drive then to Chapel Hill. I want show you the university. The place where we will go for dinner tonight is also there. It's another surprise!"

She looks with big eyes to me.

I am taking her hands. "Another surprise?!"

"Yes, I have never been there, but they have good reviews in the internet, and I think you will like this food."

"It's so nice of you!"

"It's also something I like, and we both are into trying new things. Though I have to be a bit careful with my muscles and also the rash. The food last night wasn't too good for it. In the next days, I should go on a diet and make some juices at home."

After some walking in Chapel Hill, we end up sitting in an Indian restaurant. It looks elegant, white walls, white fine tablecloths, expensive tableware and friendly staff.

Elisa is smiling all over her face and recommends that we take a big selection of small portions of different dishes so that we can try something of everything. I see in the menu that it is pricy, and she paid the most since I am here. But she wants it. I think that I still will have enough time to pay for some things.

In this moment, I am aware about how precious this time with Elisa is. The last months are running through my mind. I never experienced such an indescribable willingness, openness and love from someone. I don't know what else I need to be completely sure about her.

Monday

March 30, 2015

It's very bright; the sun is shining from a clear blue sky. I am walking from the main road where Elisa's house is into a smaller neighborhood street. It's warm enough to wear just a T-shirt in the afternoon sun. Already to breakfast time, three guys were around the house mowing the lawn. I wanted to do it, but Elisa had probably still ordered this company on Friday. Today she is busier with her work on her laptop. She also had a long phone call before I left. She worries that her work doesn't gets done good enough when she has off from Wednesday. The most part of the morning I was sitting close to her in the cats' room, was on the private laptop and read a bit in my books, also in the travel guidebook about North Carolina. At least I could do something for lunch today, though it wasn't much different than what she did on Friday. But now I felt boring, restless and impatient to be inside on this beautiful day. I think that maybe Elisa can also do her work better if I am out of sight for sometime. Be careful, she said as I left the house. This town looks quiet, but I know North Carolina isn't Baden-Württemberg. Two kids are running around at a playground, but otherwise I don't see any people. Just cars are driving by and some looking at me as if I would be an alien with my red T-shirt and my black Atlanta baseball cap. I had this experience on other trips before. If you aren't here in a park or near a mall, nobody is strolling around. It's one of the main activities for many Germans, but Americans seems to prefer car rides. I come to a nice pond. Reed is around, some insects are flying and birds are chirping. I enjoy the place and take a picture with my camera. It's too early to walk back again. I decide to walk in the other direction of the main road where I suspect is the center of this town. It seems to be like almost everywhere in States here. Some great houses, a lot of ground around … it's what Germans are dreaming, but where is the town? Where is the center? Wide roads, some nice yards, gas stations, big grocery stores, a few chain restaurants and car dealers, but where is downtown? Even every village in Germany has built a center. You see it on the houses, how close they are built, on shops, post offices, banks, churches and in bigger towns, always on pedestrian zones. But here looks often one corner exactly like the other, towns have none of their own charm, nothing unique that is typical for this town … and I see Wendell could be almost everywhere in the States. I think that I am now standing somewhere you could call downtown. It's clean, but it is not in good shape. Some stores are empty, in some shops are just junk and overall there isn't any character. A bit disappointed, I am walking back to Elisa's house. Her outdoor kitties are running away as they see me coming. I open the door with her key. She only has one, she doesn't know where the spare keys are because she never needed them.

It's something after 9 p.m. We are sitting comfortable on the little sofa in the cat's room. Lucy and Carla are moving around us. Elisa's workday has been busy, and she has concerns that she isn't able to finish all her work until tomorrow evening. In front of us, she had put up one of the laptops on boxes where we watched a travel/food show about Hong Kong on YouTube while we were eating a kind of Indian vegetable stew Elisa made for dinner.

"How did you like this show? This guy is popular on TV here. He is traveling to different countries and always trying and eating different food. Did you know the place where they have been?"

"I think I have seen this guy once or twice on TV during other to trips to the States before. Some places I know from my trip to Hong Kong last year. But not every place and some of the food he had is strange. But it was interesting to watch." I'm laughing.

Elisa is laying her arms on my shoulders and comes closer to me.

"What are you thinking right now?" She is asking like a kid, and it reminds me that she asked similar when she was at my place last year. It's like she is expecting something but I don't have a clue.

"Mmmmh, I have some nice days behind me with you, that you made another good dinner and that you are looking beautiful."

She is getting still closer to my face. I feel her breath on my cheeks.

She is asking very blunt, "Do you want to go to the bedroom? Making some love, you know? We didn't make anything in this direction since you are here?! Is everything okay?"

"Yes, everything is fine. I just wanted to be slow and careful. I didn't want that it goes too fast again …" I hesitate a bit, "But we can go to the bedroom, if you like."

"Slowly and carefully? I am your girlfriend! About what you are talking?" Her tone is suddenly harsh, and I am noticing that her eyes are looking different.

"You know about my ups and downs as you have been in Germany last year, and you know also that we had sometimes not an easy time in the past weeks." I say a bit nervous.

She is standing up and looking at me as if I would have said the most terrible thing in the world.

I am your girlfriend! You are rejecting me! Again and again! What did I do wrong that you treat me like this?"

"I'm sorry. You did nothing wrong! I just want to be careful. This is all." Her reaction makes me insecure.

"Stop! You don't have to tell me anything!" She shouts.

"I am sorry!"

"Everybody is rejecting me! My mother, my brother, my dad never cared about me, people don't like me! And you also don't like and love me."

"This is wrong. I like you, I care about you and I love you also when …" She interrupts me. "I said stop! Can't you listen? There is no need for any explanations!"

I am quiet, and she starts crying. She is running to the bathroom. I am feeling shocked about her sudden mood change out of the blue. Her outbreaks when she was at my place for nine days last year come in my mind and also her moments on the phone, especially the phone call on that Thursday in early March. Do I arrive in the reality now, I have been afraid of this before trip? I don't know what I did wrong today. Maybe something accumulated in her in the last days.

She is coming again.

"I'm going to bed now, Thomas!" She is saying with a crying voice.

Without speaking, I also got ready for bed.

Almost stiff, I lie down on my side next to her. She is crying again. I want to comfort her, but she is throwing my arms back.

"I don't want to have you close anymore! You are not loving me! You don't care about me! You don't behave like a boyfriend! What is wrong to have sex and love together? I would do everything for you! And you are rejecting me!" She cries and shouts at the same time; her eyes are rigid. She looks like a different person. I am getting scared.

"I am not rejecting you, honey. I just want be slow after what happened before."

"I don't want hear this! Slowly?! Slowly with your girlfriend?!" She is loud and rough.

Elisa jumps out of the bed and is running around in the bedroom like a wild tiger in the cage. She is crying desperately.

"Thomas, I am done with you! I can't endure your stupid and careful behavior anymore! Fuck off!" She is shouting in my direction.

She is running in the cats' room. Even Lucy and Carla seem to be very irritated about what is going on in the house now.

I am getting out of the bed too and walk to the door of the cats' room. In the dark, Elisa is sitting on the sofa, sobbing and crying.

I don't know what to do, but I think about another attempt to comfort her. Obviously she is noticing it. She suddenly stands up on the sofa.

"Stop! Don't come closer! I will jump out of this window!"

"Get down, Elisa!" I shout at her. I am moving fast to her, grab her arm and press her body close to mine.

"Go away!"

I stagger a few steps back. I am feeling paralyzed and deeply shocked.

"Come over, Elisa!"

I am getting desperate and asking myself, is this situation real? Tears are running down on my cheeks too. What can I do? I feel helpless.

Five minutes later, she is going without any word to bed. I am following her. I also don't dare to say anything. She stops sobbing and crying. The house is quiet, and I don't even hear the cats anymore. I don't move in the bed; I feel frozen. Thoughts are starting to run wild through my mind.

What can I do? There is no family or friends of hers I can talk with. I don't even know a number of her brother or her friend Martha. She mentioned in the last weeks a few times a neighbor to who she has a good contact. A lady who has family, and her name is also Elisabeth. But it's probably just a neighbor, also no real option for any help. I feel like I'm in a nightmare. I have been scared about something like this before this trip, but I hoped for best. And didn't it seem in the past days that everything is going alright? What happened tonight? What did I make wrong?

Tuesday

March 31, 2015

I am still lying frozen on my side of the bed. Maybe Elisa is sleeping, but I am not sure. I can't sleep. I have to think of myself, and I have to leave this place, I have to go home! How I can leave this place? A taxi is probably the only option. But will she let me go? Or can I let her alone? If she is acting so crazy with my presence, what is she doing alone?

I don't come to any conclusion in my mind. I am staying awake with these thoughts until the first sunbeams are coming through windows and Elisa is turning to me.

"Do you love me?"

I don't want to risk anything, but I want to stay honest.

"You know that I care a lot about you. And yes, I love you. Maybe in a bit of a different way than you do."

"Do not lie to me!"

I see on her eyes and on her tone that her mood isn't much different than last night.

"I am sorry about what happened last night, Thomas! But I can't deal with this and how you keep rejecting me!"

"I didn't sleep. I do not feel well."

She starts crying again. This keeps on for the next hour. A mix between crying, sobbing and aggressive words against me. I don't know what I can say and do.

"Oh, it's already eight! I have to get up and sign in for work!"

I stay first in the bed. Just a few minutes later, I hear her from the /computer/cats' room.

"Shit! There is nothing working! There is no power!"

I stand up and go over to her.

"No power? In the whole house?"

"Yes. I suppose that these workers out there are doing something on the power lines!" She is pointing out of the window.

She cries again. "I don't need this now! I have to call my workplace, have to change my clothes and go out to the workers!"

It's almost 9:30 a.m. until the power problem is fixed, and she has signed in at her laptop. Despite all the circumstances, her work and the trouble between us she, is making a breakfast for me.

The sun is shining bright as I walk to the pond. The beautiful weather again is deluding how I am feeling. It's the late afternoon. I am tired, sad and depressed. After I made something for lunch, Elisa came down a bit. But it's probably just because she is very distracted through work. She made a cancellation for our reservation at the Laotian restaurant in Raleigh tonight. She said that she would have to work longer because of the power problems and also because there would be so much to get finished. I am thinking that it would probably not be good idea to go there tonight. I am hoping that I get some better thought out here in the sun, but I am feeling really depressed.

Wednesday

April 1, 2015

"Good morning, Thomas! How was your night?"

"Good morning, Elisa. I slept some hours. I was so tired last night. Did you check the spot between your breast and shoulder again?"

She became worried last night as she felt something hard in her skin last night.

"I still feel it ... Give me your hand ... I will lead it to the spot. Tell me what you think."

"Yes, there is something hard or swollen. Could it be a cramped muscle? Something that has to do with the Myofascial Pain Syndrome?"

"I don't think so. I never had a cramped muscle at this place. It could be an inflammation of a lymph node. Our dinner last night also wasn't healthy again. These fried chicken pieces and hash browns we took home were very greasy. We didn't have vitamins and minerals. Further, I drank less. But I am scared that it is something serious. It's not too far away from my left breast. I should get a mammogram examination. But I doubt that my insurance will cover it. The healthcare is so bad here in this country."

"I know. This is really bad here. In Germany the health insurances cover almost anything. Just with dentists it changed."

"I hate living here in this country ... But what do you think, should I go to a doctor as soon as possible?"

"Maybe you can observe it another day. But if you don't feel good and are having too many worries. it's better if we are going to a doctor today."

Elisa is calling for an appointment and already three hours later, we are sitting in the doctor's office.

"What did she say?" I am asking as Elisa is coming in the waiting room again. The first time I see her smiling again.

"She didn't make a mammogram; she just felt the lump. She said it would be just an inflammation and gave me pills I should take for the next days. She charged it as a routine check, so the insurance covers it."

"I am glad that it is nothing serious!"

"Me too. Thank you for going here with me. I should check the oil and the tires on my car if we are going on a trip in the next days. There is a Chinese place close to the garage. Are you hungry?"

An hour later, we are at the Chinese place. I feel the for first time a bit relaxed again. We have at least a normal and nice conversation again. We both decided for chicken with rice, just the mixture of the sauce is different.

"Again, we have chicken." She says with a wink. "But we definitely should go grocery shopping later. I have to make vegetable juice tomorrow to detoxify. Do you like the food here?"

"Yes, it's good, maybe a bit too spicy."

"Can't it be too spicy for you, honey?" She is laughing.

"Yeah, it's difficult that something is too spicy. But it seems their chili shaker has a hole."

"Thomas, I have to apologize for Monday night. It happened and it's something I probably can't apologize for at all. If I could, I would erase these hours. But I can't. I wasn't myself anymore. I know that you wanted to comfort me, but if I am so into panics and fears you have to keep distance of me. If I am in such a bad spiral down, I can't handle if somebody is close and wants touch me. I didn't feel that way for years. It's not your fault."

"I don't know. But I have been obviously the trigger for it."

She is taking my hand, and we are sitting a few moments in silence.

"I have some worries about Carla. She doesn't eat much in the last days, and as we both have seen, Lucy is attacking her sometimes. Wouldn't you mind going with me to the vet tomorrow?"

Thursday night

April 2, 2015

I am very thankful for the day. It was a peaceful day. In the morning, we had different cereals for breakfast, and Elisa made for each one a glass of fresh juice. We went to the vet with Carla, and she got an injection. Around noon, we were at a farmer's market, and Elisa was proud to show me a stand from a German bakery. Not everything was really German for me there, but some things. We bought the last pretzel, a small Linzer Torte and something called "Swabian Cherry Cake." Elisa has been very talkative with the girl at the stand. I was wondering once again, if she is really highly sensitive? She was wondering about me in the opposite perspective and was asking me later why I wouldn't talk with this girl in German. I am not used to making conversations with strange people as long there isn't any need for it or I notice that somebody is interested in me. The things Elisa bought tasted good.

In the afternoon, we went to Duke Gardens in Durham. We both were enjoying the spring nature, feeding the ducks at the lake, taking pictures of the park and of each other. We felt for some time like the happiest couple on the planet. All of the heavy and sad mood was away. Though I know that it is not as before and I'm scared for another outbreak from her. What I have learned in the past days is that it can happen very suddenly.

But I am glad that we had a good day.

Friday

"What you think about this hotel?"

"Isn't it too expensive, Elisa? One hundred and fifty dollars for the night?"

She is rolling her eyes. "I would like to have something nice! It's in the center of Asheville, it looks good and they have some nice reviews."

"It looks nice, but wherever we stay there, we are there just for sleeping. We will need the car and this other place outside of the town has good reviews too, but costs only 99 dollars!"

"I wonder why it's so expensive. I am also getting impatient. We are sitting here now at the laptop for the last two hours or so!" She is saying it with a harsh voice again.

I am surprised that we are thinking about a weekend in the mountains after it wasn't a great morning because she got upset once again about my behavior or about the situation with me. Fortunately, she wasn't as down as before.

"It's the Easter weekend! I know Easter isn't so special here since it's just a normal weekend for you Americans. But maybe the people are on trips. At least the weather forecast is good."

I have my doubts if it is a good idea to make this trip. It is something we both looked forward to. But what is if she gets such an outbreak in Asheville? But it could also be a good distraction there and some fun.

"I am not used to planning trips! I checked before your arrival for things we can do there. Where we can go for lunch and dinner and I also found this hotel, this hotel I like in Asheville. The rates I have seen were cheaper. But maybe you are right that we can save these 50 dollars if we take the cheaper one."

Finally after one more hour and as we are both already weak with our nerves again, we decide for the trip and the cheaper hotel outside of Asheville. I am paying this time, and Elisa made a call if we can make a late check-in. We are getting happier and Elisa is relived that she needs nobody to feed her cats. The food and water should be enough from Saturday morning until Sunday night for them.

At 7 p.m. we are standing outside and waiting for her friend Martha. Elisa arranged that I see her tonight, and we will have dinner together at a ranch nearby and country restaurant.

Because I am sitting in the back of Martha's big SUV, I am seeing her completely for the first time as we walk in the restaurant. She is taller than Elisa, but also heavier. She makes a friendly impression and is asking me different things. Elisa and I are deciding once again for a chicken dish. Later as the waiter is bringing us our dishes, I see that Martha got fish and remember that it is Good Friday.

"Oh, I forgot that it is Good Friday!"

"Yes, therefore I eat the fish, are you religious Thomas?" Martha is asking.

"I am Catholic, but not religious. It's just tradition to eat no meat on Good Friday in Germany."

"I am sorry, honey." Elisa is saying.

"It's not a big thing. It's okay. I probably would have chosen fish if I would have been aware about it. And it would be something different to our chicken always." I am laughing.

We have a good time with Martha. I know from Elisa that they see each other every second or just every third week and their communication feels for me if I would talk with a co-worker that I don't work with every day. Nice, but casual.

At 8:30 p.m., we are back in Elisa's house. She didn't ask Martha if she wants to come in. I think she has been never in here.

Saturday

April 4, 2015

Elisa's alarm clock on her cell phone ringing.

"Is it already seven, honey?" She says sleepy.

I am already awake as usual. I am noticing once again that we have different inner clocks. While I am tired at 10 in the evening, she is just going because of politeness with me to bed, but for her it's hard to get up in the mornings. But it's maybe still the jetlag, and I am also still not used to these cats being especially active in the night times.

"Yes, we should get up soon."

After having a fast breakfast, packing some things together and Elisa's feeding ceremony for Lucy, Carla, and the outdoor cats and speaking with them in her Mickey Mouse voice, we are leaving for the interstate.

"It feels warm outside this morning."

"Yes, I saw also on the bushes and trees around your house how warm it was in the last days. It looks like spring when I arrived here. Now there are many leaves out, and it looks almost like early summer. But as we saw on the internet yesterday, it will be cooler in Asheville and the mountains."

"That's true. I think we will be in Asheville around noon. Do you think that we will make it as planned?"

"Yes. You mean driving to Asheville, having lunch there, driving to the Biltmore, going back to Asheville for dinner and then to the hotel?"

"Yep. I reserved dinner at this Korean restaurant tonight. We don't have any reservation for this South American place at lunch. But it shouldn't be a problem."

"This sounds good. I am especially excited for the Korean restaurant. I never had Korean before."

"I had it couple of times in Durham. It was ok, but also not too special for me. But this one in Asheville has great reviews. I am excited too. We also have to go next week to this German restaurant I mentioned a few times before." She laughs and continues, "We spend a lot of money on food."

I am laughing too. "Yes, we are."

"Well, this seems to be one of our common interests. But I never have been before to so many good restaurants."

"Me too. Also the food you buy at home is good quality and pricey."

"You know, the right nutrition is important for me; I want to have organic products and since you are here, I want that you feel good and I have everything you want."

"The things we had were all good, maybe except for the greasy chicken meat the other night. But I see also that it is much more expensive than in Germany. But I want pay for most over the weekend."

"You don't have to do that, darling. But it will give me some relief. On the first weekend I spent already 60 percent of the budget I planned for the whole time. I still have credit on my other card. But it was more than I expected."

"I don't wonder. You paid a lot last weekend. But I can take care of the things today and tomorrow."

She smiles and puts her right hand on my left thigh, like she did the first time from the passenger seat as I took her from the airport on November 28 last year.

I feel better and am getting curious about this trip. I always wanted do road trips in U.S. Over the many years and my trips to America, it happened just twice, once with Michael in 1996 as we were in Florida and once in the West also with friends from Germany. Though I visited already some Americans, the most had no time or money to travel around with me. I have three or even four times more vacations days as most Americans. Unfortunately, I never can drive alone a car in this country. Because of my handicap, I need extra left accelerator equipment. This makes it that

I can use only my own car at home. I know that this will not be that big of road trip and Elisa isn't used to driving too long distances, but at least we are away for one night. I hope badly that this Easter journey doesn't make any problems and that we come back safe again.

We have one short stop at a grocery store and we are buying some drinks and snacks.

Back in the car, Elisa is playing the music from the CDs I sent her. Sometimes she is also turning to different radio stations. On the horizon, we are seeing the first mountains.

"Do you see the Blue Ridge?"

"Oh yes, honey!" I reply excitedly.

"You mentioned that you have been there once before?"

Yes, it's some years ago. It was with my friend Sandy as she lived with her family in South Carolina. And it was a day trip from there, but just to the Biltmore Estate. I didn't see anything from Ashville or any other places in that area."

"I was here two times before. Twice with my parents. Once when my brother and me were still kids and another time a bit later. But it's long ago."

Around 12:30, we are reaching downtown Asheville. It is busy with the cars, and we have to drive in a parking garage. As we are getting out of the car at the highest parking level, a cold breeze is blowing.

"It's much cooler than in Wendell!"

"Yes. Good that we have the warm coats with us."

As we are walking down Page Street, Elisa is asking, "What do you think about Asheville so far?"

"It looks beautiful. In comparison to many other towns in the U.S., they have a nice downtown. A lot of small shops, restaurants, a lot to walk around and the mountains around make it better. Sure nothing really old here as in Germany. But they have a vivid and nice center."

"I like it too … Of course it's not to compare with a historic old town in your area at home that you showed me last year. But for American circumstances, it's nice." She laughs.

The South American restaurant is busy. It looks like we caught the last free table. Latin music is playing the background.

"The menu is interesting. I don't know many of the things I am reading. What kind of South American food is this?"

"I know some of the food from the time I lived in Ecuador. Some things in the menu are Columbian, these dishes here are Argentinian and a few I think are Bolivian and Brazilian."

As the waitress comes, I pointed to something where the description of it sounds good.

"Ah, you took this steak platter? I think it's good. I also thought about taking this. As usual, we select the same or almost the same." She is grinning.

"For which dish did you decide?"

"The shredded beef thing. Oh I see, we have both no chicken this time?!"

I am laughing, "Yes, no chicken this time."

"Have you ever had plantains?"

"No. What is it?"

"It's bananas. I know you don't eat the sweet bananas. But they taste different. More like a vegetable. You should try it. I will order a small portion of them extra."

It feels a kind of familiar for me as we are entering the park of the Biltmore Estate two hours later.

"Do you remember it now that you have been here before, Thomas?"

"Yes, I do. But it was during another season. It was fall, and there were nice colors to see on the trees."

"I bet that it's wonderful in fall here. I have been twice in the middle of summer before."

In the ticket office, I am paying the expensive day tickets for us. They don't have any offers when people are getting later in the day to the Biltmore and also no separate tickets for the Estate and the Gardens. We both would tend more to see only the greens.

"I am sorry, honey, that it is so expensive!"

"It's okay. But it's annoying that we have to take a complete ticket for 50 dollars for each."

One hour later.

"Thomas, please let's go out of here Or you still want to see more?" She is asking me nervous and impatient.

We were standing more than 30 minutes in the lines to get in the Biltmore house. Indeed, all the rooms are crowd. I think that it was a waste of money if we are leaving now. But I am also not too interested in this art and I have been here before.

"You don't feel good, honey?"

"It's boring, and I am starting to feel anxiety with all these people." She whispers in my ear.

"Yes, we can go outside."

The fresh wind is blowing, but the sun is shining from the deep blue sky.

"Elisa, let's go to this overview point over there!"

She is taking my hand.

"Do you still remember? The big picture on the wall in my living room is made exactly here from this place!"

"Oh yes, sure I know this picture, honey! I remember now that it is from fall and that you said once before as we had a phone call that you would have a picture from my state on your wall! You kept it a secret until I visited you!" She is smiling.

"Turn around, Elisa! It's a good place to take a picture of you."

"I am not really looking good today. And this wind and my hair. But do what you have to do."

We are walking down to the Gardens.

"There aren't many flowers to see."

"Yes, Elisa … the nature here in the mountains is still back."

"We can go in the plant houses and later to the park. There is a little creek; it looks beautiful."

We have a good afternoon and are enjoying each other. It seems that the wind is blowing our sadness from the past days away. Elisa is giggling like a little girl, taking a lot of pictures and I am surprised how much we are walking. We are going along the creek to the end of this park to a waterfall and back above over the soft green meadows. I am just enjoying the now and thinking of Eckhart Tolle's books, but also on the one from Bronnie Ware about happy moments.

Before leaving the Biltmore Estate, we stop at the souvenir and winery village. I am not too much interested in this place, but since we skipped most parts of the Biltmore house it's ok. At the end through the winery is along line for the wine tasting.

"Let's try some, Thomas! They have very small glasses. I still can drive, and I think that you can drink a bit."

Each of us is selecting four different wines. Though I am coming from a wine region, I never did something like this before.

As we are on fourth taste, Elisa is asking, "What is your favourite one?"

"You know I don't drink wine at all. I am the opposite of an expert, but I think this Gewürztraminer is a good one."

"I like it too. It's a German sort as you told before. Should I buy a bottle as a gift for your parents?"

"You don't have to this."

"But I would like to! Do think that your parents would like it too?"

"I don't know. My dad likes wine as you know. But he is picky. Elisa, let it be. It's expensive; I don't want that you spend a lot of money."

She looks a bit disappointed, "If you don't want, ok, but if I buy a bottle of Gewürztraminer for us, would you drink it with me?"

"Yes, I would do it."

"We can drink it next week with a good dinner."

It's already dark as we are arriving in downtown Asheville again. We are not exactly sure about where the Korean restaurant is. Some corners are full of folks wandering around from shopping or searching for restaurants.

"Thomas, you are better with the directions … Where should we walk?"

"As we saw on Google maps on your cellphone, I think we have to go up here on the road and probably the second to the left, I think."

"Ah … is this cold! It's almost the same as last Saturday."

"Yes, and it feels that we get temperatures below the freezing point tonight again. Do you see the big moon? It's full moon!"

"Oh, it's beautiful, honey!"

The industrial/Korean style looking restaurant is crowded, and we are glad that we reserved a table. They have a big menu, and I decide for a Bulgogi stonebowl. Elisa takes a grilled dish. The waiters are very friendly, and I sip delightfully on my fresh green tea.

"It's maybe a bit loud, but so far this place makes a great impression."

"It's not that kind of simple where I have been in Raleigh before."

"Oh, the food is coming already!"

The stonebowls are steaming. The waitress reads on my surprised eyes that I didn't have such a dinner before.

"Should I show you how it works?"

"Yes, please!"

She takes my fork and quickly stirs the egg on the top of the bowl around.

"'This bowl has 425 degrees on the bottom, so be a bit careful. Enjoy!"

Besides our main dishes, we also have small bowls with Kimchi, other pickled vegetables.

"Wow, it really tastes good!"

"I am glad that you like it. It's good and healthy."

"Everything that we had since I'm here was good, but this is definitely the best!"

"Yes! Our lunch was also good today, but it was a lot of meat."

Sometime later, we are sitting with full stomachs in the car and searching for the hotel. Elisa's smartphone is guiding us.

"Shouldn't it be here?"

"I see something in the back, that's it!"

Without thinking much, Elisa is turning the steering wheel and we are driving up to a hotel. But it isn't our hotel. As I said, it's in the back. Doesn't she see it?

"This isn't our hotel, Elisa."

"No? Why you didn't tell it me?!"

I'm noticing how her mood is changing once again, out of the blue. She is trying to find a way to our hotel, but it seems that they are separated properties. She has to drive down to the road again to take the next exit.

In the front of the right hotel, I am asking carefully, "Don't you want to look for a parking spot?

"No! I will check us in, you stay here and then we will look for a parking spot!"

She is leaving the car. Sure, she is probably just tired. But it makes me scared if her mood is changing always so fast.

The hotel room is clean and nice. Elisa is turning on the TV, and we are lying close together on one of the two beds. Each of us is taking a shower and getting ready for bed.

As I come out of the bathroom, Elisa is saying, "I prefer to sleep in this other bed separate tonight. The beds are not really big, and I need some space."

"Ok."

I doubt if space is the reason. My bed at home in Germany, which is even smaller, was good enough for her for nine nights. But it's okay for me. As long as she is peaceful and we have no other drama, then it's fine for me.

Easter Sunday

April 5, 2015

"I like the breakfast. The coffee is good and they had a lot of things to eat. From waffles, toast, bread, over-easy eggs and different juices, you can get anything."

I am smiling. "Yes, for American circumstances."

She is laughing "But you have to agree that they have a lot for a continental breakfast?"

"They have a lot. But this is not the thing that I mean. Everybody eats from plastic plates, takes plastic knives, forks, spoons, these Styrofoam cups ... look over to the big trash bags!"

"Oh yes! This is America!"

"Your country seems to be still far away from any good environment politics."

"As you know, the health care system isn't good, people who have money only care about themselves and their lobbies, shootings are daily everywhere in this country and so on, how should they care about this plastic here?"

I grin, "Therefore, I said for American circumstances, the breakfast is good."

In good moods, we are starting our day just a little later. We want to drive to Grandfather Mountain. Still on Friday, Elisa asked what I would like to see today. I thought also about Chimney Rock and Clingmans Dome. But with Chimney Rock, she wasn't sure if she can handle it with her physical condition and the other mountain is in the total different direction. The pictures on the internet looked interesting, and it's not a too big detour driving home again.

As we are leaving the interstate and driving into the mountains, I am feeling some good excitement for this day.

"It's beautiful here! We have great weather and these soft green meadows, the lovely landscape and the empty streets are reminding me of Easter in Germany."

"Yes, the landscape is here maybe like in some parts of your country."

"It looks a bit like the Black Forrest or the the Swabian Alb in my state."

"I think people here are going also to church in this area, thus so less traffic."

"Ah … could you stop here? It's a place for good picture!"

"Sure!"

She is driving on a small field road right from the highway. I get out of the car and enjoy this moment a lot on this beautiful Easter Sunday morning. It's cool, but the sun is shining bright. A big barn with a windmill and mountains in the back makes a great scene.

"Do you know that we are from the crossroad ahead, on the Blue Ridge Parkway? I don't think I ever drove from this side up to Grandfather Mountain. But up there I have been once or even twice with my parents. Some of our trips with them were nice, but often things went wrong." She is talking as I am back in the car.

The next 20 miles I am enjoying the ride on the Parkway and listening to Elisa's childhood stories.

After reaching the entrance to the Grandfather Mountain and driving up a couple of minutes through light woods, we make a stop at a parking area. While Elisa is going to the restrooms, I am preparing a little surprise. I am glad that the two chocolate bunnies and some other Easter candy survived in the back and that she didn't see it. I put the things nice on a table in the woods.

"Elisa!" I call her as she looks a bit perplexed in my way.

"Come over here!"

She gets closer and sees the table behind me, "Happy Easter, honey!"

"Oh, my darling Thomas … you are so sweet! Happy Easter to you too! I didn't expect to get more of this good German chocolate since you already gave me so much after your arrival!"

"It's tradition in Germany to hide cooked and colored eggs, but also chocolate and Easter candy on the holidays out in greens. Kids love to seek. But we are still a bit older, so I cancelled the seeking game." We are both laughing.

For a minute we are sitting down, though it's not warm. Elisa is laying her right arm over my shoulder and is kissing me softly.

We are back in the car and continue uphill. After another short stop at a big stone and a fantastic view, she looks to me with big eyes.

"I have to stop here! I get scared!"

"Park over there in this parking area!"

She is doing as I am saying.

"Uhh … please check the hand brake. It makes me nervous to look down there!"

"It's ok. Let's get out of the car for some minutes, Elisa."

"Look up to this serpentine and curves up there, honey!"

"I thought you have been here before."

"Yes, but I never drove by myself up here, and I didn't remember anymore."

"Sure, this is a difference. Too bad I can't drive."

"It's ok. We will make it up there."

I feel that she is nervous, me too. Even if I could drive with her car I would also have no experiences with such mountain roads.

"Just drive slowly. Don't mind if other cars are behind us." I try to calm her down a bit.

We are going back in the car and already five minutes later we are at the top.

In the tourist info/souvenir building, we are going up with an elevator, and wow, the view is breathtaking as we get out. In front of us is the mile-high swinging bridge.

"Please walk slowly over this bridge, honey. I will stay right behind you!"

As we are on the other side, the official path ends and there are just big stones and rocks where people are climbing even with their kids around.

"Now, I have to quit, Elisa. I don't have problems with heights, but I can't walk or even climb unsecured ways."

"I can help you if you want, darling."

"Thank you, but it's better if I stay here. If you feel safe, you can go a bit in this direction. I will wait here for you."

"Ok. Can you give me your camera?"

I'm wondering a bit if Elisa wants go with her flat, girlie sport shoes there since she is not good with heights. But I am sure she knows what she does.

I enjoy the amazing view back to the bridge and down in the valley. The nature looks still like winter here. Except of some pines, nothing is green. But it was definitely a good idea to get up here. I am watching some birds circling above the valley. More people coming over the bridge. I am turning around, and Elisa is waving from a rock. She indicates that she want to take a picture of me.

Not much later, she is back again.

"How was it?"

"Great! I took some pictures. But I didn't want to go further than this rock over there. Let's go back to souvenir shop."

We will have to go through it anyway. This is something typical American. The only things I am always buying on my trips are postcards. But maybe these shops are also a female thing.

"What do you want, honey?"

"I don't think that I need anything, maybe some postcards … and would you like to have a drink?"

"Yes, take two drinks. I think I will buy two stuffed toys for Lucy and Carla."

While she is looking for the gifts for her cats, I select five postcards. I doubt if I will write and send them as usual on my trips. I am not in the mood for it.

"Did you find something for Carla and Lucy?"

"Yes, I think these little bears are cute. Oh, your cards are nice!"

Forty minutes later, we are arriving in Boone.

"Even restaurants seem to be closed here because of Easter … look at this sign over there!" Elisa is pointing to a fast food place. In big letters is written, *Jesus is risen – we are closed!*

I am laughing. "This is one of the strange things in your country. At one hand, people are working 24/7 and on weekends the stores are open. Easter is just a Sunday here; in Germany as you know we have two holidays and many people have four days off in a row … but this simple fast food chain is closed because Jesus is risen."

Elisa laughs too. "I think it's because people are religious in this area here."

This town seems to not look special. There is no character and no comparison to Asheville. They are also nicely surrounded by the mountains. But down here are just highways, gas stations, some stores … ah, there is a sign for the old town, but I bet this is nothing more than two to three wooden houses."

She smiles. "That's just like it is, but I am very hungry now. I hope that we find something open and not too pricy. We spent a lot on food yesterday."

We end up in a kind of pizza chain that Elisa knows from Raleigh. We both order a grilled sandwich. The place isn't too busy, but the food isn't coming. She is getting impatient.

"Hello! We are waiting still more than half an hour for our sandwiches!"

"I'm sorry, guys. Let me check on it in kitchen." The teenage waitress is going to the grill desk that they call the kitchen. We almost see what they have on the grill and in the oven from our table. She is coming up.

"Oh, I am sorry. Honestly, they forgot it. You would like to have another drink?"

That's the part of her that I do not think match a shy or even highly sensitive girl.She makes a very open, friendly, self-confident and if necessary also strict appearance in talks with other people.

"Yes, please! And you give us some extra free chips since we are waiting so long?"

"Sure!"

The food is good as it finally arrives.

"I don't think we have the time to eat everything. It's already 2 p.m., we have a long drive, and I don't want get home too late. Wouldn't you mind eating the rest in the car?"

I am not used to taking food with me, and I assume that I am not good to eat this thick juicy sandwich in the car. But she has to drive.

"Hi! Could you pack up this in a bag? We need to go. We have still a long drive today." She is calling to the teenage girl.

"Yes, sure! You want to have some more to drink for your drive?"

"Yes, please."

After she took the food away, Elisa is looking to me. "Before I would not have tipped her much. But it was not her fault, and she behaved very friendly."

I put out the money as Elisa says.

As we are going to the car, I am mentioning with a smile, "This something that is better here than in Germany, the service in restaurants."

Monday

April 6, 2015

It's the early evening; we are sitting on the little sofa. Carla and Lucy don't pay much attention to the new stuffed toys that Elisa gave them last night. The room looks like a mess. Cat food is almost everywhere, things are lying around and the smell is also not the best. It's pretty warm, outside a blue sky. It's so different than the time where Elisa visited me. My thoughts are getting interrupted.

"Thomas, can I talk with you?"

We are talking the whole day, but a start like this means something bigger.

"Sure, Elisa!"

She is laying one of her hands over mine, in her look is a kind of sweetness and shyness. She is smiling a bit and her eyes are appearing big in this moment.

"You know that I love you. I have never been before so sure about a guy. But I know that my inner problems are not easy to handle. I am so sorry what happened last week. I caused so much pressure and emotional stress for you, honey … Oh my gosh … still for months!"

She starts to cry. I feel that she isn't in a mood change this time as before. I take her in my arms and kiss her on her wet cheeks.

"You are so nice to me! As nobody ever before!" She is sobbing and whispering in my ear.

"It's because you are a wonderful person! It's because I never met someone like you before. Someone who cared so much about me. It's because you are beautiful. I never thought that I would get such a girlfriend. But yes, some things are hard to handle for me. I often felt overwhelmed in the last time. I didn't know what to do, how to act, how to behave. Then are my doubts. For something like what we have, sureness is necessary. I admire your sureness so much, and I am feeling bad that I can't give it to you back in the same way."

Some tears are also running down my cheeks.

"You can't give anything you don't feel. I feel sorry that I put so much pressure on you."

"You know, it's not that I wouldn't love you. Everything that I said always was and is honest. There is physical attraction, we have a lot of interests in common, I appreciate you, and I hate myself that I am missing this final spark of sureness about us. I also feel so sorry about your past and everything you made it through."

"You don't have to feel sorry about this. It's a part of my life; I still have to learn to deal with it. Listen. With all other men, I have been in love before and it was very dramatic. And also because of the bad and sometimes even violent behavior to me, I had to stop any kind of contact with them. But I know you are such a nice and caring man, Thomas! I don't know, maybe it is possible after sometime to be befriended with each other and make trips around the world together … what do you think about this?"

With red eyes, she is looking in my mine.

It is like a heavy stone is falling from my heart. Did I understand her right? Does she think about letting me go as a boyfriend? I am suddenly feeling a big relief.

"This sounds good." I am saying with a quiet voice.

We are holding each other for the next 10 minutes.

"Darling, are you hungry?"

"Yes, I am!"

"Let's go down! I will cook something for us. If you like, we can also drink the bottle of wine." She says with a wink and a smile.

Sometime later, we are finding ourselves in the dining room. The chicken dish with some kind of oriental spiced vegetable was good. We are still sipping on our wine; the bottle is almost empty.

"It's funny. Though I am not used to drinking any alcohol, I don't feel drunk or anything different at all."

"You think so? I feel different. I am in a very good mood now. I am turned on!" She says very seductive. Her tongue is tickling her bottom lip.

I am smiling. "Let's do the dishes."

She is standing up and coming over to me, sitting on my lap, opening two buttons on her black shirt slowly and is kissing me. "Do not mind the dishes now. Let's go up to the bedroom. I feel very hot now! I can make wonderful things with you! As you know, I have a lot to give."

I don't hesitate. Maybe it's wrong, especially after our talk not long ago. Maybe I feel an effect of the Gewürztraminer though, and I don't mind about her offer and follow her fast one floor higher to the bedroom.

Tuesday

April 7, 2015

"It's nice of you honey, that you went with me and Carla to the vet today again. I hope that they find out soon why she doesn't eat much anymore. Lucy is always chasing her and this doesn't make the thing any better."

"I know how important your cats are for you." I am looking around in this still almost dirty room. It's getting dark outside. There is just the light from one laptop that makes the sight dim. I hear the fan from the bedroom and sometimes the jumps from the cats.

It seems like Elisa is following my looks. In the big shelf are some books, a lot of medicine and all the envelopes and cards she got from me. My view waves to the right to the little board.

"Do you know what these boxes are for?"

"No." Her face is suddenly changing into sadness. I feel a new tension coming up in me, what's going on again now?

"These are all the urns of my deceased cats."

"Oh."

"At least of all the indoor kitties I had. One of the outdoor cats who died a few weeks ago in a car accident is buried out in the garden. These cats were all like my kids. Before I met you, I had mainly just Lucy and Carla in my life. I made a commitment that I care about them. As my mom didn't want to have me anymore as I came back from Ecuador and I had no money, I had nothing and nobody in my life so I decided for this commitment. I helped them out of bad treatment, and they helped me. We saved each other's lives."

Wednesday

April 8, 2015

"I have reserved the restaurant tonight for 7:30 p.m. Is this okay?"

I am lying on a big blanket on the lawn behind her house as she walking to me. I lift my head in her direction, "Yes, honey. I'm curious about the food there."

She is sitting down next to me, "I am curious too and also about your opinion about it." We both are smiling to each other.

"I never had a picnic here. Well, I did nothing at all before. I spent no time here, no time in my living room or dining room. I mainly used just the rooms above as I mentioned before. But it's so beautiful out here. Even the big road in front is not really disturbing. I like it here. I learn a lot through you. Maybe we can do a walk to this pond you said tomorrow."

"Sure. I enjoy the weather and the warm temperatures after the winter."

"I understand, you probably have there in Germany even a bigger desire for spring ... Thomas?"

"Yes."

"You know for me it's hard to meditate, but you talked so much about it. Could you try to help me with it?"

"Sure, we can try it. I don't know if I am good to show it to you, but let's do it!"

"Good! What do I have to do for it?"

I smile. "Stop talking now. Just listen and do what I am saying. Sit comfortable, close your eyes, concentrate just on your breath. You may hear the noise around you louder, the birds, but also the road and other things, but this is ok. Concentrate on your breath and my voice. Start to feel your body from inside.

A few hours later.

"Are you ready to order?"

"Yes, I think we are. I will take and iced tea and the roasted chicken with Spätzle. Do I say it correct?" Elisa is giggling.

The waiter and me say almost at the same time, "Sure!"

"And a salad. And you, honey?"

"For me please also an iced tea and the schnitzel with fried potatoes and red cabbage. Thank you!"

Another waiter is bringing bread and butter to our table.

"What do you think about this place? So far about the menu and style of this restaurant, Thomas?"

"I am excited for the food. I think it's the most typical German food on the menu that we have ordered now. The rest sounds not too German. The appetizers and desserts are very American I think."

"But we should get a dessert after it. I think you would also like to have one." She says cheeky.

"Yes, of course! The place looks nice, a bit fine almost elegant, but nothing on this interior would remind you of a German restaurant."

"Yes, it's also rather pricey here, maybe the most expensive place where we have been together."

"Mmm … the bread is good. This is typical German Bauernbrot."

It takes some time until our dishes are here.

"Do you want try from me?"

"Yes sure, I can give you also a part of the schnitzel. It tastes really good and everything seems to be fresh made."

"I like mine too. The portions are also big."

"Oh, the Spätzle are very good; they are handmade. I have to admit that they are better than in the restaurant in Neckarsulm. You remember the last night from at your visit last year?" I am laughing.

"Yes. But I didn't think that the food was bad there."

"Overall it was good, but I have been disappointed about the quality of the Spätzle, and it was not as fresh as here now. But on the other hand, the prices there are maybe just one third of here!"

It's already late as we are driving home from the restaurant in Durham.

Thursday

April 9, 2015

"It was nice as we walked in the afternoon to the pond and here around in the neighborhood. I think with you around, I would be more active, honey. Also the Thai dish you cooked for dinner was great. Thank you."

"I enjoyed our walk also. There is no need to say thank you for this dinner. You cooked more times for me. Also your breakfasts are always so wonderful, you think of everything, Elisa. And I always like the juices you make."

"But thank you so much for helping to clean the house in the morning. It was really a mess!"

We are crouching once again together on the brown little sofa, and I am feeling that the countdown of the end from this trip will start soon. I don't know if should be happy that I made it through? That I fly home on Sunday? After what happened in the first week, I didn't think that I could reach this upcoming Sunday here. It was much more relaxed in the last days. But still it is very intense. In some hours I notice that Elisa keeps more of a distance from me, in other moments we behave as a couple. Sure, she probably tries to keep every outbreak and tear away from me. She knows that she scared me. Maybe it's also like a last attempt of hers to do the best to hold me in these last days here. Further, she doesn't want to get hurt by herself if she opens up to me too much again. I know this is her big issue. She became so often hurt in her life. Maybe I should have been stricter, not let her too close anymore. Because it's the circle of hurting her again.

"Thomas, when we should leave for the coast tomorrow morning?"

"You know I am up early anyway. From my side, as early as possible, then we have something from the day."

"This is good. I just have to get my credit card from the post office before we are start the trip. I don't know why they didn't throw it in my mailbox. Is it okay if we meet my brother Sam tomorrow night? He always works late at this delivery service, so I don't think that we can meet him before 9 p.m."

"Yes, it's ok."

"Ok. I will just call him now. I also have paid for the movie "Wild" online and we can watch it … But if you want I can show you some old pictures before."

"Sure."

While she is talking with her brother, I go down in the kitchen and take some drinks up to the room.

Oh, I forgot to give her the last present! Because of all of the confusion in the first week I didn't find the right opportunity. I walk to my suitcase and search for a little thick black bag with a pink loop.

With the drinks and this little bag, I am going to the cat's room. Elisa has a big carton box on her lap.

"It's nice that you have drinks … and what's this?"

"It's still a gift for you that I forgot."

Carefully she opens it.

"Oh, silver hoops! You are so sweet!"

She is kissing me.

"I hope you like them!" I say with a smile.

"Yes, they are wonderful. If you want I can wear them tomorrow on our trip."

We are cuddling together.

"Are you ready to see and hear more about my past life?"

"Yes, I am." Curious about what is coming.

"I don't think that I ever showed anybody these pictures, except Sam knows them of course too."

I see a lot of old pictures. The most are of her, as a child, a teenager and a young adult.

"This girl in these picture is very beautiful!" I say with a smile.

"This girl was maybe beautiful ..."

"No, you are still beautiful, my Elisa!"

"Thank you. But as you know, I gained a lot of weight and there are my skin problems."

"Though you are still beautiful. You have just been younger in these pictures. How old were you there?"

"About 20 years old. It was in England and shortly before my marriage. These are the parents of my ex. They were very nice people."

I am noticing that there are very less pictures of her parents and other family members, and the pictures she does have of them are very old.

"I also had no contact for some time with Sam ..." She starts to tell. "But some time ago, eventually I found out that he was also abused from my dad as I told you in December."

"Are you sure?"

"I am not completely sure, but it could be. Our dad was really a bad man."

"This sounds sad."

"Yes. And I was the one who cared about my dad in the last days before he died of lung cancer. Everybody broke up the contact to him, even his last wife. The bit money that was left I needed for his funeral. Sam was also no help ... but I think I told you this also last year?"

"Yes, you mentioned that your dad had cancer."

She pauses short.

"... but Sam was also once my guardian angel and saved my life. I told you before about how it went with the abortion. Nobody asked how I was doing, nobody asked how it happened, my parents and also my grandparents knew that I was to blame. I have been deeply frustrated and depressed. I was collecting sleeping pills and other terrible medicine I found from my mother and my grandmother. As I felt very bad one day, I swallowed them all in about 15 minutes on an evening. My mom came in the bathroom by coincidence. Instead of doing something by herself, she went out of the bathroom and was calling my dad and Sam. I took my chance and ran out of the house, over our court and hide in bushes. It was getting dark; I was starting to feel very bad and tired at once. Everything started to spin around me and I lost my orientation. My brother left with his car to search for me. He passed me, but I was in the bushes and because it was getting dark, he couldn't see me. But as he told me later, as he was out on the court he glanced shortly in his rear mirror. One day before, I got a pair of white sneakers from a sale in a small shop. Sam saw my white sneakers sparkling in his mirror. And this was how he found me in the last minute. They took me to the hospital. There I had to vomit, they pumped out my stomach and for safety reasons I stayed two nights in the hospital. That was it! A doctor told my mom that they should think about therapy. But after these two nights in the hospital, I was back in school again. A therapy or even another doctor's visit never followed. Instead, I got different pills my mom took home. Maybe all these pills were the reason for my skin irritations, weight gaining and my other physical conditions started that I have until today."

It's silent in the room. Just the cats are sneaking around. I feel very sorry about Elisa. From other remarks before, I know that this must be one from two or even three suicide attempts. But I don't want to ask, this was enough. All that I know from her, all these pieces of puzzle are making a completely horrific picture of her sad life. I know that my ex-girlfriend Veronika has also a very bad past. But maybe because the health and the social system in Germany is much better than in the US, she became a stronger person. Elisa never did get any help. Not from her family, especially her mom, not much from friends, just a bit from her therapist Stella, and she paid a lot of money for it. And I doubt if this alternative therapy are is the best in her still weak condition.

I am touching her arm, stroking her back and she is pressing against my body. But she seems to not be very sad or emotional in this moment. She told me this story about her suicide attempt as I would tell about a bad day at work.

"Honey, do you want watch 'Wild' now?"

The next two hours we are sitting close to each other on the small brown sofa and looking at the laptop in front of us.

"Did you like it, Elisa?"

"Yes, it was good. I understand why you like this movie a lot. Though it is just about a long hike, it has something about freedom and traveling. Did you understand the language?"

"It was okay. I think if I wouldn't have seen it in German before and wouldn't know the story from the book, it wouldn't be too easy, but anyway the story is very good, as you know it's real. I like the landscape and also the background music. 'El Condor Pasa' fits to it."

Friday

"Sam and I called this road the 'boring highway' when we were kids. It's really boring, and it seems that nothing changed to this time."

I am looking out on the straight interstate. Indeed there is nothing, not even many cars. The landscape looks similar as in other parts of North Carolina too, but it's still more flat.

"Thomas, do you want that I show you the house where I spent my childhood? At least a part of it. We moved around always as I told you before. It's very close to here and not much of a detour."

"Yes, sure."

She introduced me as her family house from when she was a kid. It was an old house surrounded by some meadows and fields.

Back on the boring highway, it took another hour until we reached Wilmington. Streets are blocked because of a flower festival.

It's warm and sunny as we are getting out of the car. A breeze is blowing. Hand in hand, we are walking down to the river and along the Riverwalk. We both enjoy it, and I get for the second time on this trip my excited vacation feeling.

"What do you think about having something for lunch at this café over there? I think it's Spanish?

"Yes, it's looks nice. Let us sit down at this table over here."

The location near the river is beautiful. But the portions of the dishes aren't big, and it's expensive. As always with food, we have the same opinion. She has a salad while I have a tuna sandwich.

After Elisa is looking around in a souvenir shop and I am buying some postcards, we are walking up to the town and taking some pictures of the colonial houses and the gardens. I am surprised once again how she doesn't care about her condition and is doing good. I find myself tired as we are having something to drink and muffins at another café close to the car again.

"Do you want to still see something here or should we drive to the beaches now, honey?"

"Well, I think we have seen enough here. Let's go to the beaches."

"It's already 2:30 p.m. What do you think about meeting my brother instead of tonight, tomorrow night? We would have more time now and don't need to rush on our way back."

I hesitated shortly because tomorrow night will be our last night.

"Mmh, yes. You are right. It's maybe better if we have more time now."

She makes a short call and then turns to me with a big smile.

I did it. We meet him and his buddy John tomorrow night."

"You look beautiful, Elisa."

"Oh thank you, my man. Do you like the earrings on me?" She is touching with her right hand her left ear.

"Yes, silver fits good on you, my girl."

Elisa is giggling as we both want to kiss each other at the same time.

Some time later in the car.

"I think this is already Carolina Beach. Do you want that I stop here?"

"I see on the map that it isn't too far to Kure Beach. Can we go there first?"

"Yes, no problem."

Fifteen minutes later, we are on the pier on Kure Beach.

"It feels like summer here, Elisa!"

We both look down the beach and people are in the water.

"Yes, I missed the sea. It's very long ago since I have been here the last time. Not in Kure Beach, but on other beaches."

After a stroll over the pier, we end up in the pier shop.

"Do want to buy anything?"

"Not really, maybe some postcards again." I am smiling.

"You seem to not be very interested in souvenirs."

"This is right. Do you want to have anything?"

"Maybe some ice cream?"

"Ok, what sort do you want? If it's ok, I will just try from you."

"Sure, if you don't want your own. Maybe one scoop of peanut butter and another of strawberry."

After eating the ice cream together, we are walking down on the beach. Waves are crashing, a warm breeze is blowing and once again it feels almost if the emotional troubles and ups und downs in the last days are from another life. Elisa is smiling, holding my hand and is collecting shells.

"When we were kids, we sometimes found shark teeth. It's hard to distinguish from broken shells. But shark teeth you can't break."

Just a few minutes later, "Is this one, Elisa?"

She takes the piece I give her and try to break it. "Wow, you are lucky! I think it's one!"

I find even more, and we both have our pockets full of shark teeth and different shells.

Up at the ocean walk, we sit down on a swinging bench. I am happy that she drove with me here. It still doesn't feel that my trip is coming to an end in the next days, but I know that there isn't much time left.

We are deciding to drive down on the US 421 to Fort Fisher. It's on the inland side, and the road ends on a ferry point. We get out of the car and walk up a sandy way to a few cypress trees. The wind is blowing heavy. Elisa seems to have explored a new passion. She is taking one picture after the other with my camera. Carefully, I indicate that that I don't have much free memory left. She is regretting that she didn't take her own camera on this day trip and starts to take pictures with her cell phone.

On our way back with the car to the North again, she is permanently holding her cell phone out of the window. In Carolina

Beach, we take the Canal Drive and hope that we still arrive right on time at the pier there for the sundown. I saw it before on postcards, and we both think that it should come on this road. Elisa is taking hundreds of pictures almost obsessively while driving. We find the pier, and I can take two beautiful pictures of a nice dusk. The memory on my camera is full, while Elisa is going on with taking pictures with her phone.

As we are arriving on the main road in Carolina Beach again, we are going in the next best restaurant. Elisa is getting hungry and impatient because it is already 8 p.m.

Without talking, we both notice that it is a pricey fish restaurant. But it's too late to change the restaurant. She is ordering a shrimp platter while I take the catfish platter. We have a salad before. It takes long until our main dishes are coming. I notice that the fish isn't cooked well. Elisa doesn't hesitate to complain, and it takes another eternity until the platter came back again. I pay, and it's 9:15 as we are sitting in the car again.

"We will not be home before midnight!" Elisa sounds a bit down. After this wonderful day, I am not surprised. I noticed already as she was taking these many pictures that she was a kind of hyped.

"I know." What I learned in the last two weeks is that her mood is sometimes like a roller coaster. If she has been in a very good mood the most of the day, it's just the question when she is crashing down again. I hope deeply that we are coming back safely again.

"For this price, the service wasn't the best at the restaurant. I thought before on something simpler, but we didn't have the time to search for another place."

"You are right. Something cheaper would have been also fine for me."

"Could you open some of these salt water taffies? But don't open the other bag I gave it you for your parents."

We getting on the boring highway again, and I feel some tiredness.

"Talk to me! I need some distraction." She is saying this in a harsh tone.

I am looking to her.

"Thomas, don't bore me. Please entertain me!"

I try to make some casual conversation, but it's difficult for me to make it on click and under pressure. But I have to talk. Also when her tone isn't nice, she drives and I also want to come back home.

"I don't feel well … maybe the day was too much for me."

She starts suddenly to cry.

"I don't know what is going right now. Maybe it's the boring highway or because we are so close to the area again where I had my bad childhood."

I am sure that she would have this on every other highway and on every other place now too. It's just happening because she felt so good before.

Two hours later, we are lying sound and safe in the bed in Elisa's house in Wendell again.

Saturday

April 11, 2015

I am very tired. The room looks, from my experiences, unusual in America. It's very crowded with bookshelfs, a table, a separate desk, a guitar on the wall, a mobile air conditioner is blowing, several cats are strewing around our feet. Elisa is sitting close to me on the worn-out sofa. Her brother Sam is on an armchair, and his buddy John is on another usual chair. These two guys are sharing this old flat. Elisa is talking and is the center of attention. Before this, we met them at a Mexican restaurant in Raleigh, close to this flat here. The food was good, but they prepared a kind of salsa party, and it was like our table was in the middle of the dancing floor. Elisa made it clear that we get another table, and once again I have the impression that she would be everything else, but not highly sensitive. She knows how to push things through, she knows what she wants and sometimes I even think that she doesn't notice how I or others are feeling. She doesn't see my tiredness. I also don't think that this kind of evening is suitable for the last evening together. But maybe it's also better this way, and she is protecting herself to not get too close to me again. Sam makes a friendly and quiet impression. From all the things I know before about him, he is behaving very good. Elisa told me that she mostly had to invite these two guys because of permanent lack of money. But they paid for their dishes at the Mexican restaurant, they also didn't drink any alcohol. First now, Sam has opened a can of beer. John is very chatty with Elisa. She told me before that she shared an apartment with him some years ago. I can't follow much the conversation and don't talk much. I don't want to be rude, but I feel like a child who wants go home with his mom. I know also that Elisa is used to staying up later at night. She probably just went earlier to bed in the last two and a half weeks because of me. But can't you see that I am tired? Finally, something after midnight, she looks to me and asks if I want go home. Maybe she just wants to avoid any gap of time on this evening. If this was her plan, it worked very well.

Sunday

April 12, 2015

The alarm clock of Elisa's cell phone is ringing at 7:30 a.m. She looks like she was torn off from her deepest sleep. She is always in her dreams at that time. I am already awake since the last hour. My flight will go first at 1:30 p.m. But I need to pack my things, she wants to make me a good breakfast and we don't need the stress we had last year as I took her to the airport, she said last night.

In my thoughts are also my parents. I didn't get an email or a text from my dad in the last days. I hope that everything is well with him. Maybe he is just too lazy to write me, but I don't know.

This morning doesn't feel like I would leave. I am not nervous, and there is also not much tension. I don't feel much from Elisa. She is asking if I have everything, she cares with the breakfast, gives me a love meditation CD for at home and as I want give her my last 20 dollars, she rejects it. She is like a good friend or even like a mother to me.

As we drive on the interstate and I see the area a last time, the cars and everything else around it doesn't feels as if I'm leaving the U.S. Maybe I feel this way because North Carolina doesn't look too different from Germany? Maybe because I have been more than two weeks here? Or maybe because I was too busy with the interpersonal and emotional things with Elisa?

As I check in, we are both very objective. There is still a lot of time left, but Elisa indicates that I should go through the security controls. Now some tears are running down her cheeks. I'm getting wet eyes too.

"We will see each other again, Elisa!"

"Sure, we will see each other again, my honey Thomas!"

I don't know when, and after this time, I am also not sure how. But yes, we will see each other again!

I kiss her, we hold each other and I walk to the security point. I turn a last time around and wave at her.

The empty feeling I had on my way here comes back again.

Monday

April 13, 2015

Right on time, I arrive at the Frankfurt airport. I am bit nervous if my parents are there and if they are doing well. But both are standing there as I enter the exit door with my suitcase. I am happy to see them, and we are going to the car.

They don't ask much about my trip; they are asking nothing about Elisa. My mom is entangled in her own problems. But I also don't want to tell about the issues I had on this trip. They don't understand it anyway. They probably don't even understand why I travelled there. I send a short text to Elisa. Instantly I get a response, though it's in the middle of the night there.

Nine hours later, I am sitting tired with my brother in front of the sports hall in our residential area. My nephew has his gym in there. I took some chocolate, candies and postcards to my brother's family before. Secretly, I wanted to talk with my brother and sister-in-law about the things with Elisa. I need somebody to talk to. But they are busy. Mark offered for me to come with him to the sports hall. I don't want to whine around, but I need to talk. Mark is as usual relaxed about anything. But he doesn't say much and doesn't give any comments. He just gives me the feeling that he understands and is concerned about the things with Elisa.

Saturday

I am feeling depressed. It's something after 7:30 pm. Since 11/5 I spent my time with Elisa on the phone. She was telling me something about her moving to Mannheim, a city one hour away from here by car. She would study for about five years there if everything is working well. I felt overwhelmed once again. It didn't sounds serious and realistic. She was talking about her own flat. Where does she get all this money to do this? She said she wants to take the pressure off me to live her own life here. But how will she afford this with her cats? And what is her goal? Even if she can do this in five years and what is then? She still doesn't have any job and I doubt if she would find any job in my region here. I hesitated and I didn't know what to say. She noticed it, cried and shouted that I would be creating new blocks again. Maybe she is right, but this doesn't sound like a realistic plan. These are desperate fantasies and don't make me feel good. I mentioned that the only chance would be if she is living for about three months at my place. When she is crying, shouting and talking fast, I am also getting problems to express myself good enough with my language skills. I need to write another email now, also when she prefers the personal talk.

Sunday

April 20, 2015

I have another sad 11/5 talk behind me. This time it was really sad, but not annoying or fearful. She agreed to what I wrote in my email, and we decided that it is better to end the relationship. We both cried and said that we want stay in connection as friends.

It is sad, but I feel a big relief in me. We couldn't go on this way.

I'm walking to my parents' house. The fresh spring air feels good. I breathe deeply in and out.

My parents have visitors. My mom's cousin and his wife are drinking a red wine in the living room. Maybe it's good that I don't have to talk about Elisa now.

Sometime later, my phone is vibrating. I look on the display: Elisa! I am going fast out of the room and upstairs.

"Elisa?!"

"Hi, Thomas! I am sorry that I called you again. Can you speak now?"

"I am at my parents' house. But I left the room and went upstairs. So yes, I can talk."

She sounds a bit unsecure.

"Did you mention anything about us to your parents?"

"No, my mother's cousin is here."

"Ok … Well, I thought again about everything. I think I could do it financially to pay the mortgage of my house until the end of this year. I could come then for three months to Germany. This would mean that I have difficult months ahead. I would cancel the therapy with Stella. I won't register for a yoga course

I talked about before, I won't go out for dinner anymore and so on. With all this, I could make it! What do think?"

"I don't know if this is possible. Your health is also very important."

"Yes, but the most important thing is for me is to be with you. You said that the only option would be if I come for three months and we can test if we fit together."

"This is right."

"I love you so much, I want try everything!"

"This is very sweet of you. I love you too."

"Oh my dear man … I want to let you go back to your family again. I needed to talk with you again, and it seems it was worth it. We are together now again." I hear her smile.

I am bit embarrassed, "Yes, we are together again."

"I will let you go now. Have a good night there. Thanks for talking with me. I love you"

"I love you. Bye"

"Bye, honey."

I am feeling perplexed. Was it good to stay in a relationship with her?

Thursday

April 23, 2015

In the last days, we had only nice emails. She seems to be very eager about her new plan getting here. Everything sounds perfect now. But I don't feel well. How could I tell her on Sunday that I love her? If am honest to myself, I am not sure about my feelings. I don't know what is wrong with me. An American girl loves me and is doing everything possible to get here. And I am not sure? In the last days, she even said that she could imagine having a baby with me. This was always a taboo subject for her. Her newest idea in her recent email today is that she would be able to visit me for another time in September. I don't feel well, I feel so much pressure in me and I am scared that these ups and downs are going on. I can't lie and play a wrong game with her.

Friday

I am at my lunch break in the mall. I am connecting my cell phone with the free internet there. There isn't another email, but I am getting a text from Elisa! She wants to book the flights for September today after work. I have to react and can't wait until our call on the weekend. I have to end this relationship before it's too late. I have to be honest, but how I can do it? I don't want to risk writing an email when she is alone at home. I don't know when she will meet Martha again. I have to write an email when she is still at work. It won't be fun. But for something like that, it is never a good moment and at least she isn't alone at work. I can't wait until tomorrow when she might eventually book the flights.

Seven hours later:

My dear Elisa,

I wanted to email you tomorrow or even better to talk with you on the phone this weekend.
But after I read your email, I have to write you now.
I know the time isn't good. You are at work there. But the time for something like that is never good.
Since last Sunday, you wrote some wonderful things. You removed every obstacle for us. You looked after your budget, you came to me with this idea of being here with me for three months, you talked with your neighbor, today you texted me

that you can come already in September for a visit, you even wrote such nice things which touched my heart. You said things I always dreamed about.

I should be the happiest man on earth now. But unfortunately I'm not. It's very hard for me to find any explanation for this. I should be in a love flow, but I am not. I know that I feel love for you. I care about you deeply, I find you attractive and I think there is also a heart connection. But I think there seems to be a lack of emotional love. I doubt if I can give you the love that you need and that is necessary in the next months. I know this sounds very weird and ridiculous, after I told you on Sunday that I love you. But I struggled so much with myself this week. I felt a pressure in me. It's definitely not from you or anybody else. I'm afraid that my up sand downs are going on. I can't help myself. I prayed every day this week that I get these signals and love that I want to give and share with you. But it didn't happen. I feel so sad. Especially because of you, but also because maybe I give up the chance of my life. Elisa, though I think it's better if you let me go.

I have to find myself.

I know you will need some time. The only thing that I can hope is that you can forgive me after sometime, and I can care about you as a good friend.

Your

Thomas

Three hours later.

I feel a bit relieved that I sent the email. But I have big worries about Elisa. I didn't get any response. It's bed time here, but I wonder if I can sleep. I am trying to find Martha on Facebook. Elisa mentioned once before that her friend has an account there. I found her. I write a short message and ask politely if she can check on Elisa this weekend.

Saturday

April 25, 2015

It's first 6:15 in the morning, but I can't sleep anymore. I get up and after using quickly the bathroom, I check my emails. Nothing new, nothing from Elisa! I am sure that she read my email yesterday. Before it never took long until I got a call, an email or a text back … especially if she didn't like what she read from me. There is also no response from Martha.

I write another email to Elisa and suggest a call on 11/5. This is all that I can do for now.

The morning is very slow. I had some cereals for breakfast, clean a bit, try to meditate, but I can't concentrate and read a bit in various books from my shelf. But the most time I think of Elisa. It makes no sense to check the emails again. It's still night there, and if she hasn't written me last night, she wouldn't have done it now.

At lunch I am at my parents' house as usual. My mom made spaghetti with a spicy meat sauce. Something I like to eat, but I am not hungry.

At home, I am checking my emails once again. Nothing! She could been up at this time; it's 2:30 p.m. here.

I am walking through my condo like a tiger in a cage, back and forth, forth and back. I am very nervous. Maybe it was the worst thing I ever did. I don't know how she is doing. There is nobody I can contact. Her neighbor with the same name is coming in my mind. I can't contact her neighbor. Maybe she just needs her time.

The next two and a half hours are going by so slowly.

Soon it is 5 p.m. … 11 a.m. there. My hands are getting wet. She always called me right on time. Maybe also today.

4:59, 5:00, 5:01 … no call! I have to wait some minutes still. 5:02, 5:03, 5:04, 5:05, 5:06 … nothing!

What can I do? I am checking my emails again. No new email.

I feel that I am getting crazy. What is she doing? Why doesn't she call me? A short text that she doesn't want to call me or anything else would be enough!

The only thing that I can do now is to call her. But I want to go to my parents' shop because it's the only place where I can dial a cheap number for calls abroad.

I am more running than walking. I feel hot. I want to check my emails at my parents' house a last time. But my dad is sitting at the computer. I tell him that I need the phone in his shop for a call to America. He didn't ask why, but it's maybe better.

At the shop, I dial carefully the long number. I'm fearful. One beep, the second beep, the third … just the answering machine replying.

I need to dial again and have to say anything.

One beep, the second beep, the third … "I cannot answer the call now. I will call you back!"

"Hi, here is Thomas!" I am hesitating "Sorry for my email yesterday. How are you doing? Please just let me know that you are doing ok."

I am walking back to my parents' house again. My dad is away from the computer and I can check my emails there, but nothing!

What should I do? The only final option would be to call the police there. But this idea is probably totally silly.

I logged into Facebook. Susan is online. I start to chat with her and tell her what all happened in the last 24 hours. She tries to relieve me. It would be ok what I did, and there would be nothing more I could do. She feels also sorry for her, but says that it wouldn't be in my hands anymore.

I have dinner with my parents, and after it I walk outside to a clear sky around in the neighborhood. I pray and wish that there is somebody who cares about my Elisa.

At home I'm thinking about checking my emails again. But I think on what Susan said to me, that it isn't in my hands anymore. I am not doing myself any favor if I find out that there is still no email from her. I am going to bed.

Sunday

April 26, 2015

I am again up early. Before I am going to my parents' house for breakfast, I want to check my emails again. And there is one from Elisa! Just three sentences. She obviously not doing good, but she wrote thank you for my call attempt, that she was in her bed until the afternoon and that she needs time.

This is what I wanted to hear! I feel a relief. I know she is maybe hurting and having a very bad weekend, but she is alive! I see that she sent this mail at 3:45 p.m. her time yesterday. If I would had checked my emails when I came home, I could have gone more relaxed to bed. Anyway, I am feeling much better now. Like a stone is falling from my heart.

Sometime later, I get a text from Michael. He asked about meeting for something to drink in Heilbronn in the afternoon. I agreed, I think that I need some distraction.

As we are sitting at Starbucks, I am receiving a text from Elisa.

"Thomas, may I call you if you are free?" I text back that I am with Michael in the city, but I will write her as soon as I am at home.

It's a kind of ironic. Shortly before 5 p.m., I am at home and exactly on 11/5 Elisa is calling me again.

I am hearing her sad voice and under many tears, she explains to me that my email on Friday ruined the rest of her workday. It arrived shortly before she had to give a lecture for some colleagues. I am saying that I am very sorry, and we both are crying. It is a really sad call, but no drama. I understand her and she tries to understand me. She is saying that she needs some time, maybe a couple of months, but she doesn't want to lose me. Lose me not as a friend. I'm confirming what she is saying and try to make clear what a wonderful person she is and that it would be great if we could hold on to our connection. She says that not only would she need her time, also I am used to her and would need my time.

Even a bigger stone is rolling from my heart as in the morning. I am so glad that I had a constructive talk with her. I feel very sorry, and I am thinking that I gave the chance of my life away. But though it was right what I did. Love should be no pain, no pressure and no drama.

At the evening, I am telling my parents that I broke it off with Elisa. For five minutes, they are listening to me. I don't know if they understand me. It seems that they also feel a relief. But maybe for another reason.

Thursday

April 30, 2015

In the last days, we had some small conversations by email and text.

Together with my parents, I am sitting in front of the TV. A thriller is playing. I'm happy that tomorrow is a holiday and I have off.

My phone is vibrating in my pocket. Who is this? Elisa!

I am getting out of the room once again and going upstairs. "Hello!"

"Hi, Thomas! Here is Elisa." Her voice sounds deep and broken. Hi, Elisa!"

"How are you doing?"

"Mmmh ... not bad. Tomorrow is May 1 here."

"I think of you and I miss you."

"I miss you too."

"I have just a question, Thomas."

"Mmmh, yes please."

"I think so much about you and us. Do you think that it would be a difference if I would live somewhere there in Germany and we would had met there the first time?"

I don't know what she is starting to talk about again.

"I don't know, Elisa. And I can't and don't want talk about this with you now. We can talk about this and much more in a couple of months. As you said before, we need a couple of months. I want to have you as my friend. But I don't think that it makes sense if we talk about these subjects again."

"I am sorry. Just some things came up in my mind and I wanted talk with you about it."

"At another time, but not now. I'm also tired. It is shortly before 10 p.m. here, and I am still at my parents' house. I think that they also want to go to bed soon."

"Ok, have a good night there, Thomas."

"Have still a good afternoon there, Elisa."

I press the red button.

Maybe I was too harsh this time. But it makes no sense. She sounds sad and depressed.

I walk home, and I decide to send her an email from my laptop before I go to bed. I have a kind of guilty conscience because I ended the call suddenly.

Dear Elisa,

Right now I am at home, and I will go soon to bed. I was longer at my parents' house today because of the holiday tomorrow. You called shortly before I wanted to leave.

Thank you for your call. You don't have to apologize and have never to apologize when you call me, email me or text me. You know I want to be here for you, always and also as a friend.

But I don't contact you from my side because I want to give you the time and space you need. The time to get over the pain. I think we need this time. Maybe you more than me, but also I need this time. As you called me, I noticed that it is still very fresh. No wonder, it's just a few days ago. Therefore I also can't say anything different now as on the past weekend. Maybe one day we can talk about all these things like my pressure about my feelings and more. But I don't think that it makes any sense now.

Elisa, though it's not easy and it hurts, we have to go on. Go on with our life and, after some disconnection, go on with our special connection. Though our connection will then be probably different than before, I'm sure that it is worth, and I think it will be special again. I also don't know what kind of friendship or connection we will have. But we will see.

Elisa, I know who you are. I know what a good and nice woman you are. I don't want to miss our connection and you in future. I hope that we can smile one day in person together. I want to talk and share so many things with you again. But we need the time of disconnection.

Elisa, please care for yourself and try to do things that help you to feel better. Get appointments with Stella again, try this yoga class and about a healthy nutrition I don't have to tell you anything. Even if it's hard, try to get some quality and good things in your life.

Elisa, I think there are a lot of things we can still share together, and I think we can still be there for each other. But we have to come over these wounds first.

Your

Thomas

P.S. Today as I came home from work, I watched our pictures. I hope we can watch them together one day.

Sunday

Mother's Day, May 10, 2015

Where are these bamboo table pads?

I am preparing a Chinese lunch for my parents and my brother. In the most years before, we went often out to a restaurant on Mother's Day. But the restaurants are always so full on this day. My sister-in-law is with the kids at her mother's house.

I noticed that I didn't cook anything at home since last December when Elisa was here. With everything I set out on my dining table, I think of her. I am sure that some things that I am searching now she put away. It's a shame that I didn't have guests since December. But there was also no time. I was always busy with her even when she was not here. I wonder what she is doing today? It's probably another sad day for her. I know that she is also suffering about the non-existing contact to her mom. I didn't hear from Elisa since her call at the last day of April. It's just about 10 days ago. I don't believe to hear anything from her until June or even July. I have to give her all the time she needs. But I miss her.

Yesterday I chatted with Ana in Hong Kong after a long break again. I thought of the fortune teller who told me there about the truth.

Epilogue

Tuesday

October 13, 2015

And there you are like a highway headed my way life is but
a dream I was shot down by your love my angel in blue jeans.

Delta Airlines still have the same album on their playlist. I watch out of the window, the clouds dissolve and I catch a look down to the ground. This must be the Blue Ridge! We shouldn't be far away from the Ashville area! My heart is beating a bit stronger. In about 50 minutes, I am probably at the airport in Atlanta.

What is Elisa doing now? Is she still living in her house in Wendell? Is she still working for the same company? Is she is still thinking of me?

I don't want to believe in coincidences, but I am sitting exactly six months later after I arrived in Frankfurt on a plane on the same route to Atlanta again. But I won't go to North Carolina and meet Elisa. I am just on another vacation trip to the U.S. again. This time my end destination will be Southern California without any romantic background. This is probably good.

I am still missing Elisa, and I didn't get any life sign from her. The couple of months are already sometime over. Though I would like to know how she is doing, there is no chance to find it out. I saw that her friend Martha deleted her account on Facebook. But it doesn't matter how much I think of Elisa, I can't contact her, if she does not contact me.

I wonder if she feels that I am geographically close to her right now?

The author

Martin Kettemann has a passion to travel to different countries. He not only wants to go sightseeing there; he wants to immerse himself in people's lives. He has a special longing for America, but also for Asian cultures. Though he can also enjoy face-to-face conversations, he often prefers emails, letters, chats and texts. Through private emails, he often finds access to the heart of other people and friends, helps them with different issues and get a stronger connection with them. These written conversations and personal experiences led him to write this story.

The story is in a language that is not his native language. He chose to write in English because his memories and experiences have been mostly in English. It would have been easier to write in German, but it was important for him to try it.

The publisher

He who stops getting better stops being good.

This is the motto of novum publishing, and our focus is on finding new manuscripts, publishing them and offering long-term support to the authors.
Our publishing house was founded in 1997, and since then it has become THE expert for new authors and has won numerous awards.

Our editorial team will peruse each manuscript within a few weeks free of charge and without obligation.

You will find more information about
novum publishing and our books on the internet:

w w w . n o v u m - p u b l i s h i n g . c o . u k